"Here in **A S**... is all the grandeur and excite... ...arist Russia, the suffering of the masses and the unspoiled beauty of the Ukraine countryside combined in the romantic and suspenseful story of a young English girl's confrontation with adventure at the high noon of Imperialism."

—**Fort Wayne News-Sentinel**

"Here is **A HISTORICAL ROMANCE WORTH READING . . .**
It is seldom that one book of presumably light fiction offers so much substance as this." —**Kansas City Star**

"Here is A MUST FOR THOSE WHO ENJOY AUTHENTIC BACKGROUND."
—**Buffalo Courier-Express**

"Here is A STORY WITH HEART . . . PASSION AND DRAMA." —**Hartford Times**

"Wright's heroine is a feisty, protoliberated young lady, and this is a well-constructed, creditable contribution to the genre." —**Kirkus Reviews**

About The Author

Patricia Wright is a history teacher as well as a writer. She has based this novel on actual history, and the broad outline of the book is inspired by the letters of her distant relation, Ellen Maria Hardcastle. Such accurate details bring a special element to A SPACE OF THE HEART.

A SPACE
OF THE
HEART

Patricia Wright

WARNER BOOKS

A Warner Communications Company

WARNER BOOKS EDITION

Copyright © 1976 by Patricia Wright
All rights reserved

Library of Congress Catalog Card Number: 75-17896

ISBN 0-446-89241-6

This Warner Books Edition is published by
arrangement with Doubleday & Company, Inc.

Cover art by Peter Cox

**Warner Books, Inc., 75 Rockefeller Plaza,
New York, N.Y. 10019**

W A Warner Communications Company

Printed in the United States of America

Not associated with Warner Press, Inc. of Anderson, Indiana

10   9   8   7   6   5   4   3   2   1

Contents

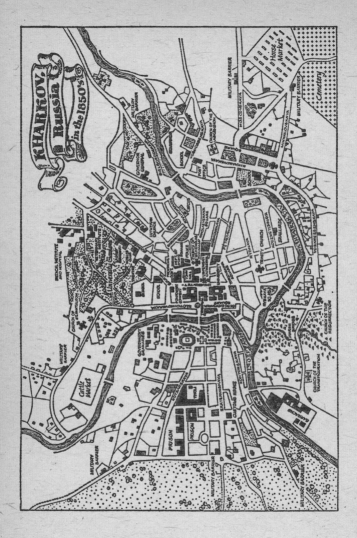

KHARKOV, Russia in the 1850's

Note

In telling this story of nineteenth-century Russia it has been throughout my endeavor not to falsify any of the facts so far as these are known, or to attribute to the characters thoughts and feelings which only subsequent events could have made clear.

There were at this time three principal divisions among thinking Russians: the Slavophiles who wished to turn their backs at all costs on what they interpreted as the degradation and soulless commercialism of the West and so preserve the pastoral simplicity and virtues of peasant life into the modern age; the Westernizers who would speed up the development of Russia that had been started by Peter the Great, regardless of the almost total divorce of Russian people, conditions, and habits from those of the West; and, thirdly, a very few who foresaw that if Russia was to escape the catastrophe which threatened her it could only be by some native blend of these two diverging schools of thought. Not by talk but in action, not in immediate democracy but in gradually tempered absolutism, not in impossible dreams for the future but in practical, honest administration in the present. And I think, even then, these few knew the difficulties inherent in the compromise they sought and the likelihood of defeat their efforts faced.

I have based the story on actual history and have tried

never to distort time or place or character to suit my convenience. The broad outline of the book is inspired by the letters of a very distant relation of mine, Ellen Maria Hardcastle, who went to Russia in 1852 and remained until 1860, for most of which time she was governess to the children of the governor of Kharkov. The conditions she found there and the reasons she went to Kharkov from St. Petersburg are those related, but the family background and her own character as shown in this book are fictitious.

All the events described did not take place in Kharkov, but almost without exception they did take place in this period in Russia. Sentiments ascribed to peasants or to other characters are those expressed at the time, including the mystical loathing of potatoes, the vain struggle of certain administrators to avoid suicidal mobilization of reserve troops, and the almost insane peculation and maladministration which resulted in the deaths of thousands of Russian soldiers who never even entered the battle area in the Crimea.

Everybody was meant to serve the state in some capacity or another, salaries were totally inadequate, and the general quality of officials was so low that by the 1850s almost everyone's position and livelihood depended on graft. If anyone attempted to stand in the way of this monstrous machine he was a mortal danger to all his fellows and crushed without mercy: in the reign of Nicholas I secret police activity reached a pitch probably not again equaled until after the Revolution. The power of the state secret police was almost unlimited: originally founded with the highest ideals and with the intention of rooting out wrongdoing from the imperial administration, it soon developed a motive force all its own and became a weapon of terror and blackmail within the government itself, resulting in the further demoralization of the bureaucracy. In 1880 it was placed under the control of the Ministry of the Interior in an attempt to curb its activities, but this had little effect—in 1911 the Prime Minister himself was assassinated by the secret police.

The names of some of the characters and places in this book will be familiar to many, but where possible I have used actual people for those less well known. General Traskine and his wife were, so far as I can tell from the letters, as depicted except in relation to General Berdeyev, who is fictitious, although they had Berdeyev relations, owned the Nipocritiy estate, and suffered as described in the cholera epidemic of 1853. Miss Faulkner, Miss Macdonald, the *Neptune*, Captain Brownless, the Simpsons, Dr. Ward, Micha and Sacha, Theodosia, the Braillards, and Chuguyev are all true.

In attempting to cover a field so vast at such a crossroads of history, it has only been possible to touch on events directly affecting the story, for while on the surface nothing of great moment occurred during these last years of the reign of Nicholas I, the flood tide of events so soon to burst on imperial Russia was even then barely under control, and with each year of control the pressure behind the dam rose. The bombs, the wild-eyed young idealists, the professional revolutionaries, the great edicts of emancipation and local government, industrialization, all these were in the future. But the future was already clearly written for those who cared to read: in the thirty years of Nicholas' reign there were over three hundred major peasant risings and the frontiers of imperial Russia were pushed forward, to the consternation of Western Europe, everywhere from the Caucasus to the borders of China.

11

Part One
ENGLAND
1852

One

There was absolute quiet in the young ladies' parlor, lately the schoolroom, at Abbotsfield House. Heads bent intently over their work, the three Lovell sisters did not so much as glance out of the window, were not distracted for a moment by the bright June sunlight or the distant misty folds of Sussex countryside.

The door opened. "Miss Susannah," said the parlormaid briefly, and without further explanation hurried away again: no one at Abbotsfield wasted time on a Friday morning. Explanation anyway was unnecessary; every Friday for twenty-five years, that is to say every Friday since Sarah Lovell had returned from her bridal weekend in Brighton and had taken over control of the rambling, attractive old house, each member of the household had had to account to her for their week's work on that morning. The under housemaid produced her tins of polish and received such replacements as were necessary, the cook made up her menus and accounted for any trifling expenditure over which she had control, the head gardener discussed the vegetables to be gathered and sown during the coming week.

Later, as children were born to William and Sarah Lovell, they were included in the pattern. Neatly kept primers and slates of sums were inspected, verses and catechisms recited, relearned, recited again and criticized.

Susannah rose at once, gathering together the pile of papers beside her, the skirt to which she had been adding some hasty, last-minute stitches, and a very attractive collage made of shells and dried ferns.

"Mama will never allow you to keep that ruching along the hem," remarked Eleanor, the eldest, looking up from a pen-and-ink drawing she was endeavoring to finish.

"She will, you'll see," said Susannah positively. "Now I am to be married Mama says that a little decoration is quite acceptable." She shut the door with a snap. .

"Susie is unbearable now, I shall be almost pleased when she is married," remarked Charlotte, the youngest. "Nell, do let me finish that sketch for you, you are making it so much worse."

"I know." Eleanor eyed it doubtfully. "I just cannot draw, or do water colors, however hard I try." She added another squiggle and sighed. "After fifteen years of lessons it must be a waste of time to persevere."

"Let me add a few lines, I know just what would make it look better." Charlotte never had difficulty in producing charming sketches of flowers and fruit, her piano pieces might have wrong notes but they never sounded wooden and dull. Her clothes were always spotless, her fingers always busy, her hair always brushed until it shone. Yet she was so enchanting, at once generous and modest, that it was seldom possible to feel more than a passing spasm of irritation at her unfailing sweetness of disposition.

"No," said Eleanor. "Mama always knows when you add something to my drawings; anyway, what is the good?" She began to shuffle together her papers as the sounds of Susannah's playing floated down the passage. "She'll go wrong there, she always does. . . . There, I said so." They both listened with melancholy satisfaction as Susannah was made to play the offending passage over and over again. "Oh, Lottie, wouldn't it be wonderful, just once, to do something different on a Friday?"

Eleanor Lovell did not resemble her sister, taking, it was said, more after her father's side of the family. Her elegant dark green dress, although devoid of decoration, set off her tall figure to admiration, but for all the modesty of her spreading skirts, the demureness of her carefully dressed hair, the grace and diffidence of her manner, her true self was not quite concealed. The gray eyes in the carefully controlled face were large and glowing with life, the thick, dark eyebrows angling toward her nose distinctly at variance with the self-effacement so rigidly taught by her mother, her governesses and half-forgotten nurse. They had been almost successful, she rarely advanced an opinion or expressed her thoughts, her sense of the ridiculous gave only herself amusement; the façade was almost complete, only her eyes were still her own.

"There, I knew Mama wouldn't mind!" Susannah swept back into the room. "She said a little decoration was just the thing for a married lady and one day next week we are going into town to buy some real lace to trim my sprigged muslin!"

"Miss Eleanor," said the parlormaid, and scuttled away again. It would have been far easier if Susannah had simply told her sister that it was her turn, but this was not allowed. It savored of slackness, of allowing the servants to expect concessions, of bringing the children up in slovenly habits, and Mrs. Lovell's sense of duty toward her dependents was far too high to give these dangers a moment's countenance.

Eleanor knocked on the library door, waited until she was bidden to enter, and then curtsied. "Good morning, Mama."

"Good morning, my dear. Your back a little straighter, I think, your left hand just gathering your skirt. Again please."

Eleanor curtsied again, head high, back straight. The library was a friendly room, full of her father's gun cases and fishing rods; only on Fridays was it turned into a place of execution. Then the cluttered desk was swept bare, the household accounts laid out, the ebony ruling stick used for the precise alignment of every minute item of expenditure laid alongside the light cane which punished the slightest clumsiness in scales or needlework.

Sarah Lovell had lived all her life in easy circumstances, waited upon by servants, gardeners, and grooms, fed plentifully, housed elegantly. But she had grown neither slack nor soft, the possibility had never occurred to her. She expected of herself and of everyone around her only the very best, and if she failed to obtain it, then she was humble enough to seek forgiveness and guidance for herself rather than them. No one knew quite how many hours she spent on her knees praying for those around her and for strength and courage to guide them aright. No one realized either that, with the years, the thin edge of her self-control was wearing away as the successive trifling failures of daily life assumed menacing proportions in the intensity of her mind. Above all she had had to admit failure with her husband: William Lovell would have been startled indeed had he known the miseries he inflicted on his wife by his perfunctory management of his prosperous timber business and by his preference for hunting and fishing rather than work. She never allowed herself to criticize her husband: even in the privacy of her mind the guilt of failure was but another burden forced onto her own already overladen conscience.

Now it was clear that she was failing with Eleanor too. She did not believe the story she had heard, but there must have been some indiscretion. "Sit down, girl," she snapped abruptly. "Let me see."

"Yes, Mama." Eleanor sat down, careful to keep her back straight, her shoulders down, her hands folded quietly in her lap as soon as she had handed over her sewing and sketches. There was a long silence in the room, apart from the metronome, still clicking after Susannah's playing.

18

At last Mrs. Lovell put the drawings aside. "They are not pleasing, are they, Eleanor?"

"No, Mama."

"They show no improvement on last year or the year before." Mrs. Lovell brought some neatly docketed sketches out of a drawer.

"Mama . . ." Eleanor hesitated. "I do try, but I just cannot draw. Charlotte can convey the feel of a tree with a few strokes, but with me . . ."

"You cannot play well either, even after eighteen years of lessons," went on her mother inexorably. "I am not blaming you but I think that the time has come for us to think about your future."

"Oh yes, Mama," said Eleanor thankfully.

Mrs. Lovell fingered the cane thoughtfully. Once her children reached the age of twenty she never touched them with it, which meant that only Charlotte now had anything to fear, though Eleanor often thought the swift retribution of the cane preferable to days of her mother's icy disapproval. "You are now twenty-two years old; dear John is already married and dear Susannah will soon leave us, although she is younger than you. It is time that you too were thinking of being settled in life."

Eleanor lowered her eyes; she had indeed been carefully brought up. "Yes, Mama."

Mrs. Lovell brought the cane down with a snap on the desk: "Look at me!" Startled, Eleanor looked up. "Your father had a very great shock yesterday when Lord St. Albyn called to see him at the sawmill." The story brought home by her husband the day before had been so incredible that she had refused to accept it. There could be no question of ignoring such an accusation but never until this moment had she believed it, as she saw her daughter's ridiculous eyebrows tighten with shock, the exaggerated swoop of them turning her face into a caricature of dismay.

"You have been meeting Christopher St. Albyn." It was a statement and not a question.

"Mama. . . ." Eleanor spoke with an effort. "I have known him for years."

"Don't lie to me! You know perfectly well I expect absolute honesty from my children. I am not speaking of a casual acquaintance, but of something a great deal more serious. Lord St. Albyn informed your father that regular meetings had been taking place. Is this so?"

Eleanor still had not recovered from her shock. She was attached to her mother, but as the distant, terrifying center of her world, by whom everything was decided but never discussed. After all the years of unceasing vigilance and criticism, she found it difficult to control panic the moment her slightest fault was discovered. She despised herself for her weakness, but at the first sign of anger and raised voices her mind shuttered and her throat stiffened so it became difficult even to control her voice. She cleared her throat nervously. "Y-yes, Mama."

Mrs. Lovell closed her eyes for a moment. Dear God, she thought, what am I to do for the best? For twenty-two years I have tried with this one, and nothing but grief has come of it; show me Your will, surely my duty must be to the others now—to dainty, vulnerable Charlotte and to Susannah, at the moment so much in need of the strongest principles to armor her for her new responsibilities? The fiery anger, which so often stirred unseen beneath her rigid control, almost overwhelmed her for a moment, but she said, quietly enough, her fingers clasped white round the ruling stick like a grip on sanity itself: "I wish to know everything, please. Your father assured Lord St. Albyn that there could be nothing in such malicious gossip. I am deeply humiliated to find he was wrong to be so confident."

Eleanor's heart was beating in odd jerks, her hands felt cold, her lips stiff, yet at the same time, somehow, somewhere, she felt warm and happy. The contrast made her voice uncertain at first but then the words tumbled out: she had wanted so much to finish with concealment, and the unexpected consideration with which her mother listened steadied her still further.

"Mama, I . . . do you remember last spring when old Mrs. Colby was ill?" She saw her mother's astonishment and hurried on. "You remember how you sent me with a basket of vegetables for her? I went across the fields and was just climbing the stile by the spinney when"—she laughed—"I was nearly shot! Christopher was shooting rabbits there, it was so close that the pellets tore my skirt a little. I cried out of course and he was full of apologies, I mean it really was very close!"

"I do not remember your dress being torn in the spring." Mrs. Lovell's mind fastened on the unexpected detail.

Eleanor gasped and only just escaped laughing; she had often thought that her mind and her mother's worked in completely opposite directions. "It was the old brown serge. I showed you the mend and said that I had caught it on the stile."

"You lied to me." It was the flat voice of a judge. Although Eleanor did not recognize it, it was also the voice of deep personal hurt and confusion.

Eleanor bit her lip. "Yes, Mama." The flow of her confidence dried up, for the Lovell children had never been encouraged to explain or excuse their actions and sheer unfamiliarity now made the effort of explanation almost overwhelming. Even when her mother said no more, the memory of that April morning suddenly seemed inexplicable to her too: just for an instant Eleanor saw it all through her mother's eyes—improper, vulgar, ill-bred trifling with sin. Yet it was not like that at all, she thought, and plunged on hastily: "We were both frightened, I think, we seemed to keep laughing and then apologizing all over again! He came with me to Mrs. Colby's and then waited to walk home with me. You will remember that I used to go there about twice a week while she was ill and he often met me and we would walk there together, sometimes

21

going round by the lake." And then running all the way home, she thought privately, so no one would notice how long it took me there and back.

"Mrs. Colby has been recovered for several weeks," pointed out Mrs. Lovell coldly.

"Well, yes," admitted Eleanor, "but . . ."

"But you have continued to behave like a common servant girl, meeting this young man on every occasion I sent you on errands to the sick or to the village, believing that you would not betray the trust I had in you?" Mrs. Lovell's disgust and fury were so great that their very intensity evaporated all feeling from her voice.

"It was not like that! It isn't like that!" As Eleanor dimly grasped the extent of her mother's distress, the need to explain overwhelmed her diffidence. "You have just said that I am too old now for the schoolroom, for drawing and piano lessons. Christopher—we—want to be married, we didn't feel we were betraying you, we were just very happy."

"To be married!" Mrs. Lovell stared at her in astonishment. "To Christopher St. Albyn? No wonder Lord St. Albyn came to see your papa; his family would never consider such a match, we are not of their world. When Lord St. Albyn's only son marries, it will be to the daughter of one of his own kind and not the child of the local timber merchant."

"Mama, please! I said all this to Christopher but he wouldn't listen . . . he said he was soon to enter the army anyway and would be independent of his father. I told him I could not possibly come between him and his family but he said . . . he said . . ." She blushed. "He said that he had never known his father unreasonable and once they had met me they would know we were just right for each other." How flat it sounded. What were words after all? How could she describe happiness, lay out contentment for inspection, show absolute certainty as if it were nothing but a sheaf of Friday drawings?

22

It had been a summer which could only be truly described within Eleanor's own mind. Everything until those weeks had had a precise pattern, an exact place in the disciplined framework of her life. Then, suddenly, everything had changed, laughter came where there had been loneliness, a future where there had been only the tedious present. Within an afternoon Christopher had become part of her life, a part so natural that there could be no going back, for without him her thoughts and her life no longer seemed to fit together.

She supposed he was handsome, although she never thought about it, but above all he was earthy, vital, bubbling with energy; without effort he breathed life into a whole side of her nature which had been atrophied by the rigid daily routine of her home. They had walked, talked endlessly, and he had even sometimes brought a pony for her to ride with him. Surprisingly, it was some weeks before they kissed.

Down by the lake, Christopher and some of his father's grooms had built a rough-riding course with dangerous, swerving jumps and unexpected obstacles, so that he could practice before his expected commission into the cavalry. The idea was to sidestep the obstacles and take the jumps with the minimum alteration of his horse's pace, and Eleanor soon found herself enrolled as timekeeper, counting the seconds steadily while he careered round the lake and in and out of the hazards on the steep bank above. The moment he finished he would gallop off with Eleanor following behind, her borrowed pony out of control but racing to catch him through the tough scrub, partly as a kind of mad hide-and-seek, partly to make up the precious minutes snatched from whatever errand she was meant to be carrying out.

Christopher was a dashing, careless rider, willing to give his highly trained mount full trust to pick its way at top speed through any obstacles, but Eleanor was far less experienced and without the confidence to allow her pony his head. Several times she only narrowly escaped real disaster on these headlong dashes, for a scratched face would be as difficult to explain at home as a broken back.

"You must be more careful," explained Christopher, grinning, when she arrived flushed and panting at his side almost five minutes after he had reached the agreed end of the chase.

"Oh, stuff! I've got twenty years of energy to use up in ten minutes' riding twice a week." Eleanor slid to the ground and began to tidy her hair and shake out her skirts. Even to Christopher she found it difficult to explain the incredible freedom that could be grasped in a few minutes without care, the way sheer speed could outdistance, for an instant of time, suffocation of the spirit. She had ridden before, sometimes illicitly on the fat pony kept for the dogcart, but more usually in carefully decorous groups at such a placid pace that all enjoyment was destroyed.

"Here, I'll do it." Christopher looped both reins over his arm and began to brush out her skirts while she swiftly fumbled her hair back into confinement— she always now carried a reticule full of smuggled combs, brushes, and ribbons.

"Do I look all right?" She craned round to watch him.

"I think so. . . ." His voice trailed off, he was kneeling, still holding the reins, picking pieces of leaf off her hem. They stared at each other, breath quickening, dying, quickening again. He did not remember getting to his feet.

The kiss was not very expert and it was utterly spoiled, yet somehow made more exciting, by Eleanor rushing off in the middle, exclaiming distractedly about a tea party at the vicarage for which she was already late.

"Thursday perhaps," she called back to him. In a way, Mrs. Lovell's rigid timetable made it surprisingly easy to plan their meetings.

Eleanor had been so disciplined and groomed for a role utterly alien to her nature that little additional control was needed to conceal her preoccupation and happiness. Christopher too, waiting through the long summer for his commission, surprised himself by the extent of his anticipation and enjoyment of her company—not just the few quick, unsatisfactory kisses but Eleanor herself, her courage, her laughter, some of the outrageous things she blurted out and then tried to recant with comical dismay.

"You see, I have never said what I thought before," she explained. "Now with you I feel I can say whatever comes into my head! You can't imagine what a relief it is."

"Oh, Nell, I do love you so." He was surprised at his own words, yet would not, could not, take them back.

"Really? Do you really, Christopher? My darling, how I love you too." His arms tightened round her, his lips seeking hers, his hands caressing, locked, forgetful, oblivious. They were both so shaken by the depth of what they had so unexpectedly found in themselves that after a moment they moved a little apart, Christopher's hands still on her shoulders. It was the sound of approaching cartwheels which at last obtruded on their consciousness, and Christopher swung away with an oath, pretending to examine his horse's foreleg.

It was the village knife grinder, immediately intense with curiosity, and they were silent for a long time after he had vanished behind the hedgerows, clattering with implements and still staring over his shoulder.

"This is intolerable!" exclaimed Christopher at length. "Nell, I can't go on like this: never able to talk to you properly, our eyes always over our shoulders or else on the time. You must come to see us and spend a proper day. I will ask my mother to invite you."

Once or twice Eleanor had just begun to wonder about the future, but she had always thrust the thought

25

away. "Come to Albyn Park? Christopher, I couldn't! Your mother would never invite me, you know that."

"She would have to if I asked you to be my wife." Christopher spoke angrily; he would not retract words he had never meant to speak, yet already some distant part of his mind was wondering whether he had not been unwise. "Nell, I should like that very much."

Eleanor picked up her basket blindly, backing away from him. "Christopher . . . no, please stay there, I can't think in your arms, I don't want to!"

"You mustn't think," he interrupted. "Once you— we—start to think it will be nothing but people and objections and not us any longer." And I am just beginning to think, he reflected miserably.

"But life is not just us, it is full of people and objections!" Eleanor was sure of her own feelings, but the dream was over. She had gladly allowed herself to be swept away day by day, week by week, but now the flood tide was suddenly rushing past her, leaving her stranded in the shadows of reality. The trouble was that her own emotions had been borne away on the torrent too, but for both their sakes, somehow she must think.

"Christopher darling, I cannot imagine more happiness than being your wife, but . . . but I couldn't come between you and your family and everything you have —we would never find contentment that way."

He brushed this aside, the need to stifle his own doubts making him even more vehement. "Why should you? Good God, my father would only have to meet you to know we are just right for each other. Anyway, I will be in the army soon so it will not be anything to do with him."

"Of course it will," said Eleanor, exasperated. "How many thousand acres is it that you will inherit one day and your son after you? Do you think your father will ever allow you to be wed to the daughter of the local sawmill owner, however prosperous?"

"Don't you want to marry me, Nell?" He grasped

26

her hand. "I am off next week, you know, we will have to decide something by then. My regiment is to be down on Salisbury Plain for a while and I am to join them there. It is all arranged now and I don't know when I shall be home again."

"You never told me it was to be so soon!"

"My God, when do I ever have the time to tell you anything as we are at the moment? It is to be the 13th Light Dragoons, my father's old regiment, and just what I wanted." His face lit up with enthusiasm. "They are due to go to Ireland soon, so I must join in time to do some training at Salisbury or I might be left behind when they leave. If it had not been for you, I would not have waited so long."

"How can anything be decided in a week?" objected Eleanor, her defenses crumbling before his certainty.

"Why not? We could not be married of course, but I can tell my father that we wish to and ask my mother to call—you know, all the usual flummery—so we do not have to go on like this forever."

Eleanor frowned, looking almost fierce with her brows drawn down, their flaring line accentuated. "Christopher, are you sure, really sure? We have been very happy together, but once everyone else is brought in . . ."

He kissed her again, silencing at once her doubts and his. "I am really sure, my love."

Riding home, the qualms he had begun to feel disappeared. He was dazzled by the unexpected intensity of his feelings, excited rather than daunted by the struggle with his father which certainly lay before him. Unfortunately he was not to be granted any time to consider the nature of the approach he must make: his father, invariably well informed where local affairs were concerned, had long been aware of the way his son had chosen to pass his summer of waiting.

Two

Christopher St. Albyn called at Abbotsfield at ten o'clock precisely, as had been arranged, but in all his life he had never before faced such an alarming and distasteful experience.

Intending to approach the subject of an invitation to the Lovells after dinner, he had instead been summoned by his father, accused of dishonesty and stupidity, and faced with an ultimatum. Lord St. Albyn himself was neither dishonest nor stupid: he had inherited vast responsibilities which he discharged conscientiously and intelligently. He was generous with his dependents, punctilious in all his dealings. He had only one son, who in due course would inherit all these things and who must therefore somehow develop the necessary qualities. For this reason Christopher was to go into the army—it was a risk for an only son, but not a great one in peacetime. There, Lord St. Albyn hoped, his son's easygoing charm would be tempered into something more durable.

The question of marrying, or even meeting Eleanor, simply never came up for discussion. Once or twice Christopher had tried to explain their feelings for each other but his father's blighting contempt almost immediately exposed his own doubts again, only shallowly overlaid as they were by the intoxication of his first serious love affair. Lord St. Albyn had viewed with equanimity the rumors that his son was spending the summer trifling with some unknown nobody, but was so coldly furious when he finally realized that the meetings were with the daughter of a respectable tradesman, an acquaintance of the hunting field, that Christopher was overwhelmed by the task of explanation.

So he had been dispatched, like an errant schoolboy who had smashed the crockery, to make his formal apologies to the Lovells and to take leave of Eleanor. "It is the least you can do," his father had said grimly. "You clean up your own mess like a gentleman. When I learned who the girl was today—and you may depend upon it that the whisper will soon be all over the county—I made this appointment for you, and you are going to keep it, no one else. In the future you will confine your activities to women who understand the rules, or else to those you can honorably approach."

Christopher was ushered into the cluttered, brightly polished drawing room at Abbotsfield, but no one came to greet or to curse him, and his carefully rehearsed speeches began to evaporate with nervousness. He roamed round the room, peering at the faint miniatures and starting when the clocks whirred and struck in unison. By the time they had struck again and the house was still utterly silent he was almost unnerved, wondering whether this was a calculated insult and if in fact he ought simply to depart.

The delay was caused by Mrs. Lovell, pale and strained after a sleepless night, flatly refusing to meet him. It was William Lovell alone who finally entered the room, so full of apologies for the delay that Christopher's stammered explanations seemed quite trivial by comparison.

Finally William laughed, for he had never taken the affair particularly tragically, indeed if anything it enhanced his respect for his daughter. "I think we had better call it quits, my boy! I believe you when you say no harm has been done, but you must know that it was very wrong of you. You have made my wife very unhappy, and Eleanor too."

"Yes," agreed Christopher miserably. "I do now. Do

29

you . . . do you think I could see Eleanor for a moment, sir? I cannot go away without saying good-by."

William considered. Sarah would undoubtedly be shocked, but this awkward, stammering boy who had so easily lost his resolution in the face of opposition was certainly not going to talk Eleanor into any rash defiance. The whole affair might well be tidier if he finished it himself. "Very well," he said finally, "but only for a few minutes here. Charlotte really should be with her, but I will tell her to remain in the hall."

· · ·

Eleanor came into his arms with a rush. "Oh, Christopher, I knew you would come! What a terrible day yesterday was—I told you it would not be easy to make your parents agree even to a visit and Mama was even angrier than they must have been."

Christopher silenced her with a kiss and surprised himself with the wish that he could blot out with kisses all need for talk, for regret, for farewell, and then just leave. But kisses and the easy happiness of summer were no longer enough and Eleanor sensed his wretchedness: "We are going to have to wait a long time, aren't we? Shall I see you again before your regiment leaves for Ireland?"

It was even worse than he had expected. Although she had been the first to realize clearly all the difficulties ahead of them, now that these were so obviously insuperable, she was the one to be naïvely confident that all would be well. He drew her to him, smothering words which were like an echo of his own conscience, hurting her in his shame and anger, crushing the mouth which had become his accuser. When she broke free they drew apart like enemies.

"Christopher?" she whispered, eyes shadowed in her white face.

He turned, kicking one of the many footstools out

of his way, and moved blindly over to the window. "It is no good, Nell. I came today to tell you so."

"No good?" she repeated dazedly.

He rounded on her, anger the only avenue of escape. "You knew it was no good, you told me so yourself. I cannot go into the army without the allowance my father pays me, and anyway no regiment will have married junior officers—it would ruin all my chances before I've even started!" At her stricken look, his anger faded. "Oh, Nell my dear, I've thought and thought since last night but there is no way out. We should have to wait four or five years, almost without seeing each other, and going our own ways—we would be strangers when we met again."

"I don't feel we should ever be strangers, however long we were parted," said Eleanor in a small voice.

He shook his head; he could not tell her the other reason that his father had given him, which certainly put any idea of marriage beyond possibility. "Come, Nell, smile at me." He took her in his arms again, but gently this time. "I will always think of you, how you laughed with me, how very happy we were; don't let us part like this."

She turned her head away. It was unbelievable that he should have changed so quickly, impossible that the conviction of two days ago could have vanished so completely, when she knew that, whatever words were scattered between them, somehow their lives had been melted together by the warmth of their love. Somehow she must fight for both their futures, and she at least had never thought it would be easy. "Christopher, what did your father truly say about us? Surely if we were quite determined, when you are of full age and with your regiment in a year or so . . ."

"Nell, will you realize that it isn't possible!"

"What did he actually say, though?" she persisted. "Could they not at least meet me?"

"He didn't say anything!" exclaimed Christopher, goaded. He was anxious to save her the ultimate humiliation of certain facts which his father had disclosed to him, and in an effort to spare her, he added disastrously: "If you must know, we never even discussed marriage."

"You never even mentioned anything about—about our plans, that it wasn't just . . . ?" It was unbelievable. She could have accepted that their marriage was impossible but her mind refused to grasp such a monstrous betrayal: that the very idea had been abandoned undiscussed at the first sign of opposition and Lord St. Albyn left undisturbed in his conviction that he had put a stop to nothing more than undesirable hedge-meetings.

"It was hopeless." He spoke sullenly now, unable to explain properly, only too aware of the way she must feel. He was anxious only to be gone, to go right away and never even look across the valley lest he should see again the break in the trees beyond which Abbotsfield stood. "Nell, I have to go, I promised your father only to stay a few minutes." He smiled suddenly: "I don't think either of us can stand much more of this. Nell my love, whatever you think of me now, remember me sometimes with kindness, for I swear I shall never forget you." He lifted her fingers to his lips, but even that was wrong, the whole of her right hand was swathed in bandages. "Hullo, what have you done to yourself?" He kissed her wrist instead.

"You were not the only one to face angry parents yesterday," said Eleanor stonily. "But I told my mother we were to be wed whatever happened, and she was so angry at our conduct that she forgot she never used a ruler on our hands once we were grown up."

"A ruler?" said Christopher, bewildered, looking at the bandages. "I've had hairbrushes and my father's riding crop in my time but it has never come to bandages."

"She used her ebony ruling stick by mistake," explained Eleanor indifferently. The abrupt change in the conversation, after all that had gone before, seemed

32

as unreal as everything else. Like Christopher, now she wanted only to go; there was nothing more that could possibly be said. Yet the only clear thought in her mind was that when he went it would be forever, that she would never see him again. Never. It simply was not possible.

But it was possible; another moment, the brush of his lips on her cheek, the click of the door, and he had gone. She stood blindly in the middle of the room, her bandaged hand to her cheek, and looked for the first time down the endless days ahead.

Mrs. Lovell felt hardly less desperate than her daughter. She had been deeply shocked by events but this did not account for the turmoil of her thoughts. Everything she had ever done or said had been intended as part of a path to God, for herself and for those committed to her charge. She had never deviated, never made allowances or concessions to lesser standards; now suddenly an incredible chasm seemed to have opened up in front of her. For all her efforts, William had failed to measure up to her standards, now Eleanor also was to be a constant source of offense, no doubt dragging down with her still other members of the household. Most terrifying of all, she sensed her own lack of control, her helplessness, her failure in all that mattered to her most. In the black fury that had gripped her the day before, she had wanted to hurt Eleanor, had not cared if it was the ruling stick rather than the cane with which she had struck out.

Life resumed its pattern, but it was a pattern which now felt brittle rather than durable and Eleanor stayed mostly in her room, quiet and withdrawn, forbidden to leave it without a maid in attendance. The others felt awkward in her presence, an awkwardness made infinitely worse by Mrs. Lovell's new rule that the sisters were to use the library instead of their own parlor and to converse with Eleanor only in her hearing.

Even William was eventually driven to protest. "You

cannot force them to do everything under supervision at their age—punished if they speak out of your hearing and Eleanor followed if she only goes down the stairs!"

"They had a great deal of freedom and it was abused," pointed out his wife coldly. "Susannah is to be wed and dear Alfred has a right to expect that he is marrying into a family of virtue where his future wife has been shielded from harm."

"But Eleanor will not harm Susannah! You are talking as if she would corrupt anything she touched. We must help her to forget, not force her into seclusion." William seldom made the effort to stand against his wife, but he was uneasily aware that this time he must, that he had a special obligation where Eleanor was concerned. "She must of course be closely chaperoned, but I will hire a companion if necessary," he ended doggedly.

"I have thought very deeply about this. I have discussed the matter with Eleanor too, for I am entirely in agreement with you that she must have occupation. She herself has no desire to go out into company and will not in any case be fit to assume the responsibilities of marriage in the immediate future." Sarah Lovell hesitated; she had indeed thought most carefully about Eleanor's future but it was a future conditioned by her own firm determination to be rid of the girl forever. For Eleanor's own sake something should be done to give her a purpose in life, but above all the rot must be cut out of the household. Did not the Good Book itself give clear guidance? If thine eye offend you, pluck it out, or thy limb then cut it off?

"What about sending her to Chichester then, to my sister Mary?" suggested William.

"Certainly not! Mary would never watch her as she should; besides, Eleanor needs occupation and service, not the reward of a visit to an indulgent aunt after the way she has behaved. I have prayed very earnestly for guidance and yesterday my prayers were answered."

34

Sarah Lovell never doubted that God answered all sincere prayers promptly and efficiently, just as she attended to her own household duties and requests. The supplicant only needed to be aware of His answer, to sift events in such a way as to make His purpose clear.

"How was that, my dear?" William was cautious, having lived for many years with Sarah's sublime confidence in the divine basis of her own decisions. He might advise or occasionally argue, but he had never yet diverted Sarah from her convictions.

"I visited Mrs. Merrilees yesterday; she was holding a small tea party for her daughter Emily, who has recently returned from Russia for a few weeks' holiday. She was telling us of her life in St. Petersburg where she is a governess, and it came to me at once that this was the solution I sought for Eleanor."

"What solution?"

"Why, that dear Eleanor should go for a year or so to St. Petersburg. She could travel with Emily Merrilees next month, for she says that several English ladies return together at the end of the summer."

"To Russia! Sarah, for heaven's sake!" William expostulated. "If the child ought to go away for a while and needs something to occupy her mind, there are plenty of other places she can go. I couldn't possibly agree to such a scheme."

"You have not reflected," said Mrs. Lovell firmly. "Eleanor needs an outlet for her energy as well as her thoughts. It would not be in her own interests for her to go away simply for a visit; as a guest she would have less occupation than she has here. Yet if she takes employment in England it is certain to be in an inferior position since she can neither draw nor play well. Her only asset is her French, and Emily assures me that all the Russian noble families speak French as their first language. In England Eleanor would always be a servant if she should go into employment, to which we could certainly never agree, but in

35

Russia the foreign governesses are honored and thought of as one of the family, since the native Russians are so completely inferior."

"No, no, I don't care what you say, it would be most unsuitable! What would happen if she should dislike her position, so far from home?"

"William, this is the answer we have been seeking, I assure you. Everything Emily said convinced me, for I felt all the objections you mention, but in St. Petersburg conditions are so different to London that they none of them apply. All the great Russian families return to St. Petersburg before the winter and English governesses are in such demand that most are able to choose from several positions, quite unlike England. But of course Eleanor must have a family to go to before we would allow her to leave with Emily. It is God's work for her, I am sure of it. Emily told me of the satisfaction they all feel at bringing enlightenment to the children there. Everyone is so kind, but with no notion of discipline for the young, that the English governesses quite hold the households together. Eleanor may not be accomplished, but she is a good manager, it would be the right sort of situation for her. I have tried hard with her all these years, but it has been to no avail; she must now seek her own salvation." Mrs. Lovell paused for breath; even to herself the explanation had been too long, too anxious.

"But who would look after her? If she shows unsteadiness of character here, surely in Russia the risks must be greater?" objected William, but he was only too well aware whose unsteadiness of character she might be said to have inherited. He also sensed his wife's determination, springing from her conviction that she had been betrayed in spite of all her efforts, efforts moreover which few men could have expected their wives to make without complaint. He was shaken by a weak man's anger that after all these years Eleanor should have cut up their peace yet again in such a fashion. Indeed the more William thought about it the more he saw that the idea of Russia did have a great deal to recommend it; he was still uneasy, however, sufficiently so to break a lifetime's rule about not questioning his wife's judgment in front of the children and to go in search of Eleanor.

He found her disconcertingly calm and detached. "Yes, Mama told me, and today she has invited Emily Merrilees over to tea so that I can talk to her."

"Eleanor dear, you know there is no need for you to go. We are always pleased to have you here with us, it is just that your mother and I are worried about your future and feel this may be right for you."

"And Mama thinks that I need to make some amends for my sins," flashed Eleanor, showing just for an instant the depths of her resentment and uncertainty. "I am sorry, Papa, but if I stay here I do not know what will become of me. I cannot speak without Mama wondering whether anything I say will give Charlotte wrong ideas and there is nothing useful I can do when someone must always be with me if I leave my room."

"My dear . . ."

"Above all I cannot endure to stay where I was so happy with Christopher! I know I must forget him and what he meant—still means—to me, but I cannot do it here. I think I must go or I shall become 'poor Eleanor,' the family ghost, before my time!" She gave an uncertain laugh, twisting some sewing in her hands.

William was aghast. Eleanor had always been so quiet, as all the Lovell girls were taught to be quiet; he might prefer Charlotte's docile sweetness but he had always been struck by his eldest daughter's calm good sense, had responded secretly to the occasional flash of humor which slipped past her guard. Now she seemed a stranger, a stranger moreover in danger of being isolated in a dream world around which the walls were thickening with every month that passed. He gazed at her, perplexed. "Do you really wish to go?"

37

"I think perhaps I have no choice any longer. Mama will listen to nothing but Russia now she is convinced it is the answer to her prayers. If it is to be Russia or nothing, then Russia it must be." She smiled faintly. "I think Mama does not consider an English family would be enough of a penance for me!" It was the Eleanor of the summer who spoke, the new, unknown Eleanor who found her thoughts more difficult to guard after the careless freedom she had enjoyed with Christopher.

Easygoing he might be, but William was almost shocked; his daughter's scarcely veiled criticism of her mother and the cynicism of her insight into Sarah Lovell's mind disconcerted him. All at once he knew how his wife felt, divided and cut off from this strange girl whose character differed so strikingly from those of the rest of the family. His guilt above all was clear and he did not shirk the thought, but it was true that they would none of them be comfortable again until she was gone.

Three

Emily Merrilees came to tea that afternoon, delighted to recount her experiences in Russia and to provide the focal point for a gathering of Mrs. Lovell's friends. Eleanor sat quietly by the window, still lost in the detachment of unbelief which had followed Christopher's departure. She did not feel as though any of these extraordinary plans were being discussed on her behalf, and when the ladies turned to her in astonishment on hearing of her determination to go to Russia, she felt like a character in a play, as if real life would resume again at some shadowy date in the future when Christopher would return.

But he will not return, she told herself fiercely, it is this which is real; she was aware of the effort she must make, now, before it was too late. She had received one note from Christopher since he left, read first by her mother and then passed on without comment. It had been apologetic, even affectionate, and she had spent days trying to read beneath the surface of the stilted words before giving up in disgust—but disgust at herself and not at him, for she knew that Christopher had been right in one thing: it was she who had known well enough how slender were their hopes of a future together.

It was Christopher's letter which had made her face this truth at last, and with it came a kind of shame that she had so allowed herself to be swept away. She was not really a dreamer by temperament, and now that she was beginning to bend her will toward breaking out of the prison of her thoughts, the constraints of Abbotsfield were more intolerable than ever. If Russia was to be the avenue of escape, then she was almost reconciled to the prospect. Apprehensive she might be at going so far, but to one who had never traveled more than a dozen miles from home it was scarcely more remote than London.

Actually, she thought, Russia sounded rather amusing, like some enormous, elegant children's party. Emily's conversation seemed to consist entirely of grand dukes, generals, and countesses, lavish balls and casual, lazy days. The prospect was alarming, but not unattractive in the stiff plush setting of Abbotsfield's drawing room.

Emily Merrilees was a plain, voluble, well-meaning woman of thirty or so, whose mother's penurious widowhood had early driven her out to work as a governess, first in London and then to St. Petersburg, when it became clear that in England her attainments

39

were insufficient for her to retain a post with any but the less desirable families. Returned from Russia after five years for a brief holiday, she displayed an invincible ease of manner which Eleanor found quite overwhelming.

"Of course our little English colony will be so delighted to have another member! We are all so friendly together that we don't feel in the least cut off from our dear homes, but a fresh face gives us such joy that I know everyone will not be able to do enough for you."

"It will be delightful for Eleanor to have such a happy circle of friends." Everything that was said deepened Mrs. Lovell's conviction of a decision rightly taken. "Although one should not think of comfort where God's calling is concerned, I cannot help feeling apprehensive for her in such a distant country. But I know I must not be selfish nor stand in the way when Eleanor is convinced that she has at last found her vocation, and Emily tells me that the need of the Russian children is indeed great, even in the noble families."

"Oh, yes indeed!" broke in Emily. "The Russians are so kind and indulgent but they have not the least notion of discipline for their children. But you need not feel uneasy, Mrs. Lovell, there are so many English there."

Eleanor said nothing, keeping her eyes lowered as she had been taught, but she could not have spoken even if it had been expected of her. She might be willing to go to Russia as a means of escape, but she had not given up hope that something less drastic might be possible, and she had intended to use this gathering to ask some of her mother's friends to recommend her to a post locally or in London. When she had made the suggestion before it had been brushed aside, but perhaps in company it would not be so easy to do so again. Surely even in a small gathering someone must have a friend or relative anxious for a governess, who would not worry too much about her lack of proficiency in drawing and music. But either because Mrs. Lovell had read her daughter's thoughts, or because she was anxious to remove from Eleanor's departure any appearance of compulsion, she had certainly now made such an approach almost impossible; already Eleanor was regarded with awe, as a martyr in a noble cause. It did not occur to her that the good ladies of Mayhurst, well aware of the cause of her disgrace, would certainly not recommend her to their friends, and that perhaps in her own way her mother was sparing her further humiliation.

"I have written to the addresses you gave me, Emily," Mrs. Lovell was saying, "and I understand that we will be able to look for a reply in about a month's time. Eleanor must have a good position to go to, and Emily has been so kind too in writing to her friend Mary Stevens, in St. Petersburg, to ask if she will call on some likely families for us."

"Mama . . ." Eleanor stopped.

"Yes, my dear?"

"Why should there be so much hurry? Would it not be better for Emily to look around for me when she returns to Russia?"

"But whom would you travel with then? Your father and I could never consider the idea of your going on your own." Eleanor met her mother's eyes fleetingly and looked away. The sooner the better, she thought resignedly.

Emily interrupted: "Anyway, St. Petersburg is quite iced up in another two or three months and you would have to travel overland, which is very uncomfortable and unsuitable. But once you are in St. Petersburg there are always so many good positions to choose from that you need have no fear. I am afraid everyone changes her situation quite shamelessly until she finds just what she wants, for of course English governesses are in great demand and no one thinks the worse of you

41

for seeking the best available—Russian households are so haphazard they scarcely notice the change!"

"How extraordinary!" Eleanor was entranced by this contrast to the relentless routine which was all she had ever known.

Emily was already prattling on: "So Mary will call on Madame Lenskaya for you as soon as she thinks your letter will have arrived—I know the governess there wishes to return to England soon. Such a delightful woman, so cultured and a friend of Count Kankrine, the Tsar's leading minister. It would be just the post for you, balls every night, I dare say, and card parties and receptions—perhaps you would be presented to the Tsar himself! I assure you it is quite unlike London and the foreign governesses go everywhere." She paused for breath at last.

"It does not sound at all the sort of situation I should like my daughter to fill," stated Mrs. Lovell flatly.

"But it is a wonderful chance! Handsome counts and guards officers in and out of the house all day long and, believe me, many of them want above all things to have an English wife; they are such much better managers than the Russians."

"Emily, please," Mrs. Merrilees remonstrated, observing the shocked faces around her. "That is not at all the way to speak. I am ashamed that you should behave in so unladylike a way. I declare, I am delighted that Eleanor will be going back with you so she can help you recollect English rules of conduct."

Eleanor laughed. "I don't think I should be a very good teacher, ma'am. I think I shall need Emily to show me the way to go on in such very grand society."

Mrs. Merrilees gave her a gratified look. "Oh well, you are both young and I'm sure you deserve a chance of some gaiety after leaving your homes to voyage so far."

"I do not wish Eleanor to go to an ungodly and pleasure-seeking household whose affairs are conducted in such a very lax and unsuitable way." Mrs.

Lovell was rigid with disapproval at Emily's artless recital of the joys of St. Petersburg.

"Come now, Sarah, I am sure it is not as bad as that. I should have thought the poor child's life so far away from home would be dismal enough without grudging her a little enjoyment. I do not suppose the governesses are asked to many of those parties, now are they, Emily? For all her fine words, she tells me life is very difficult, Russians being so ignorant that you cannot leave the least thing to them." Mrs. Merrilees tried to brush over the unfortunate impressions made by her daughter, only to hear Emily exclaim, too shrilly: "You couldn't prefer Eleanor to go to Madame Davidova's instead of the Lenskis'! She may be terribly rich but she lives in a fusty old house behind the Military Academy and has dozens of cats which she cares for far more than her one grandchild. She never entertains or goes anywhere except the stiffest court functions—they say she wears a ball gown even in the morning!"

"Eleanor will feel far happier in a quiet and orderly establishment than she would in an endless round of frivolity. I would never consent to such a thing," said Mrs. Lovell firmly.

Eleanor made no further contribution to these decisions on her future. Long training in not interrupting her elders stood her in good stead but her heart, awakened by Christopher to the meaning of excitement and gaiety as well as love, had quickened absurdly at Emily's descriptions and she involuntarily imagined the whirl of color and the quick beat of music in that distant undreamed-of world. As soon as she could speak without impropriety, however, she remarked in a neutral tone: "I thought you said their name was Lenskaya—is Lenski a shortening?"

Emily giggled irritatingly. "Good heavens, no! Nearly all Russian names and nouns have a different ending for male and female although it is the same word. The family I am with now is called Lokunin but Madame is Madame Lokunina. You will find it terribly muddling to start with—after all the years I have been there, I only speak a few words of Russian."

"However do you get along?" demanded Eleanor wonderingly.

"Everyone speaks French. Most of the Russians speak French all the time, even when they are alone."

"How about the servants, surely they cannot speak French?"

"How funny you are! No, of course they do not, but I make signs to them; they are so stupid it is all they understand anyway."

Eleanor was silent, unable to visualize people so stupid that they could not understand their own language, and when she roused from her reverie, it was to receive a list of clothes which Emily said were unobtainable or very expensive in Russia and which she must take with her. "I'll come round and see you before we go and you must ask me all the questions you wish." She dropped her voice and, looking nervously round to see if she was overheard, whispered, "Don't worry about Madame Davidova too much. There will be plenty of situations to choose from and you can always change as soon as you have had a chance to look around."

Eleanor warmed to her for the first time and whispered back: "I'll manage—for a week or so anyway!"

After the party had broken up Mrs. Lovell made no further reference to the possibility of Eleanor's departure, beyond condemning, in the most forceful possible way, Emily Merrilees' lack of breeding, good manners, conduct, and sense. It was almost the only subject on which Eleanor felt herself to be in wholehearted agreement with her mother.

As time went by Eleanor began to wonder whether after all the whole idea was to be dropped; perhaps Emily's unfortunate disclosures had revealed the enormity of the step into the unknown which was being contemplated.

The only sign that Mrs. Lovell was holding to her purpose was the endless sewing which she and Charlotte had to do, making up warm dresses and cloaks from lengths of cloth delivered to the door by the local carrier. Eleanor might inwardly deplore the drab browns and grays which her mother chose, but to someone who had never before had more than one new dress at a time the mere sight of such quantities was exciting. Charlotte or Susannah occasionally accompanied Mrs. Lovell on her monthly shopping expeditions to Tunbridge Wells, but since her disgrace Eleanor was always left behind, forbidden to leave the garden, every move watched by an anxious household fearful of blame if she should slip away.

Her brother John, with the skill of long practice, timed his visit for the September shopping day. Ever since his marriage to a rich wife three years before, he came to Abbotsfield as little as possible, but he still worked in the Lovell timber business and had been at first incredulous and then alarmed by his father's shameful hints that Eleanor might soon depart for Russia.

John was good-natured and indulgent, an old ally of their nursery days together, but it had only recently occurred to Eleanor that perhaps, now he was of independent means, he was the very person to help her. She had been racking her brains for means to talk to him privately before it was too late, so was overjoyed by his appearance on this most fortunate of days.

"Oh, John, how glad I am to see you!" She was seated with the household mending under a great oak on the lawn, in full view of two housemaids and the under gardener, but at least no one was in earshot. "Do sit down, you are the very person I most wanted to see."

He flopped on the grass beside her. "Phew! It is a devilish hot ride here, but I wanted to see you too. Whatever is all this I hear about you going to Russia? You are not serious, are you?"

45

"Oh no! It was not my idea at all." Eleanor felt almost lightheaded with being able to talk freely again. "It is just that everyone assumes I am going, so I suppose I shall unless . . ."

"But Russia, for heaven's sake!" broke in John impatiently. "What in God's name makes anyone think you should go to Russia of all places? My father told me some taradiddle about your desire to serve your fellow men and not wanting a life of luxury, but I've never heard such rubbish in my life. I could tell that even he did not believe a word of it."

"Of course I don't want to go there!" exclaimed Eleanor. "Somewhere hundreds of miles away where the people don't even understand their own language if Emily is to be believed. And then to be a governess of all things, how could I want to go? But . . . have you heard anything about why Mama is so displeased with me?"

He nodded. "I admire your nerve, but you didn't make a very good choice, did you? Whatever made you get involved with the St. Albyns of all people?"

"I don't want to talk about it. But you at least know what Mama is like—"

"Don't I just!" he interjected feelingly.

"Yes, well, it is impossible for me to go on like this, every movement spied on yet nothing to do except the same old schoolroom tasks. But after all these years of scales and drawing lessons it seems I am unfit to hold a position in an English household."

"That is certainly untrue," he broke in. "But, Nell, you can't become a governess, someone's drudge at twenty pounds a year. I certainly can't see you training half a dozen brats in deportment and the French language—it's absurd. Whatever reasons you think you have . . . this scheme has a kind of mad feel to it. You mustn't do it."

"That is why I wished so particularly to see you," said Eleanor eagerly. "Couldn't you and Blanche recommend me to a post? Perhaps have me to stay and

46

then I could go as soon as I found a situation near here?"

He shifted uncomfortably. "I should like to help, God knows. But I expect you have heard that Blanche is in a delicate state of health at the moment and I couldn't bother her with such a blazing family row as that would cause. Anyway, for heaven's sake, how could I have my sister to stay and then turn her away to a post as a governess? I've no mind to become an object of infamy in the district!"

"It would be much better for me if you would do something like that," said Eleanor desperately. "I don't even know when I am due to go, but Mama has heard from a friend of Emily's in St. Petersburg that she is arranging a post for me there with some people called Davidova who Emily says are quite dreadful. Surely people would not hold it against you if I stayed with you while I sought for a position here?"

"They could and they would," he replied shortly. "It seems that you have set your mind on going away, and if you have, then perhaps Russia would be better than England. You will never find a respectable husband here once you are a governess."

Eleanor's cheeks flamed. "But in Russia they might not be so particular?"

"Well, any Englishwoman, even a governess, must be better than a Russian, so you might do quite well for yourself if you find you can stomach them. I had not thought too clearly about it, but perhaps Mama is right, she would not suggest something she knew to be wrong." He wished now that he had not come, he had no wish for all the unpleasantness that interference would certainly bring. He was long since done with the terrible intensity of life at Abbotsfield and could not bear the thought of involving himself there ever again, no matter what the reason.

There was a long silence. Eleanor looked resolutely in front of her, at the shaven lawn bright in the afternoon sunlight, the first Michaelmas daisies just piling into bloom in the border beyond. Over the precisely trimmed hedge was the faint loom of the hills, smudged with distance and dimmed by the greenish haze of early autumn. Closer at hand the old house crouched in its heavy screen of bushes and creeper, serene, solid, familiar. It was all very beautiful. It was also unbearable. Eleanor blinked back her tears and knotted her throat until it ached. There must be something very wrong with me, she thought miserably: first Christopher and now John. I must go, it is now the only way.

Four

A fresh breeze was blowing down-river, causing the gulls to wheel and scream and the ships at anchor to shift and creak uneasily, snubbing their cables and curtsying gently to the call of the gale outside.

The *Neptune* looked hard and competent, with her sharp bow and slim black hull, the sun glancing off her yellow and red paddle box and glittering from the gilding at stem and poop. A thin trail of smoke was rising from her single funnel, to be almost immediately tossed away by the wind and driven seaward through the humming rigging.

Eleanor and Emily had stayed overnight in Eastcheap at the home of a Baltic timber importer, one of William Lovell's business acquaintances. It was as unlike Abbotsfield as it was possible to imagine: full of confusion, shouting clerks, and children playing rowdy games in the half-dark. The importer and his wife seemed quite undisturbed by the noise, which was, indeed, so great that ordinary conversation was seldom possible. The stiff parting at the railway station earlier in the day seemed almost natural compared with this kaleidoscopic new existence.

Eleanor was wakeful for much of the night, her last in England perhaps forever, the clattering footsteps and rough voices in the street outside strange to her country-tuned ears. In the bright, flat light of early morning they and their roped baggage were piled into an insubstantial boat at Tower Steps and rowed out to the *Neptune* by Mick, a gigantic Irish riverman, and the wide, strange panorama of London spread out on every side before Eleanor's bewildered gaze. Emily seemed quite unaware of Eleanor's awe and excitement; if London was so incredible whatever could strange, far-off St. Petersburg be like?

Mick maneuvered his frail little craft alongside the *Neptune* and then tossed, with effortless ease, first his cargo and then his passengers up the steep, roped companion ladder and onto the smoothly scrubbed, cluttered deck.

"There ye be now an' the best o' luck to ye both." Mick emerged up the ladder for the last time, carrying Emily's parasol in an enormous hairy fist. "It's a rough trip ye'll be having, Oi'm thinkin'."

"Do you really think so?" Eleanor searched anxiously in her reticule, wondering how much she should give him. She had ten whole guineas sewn into her petticoat —"enough to get you home again, Puss, if you don't like it," her father had said, kissing her in mingled guilt and affection the night before she left—but very little small change, no one having thought of the ferry charges.

"Thank ye kindly, miss. Ay, 'tis blowing up hard outside, but 'tis enjoyin' it ye'll be for sure."

"I do hope so, but I've never been on a ship before, you know." She smiled suddenly. "I feel as if I'd like to row back with you; it seems so strange to have left England, forever perhaps."

"Don't ye be worryin' now, miss," he replied hastily,

49

fearful of a scene. " 'Tis enjoyin' it ye'll be! Ye could have my place on the river any time for the askin'!" And with a final wave of the hand he lumbered down into his boat and pushed off from the side with more haste than care, causing an ominous scrape and a crash alongside as he did so. There was a loud yell of rage from a small figure perched above the paddle box and Eleanor recoiled from the shouted exchange of obscene pleasantries which followed, although she noticed with respect that Emily took no notice, merely beckoning to a grinning sailor lounging nearby and asking for the steward.

"I'll take your traps down for you," he offered. "The cook'll be down there some place, but the steward, I reckon, 'll be powerful drunk, he allus is, last night in port."

"Thank you very much," replied Emily composedly, again exciting Eleanor's admiration by her sang-froid in the face of these unheard-of complications. "When are we sailing?"

"In an hour or so, I'd say, on the tide. Better get yourselves unpacked like before we gets outside, be pretty rough an' all once we're clear of land." He shouldered Eleanor's trunk with a grunt and led the way across the deck and through a narrow, dark doorway in the break of the poop. "Mind the coaming, miss, there. Takes a couple o' days to get used to."

"Thank you very much," said Eleanor, stepping carefully over the raised doorway. "What is it used for?"

"Keeps some o' the water out. Floods down here ofttimes even so," he replied, patronizing her ignorance.

"Flooded right up here!" exclaimed Eleanor, astonished at the force of the sea, which she had read about but only seen once in her life and then on a day of sparkling flat calm.

"Of course, you silly!" Emily was only too pleased to be able to show off her experience. "Last time I went out it was green all over everywhere, and we had to stay in our bunks for three days without getting up."

Eleanor was silent, not really believing it, for she could not see how a ship would remain afloat once the sea was over the top of the deck, but unwilling to expose her ignorance further.

"Here we are, miss, all right and tight!" said the sailor, opening another door and slamming the trunk down with a crash. "Three other ladies and a gent aboard already an' one yet to come, so you'll be a nice snug party. I'll jus' go up an' get the rest of your traps and tell the steward you're aboard, if he's in a state to understand, which I doubt!" He disappeared like a jack-in-the-box through the narrow entrance, humming to himself.

"Well," observed Eleanor, "I don't know anything about what it will be like on a ship, but surely he is a very strange sort of man?"

"Oh, I don't know," responded Emily absently. "You are such a country girl to be sure; as a single female traveling on your own, you will find everything very different now. No one knowing who you are or caring, you won't get the respect you have been accustomed to at home, protected by your name and family. It is difficult at first and I couldn't understand why everyone was so offhand and rude when I started to travel, but you will find the same everywhere and soon get used to it."

"I don't think I shall like it," said Eleanor doubtfully.

"No, but you will not regard it after a while unless they are actually insulting. I wonder where the other three ladies have gone, I see they have unpacked, so perhaps we had better do so too if it is going to be rough outside."

There was another breath-catching crash behind them as Emily's box was heaved into the cabin and their friend shouted through the doorway, "Jus' two more to bring, soon be back, don't you fret!"

Eleanor laughed unwillingly. "Oh well, I suppose

51

I'll get used to it, although it doesn't seem very likely."

For the next half hour they were busily engaged unpacking such of their things as they would require on the journey and disposing them in a small locker and cupboard provided for the purpose. The cabin was barely twenty feet long by about ten feet wide, decorated with deep crimson hangings and carpet and lighted by two small portholes, immovably screwed down. Eleanor's nose wrinkled at the all-pervading smell which, while not actively unpleasant, was very noticeable and appeared to be compounded of a mixture of inferior soap, tar, stale cooking, half-burned coal fumes, and paint. However, the cabin itself was spotlessly clean, each blanket folded down precisely, and the dark woodwork shone with polish.

When they had finished unpacking and then wedging their unwanted belongings behind the stout bars provided, Emily and Eleanor both wrapped up in their new, warm shawls and sallied forth to investigate the rest of their living accommodation. The passage by which they had entered stretched down the length of the poop and ended in a single porthole over the stern. Two doors opened off each side, and that immediately opposite theirs was marked "Saloon," so Emily boldly pushed it open and poked her head inside. It was empty but Eleanor caught a glimpse of a long, polished, heat-stained table, a double line of dark oilskin-covered benches, and some shelves round the walls carrying a tattered collection of books, brightly polished trays held in place with hooks, and some glasses enclosed in a cabinet.

"Everything very clean and well ordered," approved Emily. "I remember the first time I went out to St. Petersburg, there was still the remains of the last meal of the voyage home left on the table when we came on board, although that was a very inferior type of ship which only carried two or three passengers."

Eleanor shivered, for it looked very comfortless to

her. "I wonder where all the others can be—is there anything else down this passage, do you suppose?"

Emily giggled. "I shouldn't go down there unless you wish to create a scandal before we even start; those will be the double and gentlemen's cabins, I expect."

Eleanor was taken aback; the cramped conditions, the idea of living at such close proximity with total strangers, perhaps for weeks, depressed her. The riverman, Mick, and then the sailor had exposed her inexperience, and the prospect of facing similar daily familiarities from unknown male passengers was unnerving. She wished, suddenly, that she was back at Abbotsfield; in her mind it was no longer stuffy and confining, it was security. Then she encountered the amused superiority of Emily's gaze and with a profound effort she took a grip on herself and steadied her breathing. I am here, she thought fiercely, I must not think of Abbotsfield again, or Lottie, or John or . . . or Christopher. But the future was too threatening to think of either, the mind cannot stay battened down forever, and she was not far from desolation when she followed Emily in search of their fellow passengers.

Once out of the stuffy saloon and into the clear, sparkling autumn air, Eleanor recovered some of her earlier excitement at the prospect of her voyage into the unknown, and she and Emily were soon introducing themselves to the group of passengers they found standing by the after rail.

"I am glad you have come, we were afraid that the rest of our cabin was going to be empty and we would have a very dull time with just the three of us. I am Miss Macdonald, Margaret Macdonald," said one of the three ladies, a tall, dark girl with a confident manner and remote smile.

Emily giggled. "We thought we would never be on board in time, everything has been such a rush these past few days! My name is Emily Merrilees and this is my very, very dear friend Eleanor Lovell, on her first

53

trip. So all us hardened travelers will have to do our best to comfort her, won't we?"

Eleanor could have thrown her arms round the neck of a frightened-looking girl standing beside Miss Macdonald when she whispered: "It is my first voyage too. I—I've never even seen the sea before or spoken to a foreigner." She bit her lip resolutely, but she looked so small and forlorn that Eleanor longed to comfort her.

The other lady was a faded blonde of middle age and a vague, monosyllabic turn of speech. Eleanor later discovered that she was in her fifties, was called Miss Faulkner, and that no one had ever heard her Christian name. She was returning to Moscow where she had been a governess for many years, taking with her her niece Minnie, whose terror of the unknown was already apparent in the few words she had spoken.

The remaining member of the party, a portly gentleman with fine red whiskers, introduced himself as Mr. Wall and kissed their hands with what Eleanor privately considered an excess of zeal in the circumstances.

"It seems as if I'm going to have a pleasant voyage," he chuckled jovially. "With so many pretty ladies to keep me company, I shan't complain if we get iced up in the Baltic."

"Is there no other gentleman on board then?" inquired Emily, a shade of disappointment in her voice.

He let out a bellow of laughter and slammed the rail with his fist. "Indeed there are! Only the captain and the officers and the crew and all the second-class passengers—not that you'll see much of them, poor devils, cooped up below with only a few square feet of deck to walk on."

Miss Macdonald allowed a faint, amused smile to slip across her disdainful countenance, but Eleanor was hard put to it not to laugh as Emily stutteringly tried to disclaim any design behind her question.

"I think there are two more passengers," volunteered Miss Faulkner unexpectedly, cutting in on Emily's embarrassment. "A Russian gentleman and his servant, so I was told."

"His servant?" queried Eleanor.

Miss Macdonald laughed unkindly. "When you have been in Russia a few days you will discover that no one of consequence there does anything for himself. Even a modest household would have twenty or thirty servants and no Russian gentleman would agree to be separated from his valet by half a dozen ladders and companionways. You'll see that he'll probably sleep in the same room as his master, only on the floor of course, just in case he wants anything in the night."

"Whatever do they do all day with that number of servants?" demanded Minnie, round-eyed.

"About half the time they sleep and most of the rest they go to parties, exchange spiteful remarks, and try to goad the servants into some action. And that is not nearly as easy as it sounds, for most of the maids are incapable of doing the simplest thing without direction and spend even more of their time asleep than their masters do. It's a fine country you're going to, I can tell you."

"Why do you go back then?" asked Eleanor, angry to see the dismay she felt mirrored on Minnie's face.

She shrugged indifferently. "I don't know. I didn't intend to, but well-paid posts are not easy to find in England. At least the Russians are undemanding and you have more freedom than you would in England. In my present position I have six servants under me in the nursery, although they are little better than children themselves unless I watch their every action."

"This looks like our Russian passenger now," interposed Mr. Wall, pointing to Mick's boat, which was beginning another laborious journey from the wharfside against the still flowing tide.

They all craned their necks but were able to see little except Mick's straining shoulders before hastily recollecting their manners and moving over to the far side of the deck, Mr. Wall remarking cheerfully as they did so: "I don't know why we should worry, though! Everyone always stares at new arrivals on board ship."

"Why, he hasn't any beard, or whiskers, or anything!" exclaimed Minnie in a horrified undertone. "Don't Russians grow beards like other people?"

All the others, even Eleanor, laughed.

"Perhaps he is young and handsome and hasn't got around to whiskers yet," suggested Mr. Wall.

"He didn't look young, so far as I could see, quite old in fact," objected Minnie doubtfully.

"Well, you will see that beards flourish particularly well in Russia and most of the peasants are more beard than face. But the present Tsar has forbidden the upper classes to grow them, so—"

"The Tsar? Oh, the Emperor! Do you mean he has actually passed a law against beards, of all things? How extraordinary!"

It also sounded very unlikely to Eleanor and she began to suspect that she and Minnie, as the inexperienced members of the party, were the victims of an elaborate legpull.

"They are extraordinary," stated Miss Macdonald flatly. "Most have whiskers, of course, and in the army they can grow mustaches, but only if they dye them the color of the regiment."

"Oh!" Minnie laughed, perceiving at last that she was being teased.

"No, seriously, dear," said Miss Faulkner. "Not red and blue of course, but in some regiments it is chestnut mustaches and horses, in others black, and so on. But do not be put off by small things which will seem strange, I have been very happy there for years."

Eleanor was grateful for these first words of encouragement since she had left home, but part of her mind could not help wondering what happened to the mustaches in units where piebald horses were the regulation. While they had been talking the usual clatter heralded Mick's arrival alongside, and they studied the new arrival covertly while keeping up an appearance of conversation.

He looked to be of that indeterminate age between thirty-five and forty-five, short and spare with a lined face and graying hair. He was also quite indubitably clean-shaven. Indeed this was the only thing which made him at all remarkable, but as neither Minnie nor Eleanor had ever seen a man of his age without either beard, mustache, or whiskers, the eccentricity was quite sufficient to make them stare.

Half an hour later the *Neptune* sailed, slipping down the silent reaches of the Thames like an intruder, gathering together expanses of gold and silver sheeting and then spilling them through her racing paddles in a shower of glittering stars, winking and beckoning to the receding shore.

The cold air and sweeping wind soon drove all the passengers below save only Eleanor, who stood beside the rail, all gloomy forebodings forgotten, laughing aloud as her hair was whipped into wild disorder and her cloak billowed madly away from her grasping fingers. At last she was shaking free from the passive acceptance which had numbed her feelings since Christopher's departure, even while the hurt and the loss had been rubbed raw yet again by the scarcely veiled relief she sensed in her family as the time for her departure had come.

She stretched out her arms with an unconscious gesture at the freely tossing gulls in their wake, and when she caught a sidelong grin on the face of one of the seamen engaged in coiling down ropes nearby, she returned it with a smile so dazzling that he had to be recalled to a sense of his surroundings by a string of curses from the mate.

She was so completely absorbed and delighted by everything around her that by the time she remembered to go below for the midday meal the others had almost finished. "I'm sorry to be late, but it was so wonderful upstairs I couldn't bear to come down."

"Shipboard food is never worth coming down for anyway," observed Mr. Wall gloomily. "You will have to learn, though, that at sea it is 'on deck,' not 'upstairs,' or you'll put the captain off his dinner."

"I'll learn," replied Eleanor confidently, determined not to be daunted by the obviously morose atmosphere. "I know I'm going to love this voyage."

"It is going to be very rough once we are out of the river, you mark my words. What do you say, Count?"

Everyone stopped talking and stared at the Russian, who was tranquilly eating his meal opposite Eleanor in complete indifference to the conversation around him. He laid his knife and fork aside and allowed his gaze to wander slowly over the row of deferential faces turned toward him before replying discouragingly, in good if careful English: "I have really no knowledge of the sea, but with this wind it will undoubtedly be rough."

Miss Macdonald sighed. "I can never keep my feet in the slightest sea. It is such a bore to be tossed about for days."

"Unfortunate," he replied politely, returning his undivided attention to his meal.

Eleanor was fascinated, in spite of herself, by such indifference and studied him covertly across the table. There was good reason for his shaven appearance, as she soon saw, for a diagonal scar ran across the side of his face and she could imagine, with a shade of malicious amusement, how lopsided even dyed whiskers would appear against such competition. She also noticed, when he later rose from the table with a distant but punctilious bow, that he limped slightly, but even this failed to reduce him to the status of a fellow human being and instead emphasized his remote strangeness.

As soon as she could, Eleanor excused herself and returned on deck to watch, fascinated, all that went on around her: the gradually increased rhythm of the paddle wheels, a sudden bustle on deck as a sail was set, and all the other incomprehensible movements carried out by the crew at the bidding of a distant autocratic figure on the bridge.

Presently Minnie came to join her, confiding that the Russian gentleman had disappeared and all the others were busily occupied in discussing St. Petersburg personalities unknown to her. Eleanor could sense her bewilderment and cold terror, and drew her hand comfortingly through her arm. "I wonder what they can be doing up at the front mast there, don't you? I cannot imagine how they know which ropes to pull when it is all such a maze."

Minnie glanced round apathetically. "Yes, I suppose so. Do you really think it is going to be very rough? This ship is not very big."

"I shouldn't think so. I think the others do not dislike to show off their experience to us! Anyway, this ship must have done the voyage dozens of times," replied Eleanor cheerfully. "Do look at that funny man, his face is so red he looks as if he is going to burst!" She indicated an immensely fat little man apparently beside himself with wrath as he exhorted a line of seamen pulling on a rope.

Minnie laughed perfunctorily but it was plain that her mind was concentrated on her fears to the exclusion of all else. Eleanor felt a quick spurt of annoyance at her for spoiling the enjoyment of the afternoon, but no one could feel annoyed with Minnie for long, she was too plainly and painfully a lost and terrified child.

They walked across the smooth planking and stood in the stern, silently watching the tossed whiteness spreading from their thrashing paddles, the flag cracking and jerking above their heads in the strong wind. When they turned away their eyes were streaming from the cold; but Minnie was also sobbing convulsively, wringing and clutching unconsciously at Eleanor's fingers until the latter flinched away with an exclamation of pain. Even after three months the ridges across the back of her hand were still raised and tender, aching easily with use.

"I—I'm sorry," gulped Minnie. "I don't mean to hurt you, it is just—just that . . ." Her face puckered like a baby's and she groped desperately for a handkerchief.

"You didn't hurt me," said Eleanor reassuringly, handing over one of her own. "England will not be very far away and you will have your aunt with you, so it will be quite homely. If you don't like Russia I expect you can always return home in the spring, can't you?"

"Moscow is m-miles and miles even from St. Petersburg and everyone at home is expecting me to enjoy the chance to travel rather than having to find a position in England. I wish I were dead." She sobbed disconsolately again.

"Nonsense!" Eleanor exclaimed bracingly, determined not to allow her own fears to reawaken. "You will have a splendid time, I have no doubt, and probably go to lots of balls and meet plenty of handsome officers." She smiled inwardly to think that Emily's trite descriptions should so quickly be of use.

"I expect they will all be like animals, as Miss Macdonald says, or else old and frightening like that one," responded Minnie gloomily, drying her eyes and nodding at the figure of their Russian fellow passenger, who was standing just below the break of the poop, staring at the receding shore line and smoking a cigar. He was wearing a long, dark overcoat with a high fur collar and, being so short to English eyes, Eleanor thought he looked like one of the wooden ninepins she and John had had as children.

"He has a very singular appearance to be sure," she agreed. "Who is he?"

"Mr. Wall said he was in the Russian army, though I don't see how he could know."

"I think perhaps Mr. Wall is one of those people who always do know," Eleanor observed. "What is his name, did he say? I heard Mr. Wall call him Count at lunch."

"Count Berdeyev. He introduced himself before you came down and I remember it because it sounds like 'beard I have' and he hasn't got one!" Minnie giggled, forgetting her sorrows for a moment.

Eleanor laughed, pleased to have diverted her thoughts. "As long as I don't call him Berdeyevnt next time I see him!"

They both laughed so immoderately with the relief of pent-up feelings that the man at the rail looked up at them, faint surprise penciled on his immobile countenance, before strolling off toward the twin humps of the paddle-wheel cases.

"Oh dear! I do hope he didn't hear," Minnie said anxiously.

"Of course not, against this wind! It is strange though to have only one Russian on board a ship bound for Russia."

"Perhaps there are some more in the other class below decks, though my aunt told me that Russians are not allowed to travel abroad without permission from their government and that even the most important cannot usually obtain it unless they are on official business. She even said that they need passports to travel inside Russia itself unless it is a very short journey."

"I can't believe that!"

"It does sound odd, but she said so and she has been there for years and years. I can't think why I ever said I'd come." Minnie relapsed into a state of profound gloom again from which all Eleanor's efforts could not rouse her. She finally gave up trying and leaned over the side in a most unladylike way to watch the pilot being dropped. He was a small, burly fellow with bold, dark eyes, who obviously took a very good view of himself. When he saw Eleanor's laughing face so close to his own as he went over the side, he blew her a kiss and then stood by the cabin of the pilot cutter bowing and waving his cap and blowing kisses until he had to clutch for support as the cutter ducked and bobbed in the *Neptune*'s wake.

"What a very ill-bred man!" exclaimed Minnie, round-eyed.

"I expect so," agreed Eleanor, waving defiantly. "But it is fun and we are never likely to see him again. He only meant to be amusing."

"Eleanor!"

"Well, he did, and I've had enough of people saying 'Eleanor!' to me all my life without you starting. I like to think of my last view of England being someone blowing me a kiss and not of a cold gray smudge on the horizon." She waved her hand at the uninviting Essex shore.

"I'm sorry." Minnie bit her lip. "I didn't mean to make you angry. I suppose now everything will be so different that I must start getting used to it."

"Not to having strange men blow you kisses, I hope!" Eleanor laughed. "That only happens on very exceptional occasions on board ship! Once I reach Russia I shall have to be the sober and steady governess of Madame Davidova, who keeps sixteen cats."

"Aren't you frightened, even a little, at going so far on your own without knowing anything about your new home? At least I am looked after by my aunt, who has been with the same family for twenty years and even brought up my new mistress."

Eleanor ran her finger along the grain of the teak rail. "Sometimes. But I think that nothing can be worse than the last few months at home. I have learned at least that it is better not to think beyond tomorrow."

"Oh!" Minnie stole a glance at her averted face, confused by this sudden change of mood in her apparently lighthearted companion.

Eleanor relaxed and slipped her arm through Minnie's again. "I wonder where all the others have got to; let's go see if we can persuade them to come up for a stroll before it becomes too dark." Together they crossed the deck, now occasionally twitching beneath their feet even in the confined waters of the river, and went below to find all the other passengers in the saloon.

"Wherever have you two been?" demanded Emily.

"Up on deck. It is lovely still, why don't you come up too? It is a shame to stay down here on such a beautiful day." Eleanor tried to push her disordered hair back under her bonnet as she caught a glimpse of herself in the saloon mirror.

"In this wind?" Miss Macdonald grimaced. "I am certainly not prepared to look like a scrubbing woman in return for the doubtful privilege of regarding a lot of water which I can see in greater comfort from the porthole."

Eleanor repressed her rising irritation, dismayed by the prospect of further endless wrangling which was revealed by the characters of her fellow passengers. She found herself hoping that the sea would be sufficiently rough for them all to have to spend the entire voyage upon their separate bunks with their minds occupied by things other than quarreling. After the last difficult weeks she had reached the stage when a lack of contention around her was the highest sum of ambition.

She thought differently next morning. She had had no idea of the depths of misery to which the motion of the sea could plunge the human body and it was a sure indication of her state of mind that she could contemplate a comfortable quarrel in a miraculously still saloon with a longing as intense as her previous dismay.

Five

The gale continued unabated throughout the next day and the following night. The wind veered steadily northward, forcing the captain to alter course in order to keep the *Neptune*'s bows to the storm. The recent introduction of paddle steamers on the Baltic run normally speeded up the journey by several days, but in really rough weather they were very much less seaworthy than the old sail packets. With each wave the paddles bit unevenly and far too deeply; as the crest passed, first one and then the other screamed and shuddered, almost uncovered by the fierce motion of the ship. Eventually they proceeded by sail alone, but the *Neptune*'s clumsy build and great weight of machinery made it difficult to keep sufficient steerageway with the few sails that could be safely set.

The passengers neither knew nor cared what was happening; the constant effort of merely keeping in their bunks was sufficient to occupy all their waking hours, and it was not only to Minnie that the *Neptune* seemed frailer and smaller with every passing hour.

Eleanor could watch the racing sea through the porthole every time the ship rolled, and often thought they had reached their last mile as the ship shuddered almost to a standstill in the trough of a wave before slowly, painfully, beginning to climb again, wearily shaking creaking decks free of water and then sliding giddily down again to do battle with the next giant wave from a seemingly never ending army.

Jars, old shoes, combs, reticules, and clothing chased

backward and forward across the crazily tilting cabin and everything was damp from a steady, persistent leak overhead. Eleanor thought she had never seen a more miserable scene and was just wondering whether she would ever be able to dress and go on deck, where she was sure she would feel better, when there was a light knock on the door.

"May I come in?" called a voice. "It is the captain."

Eleanor was startled by the idea of a man coming into their cabin, but so much that was strange had happened in the days since she had left home that she was not surprised when the others took it as a matter of course and Miss Faulkner called back to invite him in.

The captain was younger than she had expected, tall enough to have to stoop beneath the low beams and with a cheerful, vigorous bearing, although at present his face was heavy with fatigue and whipped almost raw by the wind. He ran his eye over the occupants of the cabin and smiled. "I am sorry you are having such a disagreeable voyage, but with any luck in two days' time we should be into the shelter of the Norwegian coast."

"Norway!" exclaimed Miss Macdonald.

"Yes. You see, we have had to come a good deal farther north than I would have wished because of the wind. We'll have quite a long reach south once we reach the coast."

"Are we going to be all right?" whispered Minnie shyly.

"Why, of course we are," he replied reassuringly. "It always seems worse aft here than it does forrard, but the *Neptune* is soundly enough built even if a sea like this is not quite what she would choose. You must all be feeling a mite peckish with nothing but hardtack and water these two days."

The others hastily disclaimed any desire for food, but Eleanor had reached the in-between stage, poised between queasiness when she thought of food and ravenous hunger when she tried not to. Encouraged by his friendly manner, she said hesitatingly: "I would very much like a bowl of soup if it is possible."

He laughed. "I am afraid that is out of the question. The galley fire has been out since the first night. I could send you up some cold beef and a mug of cider out of my own store, if you would like it. My name is Brownless, by the way."

Eleanor flushed under his gaze, pulling the bedclothes tighter round her neck. She was about to refuse such unappetizing fare when it occurred to her that without some form of food she would never be able to get up and go on deck, so she changed refusal into acceptance with what dignity she could muster. "Thank you, Captain Brownless. I should like that very much if it is not too much trouble."

"No trouble at all," he replied, amused. "I'm having some sent down to the Russian gentleman anyway, but I didn't think it would appeal to you ladies."

"It doesn't!" said Eleanor frankly, and then caught herself quickly. "Oh, my wretched tongue! I'm sorry, Captain, I shall love to have it of course, it is very kind of you to spare it for me."

He laughed outright. "No, don't spoil it! I really don't imagine it is what you would choose and am sorry it is the best I can supply until the fire is relit."

He opened the door. "I'll see that the steward brings your meal down as soon as possible Miss . . . er . . . ?"

"Lovell, Captain. May I . . ." She hesitated.

"Yes, Miss Lovell?"

"Captain, will it be possible for me to come on deck this afternoon?"

"On deck?" he echoed, startled. "It's very rough still, you know."

"I can feel it! But I must have some air if I am to feel better, and I would love to see what the gale looks like."

"Well," he said doubtfully, "it is certainly not safe on deck. If you really want to, you can come to the deckhouse midships, although it won't be my fault if you break something, mind."

"Oh no, of course not! Thank you very much indeed, it will be so wonderful to get out for a while. Are you sure it will be no trouble?"

"No trouble at all. When you are dressed—if you can dress—call the steward and ask him to show you the way. I don't want you out on deck in this weather." He nodded to the others and was gone.

"Well!" gasped Miss Macdonald. "Of all the forward hussies! Drinking cider from the captain's own cellar and going onto the bridge without a chaperone or anyone to look after you!"

Eleanor felt a slight qualm of doubt herself but refused to admit it. "He offered refreshment to all of us."

"But no one else took it, did they?"

"Well, I'm hungry," she said defiantly, "I shall be glad of something—anything—to eat and drink. And I can't imagine that there is much danger of anything except a wetting on the bridge of a ship in a storm like this. Everyone will be far too busy, I dare say, to give me the least thought."

Miss Faulkner interposed in her usual mild voice. "I don't suppose there is, dear, but it is unwise to become familiar with anyone on shipboard. All normal conduct and conventions are different and when you are alone and inexperienced it is easy to find yourself in an awkward situation without realizing how you got there."

"Oh!" Eleanor digested this; she already had considerable respect for Miss Faulkner. "I will be careful, but I would very much like to go."

"Of course go, but watch what you say and do, remember that the circumstances are unusual but your conduct must be just the same as if you were at home." She smiled faintly. "At home you have so much to rely on, here there is only yourself, so you must be always on your guard. It is not punishment you have to fear now, but a really disagreeable scrape."

Eleanor felt uncomfortable. Miss Faulkner was too shrewd to deceive and it was obvious that she already sensed the heady recklessness with which she was prepared to grasp her brief, unfamiliar freedom. Once in St. Petersburg, she would be circumscribed, watched, disciplined again; these few precious days were too fleeting to let slip.

There was a knock at the door and the steward came in bearing a plate of cold meat, some biscuit, and a half-full tankard of cider. "There's the dandy miss! Soon have you all to rights again; 'ave a go at this and you'll be as fresh as a lamb in no time. You jus' holler when you're ready an' I'll take you forrard." He winked heavily.

"You see?" Miss Macdonald said pointedly as the door closed behind him.

Eleanor did not reply, eating her meal in an oppressive, condemnatory silence and then hurrying into her clothes, timing her movements as best she could and closing her eyes desperately as the cabin swung about her.

Somehow she managed to reach the passage, but there the motion seemed even more violent; cider and salt beef was not an ideal diet for one balancing on the very edge of seasickness. She scarcely felt the steward's arm as she began to fumble her way forward and suddenly it was all too much, she was beyond caring when he thrust a bucket at her, bracing her against the movement of the ship while she was mercilessly sick. After a few minutes she recovered, enough to be aware of her surroundings again but too shaken and ashamed even to look at him.

But surprisingly he did not seem shocked or disgusted, laughing at her shamefaced misery. "That's the dandy miss! Soon feel as right as Moll's doll when you gets up top again, better than frowsting and fretting and throwing up down here."

"The captain said—he invited me . . ." Her voice trailed away. She was no longer sure she could manage the long journey to the deckhouse, or whether she wanted to.

"Sure, miss, I knows. I'll take care of you." He seemed to take it for granted that she was still determined to go and she lacked the energy to argue. "You just mind your step an' I'll do the rest." He wiped his nose on his sleeve and then clutched her arm with so much determination that she laughed shakily.

"That's the dandy miss," he said, grinning. "Mind your way now, I'll go first and catch you if you fall." He disappeared down a steep stairway and then tactfully averted his eyes while she scrambled clumsily after him. Fortunately their progress through the lower decks was sufficiently difficult for her almost to forget her inner discomfort and embarrassment and to feel a distinct thrill of achievement when at last she saw the captain above her and he gave her his hand up the last few difficult rungs.

"Done it like a proper little sailor, sir, she'll make a good 'un yet," the steward said approvingly. "For all I won't say she needs a bit of training where to put her feet."

"Welcome to the bridge, Miss Lovell, I'm afraid I never thought you would arrive," the captain said gravely, but with a distinct twinkle in his eye.

She turned to give him a laughing retort but the words died on her lips as she saw the sea. From horizon to horizon there was more white than green, drifts of flying spume and whipped, confused crests falling to abruptly dark depths of menace from which it seemed the *Neptune*'s bows could never reappear.

Before her unbelieving eyes the whole deck disappeared in a soapy washday of water, disconcertingly deep and green in places, and she felt she had witnessed a miracle when the bows briefly re-emerged. "Hold on—don't just stand there!" the captain yelled in her ear and she realized it was only his grip on her arm that was holding her, so completely had she forgotten everything except the magnificent, terrifying spectacle without. The bridge was perched high above the foredeck, a frail and unprotected outpost against the elements, but immediately behind it the deckhouse in which they were standing gave some measure of shelter against the berserk fury of the gale, although two portholes were smashed and the door to the bridge was battered into a few splinters hanging upon useless hinges. Two sou'westered seamen were struggling with the wheel and the captain stood braced in the doorway, occasionally shouting an urgent order to the helmsmen, the words snatched from his mouth and submerged in the unidentifiable medley of sound around them.

Eleanor wedged herself out of the way, supported against the edge of the chart table, and watched the conflict with fascinated absorption. It seemed to her a personal battle between the small, clumsy ship and the majestic power of the waters; the puny human beings were almost irrelevant—spectators and not participants in the drama. All unhappiness, all illness, all uncertainty fled before the power of the wind and her exultation in the might of the sea; her heart rose with each of the *Neptune*'s victories and quailed with each temporary defeat.

How long her body would have remained clamped in its comfortless corner as her spirit leaped and soared with the gale, utterly free for the first time, it was impossible to say, but she hardly knew where she was when she finally stirred to find the captain clutching the rail alongside her, his brows raised interrogatively.

"I—I'm sorry! What did you say?"

He laughed. "I've been asking you if you wouldn't like to go below. It's getting cold up here and will be dark very soon."

She flexed her stiff arms and cold hands unbelievingly, noting for the first time an angry glimpse of red along the sea's rim, the lack of definition between the immense lines of waves. "How ever long have I been up here?"

"Best part of two hours, I reckon. Time to go below or you will be in your bunk for good."

"Yes, I suppose so; how about you?" She felt a quick ache of pity at his haggard, salt-lined face and drooping shoulders.

He shrugged. "I shall get some sleep soon, it's quieting down a lot now."

She realized that they were talking almost in their normal voices, the mad orchestration of the storm was dying down at last with the draining light: it was no longer necessary to brace against every wave to avoid being thrown across the deck.

She smiled shyly. "Thank you very much, Captain, for letting me come up here. I could not imagine a more wonderful sight, what I would have missed if you hadn't let me come!"

"A pleasure, Miss Lovell, but I think you should go now. I hope to see you again in more agreeable circumstances."

"I can't imagine any! I think truly today has been the happiest of my life." It was the first day too, since she had known him, that she had not thought about Christopher, but it was only when she saw the captain's face change that she realized that her reply could have been more diplomatically phrased. Perhaps Mama was right to insist that yes and no were quite sufficient answer from the young, she thought, confused and unable to think of any suitable apology. "Th-thank you again. I hope I shall find my way back without any mistake."

He turned away. "I am sure his lordship here will go with you."

It was only then that she noticed Count Berdeyev leaning against the binnacle beside the helmsman. She wondered how long he had been there, surprised that he also should have wished to leave the comparative comfort of his cabin on such a day. He bowed punctiliously to her and she curtsied back, stifling an involuntary chuckle at the absurdity on a storm-swept bridge. She was also annoyed with herself at having been overheard by this stiff stranger uttering one of the thoughtless gaucheries she tried so hard to guard against.

She saw the captain say something to him and he glanced in her direction and nodded before moving over to her.

"The captain has asked me to escort you back to your quarters, Miss Lovell, if you are now ready to go." He indicated the companionway and bowed again.

Eleanor wondered whether all Russians had such unbearably formal manners as, not to be outdone in civility, she bobbed another curtsy. The slackened motion of the ship was immediately apparent below decks and they regained the saloon without great difficulty although, perched over the stern as they were there, any motion was greatly exaggerated and two oil lamps, swinging and smoking wildly, emphasized every movement of the ship.

They were met by the steward, who looked quite disappointed that Eleanor had found her way aft without his assistance. "I came forrard a coupla times, missy, but you seemed as happy as a grig so I left you. You must be powerful hungry after so long on nothing an' less than nothing, so to speak. What would you be fancying now, and you too, sir?"

Eleanor hesitated, suddenly aware of the shivering of her limbs from mingled cold, excitement, and hunger, but unwilling to face the thought of consuming a meal in the discomfort of her cabin. "Have Miss Macdonald and the others had anything?"

He shook his head contemptuously. "Likely feel better if they'd make the effort."

"Oh! Oh well, then, perhaps I'd better just have some milk and a biscuit, if you have any. I don't want to make them feel any worse."

"Them make you feel worse, you mean. Look'ee now, miss, I'll lay you a mite of summat in here, be much better than grubbing around in bed holdin' onto things all the time—the table being screwed down-like here. I'll bring both of you whatever I can find, how'll that be?"

She glanced dubiously at her silent companion but she was really too hungry to argue. "Thank you so much, I'd love that. Have you—have you anything hot?"

He winked. "You leave it to me, miss, sir."

She turned to Berdeyev and said, she hoped with sufficient formality and hauteur to impress him favorably: "I trust you will forgive me if I do not change for dinner, sir?"

He inclined his head unsmiling. "As you wish, Miss Lovell. I hope you will forgive me if I do so?"

Humiliated, Eleanor retreated to her cabin, but she was also angry, for she could not help but feel that, for all his formality, it showed a gross lack of manners to go out of his way to expose her inexperience as he had done. Her nostrils were assailed afresh by the fetid smell of the cabin, but beyond a profound feeling of disgust she found to her delight that she was no longer affected by it. As soon as she saw her reflection in the mirror she was bound to admit that there was some reason to expect her to change even under the present difficult circumstances: white salt spotted her dress and rimed her face, while patches of sea water had seeped in everywhere under her cloak. Even if the Russian had not made it impossible for her not to change, she realized that she would have done so anyway but, illogically enough, this only served to add fuel to her rising temper.

She changed hastily, with surprising ease considering the still violent motion of the ship, and was just about to creep out again when Miss Macdonald stirred. "What, are you going out again at this time of night? The attractions of the deck must be very great."

"I'm not going on deck, but to have some supper in the saloon. I hoped not to disturb you, how do you feel now?"

"Slightly better, thank you, dear," said Miss Faulkner, revealing that she also had been awake. "Have you enjoyed yourself?"

"Oh, yes indeed! As much as anything in my whole life, I think!"

Miss Macdonald sniffed disapprovingly. "What a strange thing to say. Are Mr. Wall and the captain joining you for dinner?"

Eleanor laughed as she opened the door. "No indeed! You need not have any fears for me, there is only that stuffy old Russian bowing and sneering every other moment!" She closed the door to find herself face to face with Count Berdeyev, and gasped with consternation. She could read nothing from his expression but there was an unpleasant glint in his eyes which made her moderately certain he had heard what she said.

She started to stammer an apology, but the impossibility of framing anything at all adequate froze her tongue, and the words died on her lips as he opened the door for her without apparently even noticing her efforts. Through her remorse and confusion her anger stirred again, and suddenly she no longer even wished to withdraw her words.

The oppressive silence was broken by the steward entering with a piled tray, bringing with him a tempting aroma of broth and pickles. "That's the dandy!" he exclaimed inevitably. "Here's what will put some life into you, you mark my words!" He slammed down a series of dishes, damped the tablecloth with a grubby rag, and proudly displayed a steaming bowl of greasy soup, some slightly curled warm fish, and a plate of sliced bread and pickles.

Eleanor felt her still uncertain stomach recoil before such an unpalatable assortment, but after stealing a glance at Berdeyev's unmoving countenance and the steward's triumphant pride, she sat down and helped

74

herself to the soup as the least unattractive of the selection laid before her.

Berdeyev betrayed no sign of distaste or surprise as he ate this disagreeable meal and she began to wonder whether some of Emily's stories of the Russian manner of living could, after all, have some truth in them. To accept and consume such a meal without comment surely argued a disconcerting familiarity with squalor even in noble families: it was difficult not to feel dismayed by the prospect of Madame Davidova at her unfashionable address behind the Military Academy.

The meal passed in complete silence and she was just wondering whether there was any reason why she should not suit her behavior to the company in which she found herself and simply withdraw without explanation to her cabin, when the Russian servant entered and put a small wicker-covered flask before his master. He was dressed in a loose-fitting dark shirt, belted tightly at the waist and falling outside baggy trousers; with his black mass of hair and beard he seemed to personify all her anxieties and she followed his movements with appalled intensity, as if he could give the clue she sought to the enigma of the future. He snuffed one of the lamps, which was guttering pungently in its bracket, and then withdrew with a heavy tread quite unlike the trained noiselessness of English servants, as also was the way he started to scratch himself before he was fairly out of the room.

"Will you have some vodka, Miss Lovell?" Berdeyev's voice broke into her thoughts.

She eyed the flask with misgiving. "What is it?"

"It is a type of brandy but in my homeland it is more than that—it is our solace, our forgetfulness, and also our expression of joy. You will not live long in Russia without discovering its power, I feel sure."

"Oh!" Eleanor was unable to decide whether he was joking or serious. Perhaps Russians naturally were either completely silent or else describing things in the language of fantasy. Not wishing to lapse again into their previous state of complete silence, she added: "Just a very little then. I am anxious to try anything which will help me to understand the country I am to live in."

He had been watching the colorless liquid rising in his glass, but at her words he looked up and cast her an oddly penetrating glance. "Tell me, Miss Lovell, whether I am correct in thinking that you are coming to Russia to be a governess?"

"Yes. In St. Petersburg, why?"

"In Petersburg? And why are you anxious to come to Russia? Is it so difficult to live in England, then, that you must come to what you do not understand?"

"No! I mean yes . . . why do you ask?" This strange, abrupt questioning took Eleanor aback.

"I do not wish to seem impertinent, Miss Lovell, I am merely interested." He made as if to bow slightly and then changed his mind, adding, "But then I am not allowed to bow, am I?"

"I—I beg your pardon," stammered Eleanor. She took a deep breath and said resolutely: "It was unpardonably rude of me to make such a remark and—and I apologize." She pushed back her chair.

He raised a hand. "Please do not go, Miss Lovell. Poor as this is, there is no better entertainment on the ship at the present time. You must tell me what you think of our vodka."

She sat down again, puzzled and resentful of his manner but intrigued despite her unease. She looked at the glass by her hand and, reflecting that it looked almost like water, drank distastefully.

It was as if one of those rockets John had been so fond of making in the shed behind the stables had exploded inside her head. She gasped and wept in the effort to find her breath, and when she did eventually succeed, it felt as though her throat and lungs had been blown completely smooth and open.

The first thing she saw when her stinging eyes cleared was the offensively mocking smile on Berdeyev's face; he was obviously waiting for her temper to break. With a great effort she managed to smile waveringly. "I apologize again, sir. I'm afraid it caught my breath slightly."

His smile deepened, but this time there was more genuine amusement in it. "Perhaps another drink would restore you."

"Possibly; it is delightful." She raised the glass to her lips, feeling obscurely that the whole honor of England was at stake, but even the minute drop on her tongue seared her mouth like fire. She knew he had noticed her deception but he made no comment, saying abruptly instead: "You do not seem at all the usual type for a governess."

"You do not seem at all the usual type of gentleman either!" retorted Eleanor, stung. "Oh, I beg your pardon."

He did not appear offended. "*Touché*, Miss Lovell. Have you then long experience as a governess in England?"

It had almost become an interrogation, but by now she was too confused by his changes of manner and her own inexcusable rudeness to do other than reply in a mild tone, "No, as a matter of fact I have not been away from home before."

His brows drew together, stretching the scarred side of his face and lending it such a singularly unattractive expression that she involuntarily tightened her fingers on the arm of her chair. She realized all at once the quietness of the ship apart from the endless creaking of timbers, the lateness of the hour at which to be conversing with a strange gentleman, and the extent to which the vodka had sunk in its wicker flask.

She was therefore all the more alarmed by his next question. "Where do you intend to live in Petersburg? You do know, I suppose, where you are going to work?"

"Why do you want to know?" she asked bluntly.

He looked at her a moment and then downed the

contents of his glass with a quick flick of the wrist. As he picked up the flask to refill it again, he said dryly: "Do not alarm yourself, Miss Lovell, I do not expect to stay in Petersburg more than a week or so at the worst. It has no attractions for me. I was only asking out of idle curiosity and also because I am sorry a little for someone who has obviously no idea what the future holds for her."

She was taken aback by the dismaying certainty in his voice; the utter lack of emphasis was more convincing than all Miss Macdonald's pessimism or Emily's exaggerations. "In that case, sir, I am going to Madame Davidova's but I don't know anything about her. A friend of Miss Merrilees, who is traveling with me, wrote to me of the post."

"Where does she live?"

"I am not precisely sure," confessed Eleanor, "but I believe somewhere behind the Military Academy—could that be right? Do you know of her?"

"If that is where she lives, there is not the slightest chance that I would know her."

"I understood that it was not a very good district and it seems to me that I am engaged to look after her cats rather than her granddaughter. I don't intend to stay there very long, just while I find another situation and she engages someone to replace me."

"Naturally I do not know much of the difficulties which usually confront governesses, but I should think you would be there at least until the ice melts in the spring, even assuming the post is still open. This is certainly the last ship into Petersburg this winter; why do you not go back to England where you belong, with this ship?"

"Of course I would not return so tamely to England, sir. I couldn't anyway," she added frankly, thinking of the guineas in her petticoat. In England ten guineas was an enormous sum, a whole year's wages for a governess; here, with everything to pay for, it suddenly seemed very little. "But I am told there are any number of families wanting new governesses when they come to the city from their summer in the country."

"I see." He poured himself yet another glass and her eyes widened involuntarily. "I fear you have been misinformed. To the best of my knowledge Petersburg is filled at this time of year with all kinds of unemployed officials, servants and—what do you say?— good-for-nothings, is that right? All of whom have been roused by the cold from a summer's idling and are looking for a warm household in which to pass the winter. So far as the English are concerned, there will be those who have arrived during the summer and have been waiting for the *noblesse* to return before they could obtain employment. At least that is the situation with most kinds of servants, and I cannot imagine things to be greatly different where governesses are concerned."

"It can't be," exclaimed Eleanor, appalled. "Emily. . . . Miss Merrilees swore I would be able to change without any difficulty and without the least qualm of conscience because everyone was doing so all the time."

"Let us hope she is proved right," replied Berdeyev disinterestedly.

Eleanor knew that now was a suitable time to leave and that in view of the lateness of the hour she ought to go without delay, but although she could not imagine that a man of his type could possibly know anything about the employment of governesses, she was disturbed by his information and the air of certainty with which he delivered it. She was also extremely curious and here was someone who could give her answers to all her questions about her new home, if he would. Her apprehensions and queries were now too disturbing for mere considerations of propriety to stop her attempting to obtain some of the information that was so vital for her future.

"What is Russia like, sir?" she blurted out, and then blushed for her clumsiness.

Berdeyev did not smile nor did he reply. After a moment he put his glass down exactly in the center of a series of wet rings on the table and walked, with the exaggerated care of the slightly drunk, over to the porthole. He stood gazing out into the storm-swept darkness for a long time before turning round. "How can I describe Russia for you? No one person can grasp it and words . . . words perhaps are the worst way of all. Sometimes, right out on the steppe where the distances are so great that you can see the curve of the earth, the silence . . ." He shook his head impatiently. "It is as if you had become deaf, it is so complete. Russia is like a dream, a dream that those who begin to know her cannot do without, but which one wonders sometimes whether man has not turned into a nightmare." He had been talking as much to himself as to her, fumbling sometimes for the correct English words but fumbling perhaps as much for his own true feelings. Eleanor could not think of any suitable reply, she had never known anyone who could so bewilder or infuriate her with almost every word he uttered.

But there was no need for a reply; after a moment he relaxed slightly and moved back to the table. "But that is not what you wanted to know, is it? No one can describe Russia, you will find out a little for yourself during the winter you must be there, but Petersburg is not Russia although everyone will tell you that it is. It is a different world, and the answers found there speak a different language to the problems they are supposed to solve."

"Have you traveled a great deal in Russia then?" Eleanor asked timidly, overawed by the grimness of his expression.

He picked up his glass again and nodded. "Yes, nearly all my life has been spent beyond the Urals and in the Caucasus and Caspian campaigns. Only since I got this"—he tapped his lame leg—"have I been reduced to an office clerk in Petersburg or our foreign embassies. You may be sure that I find it a most disagreeable change."

"You don't like St. Petersburg then?"

"Good God, who could like it? Everyone censored and disciplined until they are afraid to talk of anything but the latest scandals, told what to wear, which books to buy, and how to stand and walk and where to travel —" He checked himself and added in a more moderate tone: "I shall have to watch myself after a year in your country, or I will find myself in trouble."

Eleanor was not too inexperienced to realize that his unexpected eloquence was due to the quantity of vodka he had drunk, but this made it no easier to think of a suitable reply. After a pause which she was unable to fill he added seriously, "Remember one thing, Miss Lovell: in Russia nothing is the same. Nothing can be judged by what you already know and few people behave in the way you would expect. Everything is very simple and very complicated, there are no straight answers or quick solutions, and the questions which will have to be answered are getting more difficult, more urgent, and more unanswerable every year. I would certainly advise you to leave for England in the spring."

"I cannot do that. As I told you, sir . . ."

"So you have said, but I am old enough—" His mouth tightened. "I must be old enough to be your father, and I am advising you as I am sure he would, for your own good." It was clear that he took her for an orphan and Eleanor writhed inwardly. "Go home, we have a hard time ahead of us."

"I assure you, sir," said Eleanor stiffly, rising to her feet, "I have a father already to advise me, who saw nothing wrong in my coming to Russia. I do not imagine that as a governess your difficulties will be my concern."

"Difficulties have a way of making themselves everyone's concern." His speech was slurred now, but even so his English was really very good. "It is madness for a young girl to come alone, you must believe me."

Eleanor had never been so utterly out of her depth, unable to judge either his sobriety or his seriousness. As she withdrew in some confusion she managed to murmur a few polite words of thanks for his hospitality, as out of place under the circumstances as they were ignored. Her last sight of him was the total absorption with which he was draining the few remaining drops of vodka from his glass.

Six

Eleanor slept late the following morning, only waking when a fugitive gleam of sunshine struck across her face, glimmering opaquely through the rimed porthole. She snuggled into the bedclothes briefly, then stretched and yawned luxuriously. She remembered the extraordinary conversation of the night before but it no longer disturbed her; in the bright sunshine and freshness of the morning the only thing that mattered was the thought of another day of freedom and peace.

She leaped out of bed and nearly fell on her back as the stern suddenly rose through an unseen weight of water, but already she was feeling at home on the sea and began to scramble into her clothes without any thought of discomfort.

"Are you going out again?" demanded Emily querulously from her dark corner, whence she had scarcely moved during the last few days.

"Yes, why don't you come too? It looks like a lovely

morning." Eleanor chased her shoes into the farthest corner of the cabin.

Emily shuddered but Miss Faulkner remarked judiciously: "I think that I shall arise for luncheon today, the motion of the ship is undoubtedly easier."

"It undoubtedly is," agreed Eleanor, smiling.

"It was very late by the time you came to bed last night," Miss Macdonald said accusingly. "What were you doing?"

"I was eating supper and then talking to that Count Berdeyev—he is a very odd sort of man, to be sure!"

"All Russians are mad," stated Miss Macdonald positively.

"No, he wasn't mad, only—" She hesitated, at a loss to describe their conversation adequately and then ended lamely: "He drank an awful lot too."

"That is another thing you will find out, all Russian men drink too much. They have no notion of temperance when there are ladies present and their behavior is only laid on the surface for the benefit of others—it is either very exaggerated and artificial or else altogether lacking."

"Do you know," Eleanor said, carefully buttoning up her dress, "ever since I set out for Russia people have been saying that the Russians are this or that or behave in certain ways and not in others and now I don't find that I can believe it at all. I don't mean I cannot easily believe that they behave very differently to what we have been used to and expect, but I don't think you can just dismiss them as madmen or drunkards who don't understand their own language and then think no more about it."

There was a short silence before Miss Macdonald said pointedly, "But then you have only met one Russian so far and he, on your own words, was both mad and drunk."

"No, he wasn't! Yes, he drank and he said odd things I didn't understand, but that doesn't mean it wasn't my understanding which was at fault." Eleanor snatched up her bonnet and tied it tightly under her chin.

"Very noble," sneered Miss Macdonald.

"You are right, my dear Miss Lovell," interposed Miss Faulkner as Eleanor prepared to reply in kind. "The difficulty is to keep in that frame of mind after you have been there a year, and at the same time not to start condoning things which your own standards should tell you are wrong, just because that is the way they are done there. I have been very happy and the family I am with has been so kind that it is hard to criticize them, but it is too easy for us to slip back into a less civilized way of thinking under the delusion that we are seeing an improvement in the standards around us."

Eleanor recognized the justice of these words and said with her customary impulsiveness: "I'm sorry, of course I can't say anything until I have been there, but I do want to understand and fit in now it is to be my home. I could not bear to be a stranger all my life."

"There is no easy solution to the situation there, and perhaps no solution at all," said Miss Faulkner, unconsciously echoing Berdeyev's words of the night before.

Eleanor let herself quietly out of the cabin and found the passageway flooded with unexpected light from the poop door, which was propped open to allow the thin sunshine to climb weakly up the scarred paneling. She stepped over the coaming into a new world: the decks were no longer awash and although there was a heavy confused swell tossing the tops of the waves downwind, the motion of the ship sprang chiefly from the speed at which she was being driven along by paddles and half-reefed sails.

"Good morning, Miss Lovell." She swung round to find the captain behind her.

"Oh yes, isn't it? Though I don't think I could enjoy anything so much as yesterday afternoon. I almost wish it were rough again."

"I certainly don't!" They turned and started to pace the deck together. "I understand from Harry—the steward—that our Russian passenger made quite a night of it yesterday. I hope he didn't annoy you in any way?"

"Oh, indeed not," Eleanor assured him. "I should really have gone to bed but I wanted so much to hear about Russia and I hoped that he would tell me."

"And did he?"

"No-o, not really." A thought struck her. "He did say though that I might find it difficult to obtain a post as a governess in St. Petersburg at this time of year when most people are settled for the winter. How long have you been sailing to Russia? Do you think he could be right?"

"Lord, miss, I don't know. How could I? How could he either—I can't quite see our fine count troubling himself with the affairs of governesses, can you?"

"Not exactly," agreed Eleanor unhappily, but she resolutely put her uncertainty aside and repeated: "How long have you been sailing to Russia?"

"All of ten years now, I reckon, on and off, but mostly to the North German ports or Norway, Denmark, and Sweden with some odd English coasting as well. I shall be more regularly in St. Petersburg now because I have only just been appointed to command the *Neptune* and she is on the Baltic run mostly. Perhaps I shall be able to call on you there."

"That would be lovely." Eleanor was warmed by the mere thought of a familiar face from England in this strange future awaiting her. "How early in the spring can you get through the ice?"

He shrugged. "Maybe April, maybe May, it depends."

Eleanor looked around her, at the green waves shorn of their menace in the bright sun, the laced rigging swinging through the racing clouds. Suddenly she was so happy it was impossible to grasp that in a few days she would have left the *Neptune* and would be launching yet again on a solitary path into the unknown. But it was the loneliness, not the unknown, which frightened her, and she wondered whether, if she had been a boy, she would not have liked very well to voyage the world.

When she returned to the saloon for lunch she found both Captain Brownless and Berdeyev waiting for her, the latter looking understandably white and heavy round the eyes and plainly in one of his most unapproachable moods. He bowed to her in silence and replied to every remark with such stiff courtesy that both Eleanor and the captain soon left him completely out of their conversation and scarcely noticed when he left the room. Miss Faulkner and Emily, although up, also took practically no part in the social side of the meal, eating with the single-minded concentration of those whose thoughts are entirely occupied with the state of their stomachs.

After lunch they went on deck again and the captain pointed out the faint haze on the port bow that was Norway.

"Norway!" exclaimed Eleanor, standing on tiptoe and craning her neck. "Are we calling in anywhere there?"

"No, just Copenhagen late tomorrow night if all goes well."

"How long will we be there? Will we be able to go ashore?"

"Better than that, I will take you ashore if you like."

Eleanor knew very well that this was not an invitation she could accept alone, but the last few days had so increased her confidence that she replied promptly: "I am sure we would all like to see Copenhagen with you if it is possible." It was hard to believe that a week ago she had still been at Abbotsfield.

"You will enjoy every minute, I promise." The captain made a rapid recovery from disappointment. "I will be delighted to invite the other ladies along, but you will be my special guest, don't forget."

. . .

She did enjoy it. Copenhagen was rough and crude, bursting with life and noisy with new building. The half-completed Tivoli Gardens made them all gasp with its booths and stalls, raucously advertised freaks and prize fights, its trick fountains and smoking trays of fish, pickles, and spiced breads.

Yet in spite of it all she was glad to regain the *Neptune*, glad the next morning to be thrashing up the Baltic; even more than before, the little ship seemed to be a refuge, a magic, inviolate haven which she dreaded leaving.

It was a glorious day, although with the unmistakable promise of winter in its clear, translucent air and sparkling, flat-planed sunlight. The *Neptune* was heeling and dipping gracefully, chasing the razor-straight horizon as if she could already sense her journey's end.

Eleanor wore her thickest cloak and woolen shawl but her face was stung and flushed by the cold and her every sense felt alive as never before. The others were still below, unwrapping purchases and discussing their time ashore, except Berdeyev, who had not accompanied them and had sat in a blighting silence the whole of the previous evening, despite all attempts to bring him into the conversation.

But Eleanor no longer worried about his moods and strangeness and when he too came on deck she greeted him with the unthinking friendliness which kept escaping around the edges of her carefully drilled propriety, happy to share her pleasure in the day.

"Isn't it splendid weather, sir? I feel as if I had never truly lived before."

"Yes," he agreed noncommittally. "It is somewhat cold, however."

"Oh, I don't regard that; I wish that this voyage could go on forever!"

"Perhaps so, but you might find it rather monotonous quite soon," he replied dampingly. "Did you enjoy your visit to Copenhagen yesterday?"

They walked farther forward together until they were more sheltered from the keen wind. "Oh, yes indeed, I did," Eleanor replied warmly. "I thought it a wonderful city if only it had not been so dirty in the streets and the children looking so unhealthy. I loved every minute of it, I never dreamed such places existed." She smiled shyly at his impassive countenance.

"Yes," he observed dryly. "I imagine that you were a slight—what shall I say?—shock, to our good captain."

The quick color flooded her face. "Wh-what do you mean?" Her stratagem which made sure that the others came along had not entirely answered the purpose and she had not told even Miss Faulkner how, taking advantage of her entranced preoccupation with the sights of Copenhagen, the captain had succeeded in drawing her aside from the others as they watched a sword swallower, murmuring something about greater marvels to be seen in the next booth. Nor had she admitted even to herself how like a desecration his kisses had seemed after the unpracticed joy she and Christopher had known together. Somehow she had hidden her repulsion and panic, knowing instinctively that contempt and indifference would protect her more surely. Above all she had been furious at herself for her over-confidence, for her carelessness, for the arrogance with which she had so soon discarded advice which was prompted by nothing but good will. But she could not imagine Captain Brownless discussing his hopes or his disappointment with this distant personage. "What do you mean, sir?" she repeated, with rather more confidence.

"I find it difficult to imagine Captain Brownless having a disinterested motive for taking his passengers ashore," Berdeyev explained suavely, "and I feel sure from your expression that my disbelief was justified.

Accept my compliments for the skill with which you apparently—er—discouraged his attentions."

She gave an involuntary gurgle of laughter and confessed: "I think he is very angry with me because I did not have hysterics and still wanted to see the acrobats!"

Most unexpectedly the Russian's face relaxed for the first time and he allowed himself the glimmering of a smile. "Discouraging indeed. I will ask that you permit me to take my leave. I see that I must surely wish Captain Brownless good morning and discuss the delights of Copenhagen with him." He gave his usual, stiff bow and limped off, leaving Eleanor staring doubtfully at his back.

Part Two
RUSSIA
1852-1853

Seven

A deep strangeness settled over the *Neptune* as she lay at anchor in impenetrable stillness and silence. It was difficult to imagine that she was within hailing distance of her destination, and after the long bustle and endless motion of the voyage an apprehensive constraint was only too apparent among the company gathered in the saloon. It was bitterly cold and there was a constant thin scraping sound which set the teeth on edge as the surface ice already formed on these enclosed waters rubbed against the hull.

The captain had been so glad to reach the security of Kronstadt before the last of the thin northern light drained away that he had forgotten the awkwardness between them and had invited Eleanor up to the bridge for the first time since Copenhagen. Now he was closeted with the port officials and a thin drift of snow was steadily thickening into a driven whirlpool of shifting grayness.

There was a loud clatter of boots overhead and an icy draft swept into the saloon as the poop door was opened. "This way, gentlemen." Captain Brownless ushered in three men. Minnie's horror-stricken eyes widened and her lips parted in a silent scream, Miss Faulkner gave her usual absent-minded smile, and both Emily and Miss Macdonald looked resigned. Eleanor's immediate impression was one of hair, and the animal illusion was heightened by a strange, pungent smell which accompanied the newcomers. All were wearing long, full-skirted overcoats trimmed and lined with fur, round fur hats crammed down over their ears, and had long beards which melted into the upturned fur collars of their coats.

"Wish all you ladies for St. Petersburg?" asked the tallest in careful, stumbling English.

"Yes, please," they chorused after a doubtful pause.

"These gentlemen say there is too much ice for the *Neptune* to reach St. Petersburg, we shall have to unload here at Kronstadt," explained the captain. "Unfortunately the winter has set in early, but the ice is not thick enough yet for a sledge journey to be safe."

"What do you suggest we do, Captain?" asked Miss Faulkner.

"You must remain here for tonight, it is too dark to go ashore now. Then I am afraid it will have to be a hotel in Kronstadt until the ice is safe, or else the weather lets up sufficiently for a ferry to break its way through. It is about nine miles to the mainland from here."

"How long will that be?" asked Eleanor, thinking of her few precious guineas.

He shrugged and turned to the Russians, who were eying them disinterestedly, and repeated the question more slowly. The same man spread his hands helplessly. "Perhaps one week, *barishna* [miss]." He added to the captain: "I must ask now all the lights and fires go out. It is a rule. Also to see all your passengers."

Brownless glanced round the room. "These are all in the first class except one of your countrymen who intends to land tonight. I will send the steward to ask him to come, he told me that he would go ashore with you."

The other followed this painstakingly, but at the last sentence his eyes flashed and he thumped the table with his fist, making the china jump and Minnie clutch nervously at Eleanor's hand. He uttered a long explosive sentence in Russian and then, seeing the blank expressions around him, added: "Show me now this who say he come on the harbor boat. Never—never!—may anyone use the harbor boat. Also to tell at once your men to put out all lights and fires, leaving one only for my work."

The captain nodded and when Harry returned to the saloon gave the necessary instructions.

"But you cannot leave us in the cold without a fire or a lamp or anything," protested Eleanor.

"Sorry, Miss Lovell," replied Brownless, "rule of the port. We always have to do it here, though why it should worry them if we go up in flames right out in the roadstead, I can't imagine."

"Allus the same, allus the same," mumbled Harry mutinously. "Damn silly rules for damn silly reasons carried out by ruddy little monkeys looking as if they's just swung off'n a tree." He cast a disparaging glance at the silent trio by the door and sniffed. "Still up it, 'alf of 'em, if you ask me."

While unable to disentangle the precise wording of this highly offensive speech, the spokesman had no difficulty in understanding its general drift and took an angry step forward.

"Do be quiet, Harry," begged Eleanor, trying not to laugh, "or he will never allow us ashore."

At this unpropitious moment Berdeyev walked into the saloon, wearing what Eleanor later discovered was the undress uniform of a divisional general of the line. The Russians, who had turned as one man to rend this latecomer to their presence, stiffened abruptly and the leader saluted. For the first time Eleanor heard the soft, liquid sibilance of spoken Russian and she was able to reflect at the same time how unusual it was to see a man in uniform, especially one that had neither scarlet nor blue as its components. The red stripes down his breeches and piping on his tunic were the only relief from all-over green except for gold epaulettes and rank badges. Even the green was a stupid green, she thought resentfully, noting its almost bluish tinge, and all at once a realization of the utter strangeness and isolation of her position swept over her, leaving her limp and frightened.

She was saved by Berdeyev, speaking in English again: "I am leaving you now, Captain, with these officers. Thank you for a pleasant voyage." He included the passengers in his bow and added: "May I also wish you success and good fortune in your venture, Miss Lovell?"

"Thank you," she whispered, and then on impulse as he turned away: "Would it be possible for you to ask these men if we could keep at least one light tonight?"

He raised his brows. "It does not seem an unusual request."

"They say we must put out all the lamps and the galley fire and—and—everything. It is so cold!"

"I see. Do not let it disturb you." He said something to the Russians, waiting respectfully by the door. Their disagreement was obvious, but from the way in which they eyed each other no one felt inclined to risk a protest.

Berdeyev bowed again, the door open in his hand. "I do not think you will have trouble now. They will not care to risk the *pourboire* I shall give them for a few lights."

Eleanor, while grateful for his efforts, was unable entirely to hide her disapproval of such open bribery and she was chagrined to realize from his forbidding expression that he had had no difficulty in interpreting her emotions. But these were fleeting impressions as the customs officers trooped out in his wake and another blast of cold air announced the departure of these representatives of her new country.

In spite of the concession over the lights they were all too cold and depressed to wish to sit up as they had done under much worse conditions during the voyage. In gloomy silence passengers and crew alike sought the comfort and security of their berths, to shiver uneasily until daybreak in the increasing cold.

It was still snowing in the morning and Kronstadt showed up only as a dim gray hump in the gloom; it was also freezing hard and Miss Macdonald said hopefully that perhaps it would not be too long before they would be able to cross to the mainland by sledge. It was nearly midday before they saw some shrouded figures breaking up the thin ice round the ship to allow a small boat to come alongside and a few moments later a little round man bounced into the saloon, thumping ineffectually at the snow clinging to his garments and exclaiming cheerfully: "Good morning, ladies! Not quite English weather, but such as it is, welcome to Russia." His bright eyes swept the room and with his head cocked on one side he looked so much like a sparrow that Eleanor wondered whether it was a deliberately cultivated pose.

"How do you do?" said Emily interrogatively.

He flourished his hat in response. "May I introduce myself? I am Edward Simpson, very much at your service, as is my wife also. I am the British consul here, and I heard from the passenger who disembarked last night that there are several unescorted ladies aboard. We would be very pleased if you would like to stay with us rather than at the hotel until I am able to arrange transport for you to the mainland." He began to unwind a long, spotted muffler from his neck.

"Thank you very much, I am sure we would all be very pleased. How kind of you to come." Emily accepted for all of them after a hasty glance round.

"That is settled then. Are you ready to go ashore now?"

"How about the customs? They have not inspected our baggage yet, they were only here for a short while last night."

"What about me?" demanded Wall fretfully, put out at not having been included in the general invitation. "Is there any hotel worth staying at? I was most

97

particularly warned not to stay at any but the very best Russian hotels."

"I am sorry, Mrs. Simpson and I have only limited accommodation just for the ladies, but the Hôtel de St. Petersbourg in the Godspodskaya is generally accounted quite reasonable."

Overhead there was a sudden clatter and a few moments later the same three officials of the night before entered the saloon. They greeted Mr. Simpson jovially and were soon deep in animated conversation punctuated by roars of laughter and hearty backslapping. Eleanor was astonished at the difference from the suspicious atmosphere of the night before and wondered how long it would be before she would be able to speak sufficient Russian to make herself understood.

"They really are the most inefficient people! I am sorry to see our consul so sadly infected with the Russian way of living already. Why they cannot get on with checking the baggage and let us go, instead of standing around doing nothing for hours, I do not understand and never shall." Miss Macdonald gathered her things together crossly.

"Hush, dear. You will have to become accustomed all over again to things taking twice the time they do in England. I can see that your holiday has sadly unsettled you." Miss Faulkner placidly continued with her embroidery as if she expected the proceedings to last all day, as indeed looked very likely.

"If only I could speak some Russian," said Eleanor enviously. "It is easy to see that it makes all the difference: I know they will not give us half the trouble with the consul here as they would have done otherwise."

"I should think not indeed when he is our official representative."

"I don't think that will have anything to do with it, any favor they do will be because he is friendly and pleasant with them," replied Eleanor seriously. "It was kind of Count Berdeyev to call on him on our behalf."

Miss Macdonald sniffed but even she was forced to agree that there was a minimum of fuss in allowing them ashore. Each took a single bag, the remainder of the baggage being merely identified and marked for transport to St. Petersburg Customs House whence, Mr. Simpson explained, they would be able to collect it as soon as the ice was safe for heavy sledges. Their bags were not searched, each was asked only if they had any reading matter, and their statements were accepted without question. Eleanor had several books which she had left out of her heavy baggage for convenience on the voyage and they were all confiscated although with the politest possible expressions of regret. Even some old newspapers in which she had wrapped miniatures of her family were taken and her expostulations went unheeded.

"I'm afraid it is no good getting in a pucker about it, Miss Lovell," Mr. Simpson explained, kindly enough. "No foreign reading matter at all is allowed into the country although they will turn a blind eye to a recognized translation of the Bible. If they let even a newspaper through without official permission these fellows would lose their positions immediately. You will find that all your letters will be opened and also any packets you receive."

"But why? It doesn't seem reasonable!"

He shrugged. "It isn't, but that doesn't make any difference. If you don't agree to give them up you will not be able to land now or at any other time."

There was nothing she could do except hope the St. Petersburg authorities would not detect the carefully packed layers of books and periodicals in her boxes.

It was still snowing hard as they clambered into the consul's unstable little boat, the customs men's final injunction to present themselves without fail to the police within twenty-four hours ringing in their ears. Eleanor was forced to wrap her shawl right round her face to protect herself against the small, frozen crystals which were sweeping like sand across the dark water, already thickly lumped with ice. There was no one to bid them farewell from the *Neptune* and the shrouded decks, ghostly rails, and stiffened rigging seemed unreal, as if they had overstayed their welcome and this last fragment of England was already silently withdrawing from them. Not a foot stirred or light showed and Eleanor shivered involuntarily.

"I must just go and say good-by to the captain and Harry," she called to the others as they were preparing to descend into the boat.

"Don't be long, or we will all freeze!" Miss Faulkner called back.

She hurried below again and found Harry crouched over the cold stove in his little galley, mumbling obscene curses on the heads of all Russians. "Good-by, miss," he said gloomily, taking his cap off as if in the presence of the dead. "I hope you'll be all right but I doubt it. Proper 'eathens this lot, an' no mistake, sooner 'ave Injuns meself, but take your pick, I suppose." He relapsed into melancholy again.

"Do you know where the captain is? I must say good-by."

He looked at her with pity. "Gone ashore, miss, to clear the cargo. We must get out before the deep-sea ice closes the port, you know."

"Did he leave no farewell or anything?" she demanded blankly.

"No, miss. I dessay he weren't expecting you to go so soon though."

"Oh! Oh well, I suppose it was of no importance, but it is rather nice just to say farewell, don't you think?"

He rose to his feet and slowly draped an old flour sack around his shoulders. "Don't you fret, miss, I'll see you farewell off the old *Neptune* and all good luck to you."

Their last view of the ship was of his shrouded form standing mournfully waving among the whirling snowflakes, one arm upraised as if dispensing a distant blessing.

It was over a week before the ice thickened sufficiently for the regular winter sledge service to Oranienbaum on the mainland to be started, and notwithstanding the warmth of the Simpsons' welcome, they all fretted at the delay. The arrival of all foreign ships was signaled direct to St. Petersburg by semaphore and as the *Neptune* was almost certainly the last to get through that winter Eleanor found that her companions were seriously alarmed lest their respective employers might conclude they were not on board and engage someone else in their places. Secretly she was disturbed by this fresh evidence of the transitory nature of Russian domestic arrangements: in England the ease with which it was apparently possible to change a situation had seemed attractive, in Russia the disadvantages were more obvious.

The journey to St. Petersburg took over seven hours, the last part over execrable, half-frozen roads along the coast, with the body of the sledge temporarily mounted on bone-shaking iron wheels. Eleanor had never been so cold and exhausted in her life, with every shattering jolt transmitted directly up her spine by the springless structure and unpadded wooden bench on which they sat. But in spite of everything she felt her interest stir as they entered the outskirts of St. Petersburg at last. Her eyes were dazzled by the lamps and flambeaux hung outside handsome stone houses, their beams lying in golden pools on piled snow and jeweling the frosted rime which coated buildings and trees alike. St. Petersburg in the darkness was even more striking than London had been and the bustle and width of the streets, where fur-clad passers-by dodged flying sleighs and endless bells jangled merrily in the frosty air, gave an indescribable feeling of gaiety and animation to the weary travelers. The glinting lights and cloudy spirals rising from the breathing of horses and men made it seem as if the city itself was alive and burning incense to the dark, anonymous sky.

Eight

Eleanor awoke next morning in a bedroom so large and ornate that, even while she enjoyed a comfort she had never known, her thoughts dwelled uneasily on the likely size of the bill. She had already picked one of the sovereigns from her hem, and it seemed likely that more would soon follow if they were to remain long in such luxurious surroundings, so she was greatly relieved to hear that the others proposed to leave the hotel immediately after breakfast. This was a strange but delicious meal with recognizable dishes like omelette and bread alternating with trays of salted fish or pickled cucumbers.

Miss Faulkner and Minnie intended to depart that very afternoon by train for Moscow as Miss Faulkner feared that her employers also might think her stranded in England. "They soon hear in Moscow when the deep-sea ice closes St. Petersburg as all their communications must then go overland through Europe. If we do not arrive quickly they will be worried for me."

"Must you go at once?" Eleanor laid down her fork in dismay. "It seems terrible to be losing all our friends so quickly."

"I am afraid so. I have always been treated with such consideration that I should not wish to cause the least worry or annoyance. Our heavy baggage will come by carrier from Kronstadt to the Customs House here, and if we ask them, they will send it on to Moscow. In fact I think Minnie and I should soon be off, the train leaves in two hours and it always takes time to settle matters with the customs."

Emily rose also. "I will come with you if I may and make sure they have my direction at Madame Lokunina's. Then perhaps you could leave me at their house on your way to the station."

"Emily!" exclaimed Eleanor, aghast. "You cannot leave me here alone! You must come with me to Madame Davidova's, I don't know where she lives and even if I found it I should not know how to explain to the servants what I wanted and would very likely be left on the doorstep."

"Oh dear, yes, of course," said Emily, looking harassed. "Only I must be back with the Lokunins as soon as possible, for they will be expecting me. We will call first on Mary Stevens then, for she visited Madame Davidova and I do not know precisely what she may have arranged for you."

"I have the address"—Eleanor fumbled in her reticule—"and I understood from Mama that it was all agreed. Madame Davidova knew I would be coming with you on the *Neptune*."

"It should be all right then, but with Russians nothing ever is as definite as you expect, and having to do everything in a hurry by correspondence . . . but I am sure Mary will have done her best for you."

"Well," said Miss Faulkner practically, "if everything is in such a confusion, the sooner we start the better. I know that if we stay here much longer they will try to make us pay for an extra day."

"Be careful, Eleanor, when you change your sovereigns, that they do not give you paper rubles[1] instead

---

[1]At this time one silver ruble was equal to about twenty-five cents. The growing internal debt was made up by notes printed by the government and known as assignat rubles. Although sporadic attempts were made to reduce the number of assignats in circulation, inflation was such that they were worth about a third of their face value, and, after the Crimean War, about a fifth. In some parts of the country peasants and traders would not accept them as legal tender if they could possibly avoid doing so.

of the silver ones," advised Miss Macdonald. "They will certainly know that you have never been here before."

"What is the difference?"

She laughed unkindly. "Only that the paper is worth about a third of the silver, otherwise exactly the same. Aren't you ever coming?"

"How should I know what their horrible money is worth?" Eleanor's accumulated frustration and worry exploded past recall at last.

Miss Faulkner laid her hand on her arm, smiling gently. "Do not let it upset you, Eleanor my dear. Everything is strange now but when you have settled down the life is not unenjoyable if you are with a good family."

"I am not upset and I am not going to a good family. If I am going to one at all it is to a horrid old woman whom everyone knows to be eccentric if not worse." Eleanor pushed back her chair abruptly and passed her hand across her forehead. "I am sorry, it is the atmosphere in this place, I think, don't they ever open a window? I'll go up and fetch my cloak now, and I think perhaps I should take all my things with me. Then I can settle in with Madame Davidova immediately as this place is so expensive."

Only half an hour later they emerged from the hotel and scrambled into a kind of open calash on runners that had been ordered for them by the hotel. After the oppressive air inside the sparkling freshness of the morning was like a sudden transition to freedom after imprisonment. Gone was the gray murk of the day before and in its place was a luminous pale blue infinity which made every detail of the city stand out with such brilliant clarity that Eleanor's depression vanished as if touched by alchemy.

She breathed deeply. "Isn't this lovely after that stuffy hotel? I really feel as if everything were going to be all right again. What do you call this funny little cart, Margaret?"

Miss Macdonald laughed. "Certainly not a cart! This will be one of the best vehicles in St. Petersburg except for private conveyances. Both it and its driver are called *izvochtchik*."

"*Izvochtchik*," repeated Eleanor experimentally, "that is rather nice. Come to think of it, that little pony looks like a little chick scuttling along. What a funny shaggy little beast it is."

"They don't look much but under the conditions here they are twice as strong as an English horse would be, providing they do not have to carry too heavy a load."

For that first short journey to the imperial customs building, St. Petersburg looked like an enchanted city. The buildings were veiled by a shining gauze of crystals, dancing and shimmering in the bright sunlight, while floating above the irregular roof lines cupolas and spires on fire with silver and gold gave the city an insubstantial, fairytale quality.

They had a long and inconclusive battle with the customs officials who, only too obviously, had never heard of the *Neptune*, and Eleanor promised that she would return and try to check that Miss Faulkner's baggage was dispatched to Moscow when it finally arrived from Kronstadt. Privately she considered it most unlikely that she would have any success and observed as they left: "I cannot but think it is great nonsense to say that one need not learn the language here. Even the doorman at the hotel did not understand French or English although I was assured everyone would do so."

"No, but they understand most signs well enough. It is only that often they do not wish to understand," replied Emily.

"But it is so unsatisfactory like that. Why should they try to understand if we do not make the attempt to speak even a few words of their language?" objected Eleanor.

The others looked at her as if she was demented and Miss Macdonald explained patiently, "But we are

105

English! Even their masters would not *chatter* with them. You will find signs are quite good enough for most occasions, and everyone with any education does speak French and regards Russian as a peasant's language only."

Eleanor was unconvinced but could see no point in persisting and at that moment the *izvochtchik* stopped outside an imposing-looking mansion to drop off Miss Macdonald. "Would you believe it, one of the best positions in town," whispered Emily.

"Yes, I would!" retorted Eleanor. "Of course Margaret would be in the best position in town, one cannot possibly imagine anything else," and Miss Faulkner laughed.

Miss Macdonald did not look back and the last glimpse they had of her was as she was ushered very grandly into an enormous painted hall. Eleanor felt surprisingly sad at the parting; she had not found her a very congenial companion, but she felt sure that under her unemotional exterior Margaret felt as desolate as she did. If she did not look back it was because she could not trust herself to do so.

It is going to be very lonely in a foreign household all by myself, thought Eleanor. Even in St. Petersburg where there was such a large English colony, in all the everyday affairs of life, in thoughts and dreams, it would be complete isolation. Her depression, so recently banished, began to form again, deepening almost to desperation after the next parting. Minnie was close to hysterics and Miss Faulkner brusque and plainly unhappy, wishing openly that she had never agreed to bring her niece to Russia. Ill equipped as Eleanor felt herself to be for her new life, she could not think it anything short of criminal to have brought Minnie to a place so utterly removed from her comprehension.

"I do not know what she will do or how she will ever make her way. I cannot imagine why she came in the first place."

Emily shrugged. "I think she thought it exciting and

romantic as we all do when we first arrive: perhaps Miss Faulkner wanted company and so allowed her to come."

"It was very wrong," said Eleanor in a low voice, locking and unlocking her fingers in her lap.

Emily looked at her a moment and then said abruptly: "You are thinking that I did not give you a true idea of what it is like here, are you not?"

It was the first direct question Eleanor had heard her ask and she was rather startled, but replied honestly: "Yes, I was. It seems so different now to the stories you were telling us at home."

"Yes, it is different. Somehow in England one does not quite remember how it is and I thought it would be nice for all of us if you came and—and, well, I suppose I wanted everyone at home to think I was having a wonderful time and not missing all the things I could never have."

For the first time Eleanor found herself really liking Emily and she squeezed her arm affectionately. "Perhaps now there are two of us it will be more fun. Where does Miss Stevens live?"

"In the Renishnaya, quite near here. It is a lovely position, overlooking the Summer Gardens and the Agricultural Museum."

"Good heavens, I never imagined them having anything so advanced as an Agricultural Museum!" exclaimed Eleanor.

"Well, my dear, it is not really so very advanced," explained Emily. They both suddenly burst out laughing and felt much better for it, even the *izvochtchik* glanced over his shoulder and his beard stirred in what might have been a smile.

Miss Stevens was a small, gray woman with a vague, ineffectual manner. Her hair was untidy and her spectacles hung round her neck on a piece of knotted, frayed string. Several children, of whom she seemed completely unaware, were playing noisily in the background.

"Oh, Miss Lovell, yes." She spoke in such a soft

voice that Eleanor had to strain her ears to catch the words. "I called on Madame Davidova for you and she did say that she required a governess; she was much interested in your mother's letter and pleased to hear that you spoke some French."

"Thank you, it was kind of you to go to so much trouble for me. What else did she say?"

"Only something about her cats' names, I think. She did say she would be very pleased to see you when you arrived."

"So it is definite then?" asked Eleanor eagerly.

Miss Stevens smiled tiredly. "You will find that nothing ever is definite in Russia, Miss Lovell. It is, if she has not forgotten about it and if no one else has turned up meantime."

"Oh," said Eleanor blankly. She found it hard to grasp the idea of people saying they would do something and then completely forgetting about it as a matter of habit and not of accident. "Well, we had better go and see. I have her address but I am not at all sure where that is in St. Petersburg."

"It is the Sredny Prospekt, isn't it? It is the other side of the Neva behind the Cadet School—you know, Emily, the first turning after the Semenov Gallery."

"Oh yes, I know. We will have to arrange a meeting soon so that I can tell you about everything in England and we can introduce Eleanor to the rest of our little circle."

One of the children, probably feeling that insufficient notice was being taken of him, suddenly hurled himself on the floor and broke into a prolonged howl, his face screwing up and turning purple before Eleanor's startled gaze.

"Oh dear, now look what has happened! You had better go, we will not have any peace now," said Miss Stevens philosophically.

"Thank you so much again," shouted Eleanor above the din, the sounds of which pursued them down the broad staircase and across the elegant hallway.

When the door was shut behind them she could not help asking: "Is that child normal? I have never seen anyone behave so in my life. How does Miss Stevens stand it or is he not as bad as that in the usual way?"

Emily sighed. "You will find that many Russian children are shockingly spoiled and the parents will not allow you to discipline them properly. Why, if I punish my dear little Vanya you can be sure that when my back is turned his mama will be giving him sugar plums or some such thing. Once, when I was really angry and slapped him for something, she cuddled him on her lap all afternoon. The servants are worse still, so lazy and dirty, but very good-natured and willing to go to the most extraordinary lengths to gratify whatever the child wants. Of course Vanya—and all the other children too, I dare say—sees his parents having whatever they wish and hitting the servants, so when he does the same thing they cannot protest."

"What does he do then?"

"Generally nothing. He is a very sweet-tempered little boy and if he were properly brought up would be quite delightful; but although Monsieur Lokunin is a very quiet, well-mannered man, Madame has a hasty temper and sometimes hits out or throws things and the child thinks it is clever to do the same. It is not his fault."

"But don't you stop him?" cried Eleanor, revolted.

"I try, of course. I am really very fond of him but what can I do when he sees his mother doing the same things? Why, only just before I went on holiday she banished the butler to Siberia and sent his wife and baby back to her estates where they will be very badly off with no one to provide for them and no allotment of land as the child is a girl. All because they were married without her consent and she had only just found out about it when the child was too big to be hidden in the attics any longer."

"What difference will the child being a girl make?"

"Every difference. They were serfs of course, as

so many of the servants and peasants are, and belonged body and soul to their master. No serf can own anything, but in practice much of the land is distributed to them through their peasant commune at so much for each soul in exchange for rent and service. But to the Russian mind only males have souls, so when the land is distributed in the village a woman alone with a female child would get nothing. She will have to work for other peasants now her place in the household is gone. They know she has no choice and so will spare them only just enough to live if she is lucky."

Eleanor was appalled. Difficult as her own life had been, she had never had to consider existence in those terms before.

The *izvochtchik* clattered down the side of a frozen canal and now, instead of her earlier bright enchantment with St. Petersburg, she noticed the comparative daytime emptiness of the wide streets except for a few country carts and ragged walkers. In place of soaring, glittering domes floating on blue distance she noticed decaying plasterwork and garish paint. Every wall she saw, no matter how grand the building, had great patches of facing dropping off and many of the long, repetitive fronts of the larger buildings were roughly daubed with bright colors, chiefly jarring, crude reds and yellows.

"Why, it is hideous and not beautiful at all!" she exclaimed involuntarily. "What is that building there?"

"It is the back of the Foreign Office. In a moment we will be in Palace Place and you will see the Winter Palace and most of the government buildings."

"The Foreign Office? That color? All its walls are falling down!"

"Oh no. It is just that nearly all the buildings are covered with plaster so of course every year the frost flakes off any that is at all loose. In the summer they are usually repaired if no one forgets. After a hard

110

winter they look terrible, though I must say that after months of snow the bright colors are very welcome."

"I think they are awful," said Eleanor flatly. "The whole place looks as if it hasn't been lived in for a hundred years and there are too few people around to make it look lived in now."

Even she, in her jaundiced state of mind, was bound to admit that the Winter Palace was impressive, if dull, and the Admiralty with its slender, silver spire and yellow walls genuinely attractive. But after they had driven across the rough surface of the Neva, for the floating bridge was buckled and unusable once the ice began to form, and plunged into a maze of increasingly dilapidated streets behind the Cadet School and Academy of Arts, her spirits sank lower and lower and she could only gaze about her in utter despondency.

Madame Davidova's house was built of peeling, plastered brick painted an indeterminate green. The knocker, which was of very fine craftsmanship, had obviously been unpolished for decades and the steps were treacherous with accumulated ice.

Eleanor had to stifle an almost overwhelming desire to order the *izvochtchik* to drive away without even asking for Madame Davidova, but a realization of the plight she would be in unless she could find somewhere to stay, however unwholesome, while she sought a more congenial post, prevented her. It was only after several attacks on the knocker, each louder than the last, that they heard footsteps approaching and the door was flung open by a small, bent old man with a flowing white beard and an uncertain smile.

He looked as taken aback to see two young ladies on his doorstep as they were at his appearance, and he instinctively half closed the door again, only his face and beard showing round the edge. Eleanor addressed him in her best French, but he looked completely blank. She then tried in English and Emily in German but at each unintelligible sentence he re-

111

treated farther behind his door, his eyes blinking nervously.

"Don't you speak any Russian, Emily?" demanded Eleanor.

"Only a few words. Unless the emphasis is on exactly the right syllable they cannot understand what you are saying."

"Well, do try something. 'Madame Davidova, please,' should be sufficient anyway."

Emily tried a few halting words with Eleanor interpolating "Madame Davidova" and a series of nods and smiles at any pauses that seemed suitable. After a few moments, still apparently uncomprehending, but resigned to their persistence and too polite to shut the door in their faces, the old man opened it sufficiently for them to enter.

Signing for them to be seated, he shuffled off to the rear of the house and Eleanor saw for the first time that he was dressed in a most extraordinary fashion in a pink, round-necked blouse worn outside baggy breeches and tied at the waist with some knotted cord.

"What an odd dress. I don't think I shall care to live here long, there is a very nasty smell,"[1] Eleanor whispered, wrinkling her nose distastefully.

"It is the usual dress of the *moujiks*. Out in the country they wear nothing else in summer, sometimes the shirts are the most wonderful colors of silk. The smell is nothing to regard, I assure you, although the cats make it worse here. All the houses are the same while they are shut up through the winter cold."[2]

- "But it is terrible, whatever is it?"

"Ssh! He's coming back."

But instead of the manservant there appeared a

[2]The heat in Russian homes was such that in many cases fumes were drawn from the drains through untrapped sanitary appliances and the occupants suffered from partial poisoning throughout the winter; it was infinitely preferable not to be connected to any form of street drainage. Russian soaps and polishes had (and have) a smell all their own.

brisk little old lady dressed, to Eleanor's eyes, as if she had just stepped out of an eighteenth-century portrait, but in reality wearing the formal uniform of all the ladies at the court of St. Petersburg. So great was the Tsar's love of discipline and uniformity that even the ladies admitted to his presence had every detail of their dress regulated according to an elaborate code of rules. But however suitable for a court ball, rich brown velvet cut in panniers over an underdress of stiff white satin, all lavishly trimmed with exquisite lace and jewelry, could not be described as suitable for receiving afternoon callers. They both rose and curtsied as she entered, extending her hand regally in greeting.

"*Bon jour, mesdemoiselles.* To what do I owe the pleasure of this visit?" she asked in perfect French.

A cat of doubtful parentage appeared from beneath her skirts and began to rub itself against Eleanor's legs. She swallowed nervously and, trying to ignore her surroundings, fumbled for the correct French constructions. "I am Mademoiselle Lovell, madame, and I believe that a friend of mine, Mademoiselle Stevens, called on you some time ago to . . . to arrange that I should take a situation which you were offering as a governess in your household."

"I remember it, yes. But it is now long ago, mademoiselle, and I have since brought extra servants from my estate."

"But . . . but do you not also need an English governess to oversee your own servants and look after your granddaughter? I will not mind what I do, I am used to all kinds of household tasks," said Eleanor desperately.

"*Ah, mademoiselle, les Anglaises!* I have tried several since your friend called on me but all wish to change things and make everybody uncomfortable. It is too fatiguing, I assure you, and now with my good Anna Yakovlevna I am content."

Looking around her at the disorder and dirt in every

corner, Eleanor could not help but be glad that she was not to live in such a place, but all her plans had been based on entering a situation immediately. Even with the utmost economy she could not think how she was to support herself in St. Petersburg for more than a week or so. However, there was nothing for it but to withdraw with the best dignity she could manage. "Thank you, madame. I regret having disturbed your afternoon." She curtsied and turned away.

"It was a pleasure. I trust that you will partake of some refreshment with me?"

"No, thank you, madame. I have other calls to make as I must find a post as soon as possible, but thank you again."

Madame Davidova stiffened. "As you please." She walked away down the cluttered passage without a backward glance, leaving them to let themselves out of the house.

"You should not have done that," Emily said as they settled back in the *izvochtchik*. "Russians are very hospitable and it is a great insult not to accept any kind of invitation. They are never in a hurry about anything and to give as an excuse that you have other appointments is incomprehensible to them and so the greatest rudeness."

"Was that the trouble? I couldn't think what I had said to offend her, I will remember another time. But I am in a hurry—whatever am I going to do now?"

"I shall have to go back to my family. They must be wondering by now what has become of me and I will be out of employment too if I am not careful. I will ask Madame Lokunina whether she has any friends who require governesses and send you round a note in the morning."

"But where can I stay? I can't go back to the hotel, my money would be gone in a few days there." Eleanor tried to keep the panic out of her voice.

"I think there are one or two respectable lodging houses," Emily said doubtfully.

114

Oh, God, please! thought Eleanor desperately, panic no longer to be denied. Whatever am I to do? Help me! She squeezed her fingers together, tears very close and unable even to start grappling with such a disaster. "I can't go to a lodging house by myself," she said at last in a small voice. "Emily, you must see that I can't. What sort of respectable place would take me?"

"You could go to the British Embassy," suggested Emily. "They might be able to arrange something for you."

The thought of boldly calling at the British Embassy, when she had seldom been allowed even to accompany her mother on her formal calls, sparked Eleanor's erratic sense of humor and she was saved from tears by a sudden chuckle—but a chuckle which caught her throat so that she bit it off abruptly, shocked by the pit of hysteria opening before her.

"I must get back to the Lokunins," insisted Emily, calling the address to the *izvochtchik*. "I am terribly sorry, but that is really the only thing for you to do."

Emily's feeling of guilt and Eleanor's enclosing fears made their farewell abrupt to the point of indifference, but Eleanor had never felt so alone in her life as when she was driven to the embassy through the gray early northern evening. She could not think what else to do, but when she saw its vast, impressive façade her courage failed her. She stood irresolutely on the flagway outside, clutching her bags, and then turned away. When she saw a painted sign pointing to the English church just down a side turning she hurried inside without thinking, frightened by the curious stares and rough remarks she was already attracting in the street outside.

It was chill and dark in the church, but a blessed familiarity descended on her after the nightmare of the day. The pitch-pine pews and brightly polished brasses were those of any English village church and at once transported her in spirit to the sanctuary of home. Of course! It was the answer to her prayer: not the embassy, but the English minister was the person to help her: she remembered clearly the unfailing generosity with which the vicar at Mayhurst had always met the many requests for his charity.

She left the church and fearfully felt her way down the rough trackway outside, for it was now completely dark. Surely the minister's house must adjoin the church somewhere? She stumbled on the treacherous surface, her bags dragging at her arms and making it difficult to keep her balance. She was like a gambler with his last throw before disaster: nothing would stop her but if this last resort failed, then there was nothing left for further effort. She was beyond surprise or even relief when she found some spotless white-washed steps and a brass plate which proclaimed the minister's residence, adjoining the east wall of the church and exactly where she had expected to find it, too overwrought to do more than blink gratefully and stammer her name in the bright lights and bustling welcome she received.

She was conscious though of her good fortune in finding the minister, Dr. Ward, at home; conscious too of his lack of surprise at her stammered request for lodging while she sought a post as governess.

Instead he looked angry. "You are only one of many. I already have two ladies like yourself staying here while they seek almost any kind of work. It is very wrong that you young ladies are allowed to come here without anywhere to go." He hustled her into his study, breathlessly hot like all Russia houses, yet indefinably English in its furnishings and atmosphere.

Eleanor attempted to explain. "I thought I did have a post but the lady has decided not to engage an Englishwoman as their methods make her too uncomfortable."

He laughed. "That I can well believe. I do not want to depress you unduly but it may be some time before you can find yourself anything suitable, so many are seeking positions. Why don't you return to England? The *Neptune* may not yet have left."

116

Eleanor remembered Count Berdeyev's words; his predictions had proved far more accurate than Emily's easy optimism. Was there anyone in the world except her own family who did not condemn this crazy venture? "I cannot," she said doggedly. "It is difficult to explain but I could not go home now, and I am not sure whether I have enough money to do so anyway."

"I see. Well, in that case I think perhaps Mrs. Field would take you in. She is the widow of my late curate and only has two rooms on the third floor of the English warehouse behind here. I am afraid it is cold there but she is a delightful person and I really have no more room myself. She is very poor and will be pleased, I dare say, for you to lodge with her for as little as fifty kopecks[3] a day."

"That would be wonderful!" exclaimed Eleanor. She felt quite lightheaded with relief at such a quick solution. "How kind of you, are you sure she will not mind?"

"We had better go and ask her but I expect she will be pleased to do whatever she can, although you must understand that she has very little herself. I have only suggested it because . . ."

"Yes indeed. I am poor myself now and will have to practice the most stringent economies until I find a post." After only one day in St. Petersburg Eleanor had few illusions left about the difficulties of her position.

So it was settled. Mrs. Field was as delightful as Dr. Ward had promised, about thirty-five years old and quite undeterred by the many privations of her life. She supported herself precariously by teaching history to Russian children, giving Russian lessons to the English colony, and occasionally working on the books of the English warehouse. Her two rooms were partitioned off from the attics above the main warehouse as a concession by the management: adequate enough in

[3]One hundred kopecks equal one ruble.

summer, in winter they were almost insupportably cold. Breath formed as ice on glasses and mirrors and they both had to wear outdoor clothes all the time and sleep covered by the mats from the floor. Eleanor's fifty kopecks a day included supper and also a breakfast of tea and biscuits, but she could see too plainly how difficult existence was for Mrs. Field to feel able to eat more than a minimum. She sometimes bought herself a wicker carton of honey and a roll of light, cake-like bread at midday, but she grudged every kopeck from her rapidly dwindling store and spent the day walking round St. Petersburg calling on prospective employers and trying to ignore the insistent pangs of hunger. From time to time she and Mrs. Field would be invited to dinner by one of the English colony and on Sundays, as a great treat, they bought themselves some meat and vegetables and concocted a savory stew followed by pickled cucumbers and sugared fruits, both great Russian delicacies. They both looked forward to these rare treats with an almost painful intensity through an endless week of corn meal, cheese, pickled cabbage, and soup.

True to her word, Emily sent round a list of names and addresses of Madame Lokunina's friends who might by chance be looking for an English governess. Dr. Ward also suggested some possibilities and Mrs. Field occasionally came home from her lessons in high excitement with an unintelligible address scribbled on a piece of paper. So Eleanor walked day after day from one forbidding door to another over the rough cobbles and icy, treacherous ruts which characterized even the main thoroughfares of St. Petersburg. It had not yet snowed really hard but nearly every day frozen flurries would drive across the great empty squares while glimpses of the sun became more rare.

It was nearly four weeks since Eleanor had landed at Kronstadt and four of her sovereigns had disappeared. Her pride forbade her from owing Mrs. Field her lodgment money, although that kind-hearted lady repeatedly told her that she could stay as long as she pleased without payment. Even if it must eventually come to this, there would be far too little food for them to share: Eleanor would have to face the disagreeable necessity of applying to the Church for charity like any vagrant pauper. Unfortunately the Church and the British Consulate were already helping several half-starved English governesses through the winter, and there were so many out of work, she was by no means sure that she would find such help easy to obtain. She at least had found shelter while several were without provision or accommodation of any kind.

Eleanor had long since given up the luxury of taking an *izvochtchik*, although in St. Petersburg only the very poorest walked, and as the days became shorter and darker she came to dread the long, frightening journeys to indecipherable and elusive addresses. It was true that governesses and employers alike made frequent changes but it was usually by private arrangement among friends and she found her approaches invariably too late or ignored among the press of more favored or experienced applicants.

In spite of her growing anxiety over money, Eleanor had had to buy herself a pair of *veliki* or felt boots against the cold and her slender funds were still further depleted by a staggering bill from the Customs House for the carriage of her boxes from Kronstadt. She had written home to tell of her alarming position and to beg for a small draft on a St. Petersburg bank to tide her over the winter but so far had not received any reply, although she did not doubt that her father would send her money if he realized the true desperation of her plight. Unfortunately, in her first letter home she had made light of conditions and had not, at that time, had any doubt that she would soon find herself in employment even if not in the sort of situation she had hoped for. After this, and Emily's cheerful but misleading descriptions, there was no reason why they should now realize how completely changed was the position, and

119

were more likely to put her troubles down to excessive fastidiousness. In addition, now that the sea routes into the city were finally closed by ice the posts would have to go overland across Europe; it might be months before money could reach her and long before then she would be destitute.

With every passing week her prospects seemed less bright and as November drew to a close she felt obliged to cut her meals down to one a day and this, together with the fact that her clothes were totally unsuited to the Russian climate, made her feel the cold even more intensely than before. She had no money to buy furs, and cloth or wool, however good their quality, would not suffice to keep out the icy, piercing winds, while inside the superheated Russian homes they were far too heavy. She found that Russian women wore the lightest of muslins and silks indoors even in the winter and were heavily muffed in furs on the infrequent occasions they ventured outside.

Not that she very often saw inside the many doors upon which she knocked. Her almost total ignorance of Russian, in spite of Mrs. Field's careful coaching, combined with her by now threadbare and impoverished appearance, generally made it very difficult to induce any servant to take her message up to his mistress, especially as she could only spare a few kopecks to give him.

At last her luck turned: at one solidly prosperous house she was almost welcomed and called back no fewer than five times for further questions. She judged, with new-found shrewdness, that the family was nerving itself for a leap into fashionable society, for a break with a Muscovite, kaftan[4]-clad past, and was trying to feel its way past the shoals of unknown social convention in which an English governess might well prove an advantage. At the same time they shied from the com-

---

[4] A long robe, usually calf-length and originally worn by all well-to-do Russians. Generally of dark material girdled by a wide, colored sash.

plications of introducing this very odd stranger into their traditional way of life: in the circumstances a firm decision, never easy in Russia, was unusually difficult to obtain. Gradually, however, the uncertainties and hesitations grew less and after the fifth meeting, having been asked to wait in the hall yet again while the family argued, Eleanor felt that success could not be much longer delayed.

She rubbed her shabby, clumsy *veliki* surreptitiously on the carpet in a futile attempt to remove some of their many unsightly scars and stains. Mingling with the familiar Russian household smell was a rich aroma of spiced cooking and her stomach trembled irresistibly; perhaps if she were engaged she would be offered an immediate meal. She closed her eyes against a sudden dizzying wave of weakness and then scrambled to her feet as she heard quick footsteps.

"I am sorry to keep you waiting again, *barishna*, but we have decided after all that we must think further about such an important matter. Perhaps another year . . . you understand how very difficult it is to decide on such a step in a hurry, so we intend to leave the younger children in the country, at least for another winter." The words were unbelievable. Insensibly, over the past week, she had come to rest all her hopes with this worried, uncertain family, had almost forgotten her own problems in interest at theirs, had begun to like little countrified Petya and Agafa, and to visualize herself secure at last as part of their pleasant, strange, harassed household.

Now it was lost, as so much else had been lost, and she no longer even had the energy to argue: she rose blindly and hardly knew how she found her way out into the street. It was a clear day but half dark as the sun barely lifted itself over the horizon before sinking back into the darkness as if it too was exhausted by even transitory effort. She had come to appreciate why the Russians had such a passion for gilding the domes and steeples of their public buildings: the almost horizontal rays of the sun struck fiery slashes of swift light from the domes of St. Isaac's Cathedral high above her head and behind her, just glimpsed at the corner of the Winter Palace, was the spire of the fortress church of St. Peter and St. Paul on its island in the Neva, a burning needle thrust into the milky grayness above.

She stood for a moment at the corner of the Admiralty building, conscious of the sublime magnificence around her with one part of her mind, while the other was cringing at the stark grimness of her penury. She shivered suddenly as the cold penetrated into the pit of her stomach and numbed the depths of her mind, and began almost to run in an effort to outpace despair. She knew that gloom and self-pity were only additional burdens for her to carry and in the last weeks she had discovered in herself an obstinate determination to survive, somehow to win through the shadows and into real life again.

Rounding the corner of the Ministry of War, she almost collided with two army officers outside the main entrance. Deep in her own disastrous thoughts, she did not take any particular notice of them until she felt her arm grasped from behind. With a cry of fear, for this was not the first time she had been accosted as an unprotected female walking round the city alone, she pulled herself free, terror catching her throat, before she recognized the voice apologizing to her.

"I am sorry if I startled you, Miss Lovell, but I thought you were going to walk right by me. How are you?"

She found herself responding dazedly to Count Berdeyev's greeting. She had not recognized him in a long gray overcoat and round fur hat, so familiar with other officers in the capital. "I—I am sorry I did not recognize you. I am very well, thank you, I hope you are also?" she stammered when she could gather her scampering thoughts from pursuing her own affairs.

At his first sight of her face his eyebrows snapped

together and she shifted uncomfortably under his scrutiny, aware of her poverty-stricken appearance.

"Thank you, yes," he replied slowly, his glance taking in the thinness of her cloak and traveling to her eyes, unnaturally large and bright in a pinched, undernourished face, transparent with cold.

"Well, I must return to my home before it becomes quite dark," Eleanor said awkwardly in the silence that fell between them. "It has been nice to see you again and remember the happy times on the *Neptune*."

"Where do you go? May I escort you if you would like it?"

"Only just down the Galernaya, I am staying with a friend behind the English Church."

"Behind the English Church?" he queried, falling into step beside her, his accent more noticeable than it had been on the ship.

"Yes, in the warehouse. On the third floor," she added defiantly.

"I understand then that your post, I do not recall where, was not satisfactory?"

"It was gone. She had changed her mind."

"I see." He hesitated a moment and then said brusquely, "You should buy yourself some furs, you will never live the winter through in those ridiculous English clothes."

"Perhaps I will when I find a post," she answered noncommittally.

He had no difficulty in interpreting her meaning. "That will perhaps be too late. Can you not obtain some money from home?"

Eleanor blushed painfully. "I do not lack for support from my family when I need it, I assure you, sir!"

"So I see," he replied dryly.

They walked to the end of the street in silence and at the warehouse door she held out her hand. "Thank you for your company, sir. I have enjoyed seeing you again."

He bowed gravely. "May I give you my good wishes

for your quest? I hope you will soon find what you seek."

"I hope so too!" She smiled suddenly. "If you hear of a situation I shall rely on you to let me know."

As usual his face betrayed no more than rather bored, polite interest, but she had the impression that he was turning something over in his mind. A gust of wind and snow swept down the street and she shuddered as it bit through her slender defenses and seemed to numb her very nerve-ends. Berdeyev noticed her trembling fingers in their expensive, unsuitable gloves, the way she tried to hug her cloak closer, and having seen many half-starved people in his life found no difficulty in estimating her condition with tolerable accuracy.

He made up his mind suddenly. "I have a proposition to put to you which I would normally hesitate to do. I can see, no matter what you say to me, that you have no money, and no one, least of all an English-woman, can live through a Russian winter with no money. I have few acquaintances in Petersburg and as a bachelor my recommendation would do you nothing but harm anyway, but I have a cousin, who is married to the governor of Kharkov, and to there she will soon return. She was lamenting the other day that her little boy is growing up a barbarian so far from Petersburg, but naturally no one respectable will go with her."

"Why not?" demanded Eleanor. After so many disappointments she fought down a surge of hope.

He ran a finger down the scar on the side of his face: "Kharkov is over thirteen hundred versts[5] from here and seven hundred or so from Moscow. There is no railway south of Moscow and I should not expect to find any English or French person in the city, although there would be some Germans of course."

Eleanor considered this and smiled wanly. "Did you not yourself tell me that St. Petersburg was not Russia? Perhaps now I shall see the real Russia you spoke of."

There was a faint troubled shadow on his face, but

[5]A Russian verst is two thirds of a mile.

he said directly, "You are sure? Distances are so very great here and you will not find anything the same as you are accustomed to, quite different from Petersburg."

"I am sure," she replied firmly. "Things are strange enough here and I cannot go on like this until the spring and perhaps longer. If your cousin will engage me I will be very pleased to go."

"Very well," Berdeyev said curtly, dismissing the matter. "I will send round a note for you to give her in the morning. *Adieu, mademoiselle.*" He kissed her cold fingers.

"*Adieu, monsieur le comte,* and thank you very much."

"You have nothing to thank me for," he said grimly. "You are more likely to live to curse me. It is not easy to return from so far. I would not have told you of it if I did not understand the Russian winter well enough to know you will surely die if you stay here as you are at present." He left her without a backward glance.

She did not take much notice of his ominous words, so thankful was she at this happy turn of her affairs, instead scrambling triumphantly up the flights of rickety stairs to their rooms. "Mary dear! I've found a situation at last—I really think I have!" she cried as soon as she opened the door.

"How wonderful for you. Madame finally made up her mind, did she?" Mrs. Field looked up smiling from some corn meal and dried fish she was cooking.

"Oh no! The old wretch said she would not bring her horrid children to Petersburg after all. After five visits! But I ran into that Count Berdeyev I told you of, whom I met on the ship, and he says his cousin wants a governess and he will give me an introduction."

Mrs. Field hugged her. "Oh, Eleanor, I am so pleased for you! What is her name, shall I know her?"

"I didn't ask him but he said she was married to the governor of Kharkov, so she sounds very respectable."

"Kharkov!" echoed Mrs. Field, aghast. "But that is

right in the south, hundreds of miles away, in the Ukraine."

"Thirteen hundred versts, he said."

"Eleanor dear, consider. You cannot go right away down there on your own, just among Russians. It is unheard of, I dare say there will not even be a Protestant church."

"Nevertheless I am going," replied Eleanor tranquilly. "And there must be at least a Lutheran church, for he said there were Germans there. I will certainly miss Dr. Ward and all of you but I cannot continue as a charge on you indefinitely and there seems no prospect of employment here at all. I shall soon not be able even to go out because I will have nothing warm enough to wear when the really cold weather comes."

Mrs. Field bit her lip, her face anxious. "I know, but I cannot like it. I think it very wrong of that man to suggest such a thing to you, although naturally a Russian would not realize what such complete isolation from her own kind would mean to an English girl of your age."

"He did realize it, in fact I think he regretted telling me of the post, but I was most grateful. Anyway, I don't think there is much point in arguing, what else can I do?"

"It is very difficult, I know. But I cannot help hoping all the same that perhaps he will forget to send the introduction round. It would be entirely typical, you know."

Berdeyev did not forget. While they were still sitting over tea the following morning there was a knock at the door and when Eleanor opened it a young officer dressed in the green and white of the Cossack Guards was standing on the threshold. He saluted her and said in passable, if sibilant, French: *"Une lettre envoyée de Monsieur de Berdeyev, mademoiselle.* I have below an *izvochtchik* and will be pleased to escort you to the hotel of Madame Traskine."

"Oh, thank you, but please don't bother. I see it is

not too far," replied Eleanor, glancing at the super-scription on the envelope.

"I have my orders, mademoiselle, *monsieur le général* will not be pleased if I do not carry them out, and besides it will be a pleasure," he grinned engagingly.

"Then thank you, I will be out in a moment." He nodded and went off down the stairs.

Eleanor danced into the sitting room. "He did remember, I knew he would! Madame Traskine at the Hôtel de l'Europe, and the nicest-looking Cossack outside to escort me there." She rushed through to the other room to put on her cloak, arranged her shawl to cover its most worn patches, and tried to straighten out the brim of her bonnet, sadly battered by all the snowstorms in which she had had to wear it.

"Well!" said Mrs. Field, peering at the smart young guardsman below. "I thought you said you hardly knew this general?"

"So I do, but I think he felt sorry for me yesterday in my stupid English clothes. I must be off now!" She ran down the stairs.

The Grand Hôtel de l'Europe was just off the Nevski Prospekt and Eleanor, almost without waiting, was ushered into Madame Traskine's private suite, as she had sent her letter up before her in the care of a porter.

She was met in the doorway by a maid who conducted her into an ornately gilded room where Madame Traskine was still in bed, drinking tea from a steaming samovar and smoking as, to Eleanor's astonishment, a great many ladies did in Russia.

"*Eh bien, mademoiselle*, what is this that Nicolai Pavl'itch[6] writes me that you wish to come to Kharkov?" She was a youngish, rather heavy-featured woman, with a petulant mouth but an attractive smile

[6]It is usual for Russians to address each other by a Christian name and patronymic; for very close friends or relatives a diminutive is used. Here Nicolai Pavl'itch = Nicholas the son of Paul. Pavl'itch is a shortening of Pavlovitch.

which lit up her whole face on the rare occasions it was allowed to slip further than her lips.

Eleanor curtsied. "Very much, madame, *s'il vous plaît*."

"*Pourquoi?* Do you know my cousin well? It is most unlike him to be recommending a governess, *je vous assure!*"

"No, I do not know him, madame. I met him on the ship when I came to Russia and ran into him in the street yesterday. I wish to go to Kharkov because, to be honest, I can't find a post here."

"*Eh bien*, it will, I think, be very amusing to have an English lady in Kharkov! Indeed it seems very strange for you to be coming to Russia at all unescorted."

Eleanor colored but made no reply and Madame Traskine pouted at her reticence, more than half minded not to engage her. She did not particularly like her cousin and had no desire to please him but, although she had only rarely felt his anger, she had no wish to do so again. She stole a speculative glance at the shabby figure before her, threadbare gloves clutched coldly in her lap. Surely Nicolai Pavl'itch could have no interest in this pinched, impoverished, unattractive foreigner or he would not be suggesting she go to Kharkov—unless, she thought suddenly, he wished to be rid of her. The reflection of how greatly her own comfort would benefit through being able to delegate all responsibility for her child, and possibly even her household, decided her.

"Very well then, I leave for Moscow on Monday by train and from there onward we will have to travel post. I have been waiting for the new snow to harden south of Moscow before starting. It is impossible to travel on the roads except when they are snowbound or baked hard in the sun, and of the two snow is infinitely preferable. In between seasons it is impossible—but impossible! My husband remained in Kharkov, as governor he cannot be away for long, and my son also is there."

"He is to be my charge?" asked Eleanor, almost overjoyed at having at last found a home.

"My dear little Micha, yes. He is nearly three years old and of the sweetest disposition. You will have sole charge of him with two maids to assist you, and I desire you to be with him always except when I give you permission to go out."

Eleanor remembered the promise she had sworn on her mother's Bible before leaving home and had to fight one of the hardest battles of her life. Finally she said, with an almost physical effort: "I must be able to go to church on Sundays, if you please, madame."

Madame Traskine laughed. "The English and their Sundays, but yes certainly! With us we also go to church but Sunday is a day of rejoicing and most of our best entertainment is on that day, you will miss much if you keep an English Sunday in Russia—and above all in the south. I will pay you four hundred silver rubles[7] every year, and for your Sundays, you may visit church and have the day off."

"Thank you, madame," murmured Eleanor, wondering whether she would have to wait until the end of the year before being paid, but not daring to ask. A rapid calculation was enough to make her realize that this was a handsome wage indeed, far better than she had come to expect during her last weeks of frantic searching.

"You will come here on Monday morning in time for us to leave for the Moscow station by eleven o'clock. *Au revoir, mademoiselle.*" She sank back on her pillows, closing her eyes under Eleanor's bemused gaze.

"Yes, madame, and thank you again," she repeated, curtsying again before creeping out of the room. Plainly the effort of interviewing a governess at eleven

---

[7]About a hundred dollars.

o'clock in the morning was almost too much for her new employer.

Eleanor found the Cossack officer, whom she already called Yuri Anton'itch at his own request, still waiting for her downstairs. He was surrounded by plates of the hors d'oeuvres beloved by Russians and called *zakuski*, comprising every savory dish of fantasy and imagination. He rose at her approach and indicated a chair. "I shall be honored if Mademoiselle will join me," he said, smiling.

Eleanor's mouth watered at the sight of such delicacies and she threw aside all thoughts of propriety without hesitation. When they had eventually finished and he drove her back to the warehouse she was feeling immensely restored and more cheerful than at any time since leaving the *Neptune*. She ran upstairs and scribbled a note to Berdeyev thanking him for his good offices and also for the meal; she felt sure from his scrutiny of the night before that it had been his idea.

"Do you know the general well?" she asked Yuri as she put the letter into his hands.

"No indeed, I am but a lieutenant. I am at the moment on the staff here and the general has joined us temporarily on his return from your country. I believe before that he was in the southern campaigns until he was wounded—what wouldn't I do to go there!" His face lit up with enthusiasm.

"I didn't know there was a war on?"

"Not precisely a war, Ilena, but always on the Asian borders we are moving forward. I shall find my way there somehow soon, I swear it." He laughingly shook his fist. "I am bound to come through Kharkov, or at least I shall see that I do, and then I will call on you if I may."

"I should like that very much," said Eleanor sincerely.

"But what are we thinking of Kharkov for? You say you are not going until Monday, why don't you come out with me tomorrow?"

130

She hesitated; wariness had long since begun to replace her earlier frank friendliness.

"I will take good care of you, Ilena, I promise," prompted Yuri. "Perhaps you would like to go sledging on one of the new runs."

"Yes, I would," acknowledged Eleanor. He was an extremely pleasant young man, reminding her, if she allowed herself to think of it, just a little of Christopher. It was very agreeable not to be an unwanted applicant any longer but a person again, flattered, catered for and looked after. She realized suddenly that it must be safe to accept his invitation, for with one of his own officers Count Berdeyev's influence would surely be protection enough. "What a splendid idea, I should love to come!" She accepted quickly before she could have second thoughts.

The sledge runs were massive affairs, built as soon as the snows came and extending down the middle of several of the main streets of St. Petersburg. Exhilarating swoops were followed by sudden curves and then by splendid, whistling speed again. So cleverly were the runs constructed that it was quite possible to travel a switchback half mile without ever quite stopping. Eleanor had several times eyed them with longing and now in the crisp, midday brightness of a carefree holiday from worry she enjoyed herself to the full, laughing and jostling with the crowd, hanging on to Yuri's arm and besieging the hot pie seller at the end of the most successful run of all. She had for so long come to accept St. Petersburg as the dreary backdrop for her frightening dilemma, cold, hostile, and semi-civilized, that the afternoon was a revelation: briefly she became one of the privileged again and ceased to be a mere frightened bystander to the remote puppetry of other people's lives. She soon rediscovered what she had almost forgotten—life could be sweet again.

With Yuri she was accepted as easily as she had been previously ignored. When it became too cold for sledging he took her to a party held in one of the imposing mansions lining the Neva, rejecting her protests with scorn. "Every lady in St. Petersburg keeps open house two or three times a week so how is she to know, or care, who comes and goes?" and she found this to be true. She was made welcome, brought into the conversation, regaled with food and drink. Certainly Yuri was known to her hostess, but it was hard not to feel that she would have been treated the same if they had been strangers.

On the way home he took her through a series of shops which she had never even realized were shops, with their blank walls and only a painted sign to show the type of goods on sale within, and gave her a tiny silver scarf pin curved in the shape of a dagger as a memento to take to Kharkov with her. She almost wept when she tried to thank him, her emotions unlocked by kindness and gaiety when she had managed to face all adversity dry-eyed. She felt more relaxed even than she had done with Christopher, for there was no fear of a censorious family or feeling of guilt at the deception she must practice. Most important of all perhaps, after the experiences and shocks of the months since she had left home, it soon became clear that, as she had suspected, however enjoyable a time Yuri gave her, he had no intention of overstepping any limits of polite conduct imposed by their short acquaintance and her apparent friendship with his general.

When the whirlwind day was finally over and he took a punctilious leave of her, even the doubtful future was illumined by his heartfelt promise to redouble his efforts to obtain a posting south and to make sure that his route there lay through Kharkov.

Part Three
UKRAINE
1853-1855

Nine

A thin spear of sunlight lay across the unpolished boards of the nursery as Eleanor bent anxiously over her sleeping charge. His face was flushed, his fair hair clung damply to his forehead, and the coverings were wildly disordered from his constant restless tossings. She ran her fingers through her hair wearily and moved quietly over to the window and stared out into the whiteness beyond. Deep snow muffled every feature and it was impossible to tell where the boundary lay between the garden and the treacherous, ridged ice of the river beyond. Only the farther bank was clearly defined, a taut-strung gray line of quayside piled with irregular rows of wooden buildings and backed by distant glints of gold and silver light reflected from the domes in the center of the city.

As a view it was by now familiar to her, but she never tired of watching the flow of life past her window, especially now that Kharkov's great Kreshchenskaya or Epiphany fair was only two days away. Heavy country carts, drawn by oxen and piled high with corn, bales of linen, stiffly frozen fish, and barrels of spirits, surged past; strings of shaggy steppe ponies, almost hidden by their loads, plodded in their wake and were overtaken in their turn by sledges of all sizes and shapes which disdained the flimsy bridge and raced each other over the ice, their drivers' wild shouts and sharp whipcracks echoing in the still air.

Eleanor felt herself relegated to the role of bystander again and ached with longing to be with them, to feel the invigorating bite of icy air and the wild exhilaration of breakneck, heedless speed through the brittle sunshine. Their journey from Moscow to Kharkov, a week of almost unendurable cold in spite of the gift of some of Madame Traskine's castoff furs, of extreme discomfort at filthy posthouses, of uneatable food and endless glasses of steaming tea, had nevertheless been intensely enjoyable. She had not allowed herself to dwell on her first dismaying contacts with everyday Russian life and instead reveled in the excitement of it all: the full gallop at which they were driven regardless of the weather and the appalling road conditions, the five horses which were necessary in the deep, soft snow south of Kursk and the ululating, chanted endearments addressed by the *yemshchik* (coachman) to his racing team. It was as if she had been transported back to a ghostly *Neptune*, winging her way across an endless, clouded white distance beyond space or time.

No animal stirred or welcoming light broke the unlimited horizon of white, at first confined by dark, crowding trees, but as they drew steadily farther south expanding into boundless, rolling waves of vision. The few towns they passed through appeared almost apologetic at their intrusion into a vastness as elemental and unconquered as the sea itself. It was frightening, but her heart lifted to its power and she felt excited as well as alarmed by the sheer size of her new country.

It had been dark when they arrived in Kharkov at last, and she was unable to form any opinion of the city as they creaked over the hard-packed ice of the twisting streets, except that it was larger than any town she had seen since Moscow and a complete contrast to the settlements farther north, whose straight streets and vast, unpopulated squares had chilled her with their squalor and gloom. A swift kaleidoscope of light, sound, and smell flashed past her and then abruptly they plunged across a frozen river and drew up before a long, low house.

"*Allons, mademoiselle*, we are home. Welcome to Kharkov!" Madame Traskine jumped out of the *telega*[1] and ran up the three wide steps leading to the dimly pillared front door. She had slept like a squirrel for most of the week's journey, but now suddenly sparked alive, glowing and vital with energy. Eleanor followed more slowly, reluctant to face all the difficulties and uncertainties that awaited her after the carefree days of the journey.

The ecstasy of joy with which the servants greeted Madame Traskine was only equaled by the inefficiency with which they had prepared for her return. Although all the stoves were red hot so the heat was almost unbearable, no lamps were lit or food prepared and dust lay like mist in every corner. But everyone was in tears, kneeling, kissing her hand, throwing up their arms, and the happy bubble of joy and pleasure more than made up for any inadequacies of management.

Then a door opened and an immensely fat man waddled into the hall, his staggering bulk silhouetted against the faint glow of lamplight beyond. Madame Traskine moved away from the group around her, stepping over them as if they had been spaniels beseeching a walk, and extended her hand with languid grace. The gentleman kissed it, his bow scarcely perceptible, so great was his girth, a polite mumble of conventional greeting in French on his lips.

"It is good to see you again also, *mon cher*," responded Madame Traskine unenthusiastically. "Allow me to introduce to you Mademoiselle Lovell, who has come to look after our little Micha. My husband, General Traskine, mademoiselle."

Eleanor blinked at their total lack of interest in each

[1] A large covered traveling sledge shaped rather like an old steam boiler.

other after months of separation and then was almost equally astonished by the tears of near hysteria which marked Madame Traskine's reunion with her son. A priest was even at hand to achieve the appropriate blend of solemnity and rejoicing and the nursery was crowded to suffocation with, it seemed, every member of the household. On her first entry into the nursery Eleanor had hardly been able to pass the door, so appalling was the stench which greeted her. The child was crumpled into a tiny cradle and on being woken and ecstatically hugged was unable to do more than wail feebly.

Eleanor had made no attempt to clean the child or the room that night, merely placing him in the comparative comfort of her own bed, securely barricaded by chairs, sleeping herself as well as she might alongside him, half strangled by the immensely strong smell of incense left by the priest and the still more powerful odors of the room. She later discovered that the room had not been cleaned nor had the boy left it for more than an hour or so since the cold weather had set in two months before. Every time he sickened under these appalling conditions another layer of clothing was added by his concerned and anxious nurses, and the stove stoked to a new zenith of heat by his devoted servants.

Eleanor was scrubbing the floor when Madame Traskine returned to the nursery the following afternoon, watched by a wondering Micha and an alarmed and derisive servant girl.

"Mademoiselle! I assure you there is no need for such a display of unseemly energy, Theodosia will do all that you require without destroying your dignity in such a way. How is my precious Micha this morning?" She hugged the little boy tenderly.

Eleanor watched her stonily. From the strictly disciplined circumstances of her life she had never been in a position to show resentment or anger, but now she was blazingly angry, and no consideration of her dependent status was sufficient to contain it within reasonable prudence. She threw her cloth back in the bucket and rose to her feet. "He is ill and should have a doctor immediately, although I have little doubt that it is due to neglect and dirt."

"Neglect? He always has three servants in attendance and everything he could desire. You forget yourself, mademoiselle." Madame Traskine did not abandon her maternal pose but a swift spark of antagonism was struck between them.

"Servants! I dare say they mean well but they have no idea what is right for a child. Look at this room and the clothes he is wearing—they are only fit to be burned. I made him some broth myself when I found what food he was having, all prepared in the same room where dozens of servants and their families are living. It is a wonder your son is alive for you to return to, madame!" Her voice trembled as her eyes rested on Micha's thin form and listless pose.

"And what food has he been having? I left strict orders he was to have nothing but the best."

"I don't know. I have no doubt it was the best but quite unsuitable for a child his age. He should be having the simplest dishes and not caviar and spices and all kinds of drinks! He is only three years old, madame."

"Thank you, I know what age my son is. Russian children are used to quite different conditions to the English and the people here are not able to bring them up in any other way."

The mildness of her tone surprised Eleanor as did her resignation to the child's appalling upbringing, for Madame Traskine herself was both cultured and personally fastidious.

"They cannot survive in such conditions, madame," she said finally. "Many must die?"

"But of course. On my estate in some years only one in three lives, but that is natural, is it not?" She was genuinely surprised that this should be regarded as in any way remarkable and hugged Micha again. "He is kept as warmly and safely as possible and everything we can think of is done to ensure that he will live."

Eleanor felt utterly helpless; she herself had had a little brother who had died and there was scarcely a family in Mayhurst which had not lost at least one child, but the idea of a death rate of two in every three made her recoil. Her earlier anger evaporated, for there was no doubt that Micha was loved and cherished, it was just that the most elementary precautions for his safety had never even occurred to his parents. They loved him, but the idea of supervising those charged with his care and whom they knew to be incompetent for the task never entered their minds. It was not neglect or heartlessness, but simply regarded as a matter outside their control.

All these things were in Eleanor's mind as she stood a fortnight later looking out over the Kharkov River but she was no nearer to understanding than she had been on her arrival. Behind her the door opened and Theodosia tiptoed in. Eleanor had insisted on her putting on a clean shift each day and binding her hair back from her forehead, but her initial sullenness and astonishment had soon melted into good nature again in the excitement of trying to talk to this mysterious foreigner. In their enforced seclusion together with Micha in the nursery, Eleanor spent a great deal of her time pointing to things and asking Theodosia to give her the Russian word, her attempts at pronunciation provoking shrieks of laughter. Occasionally Eleanor would respond with the equivalent English word and Theodosia was fast acquiring a most enviable reputation for education in the serfs' *izba* (cabin) even if the bulk of her erudition consisted of imperfectly remembered gibberish. She was taller than was usual with south Russians, attractively dark with strong, capable shoulders, muscular arms, and a merry, lively disposition. Eleanor had high hopes that she would be able to train her satisfactorily

140

if only she could be cured of the inveterate Russian habit of granting Micha's lightest whim without a second thought.

Theodosia nodded, smiled, and laid a finger to her lips as she moved over to take Eleanor's place by the sleeping boy. Today was Sunday and for the first time since she had come to Kharkov she felt able to take advantage of Madame Traskine's concession and go for a walk and to the Lutheran church.

The sun was higher than it had been since she left England and she could feel its first faint warmth lying gratefully against her skin as she walked across the rickety wooden bridge and on to the quayside opposite. At the corner she paused, enjoying the panorama laid out before her. From the governor's house it was only possible to see part of the city and a mass of floating cupolas; because of a slight reverse slope the details which would fill in and give depth to the picture were missing. The bright sunlight struck through quivering fronds of mist which rose like incense from the jostling crowds in the narrow streets. The impression of life and vigor was exhilarating after the indifference of unlimited space, which was Eleanor's chief impression of Russia so far, and she began to hum under her breath as she carefully followed Madame's directions down the twisted, rutted lanes to the church. She was still cheerful when she came out again, in spite of the fact that for two hours she had listened to a service and sermon in German of which she understood not one word.

The interior of the church was heated to the usual unbearable level and everyone shed their furs in the vestibule. As she was struggling back into her own ancient castoffs a lady spoke to her in German. Eleanor shook her head, smiling, and replied in English: "I am sorry, I don't understand German, I am English." After a pause she added, "I am English," in halting Russian and then in French for good measure. The woman's face creased with amusement and she waddled off, to come back a moment later with another lady almost as fat as herself. Eleanor curtsied hopefully and to her astonishment the two began to laugh, pointing at her and then going off again into peals of merriment.

At length one of them wiped her eyes and said in English, still between wheezes of laughter: "I am sorry to be so rude but for you to sit through that whole endless sermon without understanding a single word is exquisite. England really is the same as it ever was, I wouldn't have believed it."

"You are English!" exclaimed Eleanor with a gasp of relief. "How wonderful! I had no idea there were any English in the town."

"City," corrected the lady automatically. "Oh yes, sometimes. Just at the moment I am the only one and I am not English any longer really as I am married to a Swiss. Even after twenty-five years of marriage he does not speak more than a few words of English. My name is Braillard, by the way, and this is my very dear friend Frau Herz. What is your name? You must come home at once and have some lunch with us."

By the time Eleanor had been borne off irresistibly in their troika, fed with unbelievably English food at Mrs. Braillard's comfortable house in the Kouznetch-naya, and teased unmercifully all through the meal she felt almost choked with happiness. She even began to respond to Frau Herz's jibes and Mrs. Braillard's outrageous comments in a way which would have seemed impossible in the bleak loneliness and responsibility of the morning. Mr. Braillard remained silent for such long periods that everyone forgot his presence, suddenly to be recalled by a dry comment in French, as apt as it was unanswerable. He lectured at Kharkov University and his wife treated him with the good-natured affection and showmanship of a ringmaster with a prize exhibit.

"Do you have to return at once to the governor's or have you the day free?" asked Mrs. Braillard eventually. "They are not scouring the city for you, are they?"

"Oh no, I was told it is traditional in Russia for governesses to have Sundays to themselves although I haven't taken one until today as Micha has been so ill. Poor boy, he was in a terrible state when we arrived."

"I expect he was. They love their children so deliriously that they can deny them nothing and then are resigned instead of repentant when they die. Would you like to come over to the Bazaar with us this afternoon? The Epiphany fair opens tomorrow and it will be a very gay sight today. My poor Armand's Swiss bargaining spirit is aroused as soon as we cross the bridge and I can count myself lucky if we do not come back with a couple of Tatar maidens if they are going cheap enough."

"Could I really come with you? I ought to be back before dark but I have hardly seen anything of Kharkov yet. What is the Bazaar and can you really buy Tatar maidens there?"

Mrs. Braillard translated this and she and her friend clasped each other in a fresh ecstasy of mirth. Even Mr. Braillard permitted himself a faint smile before replying seriously in French: "It is, unfortunately for me, not possible to buy a beautiful maiden in the Bazaar although I have no doubt I could do so under more discreet circumstances. But it is certainly possible for me to purchase a coachman or a cook provided they are not auctioned."

"How do you mean?"

"What I say. I can buy myself a domestic serf if I wish, the only regulation is that an auction hammer must not be used, but what is that to an ingenious man?"

The edge of anger behind his words cast a brief damper over the party, but it was impossible to remain serious for long with Mrs. Braillard as a companion and when they crossed the Lopàn River into the surging crowds of the Bazaar all lingering wisps of constraint vanished. Booths of every type of merchandise,

143

piles of Crimean fruit, Persian silks, Ukrainian vodka and leather, Russian metalware and cloth, tatar silver, Black Sea salt and every other conceivable product were displayed in wild confusion on every side. Frantic small boys tugged and pleaded with them to enter and buy, often not abandoning their efforts until their stronger fellows knocked them down and took their places. The majority of the people were dressed in uniform or else in sheepskins, rough loose breeches and bast shoes, or had their legs wrapped in rags and bound with leather thongs, but here and there could be seen Tatars, Cossacks, or Uzbeks in brighter colors, wearing soft leather boots and intricate silver sword belts, their clever, tight eyes and flat, dignified faces picking out likely customers from among the milling throng.

Eventually they turned to go home, but as they did so Eleanor's eye was caught by a large, gesticulating crowd gathered round an elderly merchant, impressive in flowing beard and rich kaftan.

"What is going on there, do you suppose?" she asked, catching Mr. Braillard's arm.

"Where? Oh, that is Stavchenko, one of the leading merchants in Kharkov. I don't know what the trouble is."

They moved over to listen and after a while the crowd quieted down and appeared to elect a spokesman, a young, dark-haired man with bold, restless eyes, who replied to whatever the merchant said with many gestures and emphatic jabs of his fingers at the ground.

"What does he say?" whispered Eleanor.

Mr. Braillard led them out of earshot before replying. "There is going to be trouble with young Akim one of these days, he is never content to leave things to run their own course."

"Who is Akim?"

"That young fellow answering Stavchenko over there."

"But what is the trouble?"

"There are all kinds of trouble, it is rather a case of which is uppermost at any time," broke in Mrs. Braillard. "And whatever it is, you may be sure to find Akim Akimovitch in the middle. He will wake up to find himself in Siberia or the army one of these days, which is a pity, for he is so handsome I feel my heart flutter every time I see him." She rolled her eyes dramatically.

"If it was only your heart that fluttered I would send Akim an Easter present," retorted her husband with affectionate asperity. "If the government here wasn't so dead it has not even the energy to repeat its own funeral service, it would feel its own heart flutter, but not from love, I assure you."

"Is he angry because they are serfs? I thought it was better down here in the south?" Eleanor stuck doggedly to her original inquiry.

He hesitated. "I suppose so, it is hard to say. Serfdom is so familiar to most that they do not think of it except to be grateful to their masters for protecting them from the more rapacious government tax collectors and for feeding them when there is famine. It is only when something goes wrong, or they have a tyrannical master, or a young hothead like Akim tells them something is wrong which they have accepted all their lives, that one can glimpse trouble at all and then it is terrifying to see how deeply it is rooted. Here it is almost worse than in the north, for while only about a third of the population are serfs they can see many who are free all around them. And here it is the worst form of serfdom, the *barschina* system, and—"

"What is *barschina*?"

He smiled. "It is difficult for us living in the middle of it all to imagine anyone who would not know. Apart from the domestic serfs who have nothing but the whim of their masters to live by, there are two main systems of serfdom. In the north it is mostly *obrok*, and providing the peasants pay a tax to their masters, they are often free to earn their own living if they wish, although

145

of course if they stay on the estate they must also work for the master. Here in the south it is *barschina* and most peasants must perform all kinds of services for their masters, often for four or five days a week."

"Are they paid at all?"

"It depends to whom you put the question. The landlords would say that in return they are protected, receive free use of much of their land and help when it is needed with purchases of stock and seed, even though everything they have legally belongs to the landlord. The peasants would say they are not paid, for while they accept that they themselves belong to their master body and soul, they have always regarded the land itself as theirs, even that which is occupied by the landlord. And there lies the seeds of more trouble for the future."

"Won't you come in and have some tea?" broke in Mrs. Braillard impatiently. "Armand and his economic lectures remind me of the prophets of Israel, so dreary, poor dears."

"I don't remember the prophets being interested in economics," objected her husband mildly.

"No, but everything anybody did was always worse than anything that had gone before," she retorted sweepingly. "Don't you go worrying about all these things that are no concern of ours—they will turn out all right, you'll see! Why, half the people here would starve every time the harvest failed if it was not for their masters. Are you coming in?"

"No, really, I must get back now, but it has been a wonderful day, I never guessed what pleasures were in store for me this morning."

"I shouldn't think so indeed after two hours of Pastor Schwarz!"

Eleanor gratefully accepted Mr. Braillard's offer to accompany her back to the governor's house and after a moment she ventured: "How is it that the peasants consider the land theirs? Don't the landlords own it and lease it to them as in England except that if they

146

are serfs they have to work instead of paying money?"

"Are you really interested? I can be very boring on the subject, I warn you." Upon Eleanor's assurance he continued thoughtfully: "The Russians are quite different to other peoples, not better or worse, just different. The landlords own their estates but Russia is so vast that land by itself is valueless. So the people became tied to the soil and were in the past more important than the soil itself. They cannot be parted from the land now and may only be sold with the land itself— a part of it as it is a part of them. Only personal servants and domestic serfs, being landless, may be sold freely in the open market as I told you—in theory anyway. Landowners come and go, for landowners in Russia are very improvident and do not often keep their estates for long, but as long as taxes are paid and services performed most trouble their serfs but little. There are exceptions to this of course, too many cases of wanton cruelty and extortionate rents and services for our comfort. The overseers are often worse than the owners, but for many peasants serfdom is stifling rather than onerous, a denial of human dignity rather than the terror of his life."

They walked on in silence awhile, the rough unkempt streets mute witness to the indifference of General Traskine and his provincial government. "Can they not join together in the village to refuse their services?" asked Eleanor.

"They do have a village commune or *mir* which is all-powerful. Russians are communally minded and form themselves into groups at the first opportunity. If some men from one of the villages come into town to earn money, they will form themselves into a laboring commune or *artel* and pool all their gains and share their losses. In the village the *mir* runs everything, the landlord's land as well as the rest; the *mir* divides up the strips and says when sowing is to begin. The *starosta* or headman of the village embodies the will of the *mir* and has great authority—"

147

"More than the landlord?" queried Eleanor, puzzled.

"Not exactly, for the *starosta* must often act as the landlord's agent, but no peasant would think of disobeying the *mir* once the village has discussed a matter and the *mir* decided. But as their only reward for hard work and good cultivation is to pay more tax or have their services increased, every peasant tries to be lazier than his fellow and to appear as poor as possible."

"It must be very bad for the way it is farmed," objected Eleanor. "I do not know very much about it but—"

Before she could go on, Braillard had swept on again; it was plainly a subject very close to his heart. "It is appalling, but appalling, mademoiselle! Here, on the richest land of Europe, men starve in the years when the grain does not drop from the ear into their hands. You can see how, in one way, the *mir* is the most treasured possession of the peasant because it is the only voice in affairs that he has, but in every other way it keeps the farming here at the lowest possible level. You can also see how it would be natural for them to think of the *mir*, and through it themselves, as the owner of the soil, even that of their master, and only their bodies tied to the service of their owner."

"It is very strange," observed Eleanor thoughtfully, as they picked their way cautiously through the icy ruts bordering the river. Already she could see the long, low bulk of the governor's house. "Was that meeting we saw in the Bazaar anything to do with all this?"

"No, that was a different problem altogether, although you saw the communal instinct at work. Did you notice how quiet they all were once young Akim started to speak for them? Stavchenko is a merchant who has been importing potatoes from farther north in return for cheap grain and vodka. Some of the people here believe it is a sin against God to eat potatoes and think that those who do so are punished by contracting cholera. They know they have always eaten any fruit they could get, yet Adam was destroyed by eating fruit in the Garden of Eden. They listen to the ignorant country priests when they say that these strange new apples from the soil must be the forbidden fruit which caused the damnation of man and round here there are many who follow their teaching."

"But how can they believe such nonsense, it's absurd! What harm can potatoes do them, they don't have to eat them, surely?" exclaimed Eleanor, laughing.

"A famine would force them to eat whatever they could get," he pointed out. "So long as there is enough to eat the whole affair is probably unimportant, but when there is next a cholera epidemic, as there always is every few years—"

"You can't be serious?"

"I assure you that if there is an epidemic you will see how serious I am. I will leave you here, it has been the greatest pleasure to meet you. Please feel yourself free to come again whenever you wish."

"It will make all the difference," responded Eleanor gratefully. She chuckled suddenly. "A small commune of our own. The next thing will be for us to form a pro-potato society, so we can take issue with Akim in the Bazaar."

"I can almost believe that you and my wife together would be more than a match for him; it is a spectacle I would travel far to see. *Au revoir, mademoiselle.*"

Ten

Spring, for many weeks only a restlessness in the blood and a stirring in the silent, shrouded plains, had come at last. The early rains blew over the endless spaces of the steppe, the rivers overflowed, hard-packed ice cracked and was washed away with a roar like artillery fire on the flood tide of a new year of life. Almost overnight grass grew, flowers bloomed, animals and men appeared from the long seclusion of winter, blinking at the profusion of color and variety after months of uniform cold whiteness.

The governor's house was virtually isolated while the river burst its banks, washed away the upper bridge, and deposited layers of black slime over everything within reach. The streets of the city became an unwalkable black morass and even the poorest peasant drove his own cart or else did not venture into town until the sun should bake the streets hard again. Six, eight, and sometimes ten horses or oxen had to be harnessed to drag any laden carts clear, for Kharkov was built on three feet or more of peatlike soil, unsurpassed for fertility and also for inconvenience when it happened to form the streets of a thriving township. It absorbed water like a sponge to become within an hour of rainfall an impassable bog; under the blazing sun later in the year it would dry out into a flaky, powder-dry substance which hung in a thick black cloud over the city, blotting out buildings above first-floor level and hanging in a long motionless pall behind the slightest movement of vehicles or men.

But the early spring, as the streets were drying out but before the dust had risen above ankle height, was one of the most delightful times in south Russia. The trees were in swift blossom, wild violets, their scent heavy in the warm air, peeped from beneath the corners of every house, sheets of lily of the valley replaced melting patches of snow in woods and meadows, and the voice of the cuckoo and quail sounded faintly in the blue heat which lay across the country like a welcome cloak, soon but not yet to become a stifling bondage.

Eleanor felt a new contentment, happy with Micha's recovery, grateful for the consideration with which the

Traskines treated her and for the sense of being needed and secure. She was lonely but too conscious of her good fortune in other respects to allow herself to dwell on it. Theodosia's friendliness had at least enabled her to pick up some quite fluent but rather strange Russian and they both enjoyed their stumbling efforts at conversation. Theodosia was a willing informant, telling her above all about Nipocritiy, the Traskine estate about twenty-five versts from Kharkov, from which nearly all the servants came, amused by Eleanor's bafflement at so much that Theodosia accepted as natural, above all her horror at the serfs' *izba* beside the house.

"Where else should we be, *barishna*, but in the *izba*? We are happy together there with the stove in winter and its coolness in summer, we are more comfortable than you."

"But . . ." Eleanor broke off. As so often, she had to realize that no good purpose was served by stirring up trouble when the servants themselves were quite satisfied to be herded together in one inadequately lighted room, without segregation of the sexes, with virtually no ventilation, a mud floor, and dozens of shouting children whom she was sure the Traskines neither knew nor cared whether they housed or not. The smell and noise were indescribable although the traditional house pride of the average Ukrainian was sufficient to render it somewhat cleaner than the Russian posting houses she had seen on the journey south. Whenever she sat down to a meal she had to avoid the thought that everything they ate was prepared and cooked in the *izba*. Thinking of this, she changed the subject, wishing to please: "It is much cleaner here than in those horrid posting houses. Madame says all Little Russians keep their houses cleaner than the northern Russians."

Theodosia's brow darkened. "We are not Little Russians, *barishna*, we are Ukrainians. If you wish to embrace happiness here you will never use those

151

words. Madame is not one of us or the governor either, although he has bought land and peasants here."

Eleanor was startled. "You do not regard yourselves as Russians then? Why is General Traskine your governor if he is not a Litt—Ukrainian?"

"Certainly we are brothers and sisters to our Russian neighbors, but we are also our own family, older, they say, than those of the north. Naturally we would not have a Ukrainian as governor for fear he would give his faith to his own country and not the government. It is unheard of." She was amazed at Eleanor's simplicity.

"I see. Who are 'they'?"

She looked mysterious. "I do not know, *barishna*, but there were many arrests five years ago, here and in Kiev, of those who wished for a free Ukraine and they are not forgotten."

"Akim Akimovitch and his friends?" Eleanor had seen Akim several times in Theodosia's company, since that first occasion in the Bazaar.

"Oh, no, *barishna!* Akisha[1] is only interested in our freedom from serfdom, he has such wonderful strength —but I do wish he would leave trouble alone," she added with a sudden rush of confidence, the sparkle in her eyes and the ready color in her cheeks betraying her studiedly disinterested tone.

Eleanor smiled and began to pack up her sewing. "Micha, come in now, darling, time for dinner! You know Akim well?"

Theodosia laughed delightedly. "But of course, *barishna*, he is a serf of the *barin*[2] and comes from Nipocritiy as we all do. We have wished to be married for two or three years now."

"Then why don't you?" Micha came running up from where he had been playing some mysterious game at the end of the garden and they turned to go

---

[1]Affectionate diminutive of Akim.
[2]Title of respect, i.e., her owner the governor.

into the house. "Why don't you?" she repeated as Theodosia did not answer.

"It is not possible without the permission of the *barin* and he will not agree. He does not wish to have one of his personal serfs married to a troublemaker. Many times the *barin* has threatened to send Akisha away to the army but he is a good workman and—"

Eleanor interrupted: "Do you mean you cannot marry without General Traskine's consent even if your own parents agree?"

"But of course. How could I when I belong to him as does Akisha also? I know he intends me to marry his personal servant Vassili but our steward Didi hates Vassili and has explained to the *barin* that his comfort is best served for the moment by us both remaining unwed."

Eleanor opened her mouth to say exactly what she thought of such an arrangement but, recalling the proprieties in time, merely remarked: "I like Didi, don't you? I think he is wiser than all of us sometimes."

"Everybody likes Didi—except Vassili of course. The *barin* found him nearly frozen to death one night and only able to stutter 'di-di-di.' He couldn't speak for days and nobody knows where he came from or what his real name is, but it is certain that only he could be head of the house serfs here. We all laugh at him but even our *starosta* at Nipocritiy heeds his words."

"I do hope we go to Nipocritiy soon, I have heard so much about it and it is so hot and dusty here. It will do Micha good to run around in the country too, won't it, my darling?" She glanced down at the little boy trotting by her side, her eyes softening. He was an attractive and affectionate child, although inclined to be fretful and peevish, especially on Monday mornings when he had spent the whole of the previous day in the charge of the servants and had consequently been outrageously spoiled. She was also disconcerted by his occasional lethargy when, like his mother, he would do nothing for hours on end but lie on his bed, and by his sudden spitefulnesses, which seemed to be rooted in a boredom which he lacked the energy to discharge in any other way. He had long since forgotten his shyness with her and answered chattily and at great length every question put to him, but it was in such a polyglot mixture of Russian, French, and English that she still had the greatest difficulty in understanding him. She realized it would be deeply unfair to divide his loyalties at such an early age and tried whenever possible to address him in her halting Russian, forbidding Theodosia to try out her newly acquired English. But he listened to Theodosia's English lessons and to Eleanor's whispered endearments and, being an intelligent child, soon achieved a small English vocabulary of his own which he produced at unexpected and unsuitable moments.

Eleanor took Micha in to dinner with his parents at four o'clock each day, often the only occasion upon which either of them saw Madame Traskine or her husband, for Madame seldom arose until after ten o'clock breakfast and the governor spent the day in his office. This office was the joke of Kharkov, for instead of going when necessary to the government buildings in the center of the city he had built a small office onto one side of his own house. He was so fat that to walk more than a few yards or to enter a carriage was a major event in his life, to be weighed and lamented, discussed and bemoaned for days in advance. Once it was found that the dire necessity could no longer be evaded, the entire household would gather in the courtyard, exclaiming, shrieking advice, and entreating heaven for mercy while he was supported tenderly up the carriage steps by half a dozen of the strongest indoor serfs.

Even Eleanor found herself clasping Theodosia in suspense as the delicate moment was reached when the general's shoulders had to be inserted through the door of the carriage, exhaling in relief with the half hundred other spectators as success was achieved, a

154

moment later almost joining them on their knees as only superhuman efforts prevented catastrophe when his foot slipped.

Once it was done, someone would run to the nearby church to shake the priest awake so he could come and offer prayers for the general's safekeeping. When he arrived with the sacred icon carried in procession there was an unseemly scramble as all the serfs fell on their knees and then attempted to crawl under this holy representation of the Saviour, in entreaty and devotion. Naturally, afterward the priest was entertained royally with vodka, *kvass*,[3] and *zakuski* and it was unthinkable that refreshment should not also be served to the general after so much exertion, so an impromptu party usually developed, delaying departure for several more hours.

These journeys were rare, however, and the routine administration of the province was carried on from the comfort of the courtyard office, although only occasionally was the torpor of the governor's repetitive days stirred by any semblance of work. If a particularly bold spirit dared to call, hoping for favors or a decision of any sort, he found the general amiable and hospitable, acceding sleepily to almost every demand, but as he never communicated these concessions to the relevant authorities, it soon became clear to the most optimistic petitioner that his journey had been wasted. In these circumstances the only visitors who continued to call were those who came to play cards, and for General Traskine and his staff the days and weeks passed agreeably enough in endless games of chance, punctuated by drowsy and inconclusive arguments.

The Traskine servants, loyal to their master although they did not respect him, bitterly resented the jokes and derision which his habits aroused and defended him against them whenever they could, without in any way abating their own jibes and dissatisfaction. Still, Elea-

[3] A kind of thin beer made with black bread, squeezed and fermented in water.

nor could not dislike him, since he always treated her with unfailing courtesy, including her in the tidbits of gossip which were the normal conversation at dinner and inviting her to join in his wife's round of social visits.

"You should come with us to midnight mass at the cathedral tonight, it is a very wonderful sight whatever your strange Protestant upbringing may think of our Orthodox Church." The general picked distastefully at the dried salt fish on his plate, for it was Easter Saturday and even the richest household observed the strictest fast in the first and last weeks of Lent, while the poor kept fast throughout the full seven weeks. To them, their gaunt, undernourished faces betraying their need, Easter Sunday was a joy unparalled throughout the entire year.

Eleanor had a brief tussle with her conscience. "I would like very much to come," she said doubtfully. "But I think perhaps I ought not to attend your Easter service if I am not of your faith."

"Pooh, what does that matter? It is *un spectacle très superbe*, and if we do not mind, why should you?"

This theatrical attitude was slightly disconcerting but before she could frame an adequate reply Micha scrambled up beside her. "Mama says give three kisses all, I give two kiss all," and he embraced Didi's hand as he presented the vegetables.

Madame Traskine laughed. "I was telling him this afternoon that it is the custom for the men to kiss the ladies three times on Easter morning when they see them for the first time."

"He's a proper little gentleman already, planning to kiss every wench he sees at his age," grinned Didi, cuffing him good-naturedly before continuing to hand the dishes. Eleanor had a feeling of utter bafflement as she watched the scene. I shall never understand them, she thought. Hopelessly servile materially, completely equal spiritually, kneeling in exaggerated respect one moment and embracing you with easy comradeship

156

the next. Aloud she said: "Thank you, I would like to come. What time shall we leave?"

"When we feel like it," replied Madame, yawning. "You are sure there will be no trouble tonight, Alexei? Why do you not transport that no-good Akim to Siberia while you can?"

Her husband shrugged. "I will, m'dear, one of these days. Meanwhile he is the wheelwright in Kharkov and pays me good money for permission to live here. No, there will be no trouble tonight, Easter Eve of all times."

"No money will be worth it if there is real trouble. You should not let him stay, I know you shouldn't." Her voice rose shrilly.

"What sort of trouble is there likely to be?" Eleanor thought perhaps it was time for her to intervene, seeing Micha watching his parents uneasily. Although neither he nor the servants understood more than a few words of French the note of panic in his mother's voice was unmistakable.

General Traskine pushed away his plate petulantly. "You would not understand. No foreigner can understand the ideas these crazy fools get but, like all fools, they do not remember for more than a short while and then all is well until the next time. Then that in its turn will blow over like clouds on the steppe so we need not concern ourselves too deeply. With your permission I will withdraw, my dear, business presses, you know, business presses." Didi helped him to lurch ponderously to his feet and he shambled heavily away.

"Business!" hissed Madame Traskine, watching her husband's retreating form malevolently. "A sleep and then nothing but *shtos*[4] all night long—he hasn't even the grace to play a fashionable game! One of these nights we are all going to be murdered in our beds because he is too lazy even to deal with one troublesome peasant."

"Is it Akim Akimovitch you are talking of? He is

[4] A card game played by older people in Russia at this time.

one of your own serfs, isn't he?" Eleanor had been startled by the hatred she had seen in Madame Traskine's face and sought to change the subject.

"Yes, and because of his skill one of the very few on *obrok* payment. He is such a good workman that Alexei can increase his fee for a passport and for *obrok* every year."

"A passport? It is only a few miles to Nipocritiy, isn't it?"

"Why should that make any difference? Just as we need a passport to come here from St. Petersburg, so any serf needs a passport to travel beyond his master's domains, and a freeman must get one from his commune. Otherwise how could we catch them when they run away or do not pay their taxes? I hope, by the way, that you are remembering to go to the police every month to have your permit checked."

Eleanor assured her that she had not forgotten this disagreeable and time-wasting formality but found herself quite glad when Micha created a diversion by disappearing under the table. "Come back, Micha," she said quietly in Russian. "It is rude to go without asking your mama for permission."

He peered out, looking stubborn for a moment, and then gave one of his occasional dazzling smiles. "Three kisses all, please, Mama?" He trotted over to her and climbed onto her lap, rubbing his cheek on hers.

"*Galoubchik! Mon cher, mon petit aile de paradis!*" She crooned, hugging him closely until he struggled to be put down. "It is really wonderful how you get him to mind you, Ilena Vassilievna."[5]

"It is not difficult," responded Eleanor briefly, feeling a pleasant glow of achievement. "A child is glad to have authority to run to and I grew up in a large family where we were very closely disciplined."

"All the same, I do not wish him to lose his gaiety or be denied the things he is accustomed to and has

---

[5]Eleanor, daughter of William. The usual Russian mode of address.

a right to have. There is one other thing I wish to say to you: he must speak French; English is very well in its way but French is more important to a Russian gentleman."

"But of course, madame. I try not to speak English to him, anyway until he has learned to talk Russian properly."

"The language of animals!" she exclaimed impatiently, pushing her chair back and banging Didi heavily on the shins. "Out of my way, you oaf! He is turning into a common servant child with his country dialects. I hired you to prevent that happening, so I wish you to talk French with him always, however poorly you speak it. It was a thousand pities I could not find a Frenchwoman to come south instead of you: he will be the laughingstock of his friends later with his Russian speech and bad French."

"But—but you must wish him to speak his own language?" stammered Eleanor, trying to ignore the hurt she felt at these contemptuous words.

"Certainly, but that will come. A pure French accent is the hallmark of a gentleman and can only be achieved by speaking French from the very first."

"Very well, madame, as you order of course. But it seems a pity he cannot be brought up to respect his own nation and to think of himself as a Russian and not a Frenchman." Eleanor's anger betrayed her before she could stop to count the cost of her tactlessness.

Madame Traskine paused in the doorway, then strode over to her, her face such a mask of rage that Eleanor retreated until her back touched the edge of the window frame. She felt numb, unable to speak, all her old fear of contention and quarrels returning to her across the hundreds of miles from the shadowy, bitterly remembered Fridays at Mayhurst.

"You dare to speak like that to me again and you leave this house within the hour and I will see you do not obtain another post in Kharkov!" Madame Traskine's face was within inches of hers, the first trace of opposition stripping all indulgence from her. "Be thankful you are not one of my serfs or you would be punished as you deserve. Never again tempt me to forget that you are not: you are a long way from England here." She stalked from the room without a backward glance.

Eleanor subsided limply onto a chair, her heart thumping with shock and a wave of shame engulfing her: at her heedlessness and at her cowardice. She knew she had been right, and for Micha's sake she should have found some way of convincing Madame Traskine of this instead of unnecessarily antagonizing her and then retreating into tongue-tied weakness. She also knew she had made her own position infinitely more difficult: Madame would not easily forget her defiance or her hitherto unsuspected vulnerability to threats and violence. Eleanor had noticed several times how the stifling emptiness and dumbness of her everyday life could sometimes arouse a demon of spite in Madame Traskine: she was not cruel or inconsiderate by intention but was betrayed into it by the compulsion to break, by whatever means, the unutterable monotony of her life.

Madame Traskine was not exceptional in this, it was typical of Kharkov social life as a whole, for when every family of any means employed at least thirty house serfs the slightest exertion at home was out of the question. For some, gambling gave the stimulation and drama they craved, for others drink. Above all, vendettas, intrigue, and malevolent hatreds sprang up, flourished, and were pursued to unbelievable lengths of suicide and duel, for no other motive than the excitement of the chase to which a kill was sometimes the logical consummation and satisfaction.

Eleanor felt a hand on her shoulder. "Do not despair, Ilena Vassilievna," said Didi, a silent witness of the scene although not understanding the rapid French. "The *barina*'s wrath is great but is like the summer storms, gone in a moment of time." He laid a finger on the side of his nose and squinted at her merrily. "Tonight she can wear the new cloak with the pretty patterns and a hat with plumes higher than a Cossack's boasting. She will be happy as a girl seeking her first adventure; smiling with the eyes, nodding the plumes, all this will be forgotten and over." The old man minced absurdly round the room, winking grotesquely and rolling his head so that Eleanor had to laugh.

"I suppose so." She rose to her feet again. "I shall be glad when we leave for the country. How much of the summer does Madame usually spend at Nipocritiy?"

Didi looked grave. "Some months, *barishna*, and the sooner everyone leaves for the country and the men return to their villages for the harvest the better."

"I heard the general say there was some trouble, what is it? Everything seemed quite as usual when I was in the town last Sunday."

He struck his hands together dramatically. "The balls of the Devil, *barishna*." He crossed himself and spat ceremonially in the corner, for it was well known that the Devil lurked in untended corners. "Every year more Devil's balls and now official Devil's balls. If we do not protest soon it will be an order that we must always dine with the Devil and then how shall we escape God's just vengeance?"

"Devil's balls?" echoed Eleanor blankly. "What are those?"

"Evil, *barishna*," he answered earnestly, his face wrinkling with superstitious fear. "Small like that"—he clenched his fist—"but very potent. That follower of the Devil who thinks of nothing but money has been transporting them here for several seasons but only the few forgotten of God have eaten them. Now the government farm, here in our own land, is to grow them, bringing the curse of God on our fields and families. It will be many years before God will forgive us enough for the grain to grow again as it should on land which has been sold to the Devil." Tears rolled unchecked down his cheeks and disappeared into his beard as he wrung his hands in anxiety.

Light dawned on Eleanor as she remembered her conversation with Braillard. "You mean that the merchant—what is his name?"

"Misbegotten son of the Devil's offspring! Stavchenko!" snapped Didi, his good humor returning as he rolled the insults round his tongue. "One day Akim will kill him and so would I. Our ancestors would rejoice at such a deed."

Eleanor shivered. "Yes, Stavchenko, I remember. You mean that he is importing potatoes here from the north and they are forbidden to you by your religion? In my country, you know, Didi, everyone eats potatoes and in bad years many eat well who would otherwise have little. If they grow here your children will eat better than you have done. The government should be aided in its efforts, blessed and not cursed for trying to help you."

"It is an evil," he repeated obstinately. "We will all be punished for an evil we did not want to do."

Eleanor sighed. "How do you know it is wrong for you to eat potatoes?"

"The Devil did tempt Adam with strange fruit of the earth and he did eat. If God wished us to eat them they would have grown here always; as it is they have to be brought here from other lands where He is not worshipped as He should be." Didi crossed himself. "Already our punishment is upon us."

Eleanor felt a swift trickle of alarm. She remembered how Monsieur Braillard had also said that the people believed cholera to be the inevitable punishment for eating potatoes. "Is—is there sickness in the town?" she asked apprehensively.

He nodded. "Not bad yet, with the Devil's balls barely in the soil, but it will ripen as they ripen and with the harvest many will die. Please try to understand what we do, *barishna*, we will only be fighting that this thing may not come to our own village, to

162

protect the faith we have been given." His deadly earnestness and belief were pathetic and Eleanor, standing in the heart of a very strange land with a child swinging on her arm, could think of no suitable reply. This man was respected, his advice sought by many, and his decision to defend his own was irrevocable, unswayed by any argument or logic which she or anyone else could offer. Their bodies belonged to their masters but their souls, their land, and all that was in it belonged to them and to God, and on that they would not compromise.

· · ·

She saw how much of them belonged to God that night. They entered the Uspensky Cathedral shortly before midnight to find it already packed. Outside in Sergeievskaya and Cathedral squares a vast, silent multitude was standing, occasionally chanting softly and bowing to the ground. In front of each family group was spread a white cloth on which food for breaking the long Lent fast was laid: hard-boiled eggs dyed red, patterned flat cakes, cold ham, and pyramids of sour cream cheese also dyed and studded with countless little crosses made of currants. Priests were moving down the silent lines, murmuring blessings and sprinkling the food with holy water. Everyone in the vast concourse carried a taper, to be lit on the stroke of midnight, and Eleanor felt one pressed into her hand as she entered the cathedral. Except for a faint light under the main dome where a group of priests was intoning prayers, the darkness was complete and she could sense rather than see a great throng wedged together in the pungent gloom. A continuous buzz of conversation arose as friends greeted each other, one moment chatting of commonplaces and the next prostrating themselves on the ground, whispering prayers and crossing themselves devoutly. The contrast between irreverence one moment and personal devotion the next was extraordinary and Eleanor felt baffled yet again, contempt at their shallowness warring with awe at their faith. Here in the presence of God no serf hesitated to stand in front of his master or the master to make room for his serf: all stood together, for there were no chairs whatsoever, and it did not occur to anybody to think their behavior remarkable.

High over their heads the clock whirred, preliminary to sounding the stroke of midnight, and at that instant the ikonastas doors were flung open, revealing a chanting procession of priests in their magnificent Easter vestments.

Into the silence a single voice sounded: *"Kristos voskress!* Christ is risen!"

"Vo istino voskress! He is risen indeed!" came back from the congregation in a roar which rang through the dim heights above.

At the same moment a ripple of sparkling light spread from the front of the cathedral like an incoming wave, as hundreds of candles were lit from the tapers held by the priests, passed back until everyone held his own tiny glint of faith rekindled by the miraculous resurrection of Christ. The priests burst into the triumphal cadences of the Easter anthem and the watching thousands prostrated themselves until the whole nave was a whirling mass of light, illuminating heads bent in prayer and hands raised in praise.

It was a magnificent and unforgettable sight; in the space of thirty seconds a complete transition from darkness into light, from sorrow into jubilation, from fear into certainty, and Eleanor felt a lump in her throat as she also bowed herself to the ground. Theatrical it might be to the strict Protestant mind but no one could deny the effect of such a stupendous piece of symbolism on the spirit and the heart.

After the Easter mass was over they drove to the Governor General's house for Easter breakfast through streets lit with thousands more candles and bustling with cheerful peasant families breaking their long, strict observance of Lent. Here and there impromptu dancing was beginning and occasionally a deep clear voice would soar through the chatter and excitement, sending a heartfelt chorus of happiness and thanksgiving rising to the stars, hanging so closely in the glittering sky above that they might have been the tapers of another waiting congregation.

The Governor General's house was normally empty but that night all was light and color and quick sophisticated chatter; a warm and animated scene which Eleanor, still under the spell cast by ritual and simple fervor, found almost unbearable. The Traskines were acting as hosts in place of the Governor General, who supervised the governors of two other provinces in addition to Kharkov and preferred to live on his own estates near the smaller but more congenial town of Voronezh three hundred versts away. He had only visited Kharkov once in six years even though it was the most important of the three provinces entrusted to him.

"*Kristos voskress*, Ilena Vassilievna! May I give you your Easter egg?" came a voice from behind her. Captain Boris Kyril'itch Gatchukov, one of General Traskine's aides whom she particularly disliked, was standing there holding a little porcelain egg between his stubby fingers.

"How you startled me! Why are you giving me this?"

"Always in Russia the first time you see a lady of your acquaintance on Easter morning you give her an egg with—er—your devotion. You should answer, '*Vo istino voskress*,' to my greeting, you know, though I should be able to forgive you whatever you parted your pretty lips to say."

"I'm sorry. *Vo istino voskress!* But you mustn't say things like that, it's not funny," exclaimed Eleanor crossly.

He smiled blandly. "How can I help it when my heart is slain by your slightest smile and why indeed should I wish it to be funny?" He pressed the egg into her hand.

It seemed impossible to refuse when, looking around her, she saw that all the ladies were accepting similar offerings, some made of sugar, others of enamel, crystal, porcelain, or flashing with exquisite jewelry. She said feebly, "Thank you very much, it is very beautiful," as indeed it was. Delicate pastel miniatures representing the crucifixon and resurrection, surrounded by scrolls of flowers, covered its surface and inside was a small figure of Christ in ivory. "You shouldn't give me anything so valuable! I could not accept such a lovely present—"

"Nonsense, my dear, of course you can." Before Eleanor realized what he was about his arm slid round her shoulders and he kissed her three times lightly on the cheek and once, lingeringly, full on the mouth. Her hands flew to her lips instinctively as she tried to back away from him but he laughed at her confusion. "Three for tradition and one for me, although I must say it was a very disappointing one! Next time I shall hope for something very much better, and the time after that . . ." He rolled his eyes expressively and Eleanor shivered. "Don't look at me like that, I'm not going to attack you in the middle of this very dull reception. Every lady gives three kisses to the gentleman of her choice on Easter morning."

Eleanor opened her mouth to say that he was not the gentleman of her choice but he swept airily on, taking her acquiescence for granted and folding her fingers over the little Easter egg. "There, you keep it and don't run away with the notion that I have ruined your fat employer at cards to pay for it. They make them in my village in Orel Province and it is the merest trifle, I assure you. Come and have some food, Madame has been very openhanded on our absent Governor General's behalf, I must say."

"You shouldn't say things like that, the general is your superior officer after all!" expostulated Eleanor, aware she sounded like a prude but unable to think of any protest at his calm assumption of authority over her which would not provoke some devastating response.

"Why not, my dear? Are you afraid he might have me posted elsewhere if anyone heard? I wager you six month's pay he would not."

"I would if I were in his place," she snapped, pulling her arm from his clasp.

"Not if you owed me as much money as he does," replied Gatchukov coolly, rearranging her shawl about her shoulders, his hands lingering on her arms. "I have always had a fancy to be a rich man and a landowner, and I think I shall soon achieve my ambition if he continues to lose at his present rate. Another few months like this and nothing less than the whole Nipocritiy estate with its five hundred male souls will pay me off. Then I will retire from the army and turn my attention to the many opportunities there will be here for the next few years. Would you like that?"

"I wouldn't like it at all. I think it quite wrong to gamble all those poor people and their families away at cards."

"That was not what I asked you, my dear, and you know it."

"And my answer would be the same whatever you asked me," she flashed back at him. "I wish you would leave me alone and keep your plans for those who appreciate them."

He stepped back from her, his eyes dark with anger. "If that is what you wish. But one day you will be glad to come to me on my own terms, when I am a rich landowner and you are just a struggling governess, thrown out to starve when Micha is ten years old and able to go to the pages' school in Petersburg. Once I have Nipocritiy I shall be on my way; there will be plenty of opportunities for those willing to take them in the next few years!"

She was disturbed by his words, not by the vague threats, which she discounted as being entirely typical of the man, but by his veiled references to Nipocritiy.

167

She had not yet seen the village but already it fascinated her, all the many stories told about it by the domestic serfs sounding strange and wonderful in her ears. She detailed a selected portion of the conversation to Monsieur Braillard when she visited their house the following Sunday: a shrewd and independent observer, he was an encyclopedia of information on every subject she discussed with him.

Braillard was standing with his back to the sitting-room porcelain stove, flapping his coattails as if it had been an open blaze. Swaying rhythmically on his short legs and patent-leathered feet, his good-natured face wrinkled in obvious thought, he looked more like a dancing master than a respected senior member of Kharkov University.

Mrs. Braillard always referred to him as her little monkey, but now with increasing anxiety. Censorship was becoming tighter every year and his outspokenness made the termination of his appointment all too likely. He was prepared to be silent, but if he was forced to give his views he was incapable of veneering them with any palatable gloss of untruth.

After considering Eleanor's words, his head on one side and his eyes veiled and introspective, he said, "Yes, I think your Captain Gatchukov is destined to be a man of the future, he shows a good eye for business, which is rare indeed in Russia. You could do worse than accept his offer, he is also good-looking, is he not?"

Eleanor shuddered. "Horrible man! I don't think I could ever bear to marry a Russian. I don't feel as if I had the least understanding of the way their minds are working or what they are thinking."

"No, I don't suppose you have, but if you just like them it is often enough."

"My dear Armand, you are becoming coarse," interrupted Mrs. Braillard forcefully. "Do not mind him, my dear, all Frenchmen, even when they are also Swiss, think it so terrible for a woman to be unwed that they would marry her off to anyone." Eleanor winced. "Now I've hurt you but never mind. For myself, I think Russians excessively handsome and if my little monkey finds himself clapped up in that horrid cold prison because he will tell the authorities what fools they are—well, we know they are so why tell them so?—there is no knowing but what I won't find myself a nice young cavalry officer!"

Eleanor floundered valiantly with such a slippery conversational ball but laughed all the same. "There is no risk of your losing your position, is there, sir?"

"I might," he replied indifferently. "It hardly matters when there are only a hundred students in the whole university, none of whom does any work since the censorship prevents them learning anything worthwhile. You were asking about Nipocritiy, were you not?"

"I only wondered why Gatchukov should think it such a particularly valuable estate. From the little I have seen, I wouldn't think landowning in Russia is profitable as it is in England."

Mr. Braillard waltzed gracefully round a bead-hung table, then flung himself into a chair and laid his fingertips together in his best professor's manner. Eleanor remembered with the sudden poignancy of great loneliness how she and Charlotte used to catch each other's eye and enjoy a secret laugh at the eccentricities of their acquaintance. Braillard said slowly, "Nipocritiy is about twenty-five versts southeast of Kharkov, and as well as the main village there are many scattered hamlets on the estate—it is really quite a sizable property and is also the first to be privately owned this side of Chuguyev colony."

"Chuguyev colony? Whatever is that?"

He shrugged. "A colony such as only a demented bureaucracy like Russia could have invented. Alexander I took whole tracts of crown land and made them into military reserves. Instead of the peasants being owned by the state or private landowners, they are owned by regiments, thrust into uniform almost as soon as they

169

are born and counted as part of the army. Some colonies even have breeding programs designed to produce sturdy recruits for the future. The infantry colonies are chiefly near the western frontiers but the cavalry is at Chuguyev and also at Kertch on the Black Sea steppe."

Eleanor wrinkled her brow. "Do you mean that all the peasant children are soldiers or that regiments are billeted on them?"

"Both. There is a permanent garrison there for which the peasants must provide everything, and their children are drilled and regimented, as they are themselves, all their lives, their marriages arranged by the quartermaster in the same way as he plans future stock for the remounts. All are subject to military discipline and there is no appeal except to the military authorities." His lips tightened. "Private landowners have many faults, God knows, but the military colonies are an evil, so great an evil that even here they cannot last much longer, and that is what our friend Gatchukov is no doubt counting on: neighboring landowners may find rich pickings when they do dissolve."

"But don't the people protest? To be sold to a regiment like that—it is a terrible thing!" cried Eleanor.

"How do you suggest they protest?" asked Braillard dryly, pacing the room again. "By meetings? They would be arrested. By demonstrations? They would be whipped. By strikes, arson, and murder? They would be shot or deported or drafted into the regular army and never see their homes or families again." After a moment he answered himself, but there was defeat in his voice. "Oh yes, they protest, they burn and loot, and sometimes even murder a few soldiers or police. The year I first came here, before you were born, there was what was called a mutiny at Chuguyev. I don't know how many died but it was put down in the end by taking a batch of a hundred peasants every day and flogging them, man, woman, and child, until there was no more resistance left."

170

Eleanor was silent. England, the rule of law, and accepted restraints on behavior were all very far away and there was no comment she felt able to make.

"So you see, mademoiselle, they no longer dare to be anything but stern to the point of ferocity at Chuguyev. The risings there have already been at the various military colonies have made the authorities realize that they have done the one thing no government in Russia has ever dared to do before: they have armed the very peasants who have the greatest grievances it is possible to imagine. So however slow the government is over routine matters, it reacts fast enough to any threat of unrest at the military colonies—you will see how quickly if Gatchukov should become too blatant in his ambitions."

Walking home through the quiet streets that evening, watching how the irregular roof lines shredded the pale evening sky into strips and patches of translucent light, Eleanor pondered his words. She could almost feel the static years stretching into infinity like the great distances around her, yet now she could also sense a faint stirring in the lethargy and monotony, a turning over in slumber after long rest. Theodosia, Akim, Braillard, Gatchukov measuring his opportunities, even Count Berdeyev so long ago on the *Neptune*, all in their different ways were feeling the cogs of time beginning to turn again after long ages of silent rusting.

As she passed the massive bulk of the Church of the Ascension near the Traskine house her thoughts were interrupted by a long-drawn-out wail. In the shadows she saw two figures, one kneeling and raising arms of supplication to heaven and the other lying in utter stillness. Eleanor hesitated a moment and then moved over reluctantly to offer her help, but then as she saw the body more clearly, she stood stricken, a sudden nausea hard in her throat. He was plainly beyond any help but there was nothing of the tranquillity of death here, with bearded lips peeled back in a tortured grimace

171

and the wasted body contorted in the final agonies which cholera inflicts on its victims.

Eleven

It was the first of many such bodies that Eleanor saw during the following weeks as the dreaded cholera seeped its way through the city. Although most families who could leave for the country had done so the moment the dimensions of the epidemic were realized, the Traskines were delayed by Madame, who felt unwell and alternately blamed her husband and threw fits of near hysteria, declaring that she had progressive cholera and everybody was waiting for her to die. Eleanor did her best, assuring her that she showed none of the symptoms which she saw so closely and so horribly in the gutters of the city on the rare occasions when she ventured out, but without success.

"You would all be glad if I died; I can see your greedy faces every day, but I'll cheat you, I'll cheat you yet! You will get nothing, so you had better . . . better get me well again to keep your post," she panted, glaring at Eleanor with sick malevolence when she lay temporarily exhausted by one of these attacks, in which she had thrown herself from the bed and lashed out with uninhibited violence at all who attended her.

Eleanor controlled her increasingly brittle temper with a supreme effort. "You must not excite yourself so, madame, you will make yourself ill. No one wishes for anything that is yours and certainly not myself."

"Ill? Ill? What do you mean, 'make' myself ill? As

if I was not ill enough already, probably dying on your hands for all that anyone cares—"

"Hush, madame, hush!" She barely stopped herself telling the woman just how ill she thought she was. "You will soon be well if only you would let yourself rest a little and then we could all go into the country." Wistfulness crept into her voice; longing for cool, dust-free air, for silence and freedom from the appalling drudgery of sickroom nursing which Madame Traskine would not entrust to any of the Russian servants, and above all deliverance from the fear of cholera.

"You want to go and leave me, don't you? Leave me on my deathbed while he"—she jerked her head toward the governor's office—"gambles away his fortune and mine and never thinks of his wife dying in the next room."

Despite a thin quiver of distaste, Eleanor held the hot, groping hands in her own and said steadily, as if she was speaking to Micha: "You are not going to die. You have not got the cholera, Dr. Mavurian told me so himself, and he must know with so many dying each day in the city—it is horrible to go beyond the doorstep and see them all." She covered her face, seeing again the terrible sights which held back sleep at nights.

Madame Traskine eyed her curiously. "It is often so in a hot summer, Ilena; you should not go out if these things distress you. It takes some weeks to spread to the richer areas, if it ever does." Proving, thought Eleanor sardonically, that Madame Traskine no more thought she had cholera than the rest of the household did, but she forbore to say so.

"If only the government would try to do something, madame. The people are not only sick, they are angry and sullen, there could be trouble at any time."

"What can the government do?" murmured Madame Traskine, her momentary interest evaporating.

"I don't know, but anything would be better than nothing. Just so the people felt someone was trying—it would make such a difference." She hesitated and then

173

added lamely: "I've thought and thought what the cause might be, I know it isn't potatoes, for we always eat them at home. . . ." Her voice trailed away uncertainly.

Outside the hot, early summer sun blazed down on the pall of dust which hid the city of Kharkov. The river, reduced to a mere muddy trickle by the end of the summer, was already sluggish between cracked and trodden banks, carrying with it the bodies of those who had died along its shores. Cows and oxen browsed in its fetid, smelly water, shouting washerwomen pounded clothes along its quaysides, and the lumbering city water wagons baled the liquid poison from its bed to sell to high and low alike, spreading death and suffering with every load. Even those who, like the governor, possessed a well were forced during the long drought of summer to buy city water for washing, and often for drinking as well.

The very gravity of the situation made it difficult to sympathize with Madame Traskine as she felt to be her due and when, on the following morning, Eleanor escorted Dr. Mavurian to the door after his daily visit he took some time to reply to her perfunctory inquiries after Madame's health, polishing his pince-nez reflectively. Like all Russians in official positions, including even students, he had to wear a uniform most of the time, but it was hard to imagine a more unmilitary personality and he seldom managed to look the part of a well-drilled, regulated representative of the imperial bureaucracy.

During Eleanor's period of sickroom nursing they had grown to know and respect one another although the doctor, as an Armenian and a theorist whose mind was not understood by his colleagues, was not a popular figure in Kharkov. "She is going to have a child, as millions of women do every year without the least fuss or difficulty," he said finally.

"Oh!" Eleanor tried not to laugh. "How ridiculous— I mean, how wonderful. I never dreamed of anything like that. So there is no reason why we should not go

174

into the country?" She was half ashamed of her eagerness to leave the city and its suffering inhabitants.

"Not the least in the world, in fact I have told her that for her own sake, and for Micha as well, she should go as soon as possible. She has not the cholera now, but it is no respecter of persons and—ah—pregnant women are particularly liable to the disease."

"Are they?" She was astonished; most of the victims seemed to be middle-aged or else quite young children.

He smiled slightly. "Let us say rather that I have given her that impression. My deceit is not in the least likely to be found out by either the governor or his lady since neither of them would venture into the town to see with their own eyes."

Eleanor wrinkled her brow. "I don't think it is lack of courage which stops the general going, it just never occurs to him that there is anything he can do or that it is in the least his affair even if he is governor."

Mavurian clipped on his pince-nez again, his face weary in the bright morning light. "No, it is not lack of courage. Most men, my dear young lady, and especially Russians, have courage when they are faced with an emergency. There is no time to reflect, everyone watches, honor and glory wait at the finish of a great deed. The general has many decorations and an excellent fighting record in his youth, but what good does that do when the need is to go to his office every day and see the people fed, although many would sooner starve than eat potatoes? I am not brave when I go around the streets every day, I would do better to stay at the hospital with my test tubes, far better. It is despair which makes me go, because I do not know what to do and I cannot keep away. It would be courage perhaps if I did, and spent my time seeking the cause of so much misery." He passed his hands over his eyes and said gently: "I am tired, we are all tired, and so are you. Go into the country with Micha, he is your duty and your responsibility. Do not feel ashamed to

175

leave, for there is nothing any of us can do, and courage without a purpose is a very useless thing."

They went the very next day.

Madame Traskine was miraculously restored to health and she, Eleanor, and Micha, together with twenty house servants and half a dozen wagonloads of furniture and stores, drove out to Nipocritiy, leaving the governor and his staff to enjoy their leisurely days in such peace as the crushing heat and dust would allow them, General Traskine having refused even to consider the exertion of such a journey.

In Kharkov it had seemed the height of summer but once the city was left behind it was possible to remember that it was still only the beginning of June. Eleanor peered eagerly out of the carriage windows as they creaked slowly along the powdery tracks, twisted and turned between clumps of woodland, jolted across shallow ravines, and stuck in every dust-filled hollow. They all, except Madame Traskine, had to pile out of the carriage and wagons at the slightest incline to walk alongside, since the horses had the greatest difficulty in obtaining any purchase at all on the shifting, flaky surface. The sun blazed down but a faint mist pervaded the air, veiling the further distances and filtering out the worst of the heat. A few puffy clouds rolled across the pale blue sky and a gentle breeze gave an indefinable feeling of having proceeded at an uninterrupted pace over illimitable distances.

Gradually the country opened out, the ravines and clumps of trees became more widely spaced but did not disappear altogether, the distance between inclines became wider and more regular, but not regular enough to be monotonous. Rows of fields, and freshly growing crops flowed into and out of sight, their boundaries a bright, wasteful, joyous riot of ragwort, poppies, rowans, and wormwood, the graceful shapes of birch blending the distant lines of track, horizon, and dark, occasional shade.

From time to time they passed through little gray,

huddled villages. The unkempt roofs, ragged lines of fencing, and unpainted wood were brightened by flowers, seldom cultivated but casually allowed to grow, in the thatch itself, on the middens, and looped along the carved fretwork of window shutter or sagging doorway.

Occasionally a peasant leading an oxcart or sitting beside the road would lift a hand in greeting, but mostly the countryside was infinitely empty: the spring bustle of sowing was over and by immutable custom neither haymaking nor plowing the fallow would start until the feast of St. Peter and St. Paul at the end of June. So the villagers, after a brief spell of frantic labor to get everything done after the long torpor of winter, had subsided again into lethargy, dossed down on their now cold stoves or on trusses of straw until the next spell of activity. The same pattern would then again appear with days of uninterrupted labor followed by weeks of idleness until they roused again for harvest.

Mr. Braillard had explained some of this to Eleanor and she could not help wondering, looking at Madame and Micha and the servants, all dozing happily in the most uncomfortable positions, whether perhaps this unchanging cycle had not affected the Russian character: a lifetime of semi-hibernation punctuated by frantic forays into the hostile world outside.

Eleanor loved Nipocritiy as soon as she saw it. They had left the main track and driven across open fields for several miles before they drew up in front of a little, twisted wooden house standing on a tree-fringed knoll. The house was different from most she had seen in that it was built on two stories, but the wide, unpainted, warped balcony at ground-floor level and the extravagant, inconsequential air which lay over all the decorations, architectural and domestic alike, were purely Russian.

Eleanor and Micha shared a room on the second floor, just two beds and a cupboard in a little whitewashed cell, the walls knobbly with warped planking, but she was delighted with it. She threw back the shutters, creaking protestingly on their rusted hinges, and gazed enchanted on the limitless vista of fields and long, low hills framed dimly to the east with the gray-green line of the steppe tilting away to the edge of the world.

Huddled just below them, edging the banks of a shallow stream, was a straggle of cabins and huts. A few were the familiar timber and thatch but most were whitewashed clay, for here few trees grew, only some scattered clumps of ground-hugging oak and elder clinging to the occasional fold in the ground.

"Oh, Micha, how lovely it is away from those horrible streets! Look at those shaggy ponies and—oh, some oxen! Look, darling, at their patient faces, in those white caps like old ladies."

The little boy rested his chin on the window sill beside her and followed the direction of her excited, pointed finger unsmilingly. "I like the streets, Ilena," he said at last in his curious mixture of French and Russian. Obedient to her instructions, Eleanor never spoke English to him but she still surreptitiously encouraged him to speak and hear Russian whenever she could.

"But don't you like to see all the animals and play with the other children? You'll enjoy being able to go out again instead of having to stay in the house, and here you will be able to run wherever you wish. Won't that be nice for you?"

"I don't want to, I like our own home, it's so dull and quiet here." He threw himself on one of the beds.

He was tired after the journey and Eleanor made no attempt to coax him out of his sulks, grateful for the chance to enjoy the sunshine and stillness in happy solitude. Hearing Didi laughing on the balcony with some of the other serfs as she came downstairs, she circled the house and sat down on a fallen tree trunk in the center of the little birch grove behind the rioting, overgrown garden.

178

It was still and quiet and green as the bottom of the sea; on every side sweeping waves of country ebbed and flowed, bright with the early promise of harvest. When the soft wind blew a straying curl against her cheek it was as if the whole earth moved in sympathy, so endlessly did the breeze finger through the ripening, swaying tides of grain.

She hugged her knees like a child and gazed at the horizon ten, twenty, maybe fifty miles away. How strange it was that she, Eleanor Lovell of Sussex, England, should be set down here, a speck in all this space, unknown, unheeded, a cog in other people's lives, with only her own trifling spark of thought and life to sustain her. How very strange indeed. She had thought about it before, but not so objectively; she knew herself almost unbearably lonely but somehow here, where everything seemed adrift in infinity, for the first time the knowledge was muted by the realization that she had always been alone, set apart by something within her even from her own family. She would not now go back even if she could.

After dinner Eleanor walked down to the village. Twilight had already turned the sky from blue to pale green, draining the brilliance from the untidy, beautiful cascades of flowers which seemed to hold together the crazily leaning wattle fences along the village street. No attempt had been made at gardening or neatness, or more than rudimentary repair of the worst winter damage, but the village did seem alive, individual, colorful, heart-warming after the emptiness they had driven through during the day.

Someone called a soft greeting across the dim street and there was a shuffle of bare feet before a door slammed, a brief babble of talk and laughter from some benches set under the only tree in the village. Eleanor had turned reluctantly to walk back to the house, enjoying the soft, scented air, when she saw a man coming toward her carrying a lantern. He murmured a mechanical greeting and then, realizing she was a complete stranger, stopped in his tracks, holding the lantern high.

"God protect you," Eleanor responded to his words, and then recognizing his face: "It is Akim Akimovitch, isn't it? I thought you must be still in Kharkov, when Theodosia was so sad to leave."

His face cleared and he smiled, his normally serious expression fading. "I think you must be Ilena Vassilievna, of whom I have heard much. I was indeed in Kharkov but have returned here just for a few days."

"To see Theodosia?"

He looked startled and not best pleased. "I do not know why Ilena Vassilievna should concern herself with my poor affairs."

Eleanor hastened to apologize. "I am sorry, I must have sounded very rude, but I have heard so much about you from Theodosia. I know she is always worried for you, for whenever there is trouble in the city it is always your name which is mentioned. I have become very fond of her these past months."

His expression softened. "Yes, Ilena Vassilievna, and she has told me she is very glad to be your servant and to learn from you to read and write. She is trying to teach me as she learns but I find it very hard."

Eleanor laughed. "I should think you would! I speak some Russian now, but badly, as you can hear, and hardly know how to write it at all. I wondered why Theodosia was so very anxious to learn to write, however little I could teach her, but now I understand —perhaps she sees more of you if you are anxious to learn."

He shifted uncomfortably before the accusation in her voice. "No, *barishna*, it is not true. But I have so little time. Every year my *obrok* increases as the price of the governor for not sending me into the army and I must work very hard to pay it."

"And the rest of the time you are stirring up trouble for the governor?"

He grinned briefly. "Oh, no, *barishna*, how could

that be, when the governor never leaves his own home and would not recognize trouble if she should lie in his own bed with him?"

Eleanor tried to look shocked but her dancing eyes gave her away and they both laughed, a swift, unlikely spark of friendship struck between them.

Akim picked up the bundle he had been carrying. "Tell Theodosia not to worry. I will be careful and the *barin* needs his *obrok*. But whatever happens I must go on until we are free and can till our land with the crops we wish."

After the sorrow and poverty she had seen Eleanor could only agree but, looking at his smiling, confident face, she felt afraid for him. "You enjoy the risks you run, don't you, Akim? Life is dull for all of us without some excitement. But one day there will be real trouble in Kharkov, perhaps someone will be dead and you will be blamed. Then you will not be able to come back to your home ever again, a wanderer all your life, and Theodosia will wait in vain for you."

"What do I matter? What is a dead man when hundreds lie dead every week in the streets of Kharkov? Oh yes, our masters cannot condemn us to death any more, but they can exile us by a word and by a gesture condemn us to punishments which will kill more surely than any bullet! Speak of what you understand, *barishna*, and do not think of one dead man as a sin. Think of my father's brothers flogged one by one until they died, think of my own two brothers sent into the army because they were dangerous fellows belonging to a family which had taken part in the rising at Chuguyev and were not skilled workmen as I am and so worth our *barin*'s while to take a risk and keep them! All because our brothers at Chuguyev"—he motioned to the south—"wished to petition the Tsar directly and knew no other way of doing so save by force. 'Take our children, take our money, even take our land and let us go elsewhere,' they begged, 'if only we may live in peace.'"

"This was at the military colony at Chuguyev?" ventured Eleanor, awed by the passion in his voice.

"So you have at least heard of that. Yes, it was the military slave camp at Chuguyev, may God pour His wrath upon it! Everyone, even women and children, regulated, ordered, driven, drilled every day of their lives, everyone with soldiers billeted on them and even their last chicken tagged and docketed. May the gracious Christ have mercy on their souls." He crossed himself, his face so changed and terrible in the faint light of the rising moon that Eleanor hardly recognized it, though strangely enough she was not frightened, only conscious of an infinite pity.

The quiet summer days slipped by into the even, untroubled pool of memory. A heavy, trembling heat settled over the land but, even though it was clear that the grain would be ready earlier than usual, the *starosta* would not order the harvest implements to be prepared even a day ahead of the traditional feast of Elijah. Occasional ominous mutterings and rumors reached them from Kharkov but the worst was passing without its full horror being realized, the epidemic dying down and flaring up again in disjointed, receding waves of suffering. There had been some attempted riots outside the hospital, quelled with swift, effective savagery by the garrison troops, and the bloodletting seemed to have drained the fever and danger from the many aimless, undirected plottings and murmurings. Over it all the hot, merciless sun beat down on the parched land, filtering stiflingly through the black, dusty murk which hung roof-high in the streets and spread a thin haze over the illimitable plain.

At last Taras Ivanovitch, the *starosta* of Nipocritiy, stood at the edge of the fields, running the ripe grain through his fingers and sniffing the air like a Cossack in search of Tatars. Abruptly he returned to the village crying: "It will do, my comrades! May Christ bless this crop!" and within a few minutes every soul in the village was on his way to harvest in the fields, it having occurred to no one to start before the *starosta* had given his sanction.

Micha forgot some of his boredom and ran with the other children through the fields, a pack of gay urchins, naked except for dirty white cotton shirts strung tight at neck and waist. But the village boys would sometimes be away for whole days and nights, tending the village cattle and pigs while singing plaintive songs of long-dead heroes under the bright star-strewn sky, and Micha soon became bored again by the regular tasks they had to perform. Eleanor tried to make him join them but after a few minutes he would wander off and lie looking at the sky or be found kicking dust clods through the street. She told herself that he was still very young, not yet four years old, which was of course true, but she feared for him when she saw how he turned from one thing to another, preferring to trail idly through the grass instead of running and jumping with other children his age. One of the very nice things about Madame Traskine, and indeed all those educated Russians Eleanor had met, was that she regarded it as perfectly natural for Micha to play with the peasant children. It was as if, having been born a superior being, he did not have to remember it always. One moment he was the little *barin* even at three years old, with ultimate powers over his play-mates, the next their blood brother and the victim of an elaborate joke. It was the great paradox of Russian life in miniature.

Day by day the harvest fell before striding sickles and was gathered into cracking sheaves, rustling in heavy puffs of uneasy oven-hot air, the snatches of half-chanted song wafted back to the house forming a strange background to the pleasant, idle days. The domestic serfs sang about their tasks too, their contentment a happy contrast to the strain of the last days

183

in Kharkov. Only Madame Traskine, who refused to move out of the house, regretted the gossip and gambling which had whiled away her days so divertingly in the city. As the governor's wife she had had a constant stream of visitors, officers from the garrison, officials and their wives, who arrived soon after she arose at midday and stayed until it was time to dress for an evening entertainment at one of their houses.

Eleanor had often been invited to these endless sessions and was always expected to be present when an evening party was given at the Traskines' house. Then she sat, seemingly for hours, uncomfortable and embarrassed under the unwinking stare and overelaborate compliments of the male members of the gathering, who were fascinated by her foreignness and challenged by her solitude. As time went on she became increasingly alarmed by the frank crudity of the suggestions made to her and the difficulties she encountered in making her refusals seem other than a further incitement to men seeking almost any alleviation of the boredom of their lives.

Sometimes, after several hours of sitting on the edge of her chair attempting to keep up light conversation where no conversation was intended by amorous gentlemen on either side of her, she felt physically ill, disgusted by their insistence and sickened by the heavy smell of grease and perfume and spirits which seemed inseparable from the Russian male. Yet she felt that she could not become a recluse and refuse altogether to appear in company; night after night of candlelit silence in the nursery would destroy her as surely as would a moment of inattention with the bored, half-drunk men of Kharkov's cardrooms.

But it had been a great relief to come to Nipocritiy, to be free again to be herself, and she was quite happy to go for long walks with Micha or venture occasionally on the back of one of the minute scrubby ponies which drew the village carts, amid gales of laughter from the villagers.

On one of their rambling walks, taken after the main heat of the day had passed, they came across a half-ruined church, the dome cracked and the rough masonry almost swamped by the crowding birch of a small wood.

"Don't let's go in." Micha hung back; he was not a very venturesome child.

But Eleanor was intrigued by the utter silence and desertion of the church. Who could have taken the trouble to build even a small church so far from anywhere? Why was it here when there was already a tumble-down church in the village? She parted the bushes and peered over the wall and then fell back with a gasp of horror: chained to the wall was an old, old man, filthy and unkempt, with mad eyes staring out of a tangle of hair.

"Ilena!" screamed Micha, throwing himself at her and tugging her frantically away. But when they were clear of the bushes Eleanor's common sense reasserted itself. There was no guard, no defenses, only complete silence; it was not possible that they had seen what they thought they had seen or that someone could remain chained up in a wilderness without dying of starvation. She must go back again to satisfy her curiosity or she would never be able to sleep in peace.

Not surprisingly, Micha refused to go with her, shaking his head and showing the whites of his eyes like a balky colt. Eleanor knelt in front of him. "You can see the roofs of Nipocritiy from here, can't you, darling?" He nodded. "Could you run back there all by yourself? It is no farther than the meadows where you often go with the other boys."

He scampered off thankfully, but it took Eleanor several minutes to gather together enough courage to retrace her steps into the thicket. Eventually she drew a deep breath, picked up a large stone as the only weapon she could see, and made her way carefully back toward the ruined wall. The bushes crackled dreadfully but there seemed no sign of life and, emboldened, she stood on tiptoe and peered over the wall again.

There was no mistake. It was an old man and he was heavily chained—fantastically chained indeed, with heavy links wrapped round and round his body so he could scarcely move. She licked her lips and wondered what she should do. Her instinct was to go back to the village for help but surely the old man's plight must be well known there, for she saw now that there were bowls and little offerings of food all around him, yet no one had dared set him free.

She hesitated; it all seemed so fantastic. Why go to the trouble and risk of keeping a prisoner in a ruin in a wood when the whole of imperial Russia bristled with prisons? As she watched and hesitated the dull eyes opened again and then sharpened into almost maniacal awareness the moment he became conscious of her presence. They stared at each other, hypnotized by mutual terror, and then the old man rolled over, hiding his face in his hands with a chilling rattle of chains. Immediately Eleanor's fear was swept away by pity and she scrambled down from her vantage point and began to circle cautiously round the wall, seeking for a place low enough to climb.

It was not even necessary to do that, however, for within a few yards she came to a gaping hole with a well-trodden path running through it. The obvious frequency with which the path was used made her pause, but somehow among the incoherent fears and questions in her mind she knew that she could not turn back now. She moved forward as quietly as she was able, although the precaution seemed pointless, clutching her stone and aware of the vast silences around her.

"Are you all right?" What a stupid question. Covered with sores and with only a few rags to lie on, it was obvious he must be close to death. Only his silence made Eleanor realize that she had spoken in English, so utterly had she been thrown off balance.

She was standing, feeling foolish and afraid, uncertain what to do and stricken by the filth and stench which surrounded him, when he rolled over again, only restrained from leaping at her by the great weight of his chains.

"Witch! Spawn of the Devil! Go from me, leave, I say!" He shook his fist, a face which a moment ago had seemed papery with death suddenly suffused with anger, the staring eyes set in monstrous folds of blotched flesh.

Eleanor recoiled and tripped full length over a piece of rock. She was on her feet again in a moment, but the pain of the fall shocked her sufficiently for her shuttering mind to shake into coherence again. She was ashamed for wishing to flee; no man chained as this one was could harm her.

He had hidden his head again, but this time she spoke quietly in Russian: "Your pardon, sir, for alarming you, but I wondered whether I could offer you any help? Some water from the brook or food perhaps from the village?"

She thought he was not going to answer, and when he did she wondered whether she had understood him aright as he halted and hesitated among words long unused in his solitude. "I have told you, wench . . . be gone . . . I want for nothing.

"But—but . . . why are you here? Do you not wish me to tell anyone and try to get you released?" She was utterly bewildered.

He started to pray, his voice rising higher and higher into a thin babbling chant. Eleanor began to wonder whether he could be the village madman kept out of harm's way, when she suddenly noticed with incredulity that his chains were not even locked, only twisted round a thin stake driven into the crumbling masonry of the wall. All at once it was too much and she fled, away from the dangerous solitude of the wood, away from this self-incarcerated hermit balanced on the very edge of sanity.

Out in the calm sunlight again she breathed more

187

easily, the still great heat making her reduce her pace, although no speed could be enough to outdistance her fears and conjectures. She was nearly back in the village when she saw Theodosia running toward her, apron fluttering and a long trail of dust betraying her unusual haste.

"*Barishna!* God be praised! When Micha told me where you were I feared for you. What Devil led your feet to the *starets'* wood?" She continued scolding and exclaiming, her anxiety revealed by the intensity of her feelings.

"It was very good of you to come and look for me," said Eleanor gratefully, when the flood of recrimination subsided somewhat. She slipped a hand under Theodosia's arm. "I am very glad to see you."

"*Barishna,* you must never go there again, you must promise me. You will bring death on yourself and harm to the village if you anger the *starets.*"

"I don't think I shall want to go," said Eleanor frankly. "But Theodosia, tell me, who is he and why could he bring death or harm?" *Starets,* she thought, groping through her memory, somewhere I have heard that word. Then she remembered seeing a pilgrim beg by the cathedral in Kharkov and having him pointed out to her as a *starets* or holy man, one who had sacrificed everything to a life of holy vagabondage and through whom God's purpose might therefore be further revealed.

Theodosia crossed herself. "He has been there many years, thirty seasons, some say. Once there was a monastery in the wood but all the monks have left and only the *starets* stays chained in what was once the courtyard. The people here build him a shelter in winter and take fuel and food, for he has sworn never to stir from the chains fastened with his own hands until he sees God in His glory coming to claim His land."

"But why chain himself up?"

"It is his sacrifice to God," explained Theodosia patiently. "We all make what sacrifices we can with fasts and prayer, but he has made the greatest of us all. The village honors him and we are very fortunate to have the prayers of such a saint of God to protect us, but if he is angered, then he curses us and someone will die or the crops will fail."

"That does not sound very holy to me," remarked Eleanor, recovering some of her poise but still feeling the menace—wickedness rather than holiness—with which the *starets* had filled his woodland refuge.

Theodosia crossed herself again. "*Barishna*, you must not say such things. You must never tell anyone you have seen the *starets*, for everyone here will hate you if you have angered him. We must hope he does not speak against you when the *starosta* and the *barina* visit him on Assumption Day."

"Madame Traskine?" said Eleanor, startled. "You do not mean to tell me she visits that . . ."—that filthy old man, she was going to say, but wisely pulled herself up—"the *starets?*"

"Of course," said Theodosia, astonished. "The *barina* has great respect for the *starets* and always visits him on Assumption Day when the harvest is in and we are nearly ready to leave for Kharkov again. She will sometimes visit him at other times as well if she has a special request to make. When the *barin* was losing so heavily at his cards two or three months ago she sent a special messenger to ask for the *starets'* prayers."

"And what happened?" asked Eleanor skeptically. The *barin* continued to lose fairly steadily at cards so far as she had been able to make out.

"Why, you remember when the *barin* was ill in February and did not play for three whole weeks? The *starets'* prayers were answered."

Eleanor wondered whether the *starets* had taken the precaution of sending some potion for the *barin's* food but decided it would be pointless to ask.

When they were back in the house Theodosia cautioned her yet again to say nothing of her experience and Eleanor hugged her impulsively; Theodosia was

189

plainly terrified, yet she had dared to come in search of her. But in the following days Eleanor found herself watching Madame Traskine with reawakened curiosity: it was strange and rather alarming to find her clever, idle, sophisticated employer, as well as the simple peasants of the village, apparently so much in the power of one whom Eleanor could only regard as being either mad or a charlatan. Certainly the *starets* of Nipocritiy wood bore no resemblance to the Christianity taught in Mayhurst parish church. It was some days before it occurred to her to wonder whether it bore any resemblance to the demons of rectitude which haunted her mother's life.

Madame Traskine showed no signs of abnormality or indeed of anything except the most intense boredom: all her interests and pleasures were centered on the social diversions of Kharkov—or preferably St. Petersburg—and, like Micha, she hated the isolation of the country. She sat for long hours on the veranda, chain-smoking irritably and doing nothing but stare dismally down the empty track leading back toward Kharkov. But within a few days of Eleanor's adventure in the wood a group of officers rode over from Chuguyev and soon there were always four or five and sometimes more of them lounging with her, arguing, laughing, smoking and gaming, the hot sun enhancing the brilliant white of their summer tunics and the gilding on piled saddlecloths and cavalry sabers.

The villagers resented these visits deeply; they expected the *barina* to amuse herself as best she might, but they were so sensitive to the slightest reminder of Chuguyev, whose absolute military tyranny passed them by so closely, that even Eleanor could feel their hatred and fear as each gaily clad officer cantered heedlessly by and she wondered that their horses did not stop dead like Balaam's ass before such a tangible wall of loathing.

She was resolute in refusing all invitations to join these parties except at four o'clock dinner, an unavoid-

190

able occasion when she and Micha sat together at one end of the table, thankful to be more or less ignored in the tipsy gaiety around them.

One afternoon, when the harvest was nearly gathered and the plaintive sound of chanting voices had begun to move from the fields to the threshing floors, Eleanor was sitting gazing wistfully out of the window and wondering how soon she and Micha could reasonably retire. The little boy was beside her, his eyes wide with wonder, watching one of the officers, clad only in a shirt and breeches, standing on his chair and balancing the haft of a naked saber on his forehead, its sharp, curved blade glinting in the evening light.

He nodded it into his waiting hand, flipping the blade into the table as it fell, to stand quivering among the glass and crockery. There was a wild yell of applause and he bowed gracefully, his fair face flushed with pleasure and drink.

"My forfeit, my forfeit, Maryanka!" He leaped down onto the floor and embraced Madame Traskine to the vociferous approval of his friends. She lay back a moment in his arms and then glanced wickedly at Eleanor's carefully guarded expression and Micha's fascinated stare. She returned the kiss caressingly but her heart was quickened not by the kiss but by a bubbling amusement at the splendid idea which had just struck her.

She ran her fingers down his face. "Do it again, Yasha, another and better way now."

His bright eyes teased her. "And the reward? What will you offer me better than a kiss from the lips of the most beautiful woman in Kharkov Province? Two kisses perhaps?" He pursed his lips but as he slipped his arm possessively round her waist there was not much doubt of his meaning.

She glanced at him from under her lashes. "Perhaps three, perhaps . . . who knows? But balance it on the point and not the haft and you shall have a kiss all the way from England."

There was an instant of surprised silence until the young man on Eleanor's left gave a wild hunting cry and jumped to his feet. "Go on, Yasha, on the point for a kiss from our stiff little governess!" The others shouted and laughed, all on their feet and flushed with excitement at so unusual a wager.

Eleanor pushed back her chair hastily, grasping Micha's hand, her heart thumping unpleasantly.

"Oh no, you don't." Yasha ran lightly round the table and put his hands on her shoulders. "It's a wager and I accept it. Hold her here, Aloysha, there's a good fellow, I'm not going to have my forehead cut open and then have to beat the fields for the wench!"

Eleanor struggled a moment while Micha began to wail, his eyes wide and frightened. The hands on her shoulders never relaxed their grip and after a moment she realized the futility and indignity of resisting. The young, merry, irresponsible faces around her were alight with the gambling fever she had seen so often in Russia; they were just sufficiently drunk for any thought beyond the immediate present not to enter their heads and it was she who was a fool to mind and not take the jest in good part: by showing panic she was simply adding to everyone's enjoyment. Anyhow, a kiss from a handsome young man, what was there but pleasure in that?

Two of the officers drew their sabers, saluted her with drunken deference, and then stood on either side of her, the naked, razor-sharp blades resting playfully on her shoulders. She shivered involuntarily and then remained absolutely still, whispering encouragingly to Micha: "Watch the man with the sword, dear, it will be a splendid trick if he manages it." She hoped it was disappointment she could see on Madame Traskine's face.

He rubbed his eyes and his sobs quieted a little as he buried his head in her lap. "Tell him to stop, Ilena. I don't like it, please tell him not to."

"Hush, dear, it is only a game." She met Madame

192

Traskine's eyes and smiled, trying to tell herself that it was indeed just a few drunken boys having fun, but she could not quite discount the satisfied spite in Madame Traskine's expression or shut her mind to the reckless, dangerous mood of these undisciplined and unpredictable young men by whom she was surrounded.

Yasha climbed on his chair again, rolling up his sleeves theatrically as he did so. "Hand me up one of those sabers, someone, and watch the great Yasha! Never done before but perhaps done again for such an adorably reluctant kiss!" He gestured at Eleanor's still figure and there was another shout of laughter and another round of vodka as Madame Traskine herself handed him his saber.

"Don't forget there are three kisses from me waiting for you if you do it."

He bent down gracefully and kissed her on the mouth, lingeringly and insolently. "I won't, but three—er—kisses is such a devilish odd number, m'dear." He straightened up and laid his head back, his slim body curving into a taut arc. With a flourish he laid the point of the blade on his forehead, holding it steady with the palms of his hands for an instant as he did so. Eleanor watched the slender, wavering steel, hypnotized by its curving power and threat. Then he was holding it by the tips of his fingers, a bright trickle of blood running down his face and into his eyes. A last hesitation and then his hands were away, by his shoulders, stretched triumphantly outward, before the saber clattered to the ground and he was smearing the blood from his face amid the wildly excited toasts of his friends.

"Phew! She will have to be a hot little bundle to make me do that again." He grasped the glass thrust into his hand: "A toast! To the English governess and a kiss from her lips!" The toast was drunk to more loud stamping and shouts which shook the house as he strode round and pulled Eleanor to her feet, the blood still running from the deep slice in his forehead,

193

smearing his cheeks and splotching his shirt, his eyes blank and glittering with excitement and strain.

Eleanor turned her face aside, shuddering from the horrible sight, all her resolution to make light of the affair disappearing, and for a terrible moment she thought she was going to be sick, there in front of everybody. She closed her eyes desperately as the room and that disgusting bloodstained mask revolved dizzily around her, her nostrils filled with the hot, greasy, metallic smell of him, hardly feeling her chin grasped ungently and her cold lips kissed. A second later he pushed her away roughly, still holding her wrists in a crushing grip. "What a wager! The wench is like the northern snow fields on a winter night. To think of having my looks spoiled to lie in such a Siberian blizzard! Here, comrades, you try and see how much better you can do, perhaps they don't train them the same in England and the women need a course of Russian fire before the thaw can start!" He thrust her away so savagely she staggered and almost fell, dimly hearing Madame Traskine's too long delayed protests through a stifling veil of terror.

She felt her arms seized and began to struggle violently, drunken jests in her ears and hands clutching her dress, fear and a kind of desperate anger lending her useless strength. As from a great distance she heard Micha screaming before suddenly all movement ceased and she was free and panting, half dragged across the table. Weakly she fell back in her chair and sank her head in her hands.

"Excuse me, *barins*, *barina*," said a strange voice, speaking Russian and pricking the fragile, French-speaking mood within the room. Imperceptibly, with the change of language, the atmosphere altered and Eleanor began, blindly and instinctively, to rebutton her bodice and tidy her hair with stumbling, unsteady fingers. Micha flung himself into her lap, sobbing wildly, and she began to comfort him automatically,

194

her voice still steady with the remote control which precedes shock.

"What do you want?" demanded one of the officers, rising threateningly.

The messenger at the door was a dust-stained trooper from the Kharkov garrison cavalry. "Your pardon, *barin*, I—I have a message for the *barina*," he stammered uncomfortably, handing a note to Madame Traskine and then retiring nervously to the door again.

Eleanor hardly heard what he was saying through the confusion in her mind. Blindly she held Micha's hand and walked out of the room, forcing herself not to run with every ounce of her remaining control.

She did not know how long she sat in her little whitewashed bedroom, staring at the floor with Micha sleeping the deep sleep of emotional exhaustion beside her.

When she heard the soft knocking at her door she rose to answer it without a query in her mind as to who it might be, or a care, or a hope, so apathetic had she become. There were no plans to make or angry decisions to leave for her to think about—she had nowhere to go and any alternative post in Kharkov was likely to be far worse than with the Traskines. She had not even considered it; she knew too well from glimpses of other Russian homes that the governor and his wife were exceptional in their cleanliness, careless indulgence, and European habits. She had very little money saved, having given what she could to the cholera victims, and no friends except the Braillards, whose livelihood depended on a meager salary from the university and therefore on the favor of the government.

Madame Traskine was standing in the doorway, holding a sheet of paper in her hand. She licked her lips and then said stiffly: "I am sorry for what occurred, Ilena Vassilievna. It was only a stupid prank and not intended seriously."

"It doesn't matter," Eleanor replied dully, unaware of the dried blood still on her face and lips and her ghastly pallor, which made Madame Traskine hesitate, already ashamed of her heedless malice which had so nearly led to an ugly reckoning. Finally she said reluctantly, "I have received a very disquieting message from Captain Gatchukov to say that my husband is ill, it is feared with a slight attack of the cholera."

"I am sorry," Eleanor said automatically.

Madame's eyes flickered briefly to hers and then she studied the paper in her hand again. "There is no one to nurse him properly with Didi and Theodosia and all the best servants here. I want you to go back with the messenger now and see what you can do for him."

"Me?" She was startled out of her apathy.

"Yes, someone must go and the doctor has said that I must stay in the country for my own health and for the sake of the child. I certainly cannot trust any of the servants to have the least idea of looking after him properly if I am not there."

"Very well, madame," she said wearily. "I will put a few things together and be ready in half an hour. It would be better if I went while Micha is still asleep."

Madame Traskine prepared to go downstairs, saying with a hint of querulousness in her voice: "Captain Gatchukov does not say he is very ill; naturally if he is you must send me word and I will come at once. I could not be separated from my dear husband, whatever the risks, if he were really ill."

"I will send you word, madame," Eleanor replied expressionlessly.

Twelve

General Traskine was dying, there could be no doubt of that, but he was dying very hard. His face, wrinkled, gray, and clammy, was hardly recognizable and he was scarcely conscious any longer of the agonizing cramps which continued to flex his body for hour after hour.

Eleanor prayed for him to find release in death, her groping words blurring with weariness as she forced the frightened servants to assist her tend him, herself tight-lipped and faint with the nauseating sickroom nursing, hopeless before she began. From the cholera cases she had seen around the streets she had known from the moment she saw him, frighteningly wasted only a few hours after the first attack, that there was little hope and now several hours later, with the cramps still showing no sign of ceasing, that little hope had long since vanished.

In spite of the courtesy with which he had always treated her she had found it difficult not to regard him with contempt for the way in which he ignored his responsibilities as governor, but now she could feel only a horrified pity for the stoicism with which he was meeting his agonizing death. Not once since she had entered his room nearly ten hours before had he uttered any complaint; he had even thanked her for coming and attempted a smile, a horribly grotesque contortion of the wrinkled folds of his face, crumpled as if squeezed in the fist of a giant.

The fresh early autumn dawn was breaking when Dr. Mavurian straightened up from the bedside and motioned her to follow him through to the next room.

"It is no good, is it, Doctor?" she said as the door closed behind them, her words a statement and not a question.

He shook his head. "No, I am amazed he has lasted so long. With someone as stout as he, I should have expected him to die of exhaustion if nothing else. Now he may last out the day, but certainly no more. Madame Traskine should be sent for at once and also his son if they wish to say farewell."

"I asked Captain Gatchukov to dispatch a messenger

to Nipocritiy as soon as I saw how ill he was. Do you think it wise for Micha to come?"

He shrugged. "Who can say? There seems no reason why some should contact the disease and some should not, why it should strike or why it should go. I have been tending patients all through the summer without any harm coming to me; the governor is going to die of it when he has hardly left his own house for months and the worst of the epidemic is over in the city. Certainly it would be wiser for Micha not to come but I do not think it makes any great difference."

"Nevertheless the message I sent was for him not to come and I hope he will not. His last memory of his father should not be of him looking thus." She nodded toward the closed door.

The little doctor smiled at her. "Do not worry, Ilena Vassilievna. Wash your hands each time you leave the room and see that the servants do the same if you can. Little enough, but all I can suggest; my colleagues say I am mad to think that water can affect such a disease and I think perhaps I am too. But two of them are dead and I am not."

"Is the worst really over in the city?"

"Yes, there were only two cases yesterday so far as I know. It has been mild as these epidemics sometimes go. I hear the deaths in Copenhagen have been terrible, some say nearly half the population, although I find that hard to believe." He shot down his stiff, polished cuffs and ran his long delicate fingers through his straggling beard.

Eleanor climbed tiredly to her feet. Her brief, crowded visit to Copenhagen seemed to belong to another lifetime, and yet another lifetime had passed since the drunken party at Nipocritiy instead of only a few hours. "I must get back, perhaps if I could make him drink something—" Her voice trailed away with the uselessness of it.

Mavurian gave her an abrupt, almost confidential smile and a quick sidelong glance from his slanting, secret eyes. "A waste of time, my dear Ilena Vassilievna."

"I know, but I feel I must try."

"Certainly you must try, but remember in your pity all the people lying dead in this city through his neglect."

"What has that to do with it when he is in such agony!" she burst out, unreasonably angry at his unconcern. "Unless you believe this potato nonsense, nothing he could have done would have averted the epidemic."

"Perhaps not, but it would have stopped a great deal of trouble still to come if he had attempted to carry out at least some of his duties. Now Nipocritiy will go to Gatchukov in payment of his gaming debts—"

"But surely the land will be Micha's?"

Mavurian gave a derisive laugh. "The general has gambled it all away and more besides no doubt. So those peasants will be handed over to Gatchukov, who will be interested only in making what he can from them. Traskine at least was an indulgent master, if only because he was too lazy to be otherwise."

"Ilena Vassilievna! Come quickly, the *barin*—" The girl Eleanor had left in the sickroom threw open the door, flustered yet proud to be part of such exciting events.

They both hurried into the room, turgid and horrible with sickness and suffering, to find that even in the few minutes they had been absent a great difference had come over their patient: already the relaxation of death was freeing his body from the insistent spasms with which it had been racked for so long and so unbearably.

Slowly the sunken eyes focused on their faces and the bloodless lips moved silently in a painful, frightening anxiety to speak. Eleanor knelt beside the bed and took his hands in hers, repressing a shiver of distaste at their cold clamminess. His lips moved again and a husky whisper surprised them. They both bent nearer to try and hear what he was saying.

"Poor fellow, I am afraid his mind has already gone ahead of his body," Mavurian said eventually, hostility forgotten at the last extremity of a man, no longer an enemy or even a personality.

Eleanor shook her head. "No, he's not wandering, look at his eyes. It is something to do with Micha, I think."

The dying man gasped and nodded. "Leave him—leave him in the care . . ." His voice trailed off as another spasm locked his limbs in renewed agony, but after a moment his eyes fluttered open and he whispered rapidly and distinctly, his last flicker of life bent only on racing the strides of death relaxing his tortured muscles. "Leave him—leave him, and the other child when it comes in the care of my—her—cousin Nicolai Pavl'itch. Tell him—ask him—to save what he can for them."

"Nicolai Pavl'itch who?" demanded the doctor. "Excellency, you must tell me! Where is he?"

Traskine tried to speak again but failed, his dry lips moving uselessly against each other like a gallant horse harnessed to an impossible load.

"I think he means Madame's cousin General Berdeyev," intervened Eleanor. "She refers to him as Nicolai Pavl'itch and I never heard of any other family."

"Is that right, Excellency? You wish your children, Mikhail Alex'itch and the other yet unborn to be under the guardianship of your wife's cousin Nicolai Pavl'itch Berdeyev, jointly with Madame Traskine? Is that what you wish?"

Slowly Traskine nodded and feebly made the gesture of a cross with his hand. An hour later two bearded, black-clad priests were chanting the office for the dead beside the stiffening body of Alexei Sidor'itch Traskine, lately governor of the province of Kharkov.

The stifling smell of their incense crept into every corner of the house, even penetrating into the garden where Eleanor was superintending, with the ruthlessness of complete exhaustion, the burning of all the hangings of the general's rooms, the clothes of the servants who had tended him, and also the careful scrubbing of their hands and faces.

"It is not right that we should be made to wash and burn while the *barin* lies dead, we should be mourning with the priest and commending his soul to the merciful Christ," mumbled Vassili, the general's fat and lazy valet to whom it was intended Theodosia should be married. "You are not our mistress, why should we obey you, who also obey the *barina?* We will wait until she comes, that we may show all respect for the *barin* and not play with water when I myself washed but yesterday. What can water do against anything as mighty as the disease of the Devil's balls."

Eleanor said carefully, with the precision which comes near the end of all control: "I am not ordering, but I think it will help you to avoid the infection if you wash thoroughly and burn your clothes. Dr. Mavurian has done so and he is still well." As soon as the words were out of her mouth she knew she had made a mistake. Amenable to positive orders but deaf to appeal or reason, they were already drifting away and Vassili threw his bowl of water on the ground, a satisfied smirk on his face. She felt helpless; after all, she had no authority over them and she did not even know whether washing would make any difference. Nevertheless she could not let them run any risks which she might avoid on their behalf. She was trying to marshal her sluggish thoughts into fresh effort when she saw Madame Traskine coming toward her over the grass.

The servants ran to her at once, falling on their knees, clutching her skirts and sobbing noisily. Eleanor was used by now to the readiness with which tears came to most Russians, but she was still slightly repelled by it and waited until their first paroxysm of grief had abated before joining the group.

"I wish to offer you my sincere sympathy, madame. The general knew that you were on your way and was thinking of you as he passed away." Her conventional

201

English formality sounded cold and stilted to the point of disapproval when set against a background of uninhibited sobbing and wailing from the servants gathered round her feet.

"On the contrary, Ilena Vassilievna, I was informed that his last words were of usurping my just authority over our children." The tears were trickling down her cheeks as she spoke, but she was one of the fortunate few whose looks are not marred by grief, and her eyes were bright and angry.

"He—he did place General Berdeyev as their guardian but I think he was chiefly considering his business affairs and making some provision for them," replied Eleanor tactfully. "We had already told him you were coming and he could speak very little toward the end."

"But he was quite lucid?"

"Oh yes, madame, very lucid and peaceful right at the end," responded Eleanor, not perceiving the drift of her mind.

"And I tell you he was not! It is not legal to make such an appointment—you and Mavurian had better find that your memories were mistaken or it will be the worse for you! I do not wish for anyone to tell me what I must do with my own, especially not a narrow, grasping upstart like Nicolai Pavl'itch. All the Berdeyevs are penniless as well as treacherous and greedy! Just think of every letter and document having to be sent to Petersburg before any business is transacted or I can buy Micha a new pair of drawers!"

Eleanor felt acutely uncomfortable. She had known there was no love between General Traskine and his wife but she had thought that there was at least some of the mutual affection which comes from a life shared together. But it was plain that not the slightest thought of the death of her husband was disturbing Madame Traskine's enjoyment of her wrongs. Eventually she said temperately, "I have only met General Berdeyev for a short time but I should not think he would do anything improper or interfere unless you wished it." She looked down at the still gustily weeping house serfs. "Madame, you must take care not to catch the infection. The doctor says we must wash frequently as a precaution, but when I tried to explain this to the servants—"

Madame Traskine gave an artificial, jangling laugh. "Of course, Ilena Vassilievna, you are the English girl who believes in asking and explaining, not ordering. Never ask and never show any doubt if you want a Russian to do anything." She turned to Vassili, sitting on his heels and wiping his eyes mournfully at her feet, and said in Russian: "Go to the river, remove all the clothes from your evil-smelling carcass, wash every part of your body, and burn the clothes. See that all the others do likewise."

He scrambled to his feet, sniffing despondently, but to Eleanor's amazement moved away at once, taking the others with him and mumbling disconsolately: "*Slushu, barina, slushu.* I obey, *barina,* I obey."

Madame Traskine met her eyes derisively. "You see, mademoiselle, it is the only way to deal with these cattle for their own good. You should come in now and lie down; there will be a great deal to do later and company to receive."

Eleanor followed her indoors without a word.

Madame Traskine spoke no less than the truth. The next day passed in a whirl of gaiety and entertainment. The house was full of people eating *zakuski* and drinking innumerable toasts from a table piled high with every kind of different food and drink, exchanging gossip, laughing and talking. Only when they arrived and when they left did they file perfunctorily past the general's coffin to greet him and then to take a last farewell. Had he not died of cholera the coffin would have been left open and a note of farewell placed between the dead fingers for all to see. The dread specter of cholera cut down the festivities too, for the funeral took place after only one day, a long procession of priests, ikons, and officials in full uniform winding through the old streets of Kharkov, past buildings draped in silver mourning banners. The following day, after a long service, the procession re-formed, this time with the addition of hundreds of stiffly uniformed soldiers, clerks, and school children who escorted the coffin to the city boundaries, the first stage of its journey to Nipocritiy where the burial would take place.

Out of all the solemnity and ceremony interspersed with chatter and hospitality, Eleanor retained only one lasting impression: the great Uspensky Cathedral booming with deep bass chants and lighted by serried ranks of tapers with their ironic reminder of Easter. And then above the chants and the jostling mass of mourners fighting to lay a hand on the coffin for luck, she heard soaring into the dim gloom a single voice, movingly speaking for the dead man, voicing the farewell of one pilgrim through life to those whose span was not yet completed:

> "Grieve not for me,
> No longer do I sojourn among you, but
> Pray earnestly that I be received into the
> Light of life."

Thirteen

Immediately after the funeral they were plunged into another whirl of gaiety: there were mourning visits from friends and official connections, a reception to thank acquaintances for their interest, and then a fresh round of visits as Madame Traskine repaid all these calls in her turn. Micha, and therefore Eleanor, had to be present at these occasions, seated stiff and uncomfortable on the edge of their chairs in tight, formal clothes, both frankly rebellious at their confinement as the long, last days of autumn drew remorselessly on toward winter again. Although Russians never wore black for mourning, Eleanor had had to spend most of the little money she had saved on some light gray silk to make a suitable dress for these occasions, and she was guiltily pleased both by the extravagance and by the way it fitted her. But the drab color and severe lines she had felt to be necessary did not flatter her dark hair and gray eyes, or her youth: she was thin to emaciation and a few strands of gray were already appearing in her hair, which no longer curled up as stiffly as it had. Only the still ready laughter in her eyes, her softly curving mouth, and the deep childish cleft in her chin betrayed the fact that she was not yet twenty-four years old.

She sat quietly and mostly unheeded during the endless chatter of those weeks, for while Madame Traskine would never have dreamed of dancing yet at the public assemblies held at the Nobles' Club in the Soumskaya, she would have thought it odd indeed not to turn the obligatory hospitality of the mourning period into as festive occasions as possible.

Eleanor was interested to see the almost proprietary air which Captain Gatchukov assumed in the house and wondered whether he had already drawn up an inventory of the property he expected to see transferred to him as soon as General Traskine's affairs were cleared up. That this was likely to be a long and complicated process was already clear, for Vice-Governor Ilyin, appalled and dazed by the sudden responsibilities thrust upon him, had informed his superiors of General Traskine's wishes about the guardianship of his children and property at the same time as he informed them of his death. Madame Traskine had been furiously angry when she learned of this on her return to Kharkov from the burial at Nipocritiy, for the appointment had been so irregular and unofficial that she had hoped, not unreasonably, that no notice would be taken of it. Now, however, all the gigantic bureaucratic machinery of the Empire had been set in motion and it might be years before a decision could be obtained; it was more than likely that only a massive expenditure of bribe money, which she was quite unable to afford, would make it a favorable one.

So it was not surprising that she expressed her grievances with such vehemence that every cardroom and social gathering hummed with delighted speculation over the methods she might use to cut loose from her predicament, for Marya Fedorovna Traskine was still only in her thirties, and all chance of remarriage would be lost if she could not somehow free her patrimony from the grip of the government and from her husband's creditors alike, in time to provide herself with an adequate dowry.

The first obvious step was to blacken her cousin's name, which she embarked upon with such single-minded vindictiveness that few in Kharkov could doubt that her children had been left in the care of a monster of corruption and greed, but this was unsatisfactory since it offered no immediate prospect of achieving more than purely personal satisfaction. As the weeks drew on Madame Traskine began to lay other, more long-term plans and if the matter had not been so serious her enjoyment would have been intense. Life now had purpose and excitement, she had to calculate and plot, keep Gatchukov happy and even flirtatious while slowly, carefully, beginning to prepare his downfall.

Eleanor was unable to appreciate the extent of Madame Traskine's fears and difficulties, although the drama and enjoyment which she was drawing from the situation were obvious enough, and she became more and more bored by the endless scurrilous speculation into which the small talk of Kharkov had degenerated since the governor's death. She found herself almost longing for a duel or a scandalous love affair which would offer some relief from the monotony as she had to sit in her corner with Micha, hour after hour, drowsy with heat and tedium. But by the middle of October it was still the same, nothing had happened, nothing had changed, she was still listening, although her thoughts were usually far away, wondering perhaps when she could expect another letter from home. The family conscientiously took it in turns to write to her once a month, and while the grudging spirit in which they did so shone through the stilted news and moralizing sentiments with which everyone but John and Charlotte regaled her, she looked forward to these occasional links with home and normality for days before she could possibly hope to receive them.

"She is certainly very upset about it all," remarked a voice in her ear and she looked up, startled, to find Dr. Mavurian, shrewd and alert as always, by her side.

"How nice to see you again, Doctor, how are you?"

"I am well, thank you, Ilena Vassilievna," he replied precisely. "I am afraid, though, that your charge is not behaving as well as you could wish," he added acidly, as Micha upset a table with a shriek of joy and a loud clatter of crockery.

Eleanor started to her feet, but no one else took the slightest notice and two servants hastened to repair the damage. At once Micha struck out viciously at one of them with a broken tea glass, leaving a long red slash down his arm. A woman laughed while the wretched servant stood nonplused, blood welling from the cut and dripping onto the polished boards.

"Come here, my lovely, come and have a sugar cake with Mother. Ah, my little one," crooned Madame Traskine, laughing. "Oh, do go away and put your hand in some water and stop dripping all over the floor!" she added irritably to the servant. "Ask Didi to give you some bandage and a small carafe of vodka."

"Thank you, *barina*, thank you!" The man grinned delightedly and hurried off.

"Excuse me, madame, I will take him and put him to bed," Eleanor interposed.

"Why? It is only six o'clock." She was astonished and her arm tightened around Micha's shoulders.

Eleanor drew a long breath and tried not to sound dogged. "He has been very naughty and should be punished. I would like to put him to bed immediately."

"He was only bored and clumsy, he didn't mean to knock the table over. None of the china was valuable, was it, my pet?"

Eleanor retired defeated; she could not argue with her mistress in public under the supercilious gaze of most of the dignitaries of the city, to none of whom it had apparently occurred that what she wished to punish was not the breakage of crockery.

"You cannot understand us at all, can you?" remarked Mavurian interestedly.

Eleanor smiled ruefully. "No, and I am not sure I want to when Madame encourages Micha to behave so badly. Of course the poor child is bored with so many unsuitable parties, I could not blame him for knocking something over, but just to laugh when he could have seriously injured that poor man is dreadful. Whatever sort of person do you think he will grow up to be, encouraged as he is to behave so heedlessly?"

The doctor considered the question on its merits. "Lazy, bad-tempered, good-looking, charming, and useless," he said eventually.

Eleanor laughed, her annoyance evaporating. "Just exactly that! If only I was left alone to manage him I am sure I could make him think a little more about what he does. As it is, I am doing no good here. I can teach him very little and it is probably better for him never to do as he is told than be able to appeal to his mother whenever I am strict with him."

"What else can you do?"

She grimaced distastefully. "That is just it, isn't it? I cannot leave Kharkov and everywhere else would be the same."

"Far worse, Ilena Vassilievna, believe me, far worse. Here you are comfortable and in civilized surroundings, although perhaps you do not always think so. Elsewhere the merchants are just primitive boyars at heart, and so far as I know Madame Traskine is the only lady in the city who has ever traveled beyond the borders of Holy Russia. I wonder what she will do when the new governor comes? She will not like losing her position as first lady in Kharkov and giving up her home at the same time will make it worse."

"Giving up her home?"

"Well, yes, naturally. It is the governor's house."

"Of course it is," said Eleanor thoughtfully. "She will certainly not like that. No preparations to move have been made so far. Do you suppose Ilyin will be promoted to governor?"

"My dear Ilena Vassilievna, just look at him!" protested Mavurian scornfully, indicating the vice-governor's unimpressive figure, his back permanently bent into a deferential bow and his hands nervously stroking the seams of his trousers. "He is so deeply involved trying to think of a different reason every day to explain to Madame Traskine why he should have written to the Ministry of the Interior and to General Berdeyev instead of keeping quiet about the whole affair that I should think he will be asking for retirement as soon as the new man arrives."

"I suppose so, but General Traskine was not my idea of a governor either," said Eleanor doubtfully. "I cannot see why everyone is so excited about General Berdeyev being guardian to Micha. I have met him and I should think he would do it very well. Anyway the appointment would not be legal without a document of some sort, would it?"

"It entirely depends on what you mean by legal. It might suit the government very well to have Nipocritiy administered by one of their own officials instead of handing it over to Gatchukov, who is certain to create discontent there, right on the borders of Chuguyev where they least want it. If that is the case, then legality will not matter and no court in the land would find for Madame Traskine. That is what they are afraid of." He nodded toward Madame Traskine and Gatchukov, deep in gesticulative conversation at the other end of the room. "They have made General Berdeyev the scapegoat for all their fears. I would not be in his place if ever he has to deal with them at first hand."

"Why should she care if he administers Nipocritiy for her? She cannot want it to go to a man like that, surely?"

"The debt to Gatchukov, and others too no doubt, still stands. If the land cannot be sold Madame will find herself poor indeed, for she will lose even more when emancipation comes to the serfs, as will all the landowners. If General Berdeyev stops her realizing what she can on the land now and it becomes worthless in a few years, she will never forgive it."

"Emancipation is coming?"

"It is coming," he agreed.

"Oh, I am glad, I am so glad," Eleanor said fervently.

"Are you, Ilena Vassilievna? Sometimes one wonders, and so will you if ever you see what they can do if they get out of hand. I must go now, *au revoir, mademoiselle*," he added hastily and, bowing clumsily, made off across the room. A moment later he was back by her side. "I need not warn you, I am sure, not to repeat anything I have said to you. I do not wish to find myself being entertained by Colonel Suikevsky and his friends." He nodded to her and shambled away again, his haste explained when Eleanor saw Suikevsky's glance follow him, a coldly speculative look in his eyes.

Suikevsky was well known to her by repute, a man alternately shunned and fawned upon by the townspeople. Tall, dark-haired, with flourishing mustaches and fresh, ruddy complexion; only tight, unsmiling lips and the eyes of a gypsy horse thief prevented him from being an outstandingly handsome man. He also had a strange habit of posing his sensitive, beautifully manicured hands on the dark arms of his chair or hooked negligently into his sword belt, so that those facing his interrogations became almost mesmerized by them. For Colonel Suikevsky was head of the State Gendarmerie, or the Third Section of His Majesty's Own Chancellery as it was more properly known, and the sky-blue tunic and black breeches which he and his men wore marked them out wherever they went as enemies to the ordinary Russian, be he landowner or serf.

Eleanor had had it explained to her that he was the head of the secret police in Kharkov Province and many darkly horrible and mysterious stories of his doings had been recounted to her; hitherto she had discounted most of these, for surely everyday life in Kharkov was too trivial to be of the slightest interest to the secret police even if it was possible to accept their existence. Now, as Suikevsky's impersonal gaze rested on her face for a moment, she found that she did believe at least some of them.

Eleanor was retreating into the harbor of her own thoughts again when she became aware of Didi standing in the doorway indicating Vice-Governor Ilyin to a tall, bearded man still dressed in heavy outdoor furs, stained and wrinkled from travel and spotted with the first snow of winter. Although obviously a peasant, his face was vaguely familiar, but she was at a loss to place him as he strode across the room, completely at ease and seemingly unaware of the stares and dying chatter around him.

He halted before Ilyin and pulled off his disreputable hat. "You are the Vice-Governor, *barin?*"

"Yes, yes, indeed I am. But I cannot see anyone now, really I do not know what things are coming to when anyone can push their way into a lady's drawing room! Go away at once!" Ilyin waved his hands agitatedly at the immovable figure before him.

"Your pardon, *barin*, but my master the new gov-

211

ernor has just arrived in the city and sent me to find you. He wishes to see you at once and to hear what is being done about the buildings on fire to the north of the town barrier."

Utter stillness stretched into every corner of the room before Ilyin licked his lips and echoed stupidly: "On —on fire? I haven't seen . . . a new governor too . . . Oh, gracious Christ preserve us! Where is your master?" Eleanor had the impression he was about to go down on his knees and cross himself.

"At the hotel, *barin*, if you would follow me." The man turned on his heel without a second glance at anyone in the room and the wretched Ilyin trailed behind him, so overwhelmed by events that he completely forgot to take leave of his hostess until he was brought back to a proper sense of his surroundings by Madame Traskine's voice cutting through the iced silence, a hot wire of contempt.

"One moment, Excellency, before you bid us all *au revoir* . . ."

"I beg your pardon, madame." He stopped, confused, eyes haunted, back bending even more abjectly and his fingers clutching nervously at his skimpy stomach. The picture of a Russian administrator, thought Eleanor, smiling to herself.

"Your apology is accepted, Igor Dmitr'itch." There was no doubt that Madame Traskine had a regal presence when she chose. She transferred her attention abruptly to the messenger, waiting with barely suppressed impatience by the door. "Tell me at once, you, who is your so peremptory master?"

Before the man could reply Eleanor had suddenly placed him in her memory and she knew what his answer would be: "His Excellency Nicolai Pavl'itch, General Berdeyev, *barina*."

Fourteen

Eleanor woke the next morning in a state of pleasurable excitement; she had the feeling of events starting to run again after long stagnation, be it for good or ill. Even Micha was affected by the restlessness in the air and was unwilling to play, fidgeting round the room, scuffing up the rugs, and kicking the furniture until Eleanor could stand it no longer and started to tell him a fresh installment in the life of a family of Mayhurst rabbits called the Gruffies, which was their private epic.

". . . There was nothing that Baby Gruffy liked so well as slipping away when his mother and father were out shopping . . ."

"What did they shop for?" interrupted Micha.

"Oh . . . cheese cakes and loaves made of chopped grass, and as it was spring they were also looking for a new hat for Mrs. Gruffy. She had set her heart on one trimmed with dew-pearls."

"And cherries on the top like you told me?"

"Perhaps, but they really come later. Well, anyway, Baby Gruffy on this bright spring morning wriggled through the thick thorn hedge and jumped and ran and chased his own shadow across the fields until . . ."

"What is happening, Ilena?" Micha jumped to his feet breathlessly. Eleanor had been aware for the past few minutes of subdued scurrying outside the door but now there was a loud wail and a moment later Madame Traskine swept in, her cheeks flushed and her eyes glittering with excitement.

"Put your wraps on quickly, Micha dear! Come,

mademoiselle, there has been shooting in the square, we must go and see what it is all about,"

"You are surely not going to take Micha!" expostulated Eleanor as the little boy started to scramble into his furs with a squeal of delight. But she was already gone, her heels beating a wild, excited tattoo on the boards, and Micha raced after her, dragging on his heavy coat with frantic jerks.

Eleanor followed reluctantly, the happy, restless anticipation of the morning abruptly swamped with misgivings. She knew that nothing would dissuade Madame Traskine from her desire to take part in anything breaking the monotony, even a public execution; equally she could not be trusted to remember that she had Micha with her if any emergency should arise.

"Ah, here you are. Come along then, Micha, walk with me and don't run away. If you are found outside alone, now a new governor has taken your father's place, he would probably have you shot too." Micha blanched and clutched at Eleanor's hand but Madame Traskine took no notice, hurrying across the courtyard and leading them down the road at a great pace, the unexpected diversion acting like a tonic on her bored and restless spirit.

"I see that my cousin Berdeyev has wasted no time in creating a riot and making himself as thoroughly unpleasant to everyone here as he has always been to me." She cast a sidelong glance at Eleanor to mark the effect of her words; she had almost forgotten that she was not the only person in Kharkov to have previous acquaintance with the new governor, nor did she care now she had remembered it.

Her principal energies might be devoted to the almost hopeless task of wresting her monies and estate from the insatiable, anonymous imperial bureaucracy, but she was far too feminine not to feel the need to personalize her hatred and fear. She was also quite astute enough to realize that the appointment of Count Berdeyev as governor of Kharkov could only mean that the Ministry of the Interior had seen its chances too, possibly—most alarming thought of all—suspected that the fall of revenue from Kharkov Province in recent years was not unconnected with the late governor's gambling debts and had chosen the one man now able to inquire, as of right, into both sides of his activities.

The advice of the *starets* had done much to determine the immediate course of her actions: she had known when she consulted him that such a holy man could never understand the details of her difficulties but she had explained that she was menaced by powers of evil which her woman's strength alone could not oppose successfully. There had been a long silence in the shadowy wood, a silence of prayer and thought and power reaching out to her. "You are wise, my daughter." The *starets*, as always, mumbled and choked on his words as his body was possessed by a strength far beyond his own. "When opposed by power stronger than yourself, power which is born of the Devil and against the blessing of your *starets*, you can only call on those greater yet in power, in heaven and below on earth." It was a mysterious and baffling message, as all the holy man's messages were, but as always it had only needed time and reflection to supply a meaning: who could be more powerful than her enemy? The Governor General? Hardly. If he had not visited Kharkov in three years, he was unlikely to be much use now. Then, like a flash of the miraculous light which she firmly believed it to be, inspiration had come, fitting her already dimly conceived plans too closely for it to be coincidence. Colonel Suikevsky. Few men were more powerful in provincial Russia than the colonel of State Gendarmerie, responsible only to the Tsar himself and to his own ubiquitous organization. The appointment of Berdeyev himself as governor only confirmed, with delight but without surprise, the rightness of her choice, for any colonel of provincial Gendarmerie had a vested interest in unseating or blackmailing a governor, and

215

of all the men of her acquaintance Berdeyev was surely one of the most vulnerable to police pressure. She foresaw an amusing winter.

Meanwhile, whatever she might be able to achieve in the future, the first priority was to repudiate absolutely any authority Berdeyev might feel he should exercise over herself and Micha now he was here. There was something almost touchingly gallant in the way Marya Fedorovna Traskine was preparing to do battle with the whole of official Russia, an enterprise not many of her compatriots would have cared to attempt.

As they proceeded nearer the center of the town their footsteps were the only sound in the still morning air, everywhere seemed deserted, and in the Nicolaevskaya, the richest residential street, the sound of the wind was like the muttering of a distant crowd and even Madame Traskine hesitated.

"I have no doubt my ruthless cousin has been satisfied with nothing less than putting the whole city under martial law and we will probably be shot if we go any farther. Any fun and excitement there may have been is over now."

"Maryushka!" a penetrating whisper came from overhead and Micha jumped nervously. Eleanor recognized one of Madame Traskine's most devoted companions, the fat, excitable, tightly corseted wife of the city treasurer. "Whatever are you doing out this morning? You have no idea of the danger we have all been in, we might be dead in our beds." She spread her arms dramatically and it occurred to Eleanor that she too was enjoying herself more than she had enjoyed anything since her debut in St. Petersburg thirty years before.

"We came to see what was going on but it all seemed so quiet—"

"Hush, not so loud! Anyone may be listening!"

Madame Traskine looked annoyed at being interrupted but nevertheless lowered her voice obediently. "What has happened? Have you seen anything?"

216

"Seen anything!" Her friend forgot the need for quiet at once: "It has been like a nightmare! Such goings on, my dear, as you never would believe: first the whole garrison called out and clattering through the streets, preventing anyone having a wink of sleep, and then—"

"Just when we were settling down again—" chimed in a voice across the street; already heads were appearing in many of the nearby windows and the excited owners joining in on an inspired recital of the night's events. One made a comment, another capped it, a third disagreed, and soon the tension was broken all down the street, doors opened, windows were flung wide and gruff greetings exchanged.

Pent-up feelings released themselves in conviviality and a party soon began in someone's house in the inconsequential way in which the best Russian parties often did begin.

From the conversation Eleanor gathered that the garrison had been called out from its barracks during the night, that the city had been a mad swirl of soldiers for most of the dark hours, and in the cold light of early dawn a running fight had developed, nobody knew with whom, since when most of Kharkov's inhabitants had prudently stayed indoors.

"You see what life will be like now this terrible monster has come to replace my beloved Alexei, rioting and incompetence at every turn until no one will feel safe." Madame Traskine's voice rose, shrill and delighted, above the chatter. "Can you wonder that I will fight to the end against my beloved son being ruled by such a man?"

A powdered, pomaded gentleman put his arm round her, tears running down his cheeks. "I feel for you, we all feel for you, we all do more than feel for you." He nodded solemnly, hiccuped, and tossed off another glass of vodka someone handed to him. There was laughter and some cheers, a new vortex of speculation and gossip created by the swirl of novelty alone, but as talk and argument eddied and flowed around the room it was always Madame Traskine who was the center of the most scurrilous and hilarious group.

Eventually Eleanor fought her way through the throng and shouted in her ear. "I think I should take Micha home, madame, would you like me to send the carriage for you?"

"No, I will come with you. This is no longer amusing and there is an assembly this evening to which I have long looked forward." Of all those in the room Madame Traskine alone was entirely collected and Eleanor could tell from her ready, bubbling gaiety how well pleased with herself she was. The assembly would provide another excellent opportunity to further her purpose while everyone was still nervy and worried by the events of the previous night.

Madame's complacent mood lasted all the way home and Eleanor reflected that the winter, always the season above all when gossip and malice flourished, was going to seem very long if this was to be a fair sample of the pattern of events. As they turned into their courtyard they saw some horses with green and gold military saddlecloths, tethered under the charge of a trooper. He spat out the straw he was chewing and stiffened to attention as they approached.

"Who is here?" demanded Madame Traskine sharply.

"His Excellency the governor, *barina*," the man replied, sketching a salute, his eyes fixed on a point in the sky. Micha gave an involuntary cry and cowered back against his mother, who smiled approvingly at him: her strategy was already repaying the sleepless consideration she had given to it.

She took Micha's hand and propelled him forward. "Come, mademoiselle, let us go in immediately. I trust that His Excellency has at least confined his attentions to my poor husband's office, though I should not be surprised to find him ransacking the house."

Fortunately she spoke in French so the trooper could not understand what she said, but Micha's eyes widened still further at the thought of finding this monster in his own home. Eleanor could hardly contain her anger, only too aware of the wickedness being sown in the child's mind, but unable to see any way of countering it before it was too late.

As they reached the front steps there was the sound of voices and a group of officers came out of General Traskine's office building. Instinctively they stopped and Eleanor thought, from the gleam in Madame's eyes, that this chance meeting fitted in extremely well with her plans. She had time to hiss a further caution at Micha before one of the men detached himself from the group and walked over to them.

"I trust that I find you well, Marya Fedorovna, and Micha also," Berdeyev said politely, bowing over her hand. "I have to condole with you on your tragic loss and ask you to accept my apologies for not arriving here in time for the funeral."

Madame Traskine made no attempt to return his greeting, half shutting her eyes and flicking her gloves impatiently against her side. He looked at her in surprise and after a long moment added stiffly: "I am sure it must have been a sad blow to you."

He knows perfectly well it wasn't, thought Eleanor, entertained in spite of herself by the ridiculous charade.

There was still no response, so after a further hesitation he continued: "I am sorry to have to burden you with my presence and that of my staff at such a time but I am sure you will understand that I wish to acquaint myself with such papers as there are"—Eleanor hid a smile at the ironic note in his voice—"in my predecessor's office as soon as possible. I shall be very happy for you to stay in this house through the winter if you wish and will try to trouble you as little as possible."

Madame Traskine emerged from her strategic silence with a snap: "I am delighted, though surprised, to hear that as well as usurping all my natural rights you do not wish to make me immediately homeless as well!"

His brows rose. "Your natural rights? In what way

have I interfered with you?" He turned to Eleanor and made his remembered stiff bow. "It is pleasant to see you again, Miss Lovell, I trust that—"

Madame Traskine interrupted: "Will you leave my property at once or shall I summon the servants and have you removed?"

His eyes narrowed and he regarded her in silence a moment as if seeking a reason for her behavior. "I have to remind you, my dear cousin, that this is not your house but, on the contrary, mine so long as I am governor of this province. However, it will suit me better to live in the Government building in the center of the town during the winter and I am entirely willing for you to remain here as my guest during that time. My staff will, however, be occupying the office here for the next few days transferring anything of interest to the government files. I trust I make myself plain?"

Eleanor wished there could be some opportunity to warn him of the bitter resentment and antagonism Madame felt toward him and which she was fostering, for her own purposes, in the city. But she was helpless; as usual there was nothing she could say or do which would affect matters, except possibly to make them worse.

As if reading her thoughts, Berdeyev added in a slightly more conciliatory tone: "Is there anything I may do for you while I am here? I understand Alexei Sidor'itch asked that I should give you any assistance I could before he died and I shall naturally be pleased to do so."

He could not have chosen to say anything more unfortunate. "You will kindly not mention that monstrous affair, indeed I would not be surprised to find that all my sainted Alexei's money was already in your hands and my poor Micha a pauper for life! I'll petition the Tsar himself before I will agree to such an injustice."

Berdeyev was apparently quite unmoved by these histronics although Eleanor felt reasonably certain that his dislike and anger at the scene so unnecessarily thrust upon him were even greater than her own.

He ran a finger down the scar on his face, a gesture she remembered as having denoted uncertainty or irritation. "I understood from the letter I received that Alexei Sidor'itch merely gave me the privilege of disentangling his affairs and those of his family as best I could. I had not, until this moment, believed you might have reason to fear injustice." But even as he spoke he was remembering uneasily his instructions from St. Petersburg and knew that there was reason for his cousin's rage. He tried again. "Marya, there is no need for us to quarrel and this is neither the time nor the place to discuss such matters. I shall be pleased to wait on you tomorrow to explain the position so far as I can. I certainly have no desire to interfere in anything that is not my concern, but unhappily this is now my affair whether I wish it or not."

"Discuss the matter indeed! As if there was anything to discuss except to tell you to leave me and mine alone and not try to impose your evil tyranny on us as you are doing on this unhappy city. No doubt you are delighted that, although you have been here less than a day, already there are many lying dead who yesterday were alive, and the whole town in fear of your excesses!"

His face tightened. "Have the goodness to explain if you please. Who lies dead from my excesses?"

"I suppose they are so many you cannot keep track of them any longer? We have just come back from the Nicoloevskaya and have heard terrible stories of how you allowed the garrison to terrorize and loot the town during the night. I suppose you thought it right to start as you meant to go on, Your Excellency?"

Instead of the explosion of anger which Eleanor expected, to her relief and surprise Berdeyev appeared faintly amused by this recital. "I am sorry if the imaginative citizens of Kharkov are living in anxiety but I really cannot be expected to cure them of nightmares. Part of the garrison was called out to fight the fire some fools had started in the potato warehouse. On their way they encountered a group of peasants who had somewhat unwisely remained to admire their handiwork and a detachment chased them back to the city. I believe they slightly wounded one but he still managed to run fast enough to escape. I can see that a great deal of training will have to be undertaken before the regiments here are fit for war."

"For war?" queried Madame Traskine, momentarily diverted.

"Yes, war. The Western Army has already been mobilized and is assembling on the Danube. The news when I left St. Petersburg ten days ago was that the British fleet had passed the Dardenelles."

Eleanor gasped. "Surely there isn't war between England and Russia?"

"Not yet, Miss Lovell, and we must hope there never will be. Even if this great disaster should come on us all it will make no difference to your position here. The imperial Russian government does not make war on women and neither do the Russian people." But do they not? he wondered, remembering certain incidents on the Central Asian plain.

Madame Traskine tapped her foot impatiently. "Never mind that! Do you go back to the army then? I cannot imagine you enjoying being a governor after so many years on campaign."

"No, I do not return to the Army of Operations. I was declared unfit just before the news arrived that Alexei Sidor'iteh had died and that was one of the reasons I was appointed here." His voice was expressionless but his disappointment was clear enough.

Madame Traskine smiled maliciously. "I am sure your comrades are as sorry as we to hear of your misfortune."

"I hope so, for it would mean they were quite brokenhearted, would it not?" he countered and then added seriously: "But I am here as a soldier also, for if there is war with Turkey, as now seems inevitable even if England and France do not join in, Kharkov will be of major importance as a supply center. It has been, for you perhaps, an agreeable game we have played here this morning, but I would advise you most strongly in the future to reserve your animosity for our private ears. I have no desire to interfere in your concerns further than I must, but I shall have to see that Traskine's commitments with regard to Nipocritiy do not disturb the peace of the province at such a vital time, and that any investigations which are ordered into his administration are properly carried out. I can have no mercy on anyone who tries to create disorder here, whoever they may be." He turned away without another word and signaled for his horse.

Fifteen

Late in February Madame Traskine was delivered of another boy, Alexei Alex'itch after his father but at once called Sacha by his family and adoring attendants. He was a contented, merry baby, soon smiling and laughing at all who came near him and the minimum of trouble to look after. Eleanor loved him as if he had been her own and from the first he appeared to regard her as if she were indeed his mother. Her days took on new meaning and she had to watch herself carefully lest Micha should have cause for jealousy, for, try as she might, she could not love him as she loved Sacha. She felt sorry for him, angry at the fears and prejudices planted in his mind by his mother, by the superstitions around him, by his own unpredictable nature; but love was not hers to give or withhold—it was there or it was not there. For Micha

223

there was sympathy, affection, protectiveness, understanding, for Sacha, without her willing it, there was
something infinitely greater to which it was impossible
to put a limit.

During her long confinement in the house Madame
Traskine had been unable to prosecute her private
vendetta against the new governor with the vigor she
would have liked. Berdeyev had also been fortunate in
that he had taken office at the beginning of winter when
every Russian peasant who could returned to his home
or to his winter occupation of long-distance carting.
Pleasure, violence, merrymaking, and rebellion alike
were submerged in the general preoccupation with
staying alive and warm. Even his first action, prohibit-
ing the sale of grain except to the government, was
received with resignation rather than open fury.

The need to start conserving stocks for the army
made this move inevitable but Madame Traskine was
quick to perceive her opportunity and it was not long
before everyone in the city was openly discussing the
fabulous sums the governor was amassing from his
dealings in grain. This in itself was not felt to be particularly shocking as all officials were expected to maintain themselves through their peculations and most
governors amassed fortunes during their terms of office.
But once Madame Traskine had recovered from her
confinement the rumors redoubled, particularly as to
how he was allowing his cousin and her children to drift
toward penury in order to safeguard their estate for
himself, and feeling at once became more hostile, for
meanness was felt to be a far greater sin than mere
corruption.

In March came news of an Anglo-French alliance
and then at the beginning of April an imperial proclamation arrived from St. Petersburg and was read to an
apathetic crowd from the steps of the cathedral: England, France, and Turkey were at war with Russia.
Rotten with disease after a miserable winter camped

in the open, the huge Russian armies on the Danube began their long march southward.

No one in Kharkov dreamed of blaming Eleanor for the hostility of her countrymen but they were pained and angry at such unwonted interference in what was plainly a domestic quarrel between them and the Turks, and quite at a loss to understand why so-called Christian nations should take the part of the Infidel. Conversation died down awkwardly when she entered a room and mothers, whose sons were already on their way out of town after years of comfortable garrison duty, gazed at her reproachfully.

So she went less and less frequently into the drawing room when Madame Traskine had company and tried not to think of the many months which might lie ahead with no news from home. Letters had come to be an anchor of a whole part of her life; stilted and formal though they might be, she longed for them desperately, counting the hours if they were a day late. Theodosia and Micha shared her excitement and quite felt the Lovell family to belong to them as well, although both were puzzled by some of her evasions and reticences to their curiosity. Micha quite lost his sullenness when the "English" letter arrived and he and Theodosia would ply Eleanor with questions and discuss endlessly the lightest event which stirred the calm of Mayhurst.

They were both thrilled when, toward the end of April, Lottie's letter came announcing her engagement to a local farmer, a respectable if not a brilliant match. She sounded incoherent with joy and Eleanor was kept hard at work all morning inventing a description of a typical Sussex farmhouse and describing an English wedding to her rapt hearers. In the afternoon while Micha slept, she reread the letter to herself and had to blink back the tears which stung her eyelids. She told herself that they were tears of joy for Lottie's happiness, but in reality it was Lottie's happiness which was acting like a catalyst for her own aching loneliness, solitary and almost forgotten in an enemy country two thousand miles from home.

Sacha gurgled and held out his chubby arms toward her and she snatched him up and hugged him to her, laying her wet cheeks alongside his and feeling the soft down of hair like mist on her hot forehead. Micha awoke and she swept him into her arms too before he could see the tears in her eyes and they were soon jumbling together, growling like bears and hissing like snakes, and if Eleanor was nearer to tears than laughter Micha did not notice it.

Theodosia put her head round the door, her eyes round and frightened: "*Barishna*, the governor is here and the *barina* will not see him. Didi is out at market and none of the others will dare to tell him—so black he looks at being kept waiting outside for many minutes while the *barina* does not appear."

"Won't she see him at all?" asked Eleanor.

"No, Ilena Vassilievna! 'Tell him to go and not come forcing his way into my home,' she says, and goes to bed straight away with a headache. What am I to do, *barishna*? The governor will surely have me exiled if I take him such a message." She was trembling and Eleanor realized just how deeply Madame Traskine's troublemaking had struck.

"Nonsense, Theodosia! The governor is a just man and would not blame you for a message you brought. Though I think I would simply say that the *barina* is not well if I were you," she added, smiling.

"No, *barishna*, I dare not!"

"Very well then, I will tell the governor if that is what you wish. You had better come with me and see that he is not angry with me, then another time you will not fear him."

"Please, no, *barishna*. It would do no good for me to come. I would be no protection for you against him."

"I did not mean that you would protect me, there is no need—" began Eleanor and then, seeing it was hopeless, broke off and held out her hand for Micha.

226

"Come on, Micha, you shall greet your cousin in your mother's place and show him what a big boy you are now."

But her careful attempts to overcome his fears during the past weeks, and to counter Madame Traskine's constant horrific fabrications, had gone for nothing. All his shallow self-confidence evaporated before Theodosia's obvious terror and he cowered back on his bed fearfully. Deciding it was better not to insist on his obedience than risk an unpleasant scene before the governor, who was probably already in an inflammable mood, she left him there and ran into her own room to bathe her face and tidy her hair.

Berdeyev certainly did not look in an ungovernable fury when she first saw him. He was standing on the veranda outside the front door idly inspecting a small faded ikon which hung on one of the doorposts, but there was a certain stiffness in his attitude and in the pointed way he had remained outside the house which showed that Theodosia's fears were not altogether unfounded.

"I am sorry. Didn't Theodosia invite you in? I must give her a terrible scold when I see her!" Eleanor said cheerfully as she stepped out beside him, but her heart quaked when he turned to look at her.

"Good morning, Miss Lovell. Do I understand that the Traskine household is now so poor, owing to my depredations, that the governess has to answer the door, or is the female who admitted me so busy crossing herself that she will be unfit for duty for the rest of the day?"

After a moment's hesitation Eleanor decided that there was no answer to either of these questions and replied quietly, her voice jumping a little from nervousness: "I have been sent with Madame Traskine's apologies, but she is indisposed today and will therefore, with many regrets, be unable to see you."

"Indeed? You might as well be as outspoken as the rest, or is it only behind my back that people whisper these things? Madame Traskine is no more indisposed than you are."

"No," she acknowledged, her eyes twinkling irrepressibly. "But it seemed less rude to put it that way, for I am afraid she will not see Your Excellency." Her tongue fumbled momentarily over the difficult Russian.

He relaxed slightly. "Your Russian is good after such a short time. I congratulate you."

"It is nearly eighteen months now." Eleanor tried not to let the depression sound in her voice. "Wouldn't you like to come in for a few minutes? I think you have not seen Sacha, he is growing into a fine boy."

"At least he would not cower away from me yet as his brother does." The anger was back in his voice. "Thank you, no. I prefer to remain here while I am so unwelcome a guest. I should be grateful though if you would carry a message to Marya Fedorovna for me. As she will not answer letters there appears to be no other method of transacting business with her."

"Yes, of course. What is it?"

He said slowly, "Will you tell her that I have now definitely been ordered not to sell Nipocritiy in settlement of Traskine's debts except to the military establishment at Chuguyev. Accordingly I have no alternative but to take out a mortgage on the whole and use what cash assets I can raise."

"I am so glad you will not sell all those poor people to Chuguyev! They will be so grateful and so am I."

"Save your thanks, Miss Lovell, I have sufficient trouble on my hands at Chuguyev itself without inflaming every estate on its borders," he replied brusquely. "I certainly do not expect Marya Fedorovna to see it in at all the same light as you, but there is nothing I can do about it, my instructions are clear and I cannot keep Gatchukov waiting for his money any longer."

"That horrible man! I wish you could get him transferred."

"He no doubt feels that to have an Englishwoman as his wife would add to his stature as a local landowner,"

228

he observed caustically. "If you would have the good-ness to convey my message to Marya Fedorovna . . ."

Eleanor whisked away, glad to hide her burning cheeks: ostracized Count Berdeyev might be, but he certainly seemed to have kept his finger on the pulse of Kharkov gossip.

She found Madame Traskine reclining on a sofa, eating sugared plums and smoking. No matter how long she lived in Russia, Eleanor was sure she would never become accustomed to seeing women smoking or to the habit of drowsing endlessly through the day whenever entertainment did not offer itself.

"General Berdeyev is here, madame," she said, feel-ing her way cautiously. "He would very much like to discuss some business with you if you could spare him a few minutes."

"I have already informed Nicolai Pavl'itch that I am indisposed today and unable to grant him an interview."

"But, madame——"

"Enough!" She waved her cigarette in the air. "I have no wish to discuss anything with him, least of all my private affairs in which he has no right to interfere. Has he gone or is he inspecting my few remaining possessions?"

"He declined my invitation to enter the house while he is not a welcome visitor here," Eleanor reflected that, from the disappointed expression on her mistress' face, he had certainly been wise to do so. She took a deep breath. "He asked me to tell you that he has instructions not to sell Nipocritiy except to Chuguyev and that there-fore he must mortgage it and use other means to pay General Traskine's deb—er—liabilities."

Madame Traskine leaped to her feet, her face suf-fused with a wild anger but her mind racing as she sought to reassess her scattered plans. To throw away money paying Alexei's debts was folly enough when with Suikevsky's aid she was close to evolving a scheme which would evade such a disagreeable neces-sity, but to have Nipocritiy unsold and burdened with

229

debt would be a disaster. It was doubtful whether such an immense mortgage as would have to be raised could be discharged even by the time Micha and Sacha were of age; it would quite certainly end any possibility of raising a dowry, without which her own remarriage was impossible.

"I'll see him broken first! Tell him no. Never! Never!"

Eleanor stood her ground, unable to understand Madame Traskine's calculations, contempt lending her strength. "But, madame, what can he do if he cannot sell Nipocritiy? Gatchukov will wait no longer to be paid and it is not right to make him."

"Why can't he sell Nipocritiy to Chuguyev then? Tell him he must sell. By the time Micha and Sacha are grown an estate down here will very likely be no good to any of us. The need for money is now, to get us all established again, away from here, please God."

"Madame, why do you not see him to explain all this? Although General Berdeyev did tell me that he did not feel it safe or right to sell Nipocritiy to Chuguyev."

Madame Traskine looked thoughtful but shook her head. "No. If once I discuss anything with Nicolai Pavl'itch I am acknowledging his right to do so—and I do not! If he must interfere, then he does so at his own risk. Nipocritiy must be sold, to Chuguyev if necessary, for the best price he can get. It should bring us enough for our needs and he will not have to concern himself any longer with my affairs." Especially when I have no intention of paying Gatchukov, she thought with pleasure.

"You cannot wish to sell Nipocritiy to Chuguyev! Why, the peasants dread the very name, anything would be better than that," cried Eleanor, appalled. "Please, madame, do not suggest such a thing."

"You forget your position, mademoiselle. You are not paid for your opinions but to do as you are told. Kindly convey my message to the governor and then return to the nursery at once. Do not forget that you are an enemy of Russia now, and if I found myself unable to employ you, you would find yourself a thousand versts from the nearest British consulate, perhaps put over the Turkish frontier unprotected, since Turkey is now your gallant ally." Madame Traskine could seldom resist the opportunity to crush the slightest sign of opposition to her will; she found pleasure in looks of fear and subservience around her, even if she seldom carried out her threats.

Eleanor felt her mouth go dry; it was a horrifying possibility of which, in the quick anger of the moment, she felt Madame Traskine to be quite capable. She had a daunting vision of herself trudging from house to house as she had done in St. Petersburg, begging for a post from Madame Traskine's friends. Good-natured though most of them were, among the artificial excitements of total idleness such a situation could easily become the latest joke of the city from which it would be the act of a spoilsport to rescue her.

Madame Traskine herself was already considering more important matters. "If the government is so anxious to buy the estates near Chuguyev, then Nicolai should be able to obtain a good price. If he claims to be acting in our interests, that is his duty. Tell him so, as he seems to be using you as a messenger."

"I do not think that he will sell to Chuguyev," said Eleanor stubbornly. Then she added hastily, despising herself for the attempt to placate Madame Traskine's anger: "It is not that he does not wish to do what he can to meet your desires but he is afraid of a rising if he did so, perhaps spreading to the other estates nearby."

"Pooh! Nicolai Pavl'itch was ever frightened of shadows! Tell him to have them all rounded up and taken to the barracks at Chuguyev before the sale is announced, they will be docile enough then."

There was nothing to be achieved by staying any longer and further protest might easily provoke real disaster for Eleanor herself. Her conscience told her

that she should have fought harder, argued more per-
suasively, but the words simply would not come. Once
out of the door, she leaned her forehead against the
cool whitewashed plaster of the wall outside. She was
in General Traskine's bedroom, since in common with
most Russian houses all the rooms on either side of
the hallway intercommunicated with each other, and
she was grateful for its shrouded gloom in which to
recover from the shock Madame Traskine had dealt
her. Gradually, over the past year, she had begun to
feel secure, involved with those around her, so that
some of her corroding isolation, if not her loneliness,
had slipped away. Madame Traskine might not carry
out her threat but her words had highlighted the truth,
that everything Eleanor thought she had gained, even
Sacha, could be swept away again for nothing more
than a whim or a passing fit of temper. It was only with
a great effort that after a few minutes she managed
to grip herself again, thinking, I survived Mayhurst and
St. Petersburg, I will survive this, I have not come all
this way to be defeated now.

She found Berdeyev still on the veranda, leaning
moodily against one of the skillfully carved pillars, his
hands deep in his breeches pockets.

"I am sorry—" she began nervously.

"It is for me to apologize, I should not have sent you
with such a message. I heard it all." He nodded to
Madame Traskine's open window at the end of the
veranda and kept his own voice low. "If she will not
listen to reason I shall have to proceed as I think best
and inform her of what I have done."

"Will that be legal?" asked Eleanor doubtfully and
then, aware she had fallen yet again into the trap of
impertinence, mumbled a shame-faced apology, expecting a cutting rejoinder.

Instead, he said almost gently, "You have no cause
to reproach yourself, Miss Lovell." There was a rare
glimmer of a smile as he added in his accented English:
"You are of course correct, it would not be legal, but

here I am the law and my orders come from Petersburg whence lies the only appeal. I do not think such an appeal is likely to succeed in the present circumstances."

Eleanor could not help smiling back, amused above all to find that her law-abiding British soul could still be shocked by such methods after eighteen months in Russia, but in place of protest she found she could only be glad that Madame Traskine was to be discomforted. She said irrelevantly, "It is lovely to hear English spoken again, it is almost a foreign language to me now. Sometimes I find it quite difficult to phrase my letters home correctly."

"You are still receiving your letters without difficulty?"

"Oh yes. I had one today telling me my sister is to be married and of all the family celebrations and preparations." She managed a swift, unhappy smile, all her former desolation flooding over her again. "Will—will the war make any difference to the posts, do you think, sir?"

He pulled on his gloves, his eyes on her face. "I should think not. They will no doubt come through Prussia and Austria, both of whom are neutral at the moment, though for how long I would not like to say."

"But Austria is Russia's ally, isn't she? Everyone says so and how the true monarchies are going to unite against foreign aggression and use their power to keep anyone from spreading liberal ideas, though it doesn't seem to me that Russia needs much assistance in that."

"It is fortunate that you are voicing these sentiments to me and not to my friend of the police, Suikevsky. Watch what you say, the most innocent words can be dangerous these days. You should be doubly careful now with our countries at war, although naturally you can count on the protection of the provincial government if you should run into the kind of difficulties my cousin suggested to you in the heat of the moment." He signaled to the trooper holding his horse. "*Au revoir*, Miss Lovell, and thank you for your assistance."

233

He mounted and wheeled his horse but Eleanor, although grateful for the tacit offer of assistance, was determined to make one more effort to make sure that Nipocritiy was safe. "Please stop a moment, General." Berdeyev at least would not stoop to threats and bluster to keep her quiet.

"What is it now?" he demanded, and his mount fretted and sidled impatiently.

"I'm sorry. But please, you will not sell Nipocritiy to Chuguyev, will you?"

"Why? What is Nipocritiy to you?"

"I don't know, nothing, I suppose." She thought of the rippling plains, the wide peaceful sky rimmed with feather-light cloud, the good humor and kindliness she had found there in spite of all its laziness and dirt. And the terror and hatred of Chuguyev which was with the villagers whenever they looked to the southern horizon, the way they crossed themselves and spat even when the wind came from that direction. "Yes, it is. In the few weeks I was there, I don't know how to explain it, but it came to be a kind of home to me and everyone was very kind. They are so terrified of Chuguyev, I couldn't bear—"

"Be at ease, Miss Lovell, you are an able advocate and I myself have no desire to aggravate an already difficult situation on the estates bordering Chuguyev. I will not sell it." He touched his cap with his whip and cantered out of the yard.

• • •

Another Easter came and went, bringing another miraculous reawakening of the countryside, with wild flowers springing up everywhere even before the last snows were melted. Yet again the long-drawn solemnity of Lent was transformed into praise and rejoicing so that it seemed as if the world really was born anew on the first stroke of Easter morning. Only this year of 1854 the rejoicing was muted and the prayers were for peace, for peace soon so that the levy of eight recruits out of every thousand male souls would not be needed; that the long, ill-fed, scavenging lines of soldiers marching through the province might cease before the time came for harvest.

For Madame Traskine and her friends, except for the few with husbands or sons at the front, the war added a pleasant extra spice to the gaiety of the season. A grand ball had long been planned for the middle of May, chiefly as a send-off for the officers of the 6th Light Cavalry Brigade, the latest unit to receive orders to move up to the Danube front from Chuguyev, but it would also be the climax to the season, the last large social event in Kharkov before all the leading families dispersed into the country during the heat of the summer.

Eleanor had been doubtful of the propriety of her attending such a function when all these young men were off to fight her country's allies, but Madame Traskine brushed her protests aside. "Nonsense, Ilena, you are our guest, it is nothing to you what mad schemes your country may follow—though to uphold the infidel and side with French republicans, even if they call themselves an empire at the moment, is too much as I do not mind telling you! But of course you must come to the ball, I would be ashamed for you to miss such an occasion when we have three months in the country ahead of us." Madame Traskine was at her most charming, as excited as a child at the prospect of the ball, and it was impossible to remember the casual spite she could also so easily display,

"But I have no dress suitable for such a grand occasion," objected Eleanor.

"I have the very thing and you are so clever with your needle, I am sure you will be able to make it fit you before Friday. Come, I will show it to you and see if you can still resist coming then."

She dragged Eleanor off to her room, still protesting halfheartedly, but when she saw the dress she could protest no longer. Of deep blue silk slashed down the front to show a flounced lace underskirt and cut low over the shoulders, it was the kind of dress Mrs. Lovell would have unhesitatingly declined to allow any of her daughters to wear.

"It—it is beautiful, madame," she gasped.

"It is yours, Ilena. Since Sacha was born I can no longer wear it and anyway I have my new gown just arrived from Vienna."

"For me to keep? Oh, thank you, madame. I have never had such a dress before. Are you really sure you wish me to keep it?" She ran her fingers down the stiff folds admiringly.

"Of course I wish you to keep it, I have told you it is no further use to me. So you are coming to our ball now, Ilena?"

Eleanor laughed. "I don't think I could refuse! I would love to come, thank you so much for asking me."

Madame Traskine shrugged and yawned, losing interest as soon as her point was gained. "It is the last of civilized life we will see until the autumn. How I hate the country! If only this horrible war had not started perhaps we could have visited Paris this summer, and if only Nicolai Pavl'itch would stop interfering, we might be able to go to Petersburg next winter."

Madame Traskine was disappointed in the results of her campaign against Berdeyev; the reasons for her hostility were too widely known for it to carry much weight. Although all were united in disliking his uncompromising and ungenial administration after the easygoing incompetence to which they had become accustomed, and it was widely believed that he had cheated his wards and was indulging in the customary fraudulent practices of provincial governors, such things were too common to occasion more than casual envy. But whatever hopes of reconciliation Eleanor might cherish she was forced to recognize that they were ephemeral whenever she saw the expression in her employer's eyes at the mere mention of her cousin's name. This was no transitory hatred conceived during the boredom of winter to die with the rain in the heat of summer.

Unknown to Eleanor, or indeed to most others in Kharkov, Madame Traskine's other plans were proceding more smoothly. Colonel Suikevsky was a frequent visitor to her house and it was whispered that he now transacted more business there than he did at State Gendarmerie headquarters. The servants nervously crossed themselves every time he or one of his innumerable messengers passed the threshold and even Madame Traskine's friends found it difficult to be at ease in his company. Gatchukov especially was visibly disconcerted to have Suikevsky's cold policeman's eye cataloguing his every movement and sweated with fear when he heard talk of investigation into the financial chaos left by General Traskine's administration in Kharkov.

Gatchukov was uncertain whether an investigation into provincial finances by Berdeyev or his private involvement with Suikevsky gave him the most cause for alarm, but however threatened he felt, he was determined not to abandon his hard-won claim to Nipocritiy. Certainly he would have to proceed with caution, but at least one factor in his favor was the hatred and suspicion with which every provincial administration regarded the State Gendarmerie. In Kharkov this was undoubtedly worsened by the Traskine affair if, as seemed likely, Suikevsky was about to throw his weight behind Madame Traskine's attempts to regain possession of her lands. For a resourceful man all was far from lost.

Sixteen

The evening of the ball was enchanted, the early stars sparkling in the pale green light of evening and seeming to join the hundreds of candles and fairy lights within. As this was a city reception in honor of the Light Cavalry Brigade, the ball was held in the absent Governor General's residence and the Kovlikovskaya was jammed with carriages and droshkies bringing guests from far and wide.

It was the first ball Eleanor had ever attended and she was full of anticipation, delighted with everything and aware that the remade dress fitted her perfectly. She was slightly disconcerted to find that it was still possible to wish that Christopher could see her in it, but resolutely turned away from the thought and instead watched, entranced, as officers dressed in every color imaginable waltzed and mazurkaed around the room accompanied by ladies in dresses encrusted with layers of precious stones, some larger than any she had ever seen.

As this was an official function Berdeyev was receiving his guests at the head of the steps, but Madame Traskine flatly refused to meet him and Eleanor had perforce to accompany her, although she was acutely conscious of the discourtesy. She was soon left alone when Madame Traskine was whisked away by an inebriated youth in the blue and white of the artillery but within minutes found herself monopolized by Suikevsky's policemen, whom everyone else carefully avoided: Odzanov, Suikevsky's aide, in particular she found impossible to shake off without dangerous rudeness as he spent the greater part of each day at the Traskine house. He was a good dancer and his companions were pleasant enough, but once she was seen to be dancing with secret policemen no other partner presented himself and she was in danger of being uncomfortably isolated for the whole evening with a group from which any Russian girl would have been instantly separated by her family.

She was almost glad when Gatchukov marched her firmly away while Odzanov was fetching her some lemonade. "What do you mean by making a spectacle of yourself with those police dogs in front of the whole of Kharkov? It is not at all permissible in one who is to become my wife."

She pulled away from him, gratitude immediately swept away by anger. "I am not going to become your wife, I do wish you would get such a stupid notion out of your head! How can I refuse to dance with someone who is in and out of the house all day long?"

"Of course you should refuse," he interrupted. "Leave all policemen alone, my dear. Your household has a bad enough name already with Suikevsky there half the day and that dirty thief Berdeyev paying visits to try and sweeten Marya Fedorovna so he can get his hands on the little there is left at Nipocritiy."

"I wish you would realize once and for all that it is nothing to do with you what I do or how I behave. I will never become your wife, so it is no good going on asking me," Eleanor said tartly. "And I do not want to hear any more slanders about the governor either, he has always been very pleasant and considerate to me and I do not believe one word of these stories everyone is telling about him."

His eyes were suddenly intent. "Do I understand that you know our distinguished governor well?"

"No, of course I don't know him well. I traveled out from England on the same ship and he recommended me for this post with his cousin when I was desperate for any situation in St. Petersburg. I know you want him to agree to sell Nipocritiy to you and I am glad he will not."

Gatchukov appeared not to hear her, taking her elbow again and steering her out of the ballroom and onto one of the softly lighted balconies overlooking the garden. A gentle, blossom-flavored breeze stirred the green filigree of early leaves touched in from the surrounding darkness by ranks of colored lanterns looped along the balustrades, and Eleanor breathed in gratefully. In daylight the Governor General's residence had an abandoned, mournful air, but in the darkness rotting steps and rioting weeds alike were hidden.

Gatchukov lit a cigar reflectively, his thoughts obviously far away; she was glad of the silence and took care not to disturb his mood lest he should reutrn to the subject of their marriage, which he still appeared to regard as a foregone conclusion if only he asked her often enough. She remembered Berdeyev's uncomfortably acute comment that Gatchukov would no doubt consider it added to his stature as a local landowner if he had an English wife, and she shifted uneasily.

As if her slight movement had marked the conclusion of his train of thought, Gatchukov tipped the fine ash from his cigar and said softly: "You are glad that the governor will not sell Nipocritiy to me. How do you know that he will not?"

"It is common talk—"

"It is not common talk as you would know if you went more into society. The scandal is that he has appropriated it to himself and will sell it on his own behalf to the highest bidder if he can. I repeat, how do you know that he will not sell it?"

Eleanor flushed uncomfortably, but there had been nothing secret in their conversation so far as she knew, so she said boldly: "He told me he would not, but if you have a rightful debt against General Traskine's estate I am sure it will be paid."

"It has been paid," said Gatchukov grimly. "In assignat rubles."

Eleanor could not restrain a quick gurgle of laughter. "That is all right then. Why don't you tell the people here so that those horrible stories will be stopped?"

"And make myself the laughingstock of the whole city? I won from Traskine in fair play—Nipocritiy and not a lot of worthless paper."

"If that is so, why are you paid in assignats and not in land?" asked Eleanor shrewdly.

He threw his cigar on the ground with a violent gesture. "How was I to know that that fat son of a pig would die? The debt was one of honor and I knew he had no money to pay it, it would have to be met by selling his land. I won too much and I knew too much about the swine not to be able to demand payment on my own terms. But what do I find now—"

"You find," said Eleanor with satisfaction, "that, instead of having to deal with a lazy, stupid man who would go to any lengths to avoid losing a very profitable position, you have an energetic, honest administrator under orders not to sell lands you thought would be the start of your fortune. I tell you again I am glad this is so." She rose to go, miserable suddenly that the ball, after the excited anticipation with which she had prepared for it, had failed to give her any pleasure at all. But he was too quick for her, grasping her wrist with one hand and forcing her chin back with the other.

"Not so quickly, my little governess! You cherish such affection for our governor, perhaps you would like to use your influence on my behalf. If I had you for a wife perhaps he would let me have Nipocritiy, since you both seem to have such a high opinion of each other's abilities. You could promise we would not resell it and he would believe an Englishwoman."

Eleanor stood perfectly still, trying not to feel alarmed, and said contemptuously, the blood beating painfully in her ears: "It is not resale you want it for, until you have first drained everything you can from it. He is not such a fool as to believe anything you promised and I have done nothing but tell you I will not become your wife. Now will you please let me go."

His grip tightened. "Perhaps one day you will be only too glad to marry me. You are an enemy now, remember, with no rights. If the government should decide to deport you across the Turkish frontier, what would you do on your own? You would be glad to marry a Russian citizen then, I think." He laughed abruptly, knowing his words had struck home, but not realizing they also revealed the likelihood that he and Madame Traskine had been discussing her situation together. I suppose it was Gatchukov who told her to make sure I came to the ball, thought Eleanor drearily, and then with sudden panic she wondered whether he had enough hold over Madame Traskine to force her into dismissing her governess in the hopes that it would indeed frighten her into marriage.

As if reading her thoughts, he pulled her to him. "You see, Ilena? You will be glad indeed to come to me if that should happen, as it might at any time." He kissed her, carelessly at first and then with hot, thrusting desire, the heavy, greasy smell from his pomaded hair stifling in her nostrils.

She struggled violently, no longer able to command the detachment which had so baffled Captain Brownless at Copenhagen. Instead the horseplay at Nipocritiy had bequeathed a quick, flaring terror which stiffened her muscles and almost blanketed conscious thought.

"Wassa marrer, someone troubling my li'l governesh?" broke in a strange voice, blurred and uncertain with drink. Gatchukov released her and swung around, his eyes wild and staring with quickly stirred lust and his hand falling to his sword hilt. Eleanor half fell back against the balustrade, her hand pressed to her bruised mouth and her breath coming in shuddering sobs.

"Who the devil are you?" demanded Gatchukov.

The figure swayed slightly. "Not the Devil, just his

re-represh-represh-entative, at your service. What'sh you doing to my governesh?"

Gatchukov tightened his grip on his sword. "Your governess, you drunken swine?" He rounded on Eleanor. "Who is this?"

She shook her head dumbly and the man wagged his finger at her with drunken solemnity. "There, you don'-remember your poor Yasha, when I had—had my head cutsh open for your beautiful eyes and a cold Shiberian kiss for my trouble. Shame, my love, shame!"

She recognized him now and it was as if the two incidents became one in her mind. Yasha the cavalryman from Chuguyev, who must be one of those in whose honor the ball was being given and who, for some extraordinary reason, seemed to feel that his feat with the saber last summer still gave him proprietary rights over her. She said hesitatingly in reply to Gatchukov: "He—he is one of the officers who came to Nipocritiy to visit Madame Traskine, and he kissed me as a reward for a silly wager they laid." She began to smooth her tumbled dress and untidy hair with trembling fingers.

Gatchukov sneered. "So you had a fine time last summer, whoring with every pair of mustaches between here and Moscow, for one so prim and proper with me."

Yasha let out a yell of rage and flung himself forward, flailed drunkenly a moment, and then tripped over his scabbard, while Gatchukov never even moved except to draw his sword, standing easily as Yasha struggled off the floor.

"Oh no, please!" Eleanor grasped his arm. "He is drunk and doesn't know what he is doing. You mustn't fight him now, it would be murder!"

Gatchukov threw her off roughly without even looking at her, flexing his blade in his hands, the pale candlelight glinting wickedly on its blue length. For the first time Eleanor became aware of a crowd collecting around them, of eager whispers floating in the tense atmosphere. Yasha stood in the middle of a small circle of his brother officers, dense and still half fuddled

243

with drink, but quiet and sullen as consciousness of his position slowly penetrated his dulled mind. He drew his hand repeatedly over his forehead and touched the hilt of his saber reluctantly, knowing he could barely see his opponent's movements. Gatchukov made a fake pass through the air and grinned in savage satisfaction as the boy flinched, the desire within him served as well by an execution as by a woman. The crowd rustled expectantly and Yasha shook his head, desperately trying to clear his vision before it was too late. It was death facing him and he knew it.

Eleanor forced herself forward again on weighted legs and spoke in an urgent undervoice to Gatchukov. "Please do not force him now. There is nothing to fight over, nothing at all, he is only a drunken boy and will apologize if you give him a chance, although it is you who should apologize and not he."

"Do not interfere in what does not concern you," he replied coldly. "On your own showing he molested you at Nipocritiy—"

"As you are doing here and as every man seems to think he has a right to do to an unprotected foreigner if he can!" cut in Eleanor, still keeping her voice low, but fear momentarily overmastered by anger.

"That has nothing to do with it, I am able to defend my own."

"I am not your own! Will you never—"

"Enough! Come, sir, on guard!" Gatchukov pushed her away contemptuously and feinted wickedly within an inch of Yasha's nose, who recoiled, stumbled, and nearly fell. He regained his balance by a supreme effort and came on guard gamely enough, every drop of color drained from his face, his sword arm wavering uncertainly in the flickering light.

Gatchukov feinted again and thrust, knife-swift and deadly. Yasha staggered, half parried, and avoided the point by a miracle. It would all have been over within a moment had not Eleanor grasped Gatchukov's arm with all her remaining strength, fears forgotten in

244

determination to avoid disaster. He turned on her, hardly aware of what he did in the swift insanity of the moment, his body taut and unheeding in its awakened desire to kill.

A moment later a cold voice said: "Will you gentlemen kindly reserve your brawls for the parade square where they belong, rather than exhibit your lack of manners in my ballroom?"

Eleanor sagged against the wall as Gatchukov swung away from her to find Berdeyev standing between him and Yasha, one hand on the chased gold pommel of his dress sword.

Gatchukov said thickly, "Out of my way, Your Excellency, I have a quarrel with this young scoundrel here and by God I mean to finish it."

Berdeyev studied Yasha a moment and then said flatly: "He is drunk, there is no credit in killing a boy half your age who can hardly see his own blade. While I am here the law will be enforced and anyone found dueling will answer for it to a court-martial, whether I hear about such a duel before or after it has taken place." He turned to Yasha's companions, quiet and sobered now by the events of the last ten minutes. "Return to your unit at once; any of you found in this city in half an hour's time will be put under close arrest. You will have a more useful opportunity to prove your courage on the battlefield in the months ahead."

The crowd swayed and parted wordlessly to let through the brightly dressed, melancholy group of officers supporting Yasha in their midst, and then closed again into a tight ring of avid faces as Berdeyev turned to Gatchukov, the distant tones of the orchestra serving only to emphasize the area of silence around them.

Eleanor glanced at Gatchukov's face and was afraid. She had the feeling that he had already forgotten his momentary overmastering passion and was considering, with racing, absorbed intensity, the unexpected situation in which he found himself, exploring possibilities and laying plans with lightning speed while the silence lengthened and the press of guests grew ever larger.

It was Berdeyev who broke the brittle bubble of tension by turning politely to Eleanor and offering her his arm. "Come, Miss Lovell, allow me to escort you to Madame Traskine. I apologize for the deplorable manners my guests' have seen fit to adopt before you."

Eleanor felt his cool glance on her disheveled appearance and knew, to her shame, that he was not referring only to the abortive duel. She did not look up when she laid her hand on his arm, but as they turned to go Gatchukov's voice rang out, "One moment, Your Excellency!"

Berdeyev halted. "Well?"

He said deliberately: "You have seen fit to interfere in a private quarrel and then to criticize my conduct and manners—"

"It is your own behavior which has laid you open to such criticism," replied Berdeyev evenly. "I advise you also to return to your quarters and we will continue this discussion tomorrow."

"You talk to me of conduct and manners! I thought we had seen everything when Traskine was governor but now, instead of a useless, lazy parasite, we have a power-crazy army breakdown pilfering even from his own wards!" As the full sense of this outrageous tirade dawned on his listeners an audible gasp went up, but behind the calculated insult of his words Gatchukov's eyes were cold and watchful, gauging the effect of his hastily conceived plan. The inevitable inquiry into the tangled financial affairs of the province was coming uncomfortably close to Captain Gatchukov, among others, and the removal or incapacitation of the governor would undoubtedly help to slow or confuse matters at such a crucial stage. At the very least a public quarrel, whose origins would be obscure long before a trial or inquiry could be started, might well enable him to maintain that any future accusation Berdeyev made was activated by private malice.

246

Eleanor felt Berdeyev's arm rigid through the smooth cloth of his sleeve and his face became perfectly white, the long scar standing out dark and wicked against his pallor. After an endless minute his muscles relaxed and when he spoke it was as if his voice came from a great distance. "You have been paid your just debts and your opinion of my administration is not of the least interest to me. I do not play this game your way, nor do I intend to subscribe to the terms you lay down. I have said that dueling is illegal, for me as for you, and any further remarks of the kind you have just made will find you posted to one of our Siberian garrisons as a private soldier, and not with my sword in your gullet where I would have the greatest of pleasure in putting it."

Eleanor looked fleetingly at his face in the stunned silence which followed; she saw the trickle of sweat running down the side of his jaw and realized the effort of control his answer had cost. She sensed also the intensity of his desire to accept the challenge forced on him and so assuage at one blow all the long frustrations and hatreds that had soured his months in office. She saw too the expressions of incredulous horror and disgust around her as it was realized that he was not going to exact vengeance for the unbearable insults that had been spoken: and the look of unbelieving surprise on Gatchukov's face as he watched his plan succeed beyond his wildest imaginings. To wound or possibly kill a governor in a duel carried great risks which only the desperation of his position justified; this way, humiliation and discredit would be achieved without any penalty at all.

He threw back his head and laughed full-throatedly. "A coward as well as an army throw-out! My God, how low will you stoop?" He flicked his sword and made a mock, contemptuous pass at Berdeyev's still figure.

In that moment Berdeyev moved, grasping the weapon round the blade and in one swift movement sending Gatchukov sprawling off balance and reversing it into his own right hand. Before Gatchukov could collect himself in his dizzying fall from the heights of intoxicating success the point was at his throat, its naked menace flattening him desperately against the wall.

For a long moment neither man spoke, their heavy breathing harsh in the stretched solitude around them. Gatchukov ran his tongue over his lips, his eyes dilated with shock and fear. He tried to speak but as he read the hardly bridled purpose in Berdeyev's face the words would not come and the saliva ran dry and bitter in his mouth.

The seconds spun out into fragile threads of endless time, without track or meaning, until Berdeyev spoke, his voice clear and expressionless. "I have warned you that your terms are not mine: we are no longer playing an amusing game by gentleman's rules of honor and pleasure, we are at war. We have neither strength nor energy nor time to waste on petty quarrels and imagined slights." He lowered his sword arm and looked at the blade contemplatively while Gatchukov's hands went automatically to his throat where a single trickle of blood testified mutely to the closeness of his escape. Berdeyev laid the sword down quietly on a table and let his gaze rest on the breathless gathering of faces around him before walking back to Eleanor. "Come, Miss Lovell, I will restore you to Madame Traskine."

The crowd parted again without a word to let them through.

Back in the ballroom they stood watching the couples who were still dancing; it was only half an hour since Eleanor had left the floor on Gatchukov's arm, and if the gilded pendulum had not been swinging placidly below the ornate clock face on the wall she would never have believed it. Dimly aware of how Berdeyev's already difficult position in the city had been further complicated by the events of the evening, she stumbled miserably into a halting apology, gripped in the black depression of reaction, but he cut her short.

248

"What is done is done, though I should be obliged if you could confine your friends' desire to fight over you to occasions when I am not their host." He looked at her quizzically.

She felt the ready color rising in her cheeks. "Yasha is not a friend. I—I don't even know his surname. There was a stupid wager when he called on Madame Traskine at Nipocritiy last summer, but that was the only time I met him."

"Indeed? And might I know the subject of this wager?"

"I suppose so," she said reluctantly. "Madame wagered him that he could not balance his saber on his forehead by the point. It was a boy's trick, no more, and they were all drunk."

"It appears to be his usual custom. What was the stake in this enterprising wager?"

"I was," she answered quietly. "But they were only after a kiss and some fun—for them."

"I see," he said dryly. "You must have a very high opinion of Russia. Was my cousin a party to this scheme?"

"What does it matter? It is all over and done long ago and I was glad of Yasha tonight although perhaps he should be even more grateful to you." She glanced down and saw a spreading stain on the side of his breeches. "You're hurt!"

"Yes," he answered indifferently, pulling his left hand out of his pocket. There was a deep cut across the palm where he had grasped Gatchukov's blade, from which the blood still flowed sluggishly, soaking the handkerchief he was holding.

He smiled unexpectedly. "There are more tricks learned in a barrack room than how to duel like a gentleman. Gatchukov will never make a good soldier for all his ability and ambition, his tactics must have been learned in the cardroom. His first campaign would have taught him that when you are winning is the time you have to be most careful. If he had put his sword back in his scabbard when I refused to fight him, I and not he would be full of apprehension this night."

Seventeen

Almost immediately after the ball the entire Traskine household was plunged into a frenzy of preparation for the summer-long move to Nipocritiy. Madame Traskine and her friends paid endless farewell visits to each other while Eleanor and the servants packed all the household effects into a long line of high-sided bullock carts dispatched from Nipocritiy. This year they were to leave before the end of May to avoid any threat of cholera and the house was to be shut up except for Vassili, who was left behind as caretaker. Madame Traskine openly rejoiced in the fact that her long campaign against the governor had at least borne sufficient fruit for him not to consider claiming the house that was rightfully his, even thought it would stand empty the whole summer through while the center of the city sweltered oppressively in a blanket of dust.

At last all was ready, the rooms stripped, servants piled like squalling litters of kittens on top of the last loads of necessities, Micha and Sacha wedged into the carriage with their mountains of hand-embroidered summer clothes, Madame Traskine persuaded that her ostrich-feather bonnet and hamper of muslin country dresses were safely packed into place, and the procession lumbered slowly out of town, a long bolt of black dust unrolling behind their wheels and hanging, still and choking, in the motionless air.

"Oh, I am so glad to see the country again, I thought today would never come!" exclaimed Eleanor, hugging

Sacha tightly on her lap against the bone-jarring jolts of the carriage.

"If it wasn't that Kharkov is impossible to live in during the summer I would never come near the country. It's so dull and I can never forget the half dozen or so landowners murdered on their estates every summer. I hate it and I can feel it hating me back." Madame Traskine shivered suddenly.

"I hate it too," said Micha sullenly.

At Nipocritiy Eleanor had sensed a massive indifference to the Traskines, as if their presence was accepted but lacked significance to the life of the area: such hatred as existed was directed at Chuguyev. Even so, Madame Traskine's words chilled her, made her wonder about the happiness she had found at Nipocritiy the previous year and, as the morning mist blew past the coach windows like steam, she hoped that Micha had not really understood what had been said. "You will like it when you are there, darling. Your mother has all her friends in the city, so naturally she doesn't like being away, but it will be lovely for you to be able to run about and play where you wish. Perhaps this year the *starosta* will let you ride his horse."

"I hate it," he repeated stubbornly.

Madame Traskine laughed and stroked his hair. "He will grow up into a true son of mine with nothing of the Traskines, or the English either." She watched the expression on Eleanor's face with lazy enjoyment. "And it is no use you tempting him with stories of riding the *starosta*'s horse either; many things have changed at Nipocritiy now my cousin's long arm has stretched out to it from Kharkov."

"How do you mean, madame?"

"We have a bailiff at Nipocritiy now, a vulgar, canting German, who tried to make everything run to order and would certainly not permit a waste of time like letting the little *barin* ride on a horse."

"But why?" asked Eleanor blankly.

"Because, as you should know by now, Nicolai

Pavl'itch can leave nothing as it is and everything must be orderly and run with dull army discipline. He should have been a German himself. Would that he were, or had never left Siberia!"

"Was he in excile there or something then?"

"Not exactly, or he wouldn't be governor now. No, his father was a Decembrist[1] and when the conspiracy collapsed he was sent to a village in the wilds of Siberia somewhere and his wife chose to follow him there with Nicolai, who was then about ten years old, I suppose, more fool she. Nicolai came to Petersburg some years afterward when he started his military training but his mother was not allowed to return even when his father died, although Nicolai had the impudence to petition the Tsar for her."

"What happened when he did that?"

"He had his commission refused for all the guards regiments and had to take up an appointment to the Army of the East. I believe he spent the next few years establishing some backwoods settlement at Dead Bay on the Caspian—a pity he didn't stay there," she added vindictively.

"How did he come to be in England and then governor here then?"

"You should know that well enough," she snapped. "He was in the East so many years we had forgotten about him, but then he was wounded in some sordid skirmish four or five years ago and I saw him a few times while he was convalescing and attached to the Moscow and St. Petersburg garrisons. He was never fit to get around much, though, and I thought his appointment to England just an excuse to be rid of him, for the Tsar has never forgiven any of the families of the Decembrists. It is obvious the government know

[1] A military, vaguely liberal uprising against the accession of Nicholas I in December 1825. The Decembrists demanded the accession of the Grand Duke Constantine, his younger brother, and the granting of a constitution to Russia. The rebellion was easily suppressed but Nicholas always cherished a grudge against the Decembrists for giving his reign such an inauspicious start.

they have a grip on him and they have placed him in Kharkov as one of their creatures to help in looting us all. Many of the landowners here are not rich even if the Golitsyns do have nearly five thousand serfs up toward the Kursk border, and the Petersburg officials can feather their nests more easily at our expense if they have a governor they can stop getting rich on his own account."

Eleanor puzzled over this. "You think, then, that the government intends to—"

"How should I or anyone else know what the government intends to do? They do not even know themselves. All I know is, that with such a background he should be easy to dislodge but Colonel—"She caught herself and continued in a different tone: "It is difficult to know what backing he may have negotiated before he came here. The governor's *vzietka* or squeeze is well known enough, but if he was sent here because the Petersburg officials knew they could share it with him since the Tsar will not listen to his side of any dispute, then affairs may be more difficult."

Eleanor remained thoughtful for the rest of the journey. It was difficult to imagine so aloof and self-contained a man as Count Berdeyev being subjected to such pressures and she wondered whether he was aware of the close partnership which was being forged between his cousin's hatred and Colonel Suikevsky's professional rivalry.

Nipocritiy was indeed changed from her memories of the year before. Then they had not arrived until nearly midsummer and a busy, if sometimes misdirected, purposefulness had prevailed. This year the early cultivations were done, harvest was still nearly two months away, and the village was wrapped in a heavy, lackadaisical stupor from which it seemed impossible that it would ever rouse. Rudimentary haymaking was proceeding at a shambling rate but for much of the long, hot daytime hours scarcely a figure moved in the heat haze quilted suffocatingly over the parched land.

Then, as June ended, the weather changed. In place of the endless opiate of drugged blue skies, heavy clouds banked against the southern horizon and then, driven by gusts of wind into a steady concentrated fury, came the rain. Day after day the sodden gray circumference of the earth met the pitiless gray arc of the sky, and the early promise of harvest sank into a morass of swamped, rank growth, seeds unripened in the crumpled sunflowers and broken ears of grain.

"What are you going to do?" Eleanor had called in at the hut of the *starosta*, Taras Ivanovitch, on her return from a long, rain-whipped walk around the fields which left her filled with a terrible kind of pity as she saw the havoc being wrought in all that stood between the villagers and starvation in the coming winter.

He shrugged. "It is as God wills, *barishna*, there is nothing we can do." He was lying on top of the stove which filled one side of the larger of the two rooms which constituted his home. The walls were freshly whitewashed and a small lamp was burning in front of the ikon in the corner but through the long idle weeks he had made no effort to prevent the weather running unchecked through a large patch of thatch displaced by the spring thaw.

"Tea, *barishna?*" His wife Lukerya drew a little of the hot, faintly flavored water which passed for tea from the samovar and handed her a sugar lump.

"Thank you, Lukerya Petrovna," said Eleanor gratefully, bowing to the ikon before settling down on the narrow bench that ran round the walls. She placed the sugar between her teeth and drank a very little through it: now she had been offered tea she would be in Taras' hut for at least an hour and the sugar must be made to last for the whole of that time.

"Ah, *barishna*, this is a bad year for us." Taras crossed himself. "The curse of the Devil's balls is over all the land, the grain cannot live in the same soil."

"Can you not harvest some of the riper sunflower

seed and dry it on your stoves?" asked Eleanor cautiously.

He spat and answered sourly: "If God wills there is yet time for a harvest, but if we are not forgiven, then we cannot set ourselves against His curse."

"But surely, Taras Ivan'itch, it cannot be God's purpose for you to starve?"

He looked at her in astonishment. "But of course, *barishna*, if we have sinned."

"But would He not expect you to try and save what you might?" Eleanor persisted.

His eyes veiled and she sensed his withdrawal from her interference as well as his utter lack of interest in doing anything to forestall the disaster which would threaten the village in the winter. "What can we do? In due course, if a harvest is intended, the clouds will pass, otherwise"—he shrugged again fatalistically—"it is the *barin*'s affair and not ours."

"The *barin* is dead and the *barina* will need all her grain for sale." Eleanor knew she was unwise to interfere, but sought any means of puncturing his apathy.

"Your pardon, *barishna*, but we have a new *barin* in the governor and the German son of a diseased cow he has put here as bailiff."

"Oh!" She was at a loss. The complicated ownership of Nipocritiy was beyond the comprehension of the villagers and she was not surprised at their resentment.

"Ever since he has tried to make us grow Devil's balls he has called the rains upon us as a judgment from heaven, may his feet wither on his body." There was venom in every syllable.

"He only seeks to ensure that you will not starve when the grain is beaten into the ground. Surely there can be no evil in growing something given by God for us to use?"

"That is not for us to say, *barishna*. Always we have grown what we know here, whatever the season may be. When the *barin* visits us next he will have to look far to see the infection on our lands."

"Is no one in the village growing them?"

"The *starets* has spoken, *barishna*, and who are we to question him?" he answered obliquely.

It was no use to argue with such monumental conviction and his impatience with female questioning was becoming only too obvious, but Eleanor was in a thoughtful mood as she splashed her way up the village street some time later and she was hard put to it to welcome Karl Spolden, the bailiff, when he fell into step beside her, exclaiming in unfeigned pleasure at the meeting. He was a Russian-German from the German settlements on the Volga, used all his life to the orderly, industrious habits of the colonists there and now utterly out of his depth at Nipocritiy. He was personally outraged by the peasants for not tending the land with the daily, unremitting, methodical labor of his compatriots, and bewailed continually his own foolishness in cutting adrift from his parents' snug farm near Nicolaevsk.

"Ah, Fräulein Lovell, to see your face after the surly snouts of these pigs and less than pigs! It is unbelievable that today, when the rain at last is barely a drizzle, there is not one man in the fields, and to all my orders I find but drunken hulks in every corner. It will be fine before evening, I can feel it. The sunflowers could be staked, the ditches scoured, there is much that could be done to lessen the damage."

"It is not yet harvest. Last year when I was here they were working very hard," Eleanor tried to encourage him. "And I do not think you will find many drinking anything much stronger than tea; they get drunk to celebrate and they have nothing to celebrate now."

"Perhaps, but they do nothing. There is much that might be done now. The land is good, wonderfully good, better than any I have ever seen. To starve on such soil as this is a disgrace, and insult to the good God! It is not fair that cattle like these Russians should inhabit such land so that they may work six weeks in every year and spend the rest of their time in idleness."

"Oh, come, it is not as bad as that, there is plenty of work done when the weather is fine."

But he would not be comforted. "It does not rain every day and now they are also going out at night and uprooting the potatoes, the one crop which might do really well this year if it clears up later as I expect. Are they all mad that they will destroy their only hope of avoiding hunger? What I am to tell the governor when he comes again I do not know."

Eleanor was touched by his bewildered resentment but at the same time could not avoid a feeling of awe at Nipocritiy's gesture of faith, made even at the cost of starvation for the whole village. "You must try to see it their way, Karl Karl'itch," she said gently, falling unconsciously into the Russian manner of address. "If they hold it a sin to eat potatoes, to them it is better to die than imperil their souls, as we perhaps would feel it better to die than do some dishonorable action. In a way it is a fine thing that they do and we should respect them for it, although it is exasperating to us."

He grunted, unconvinced. "Meanwhile there will be no profit from Nipocritiy this year and I shall be blamed. Any grain we do manage to save will have to be stored to keep these oafs alive until next year, more's the pity."

"You must not speak like that," she said quietly. "One day when they are free they will learn. How can a serf be expected to value or be interested in land which is not his?"

"But the governor values his profit," he said brutally. "He doesn't want the Traskines sponging on him for the rest of his life and who is to blame him? Why do you think I am here except to squeeze something out of the place? Although how he expects me to do it unless I have a free hand to make them obey me as I see fit, I do not know."

There was something singularly disagreeable about such a blatant attempt to extract the maximum return from the Traskine estates. Perhaps there were, after all, some grounds for Madame Traskine's resentment. Finally she said, with a sigh: "Have you tried enlisting the aid of the *batyushka?*[2] She wondered whether Spolden had yet discovered the *starets*.

Spolden uttered a wicked and mercifully unintelligible German oath: "Have you seen the *batyushka*, Fräulein?"

"Yes," admitted Eleanor, "I have."

"Well! Sodden with drink half the day when he can peddle the services of his altar for some liquor, and the rest of the time whining round having doors slammed on his long nose and seeing what he can beg! Last time I saw him he was kneeling beside some old woman's deathbed pronouncing a blessing with his hand under the pillow feeling for her savings."

"I suppose it is difficult for them when they are not paid anything," said Eleanor excusingly, but she too had been startled to encounter the *batyushka* after a recent christening, reeling with drink as he went from house to house, begging for a little vodka in payment for a blessing. "I wonder they have any religion at all with their priests and holy men the way they are."

"Religion!" he exploded. "They are not religious at all! Superstitious if you like and walled about by belief in magic and ceremonial, but anything with more powerful magic or stronger appeal could take its place and they would never know the difference."

She was saved from replying by the sound of hoofbeats. Soon two horsemen appeared, picking their way delicately down the spongy lane toward them. The figures resolved themselves into Berdeyev and a young officer whom Eleanor vaguely recognized as having seen in his company before and whom she rightly assumed to be an aide-de-camp.

"The governor!" uttered Spolden in horrified accents. "And he has come by way of the potato field when I

[2]Little Father. In this sense the parish priest, but such was the patriarchal feeling in Russia that soldiers might address their officers thus, peasants their landowners or even the Tsar himself.

thought him safely settled in Kharkov at least until better weather came."

"Good morning, Miss Lovell, Spolden." Berdeyev drew rein before them and shook the rain from his sodden cap.

"Good morning," replied Eleanor, rather coldly after the bailiff's revelations.

"Good day, Excellency," murmured Spolden, bowing deeply.

Berdeyev contemplated them both in silence a moment and then said in English: "Do you think my cousin would receive Volodya Sergeivitch and myself to a meal when our business with Spolden is done?"

As always on the increasingly rare occasions when she heard her native tongue nowadays, Eleanor felt a quick constriction in her throat and it was with difficulty that she answered: "I will go and see if Madame is up yet and inquire."

He nodded and dismounted, turning to Spolden. "You seem to be having some difficulty in keeping the potatoes in the ground, Karl?"

Eleanor heard the beginning of a long explanatory protest from Spolden as she made her way to the house, slightly nettled by Berdeyev's irritatingly offhand manner. I am not his servant, she thought resentfully, and then laughed at herself, for she was indeed at everyone's call; everyone knew that she could not leave the Traskine household any more than could a serf, whatever the provocation. Although Madame Traskine would not lightly be rid of her with no replacement nearer than Moscow, short of actual dismissal she was in no position to protest against any treatment that might be her portion. To be a single woman with virtually no money, no friends and no fellow countrymen within hundreds of miles, living in enemy territory in time of war, was truly one of the most invidious positions possible to imagine.

Eighteen

The usual babble of voices greeted her when she opened the door. Although several regiments had left Chuguyev it seemed to make no difference to the number of officers who visited Nipocritiy to while away the tedious hours in aimless talk and reckless, unbridled gambling.

"Well, what is it?" demanded Madame Traskine, feeling Eleanor standing beside her. The talk died down and the men eyed her in a way which she still found difficult to accept.

"General Berdeyev is here, madame, and is speaking with Karl Spolden."

"Well? I cannot do any more to stop him pilfering my poor children's patrimony." She spoke almost absently; it had been said so many times it had become a bad joke rather than an insult, and she was too intelligent not to be aware of this.

"He has asked whether he and his aide might break their fast here before continuing their journey," Eleanor said as tactfully as she could.

Madame Traskine silently considered refusing but decided she would look much more effective as a persecuted widow and threw up her hands in resignation. "Not satisfied with taking all that is ours, now he even forces his presence upon me! I beseech you gentlemen as you are men of honor not to desert me."

There were some rather embarrassed disclaimers and half laughs as Eleanor went out, feeling rather nauseated, to ask Didi to send a message to Berdeyev to say that he would be a welcome guest at dinner.

Didi cast up his eyes to heaven, "Welcome, *barishna!* As well say the Cossack is welcome under a flag of truce in a Tatar encampment, or a dog in the snake's lair. It would be better for the *barin* to speed his departure and sup on his return to the city."

"You call him *barin* too," Eleanor said curiously. "Yet he does not own Nipocritiy and I still find it hard to believe that he is enriching himself, whatever the gossip of Kharkov may say."

He shrugged. "As to that, *barishna,* who can know? Naturally, as he has the ordering of us he will enrich himself, but what will he get from us compared to the wealth of Kharkov which flows into his pockets? The *barina* does not trouble herself with us so our orders must come from the governor, who is now our *barin.*"

Eleanor had by now seen enough of Russian officialdom to know that corruption was so much the rule that even the simplest business could not be transacted without a bribe. Her own monthly visits to the local Gendarmerie to have her papers stamped had been interminably unproductive until she had realized the necessity of bribing the clerks. Since she found herself quite unable to argue against his conviction that governors and governments existed for the sole purpose of swindling those committed to their charge, she retired upstairs in search of Micha.

His rest hour was over, but he was still lying on his bed, staring at the ceiling. As he grew older he was moodier and less tractable than he had been and Eleanor sometimes felt that Madame Traskine was actively fighting any control she might have had over him, just for the pleasure of demonstrating the strength of her hold over her son. More and more Eleanor had to disguise the love she felt for Sacha, no longer so much for fear of rousing Micha's jealousy as to guard against the likelihood that Madame Traskine would seek to use her love as a weapon against her, and eventually against Sacha too.

261

She shook the rain off her cape. "Come on, lazy-bones, time to get up."

He flopped over on his face. "What is it for dinner?"

"I forgot to ask, but something good, I hope, because there is going to be quite a party of us."

"I'm tired of the guests we have here, I wish we could go back to Kharkov."

She had been wondering how she was going to make him face Berdeyev and this seemed as good an opening as she was likely to get. "Well, today is different, so it will be a pleasant change. The governor has come to have a look round Nipocritiy and find out how we are all doing in the rain, so he will dine with us."

He settled back on his bed. "I'm not coming, I hate him!"

"You must come, you are only repeating wicked gossip and it is not kind. You are a big, brave boy now and must not pay attention to such childish fears."

"Mama says he has the evil eye, she will not make me come." He turned over again and closed his eyes.

She did not know what to do. She could hardly criticize the boy's mother openly to him, but if she insisted on his obedience as she ought, then he would exploit his mother's attitude to create an endless series of tearful scenes, which would certainly be extremely embarrassing both to herself and to Berdeyev before his junior officers. In the end she left him, but with strict instructions to Theodosia that under no circumstances was he to be given any dinner.

"If he will not come downstairs for it, then he cannot have any," she said in his hearing, but he only hunched a shoulder and would not look at her.

"Ah, the poor little one, thou art frightened, my dove," cried Theodosia, hugging him tightly.

"You are not to sympathize with him!" exclaimed Eleanor. But she knew it was hopeless; as soon as her back was turned Theodosia would be tiptoeing down to the kitchen and bringing up dainty morsels to tempt her young master's flagging appetite.

It was therefore in a somewhat brittle mood that she went downstairs, to find the party already seated around the table. She slid quickly into her place beside Micha's empty chair, murmuring an apology for her lateness, confused by the certainty that Berdeyev would know why Micha was not with her.

"Who shall blame you for being late at such a gathering as this?" replied Madame Traskine disagreeably.

One of the officers whom Eleanor knew as Kyril Nicol'itch cleared his throat uncomfortably and turned to Berdeyev. "Is there any news of the war, Excellency?"

"Yes, Lieutenant, there is," he replied. "The English and French landed at Varna and our troops pulled back to this side of the Danube three or four weeks ago, although the news has only just reached here."

"Back across the Danube?" echoed one of his companions, Boris Ivan'itch. "It isn't possible, the miserable English and French could never defeat our army in a year, let alone a few weeks."

"There has been no battle except with a few Turkish troops outside Silistria. The army has withdrawn in the face of a threat to its flank and now the Austrians have occupied the Danubian provinces."

There was a stunned silence. "I don't believe it," stated Kyril flatly. "The Austrians are our allies, they would never side with the Infidel against the Holy Church."

"What everyone forgets," observed Berdeyev mildly, "is that the era of the Crusades has been over in Europe for the past many hundred years. We are out of date and Europe is not interested. What they are interested in is finding Russia one day on the shores of the Mediterranean or the Indian Ocean and they will do anything to stop it—including allying themselves with Infidels or the Devil himself if need be."

"You take the defeat and disgrace of your country very quietly, Your Excellency, or is it that you are happy so long as you can stay in the back area growing rich in idleness off the stores that flow through Kharkov?" mocked Madame Traskine.

"My God, is there nothing you won't say?" he demanded, almost too startled to be angry. "I have fought for my country many times, Marya Fedorovna, and I serve now as best I can. I am but stating facts which I made known to His Imperial Majesty on my recent return from Europe. Blindness will not help us now, any more than the senseless slaughter of our best troops, my own comrades. Least of all will petty quarrels among ourselves."

"The day will come," broke in the third officer, who had been silent until then. "The day will come when we will teach the rest of Europe a lesson they will never forget about the greatness of Russia, and sweep the corruption of the West out of the way forever!"

Ignoring Berdeyev's warning look, Eleanor moistened her lips. "You are quite wrong. I wish you could go to England and see how we are ruled, with a free Parliament and laws which everyone respects. Everyone in absolute freedom and—" She broke off, unable to give them any sense of the atmosphere of England, and ended softly: "It is a wonderful country and I love it very dearly."

"Parliament! A pack of overfed, scrounging rascals crying up their own wares to get themselves elected and then forgetting everything except themselves until the next time! Our Russian comradeship and the strength of the *mir*[1] is much above that!"

The other two chimed in like a chorus. "Ignàt is right—look how your people are herded into factories and left without land or a village to go back to! Why, our peasants are unspoiled by money and share everything. However far they go or however long they work in the towns they have the right to a piece of land and a place in their *mir* to come back to! We will never have beggared, landless mobs like yours!"

[1]The village community.

"This topic is now closed," interrupted Berdeyev coldly. "Miss Lovell is a guest in our country and it is the height of discourtesy to speak as you gentlemen are doing in her presence."

"They are my guests and they have a perfect right to talk as they wish in my house, for all that you may treat it as yours!" cried Madame Traskine shrilly.

"As you say, of course, Cousin," responded Berdeyev politely. "I am merely reminding them of their rightful conduct as officers in His Majesty's service, which reminder I trust they will not lightly disregard."

The three officers stiffened angrily and Ignàt dropped his hand to his sword, but after a moment thought better of it and changed the gesture to one of smoothing his tight-fitting tunic.

Madame Traskine knew no such restraint. "Then next time you come to Nipocritiy you had better have your meal sent to the bailiff's cottage since you are such a believer in Germans and other Western trash!"

"Madame . . ." Eleanor pushed back her chair, unable to bear any more.

"Sit down, child, I didn't mean you," she said testily. "But to have that German brought here to Nipocritiy without even telling me of it, ordering us all about and making the serfs even surlier than usual, is too much."

To Eleanor's surprise, Berdeyev masked the anger he must be feeling and replied with his customary detached courtesy. "I did tell you, although doubtless you tore up the letter unread. As you know, there have been certain difficulties over consulting with you about matters here, so I have had to proceed as seemed to me best. Since I cannot often come here I felt it necessary to appoint a bailiff who was both industrious and knowledgeable; unfortunately only a German possessed these desirable qualities. If you should wish to talk over these arrangements further I am quite at your service when your guests have departed."

Volodya, a nice-looking boy of about twenty with the broad face and merry eyes of the Great Russian, broke

265

the silence which followed with a tactful inquiry to Madame Traskine about a party she had attended at Chuguyev.

"It was wonderful!" she exclaimed, her mood changing at once. "It is gay over there, although I miss so many friends from last year. Perhaps now the war is over they will be coming back again."

"The war is not over. One battle is not the whole war, Maryushka. We can fight the Austrians as well as the English and the French if they wish it that way," Ignàt declared belligerently.

"Oh, how you do run on about the war, what does it matter if the English protect the Turks or the Austrians camp on the Danube? It is so dull when all you can think of is war, war, war! Soon there won't be any officers left in Kharkov and then what are we poor ladies going to do all through the long winter?" Madame Traskine smiled out of the corners of her eyes, first at him and then at the other young men seated round the table, sending a hot tide of embarrassment into Volodya's youthful cheeks. It was so absurd that Eleanor bit her lip to prevent herself smiling. When she looked up she found Berdeyev watching her and knew instinctively that he also was amused although no hint of it was allowed to appear in his expression.

Ignàt ignored Madame Traskine. "The war is not over, is it, Excellency?"

Berdeyev shook his head. "No. Another levy of six in every thousand souls is to be drafted into the army soon."

"When will Chuguyev be fully mobilized, and the rest of the garrison troops? The last levy has not yet been fully met in this province, has it, Excellency?" Kyril pushed back his chair as if he wished to be off to the wars that very instant.

"That is so, and I doubt whether it will be met before Christmas. I certainly do not intend to mobilize any more men from Chuguyev at present."

266

"Then what about this new levy? My brother in the Ministère de la Guerre in Petersburg wrote to me that already some provinces are starting on this new draft."

"Yes, in the areas around Moscow, I believe, where supplies are more plentiful than here." Berdeyev was clearly unwilling to say more but Kyril belonged to an immensely wealthy family, rumored to own more than a hundred thousand male souls, and he had never had to consider the wishes even of superior officers.

"Then why are so few going from here? Chuguyev is our first reserve and there are still two good regiments left there. I would have thought we would all have been in battle by now."

Berdeyev smiled. "I appreciate your anxiety, but there is no fighting in progress anywhere, except some skirmishes in the western marshes, for which purpose there are already about a million men under arms in addition to our forces elsewhere. We do not yet know whether the English and French will go home now the Austrians have occupied the Danubian provinces. Having come as far as this, I dare say they will press on a little farther for the look of the thing if nothing else, but even if they do I have no intention of mobilizing many more men from this area in the immediate future."

"But you have orders to start raising more soon! By the living God, one would think you wanted these Western barbarians to trample the soil of Holy Russia."

Berdeyev's patience finally snapped. "Your youth is barely sufficient to excuse your manners, which, permit me to inform you, are a disgrace to the name you bear. For your information, there is not the remotest chance of even those already mobilized being equipped or transported to the field of action or receiving sufficient supplies to maintain them there. To strip this area of troops and then mobilize a rabble of disaffected serfs will not in any way assist in the defeat of the Allies but will merely risk an uprising on the scale

of Pugachev's.[2] I suggest you have now exceeded the
indulgence which even your long-suffering hostess is
inclined to extend to you, and it is time you returned
to your military duties, a greater attention to which
would find you better equipped for the war you crave."

Without a word the three young men rose to their
feet, kissed Madame Traskine's hand, and filed out of
the room. They could be heard shouting for their horses
and finding fault with each other for their withdrawal
on the veranda just outside the window.

"It is really too bad of you, they were not on duty.
What will I do for the rest of the day now? This is my
home, although I am sure you would not think it any
longer, and it is not for you to say who I invite or how
they behave. Wherever you go, there is always argument
and unpleasantness." Madame Traskine rearranged
her shawl petulantly.

"There is indeed," he agreed, his face drawn and
weary suddenly. "But there is a limit to the amount of
insult I am prepared to take and it is certainly my concern how the officers of this province bear themselves.
They were all being extremely tiresome, don't you
agree?"

"No, I don't. I suppose you do not believe in the
destiny of Russia or our mission to the commercial
decadents of the West?"

At that his expression relaxed and he burst out
laughing, the first undisguised amusement Eleanor had
seen him show. "My dear Marya Fedorovna! I can see
you have been mixing with the young firebrands at
Chuguyev—it is one of those dramatic young idiots
speaking to the life."

But she would not be diverted and her face was still

2Pugachev led a mass uprising of serfs, Tatars, Cossacks, and
every kind of disaffected peasant in 1771, overrunning vast areas of
country from the Urals almost to Moscow itself. Thousands of landowners and merchants were killed and tortured and several detach-
ments of troops sent to quell the rising deserted to the insurgents.
When order was restored, whole districts had been laid waste and
the government was equally savage in its reprisals.

and serious as she asked again: "Well, do you believe in Russia's future, Nicolai?"

His eyes narrowed and after a pause he replied enigmatically, "Perhaps I was fortunate to come here on a day when you were not entertaining Colonel Suikevsky. You may tell him with my compliments that I remain what I have always been: a faithful servant of His Majesty and our country. Volodya, will you please order our horses, we must not impose ourselves any longer on Marya Fedorovna's hospitality."

"But I do not understand, Nicolai," complained Madame Traskine, flushing. "This has nothing to do with Suikevsky, I was just asking for your opinion."

"And I gave it to you. While I am here I would like to discuss with you the various instructions I have given Spolden before these become a fresh source of grievance. Even if the weather changes soon famine will be unavoidable so long as these fools continue to distill their reserve grain and root up the potatoes. In addition to preserving enough for this area I need to increase my purchases for the army, especially if the British and French invade south Russia, for Kiev and Kharkov will then be the main military supply centers."

"You will need half the army to enforce sales of grain at this time of year! And don't you start taking from Nipocritij until we return to Kharkov, it frightens me here alone."

"Have you had any trouble with the peasants?"

"No, but I hate the way they watch me and if you start seizing grain God knows what could happen." She shivered suddenly, hostility temporarily shelved. "Have you heard of the *starets* here?"

"In the wood over the hill? Yes, I have heard of him. From what I have been told, I can blame much of this potato nonsense on him."

"It is not nonsense. Just look at the rain we've had this year. He is truly a holy man. When he blesses or curses he has the power of God and he is certain that the potatoes are bringing this misery on us. No one in this district questions anything he says."

"Even you, Marya?"

"Well, of course even me," she snapped angrily. "My God, I've even watched one of the serfs die when he cursed her. If he is sure that the potatoes are the source of our trouble, then it will not matter what proclamations you make, you will not be able to keep them in the soil. If distilling is to be illegal too, then the province will not receive its liquor tax and you will not be able to pay for your purchases anyway."

He smiled faintly. "Do you know, Marya, you ought to be on my side, you are much too clever for your own good. Of course the administration has no money to pay proper prices, so I shall have to seize much of the grain I need, for all our sakes. I do not doubt that your *starets* can make potatoes into the source of all our troubles if he wishes, but if I just remove him there will certainly be a revolt, here where I can least afford it."

"Is that all you think of?" Her voice was rising with hysteria and she mocked his tone: "You cannot afford it? What about us, murdered in our beds and probably worse?"

"I have said that I will not do it, but you would certainly be wise to return to Kharkov before the harvest. I will not take over the surplus stocks here until you have left."

She leaped to her feet. "Not even then! The *starets* will tell them not to part with the grain!"

"You will be safely away by then. I must have all the spare grain that is available."

"His power is the power of God, there is no place to go that is safe from that." Scorn and fear made her voice shrill and unsteady. "You cannot stop distilling either; more than half my income came from sales of liquor last year and this year it will be all I get with the harvest so poor."

He kissed her hand formally. "But then if I had

270

usurped your patrimony it would be my income that was suffering, would it not? I will instruct my rural police inspector to keep an eye on you here but do not forget to present my compliments to Suikevsky on the next of his all too frequent visits." He bowed again and was gone, leaving her apprehensive and suspicious, worried by his obvious knowledge of her doings.

It was true that Suikevsky, protected from the rain in a fine black and gold carriage, was a frequent visitor to Nipocritiy, but it was with feelings of unusual relief that Madame Traskine saw it draw up before the house two days after the governor's visit.

Suikevsky heard her out in silence, one elegantly shod leg crossed over the other, his hands beating a slow tattoo on the arm of his chair. He dismissed her fears over a rising at once and fastened instead on Berdeyev's comment over mobilization.

"I fear, Marya Fedorovna, that you must have been very crude in your questions." He laid his fingertips together. "It is clear that he is too wary to commit himself and the province has never been so quiet— damn his soul to hell! He must have friends in high places to have come as far as this with a Decembrist for a father, but one slip would surely be enough: His Majesty is never on the side of anyone from a Decembrist family."

"I know that," said Madame Traskine irritably. "But we need to be sure that the inquiry over the provincial money is closed down too, and then there is Gatchukov still to deal with."

Suikevsky flicked Gatchukov aside. "I could arrest him today and he would disappear forever, but it is not safe as you well know while he is a witness to Traskine's frauds and the inquiry continues."

"And your frauds, Piotr Dmitr'itch, and yours. Do not forget our bargain," said Madame Traskine coldly. "I know quite well why you never reported unfavorably on Alexei when the Third Section is the Tsar's own watchdog over such as he. What a feather in the cap of any colonel of Gendarmerie to unseat a governor, yet you never did it."

Suikevsky did not look up and his hands were still on the arms of his chair, but had she seen his eyes she could not have failed to recognize the extent of her own as well as Gatchukov's danger. Nothing could be proved against him, he had no fear of the financial inquiry Berdeyev must be conducting, but until it was over he could not touch Gatchukov; while Berdeyev was there the inquiry was bound to continue and with it the close interest of the Ministry of the Interior in the province's affairs. If Berdeyev could only be prised loose, then in the inevitable confusion and vacuum of power which would follow, all the loose ends which remained so aggravatingly out of Suikevsky's grasp could be tied up in the interests of the State Gendarmerie. The Traskine estate was only a minor consideration to Suikevsky, one of the many sources of profit which could be expected to accrue when police tentacles were firmly fastened onto all aspects of provincial administration, a process which the death of General Traskine had temporarily interrupted.

Madame Traskine knew that in Suikevsky she had an invaluable ally, had not the *starets* himself guided her choice? But in her self-absorption, she forgot that the mainspring of her action might be but a cog in his. She continued thoughtfully: "He will make many enemies among the military and in the Ministry of the Interior itself if he really intends to ignore orders to mobilize."

Suikevsky stirred, his eyes veiled and secretive again. "It would not be enough for our purpose if the war remains as it is at present. Half the provinces in the Empire are more behind than this with their quotas. If the war spreads and he persists in his disobedience, then there is a chance that I can usefully bring it to someone's notice and we will also have to see what troubles his grain seizures bring." He struck his hands together in exasperation. "My superiors in Petersburg are saying that if I cannot upset a miserable backwoods general I had better go to the East myself and learn his tactics."

"What can it matter to them?" queried Madame Traskine. She realized quite well that the more confusion Suikevsky could spread in the provincial administration the better any dealings he had had with her husband would be covered, but she was intrigued by the way he was able to take for granted the support of the hierarchy of the Third Section in his personal vendetta.

"Their promotion depends on it just as much as mine does," he replied shortly. "We are employed to find irregularities, which everyone knows exist, so if we do not find them the Empire is in danger and we are failing in our duty. When your husband was here my task was simple: I could choose or not choose to get him dismissed, but my superiors were well pleased with what I did report—" He broke off. If she did not know how her husband's venality had laid open everything in the province to police penetration, he certainly did not intend to enlighten her.

"But the longer Nicolai stays, the more difficult to be rid of him. We must not hesitate too long looking for the right opportunity," Madame Traskine pointed out.

"Certainly, but the opportunity must be carefully chosen nevertheless."

She hesitated and then said slowly: "Do you know my English governess Ilena Vassilievna?"

Suikevsky made an inelegant gesture. "Yes indeed. A colorless mouse of a woman with dangerous ideas whom I should be compelled to investigate were she not English."

"Yet we are at war with England."

He waved his hands. "The opinions of West European barbarians are not my affairs. Let them wait until they bring destruction on themselves."

"But she would not have any protection from her government now if you should wish to question her?"

"Naturally not, but I have told you, she is of no

interest to me. I would not be supported in Petersburg if I took action against a solitary foreign woman, be she English or any other nationality save Jew or heathen. At the least I would be in trouble for putting the Third Section in the position of having to support me on such an issue. Dismiss your servants if they displease you, Marya Fedorovna, your domestic plots are unimportant to me. It is our beloved governor and not a half-witted governess who is my concern."

"Precisely." Madame Traskine spoke softly and the silence lengthened until, aware of something behind her words, Suikevsky lifted his gaze from the floor and stared at her.

"What is your meaning? There is nothing between your foreign mouse and our dear Excellency, is there?"

She gave a crow of laughter. "At last your great policeman's intellect has seen what has been under your nose for these past weeks! I am almost sure there is something between him and her, but between her and him"—she paused thoughtfully—"I do not know for certain. Perhaps. But that is not important. It might be sufficient, don't you think, for Nicolai Pavl'itch to be willing to take risks for an Englishwoman with dangerous ideas, now we are at war, as he so delights in telling us?"

Suikevsky leaned back in his chair, whistling soundlessly through his teeth and forgetting even to pose his hands. At last he said, like a man reluctant to believe his good fortune: "You are sure of this?"

"I have told you I am not sure!" she exclaimed impatiently. "But a man cannot deceive a woman very easily and I think I am right as far as Nicolai is concerned."

"Then what do you suggest?"

"You would think it was I who was colonel of State Gendarmerie and not you! I have given you a vital fact that you should have known for yourself and you ask me what to do with it!"

This time he did look up and before the terrible look

in his eyes the laugh froze on her lips. He said softly: "Your words are like the wild animals of the steppe, that toss and stray wherever they will until the day comes when they find themselves within some hunter's bag and wonder how they came there, for they will never again see the light of day." The deceptive, undeceiving veneer had vanished and in its place was naked menace. After another long silence, he added: "Now you will tell me at once the purpose to which you propose to put your convictions about Berdeyev and the Lovell woman."

He dropped his eyes again to contemplate his fingers straying among the silk tassels of the chair covering, but it was some moments before Madame Traskine could make her dry lips obey the behests of her panicking mind. She had been tempted by her acquaintance with Suikevsky to overstep the bounds of respect and obedience with which every Russian treated the secret police and it was only now, when she had gone too far to retract, that she was suddenly shocked into an awareness of the risks she ran by allying herself with Suikevsky. How many attempted to use the secret police for their own purposes and survived to tell the tale? But it was already too late to ask such a question, even if she was willing to give up all hope of recovering her estates, which she certainly was not. She said hesitantly, "I thought—I thought perhaps, as Nicolai is too clever to be trapped, it—it might be possible to use Ilena against—to force him into meddling in police affairs if you arrested or seemed to be threatening her. If he does nothing, then we are at war with England. No great harm is done and she can be released in a day or two. Surely there is something about which you could question her?"

"Undoubtedly. Even to remark that the weather in Russia this summer has been unfortunate could be treasonable under certain circumstances."

Madame Traskine shivered. Newly worried, she was now also half ashamed, but after all no real harm was intended toward Ilena. A day or so at police head-quarters, no more, and for Berdeyev, who was her enemy, she felt no pity. She continued slowly: "I could tell Nicolai where she was and ask his aid. Then if he should intervene you would certainly have a complaint against him, for the Third Section and its actions are no concern of a governor."

Suikevsky shook his head but he was smiling, his thin lips scarcely parted. "In itself it would be a petty complaint and no use for our purpose. But the contrast between his solicitude for our enemies and his refusal to mobilize any further recruits from this area could be useful, especially as he has also held an appointment in London. Certainly he has no authority to make me release her although he will know that I must do so eventually." He tilted his chair and closed his eyes, considering. He had no intention of revealing all his plans, but it was not impossible that in Ilena Vassilievna he had found the lever he needed.

Abruptly he roused and twitched his cloak around his shoulders. "*Au revoir, ma petite.* Forget this conversation for now, it may be weeks before we can move. He must be given plenty of time to mobilize, for it is his failure to do this which can be made into a major issue. Without it all these petty schemes are valueless. Your servant, madame." He bowed mockingly and a moment later she heard the sullen sploshing of his carriage wheels past her windows.

She wept with remorse as the vehicle swung out of sight. She would do all she could to see that their plans were successful but she resolved to be particularly nice to Ilena during the next few weeks.

Nineteen

The weather changed at last and September was breathlessly hot and humid. Everywhere the peasants toiled to save what they might of the harvest, realizing only too well the menace of the coming winter and accepting the changed weather with prayers of gratitude for their forgiveness. But from the *starets* of Nipocritiy and from other holy men as well the word of God against potatoes still traveled far and wide and those crops that were harvested often sparked off violent scenes as they were seized by the government at ridiculously low prices. Apprehensive of the future and deprived of drink, the peasants everywhere were in a dangerous mood as they watched the soldiers and rural police destroy their stills and impound any surplus grain they could find for the use of the army, but the countryside was not yet aflame, the work in hand too urgent to admit of any distraction while the fine weather lasted.

The news that the Allies had landed at Eupatoria in the Crimea was received with the apathy of extreme disinterest, as was the imperial bulletin announcing a glorious victory to Russian arms on the Alma: was not the Russian army the mightiest in the world, for which their taxes, their toil, and their sons were yearly demanded? It was with bitterness and incredulity that the citizens of Kharkov learned that the Alma had after all been a defeat and not a victory. An incomprehensible defeat, for the Russians had been entrenched in the strongest position in the Crimea and still their defenses had been stormed, uphill and under appalling conditions, in the sight of all the fashionable world of Sebastopol picnicking on the neighboring hills.

Struggling hospital wagons began to jolt painfully into Kharkov, carrying the pitiful bodies of British, Turkish, French, and Russian soldiers, too often dead and dying from lack of attention and hardship in the open upsprung carts. There was no room for them all in the small hospital, so part of the barracks was cleared and used, together with some school and warehouse buildings. Those who did not die had only their own strength to thank, for there were virtually no medicines available, no bandages or lint except those wound by the ladies of Kharkov in gay bandage-wrapping parties, and only two doctors who had any skill in their profession.

No one believed the next imperial proclamation of victory, this time at Balaclava, but it was clear that the fighting had been heavy and confused and soon many more terrible hospital carts would be finding their way through the long, suffocating dust clouds to the south to mingle in inextricable confusion with supply and munitions convoys coming from the north.

From the first Eleanor had gone daily to the temporary hospitals although there was little enough she could do except to bring some spark of comfort to men of all nationalities dying far from home, and assist Dr. Mavurian as best she might in his almost hopeless struggles for the lives of men condemned to death long before they reached his care. She had obtained permission for her daily visits from a still repentant Madame Traskine, whose kindness to her in the weeks following Suikevsky's visit had been inexplicable. As the weeks ran on she spent less and less time with Micha and Sacha, and if she had not been so unutterably weary, so shocked and nauseated by what she daily saw, she would have been conscience-stricken by her neglect of them. But the lesser duty was swallowed up by the catastrophe at their gates, unacknowledged and unseen except by some of the peasants women who also came, looking for relatives and to bring small scraps of food and covering for friends and neighbors.

So far as was possible the English and French wounded were separated and put in the Tivoli building, but in their torment it was often difficult and unnecessary to tell nationalities apart. All were bearded, filthy, agonized, frightened, and helpless; mere nationality was no longer relevant.

Every day Eleanor let herself out of the Traskine house at first light, still heavy and stupid from brief hours of restless sleep, and picked her way through the tethered army horse lines in Mikhailovskaya Square to start her morning visits. Sometimes she would encounter one of the doctors and assist him as best she could, but more often she saw no sign of anyone giving the wounded even food and drink and had to labor down the endless rows with water and what scraps of food had been issued for that day. There were twenty soldiers from the garrison on duty at each hospital but most of them had never seen battle and so had none of the old soldier's concern and hardiness, only a peasant stoicism and indifference to suffering which came from generations of acceptance of whatever a harsh and arbitrary fate should send.

When Eleanor arrived at one of the wards they would do her bidding, help her with buckets and distribute such food as there was. Under her direction they would even render what assistance they could to the suffering and remove the corpses of those who had died during the night but she knew that once she had departed they lapsed into lethargy again, talking and storytelling without a thought for the sufferers around them.

At first she had been angry, then despairing, now philosophical: there was so little anyone could do with the means available, least of all these clumsy, unimaginative peasants. She also realized that it was not deliberate callousness which made them so heedless, it was life; if a similar catastrophe should overtake them, they would not themselves look for assistance, or pity, or mediation in their fate. It was ordained. It was enough.

But Eleanor, going from one leprous building to another as the endless nightmare weeks drew on, was not content or fatalistic. As she saw the indifference which was allowing these things to happen, the starvation which threatened the few who struggled their way back from death while gay parties were still given nightly in the city, she was possessed by a cold, bitter anger against the authorities in whose power alone lay the impetus to relieve the distress which in another country might have been achieved by individual responsibility and conscience.

Several times she summoned up her courage and called at the Provincial Government building in Universitetskaya and asked to see the governor but each time he was engaged, or absent, or on a tour of the provinces until she realized that either he did not wish to see her or her messages were not being delivered.

On the last occasion she saw Volodya, abstractedly reading some report, the mud of long travel still on him. He greeted her politely enough but on hearing her request said awkwardly, "As you can imagine, the governor is very busy at the moment. I don't think he is seeing anybody except those with urgent business."

"My business is urgent unless perhaps it is not important to the governor that a hundred men are dying every week in the city's hospitals."

He flushed and replied stiffly: "We do what we can, mademoiselle. I will inform the governor of your concern, but there is little we can do and our affairs are with the living."

She had been so much enraged by his unconcern that she made no more attempts at a meeting, which it was plain would produce no result. After her morning's visits she would change her soiled clothes and sit with Micha and Sacha, too tired and numb to attend properly to them and too bitter and disgusted by what she

280

had seen to care. Gradually, as the humid heat of September turned into more rain and bitter winds in October, in this the strangest of all seasons, even Sacha no longer smiled at her approach and Micha was sulky and rude by turns, for which she was unable to blame him, knowing her inattention to their needs. After they were in bed she would make her way again round the hospitals, an ordeal she came to dread as the evenings grew darker.

By the end of the month it was too dark for her to be able to walk farther than the barracks hospital, but even so the last few hundred yards lay across open marsh dotted with dilapidated shacks and mud huts and she was always relieved when she reached the barracks gates even if the desperately poor people living there usually greeted her kindly enough. The one occasion when an old beggar refused to leave her alone, whining for bread and then trying to snatch the packet of scraps she was taking to the hospital, he was indignantly bundled away by an old woman with a wooden washing paddle although she was scarcely better off than he.

One evening she saw an indistinct figure waiting by the marsh bridge and all her fears reappeared with a rush before she recognized Akim Akimovitch. "I am sorry to have frightened you," he apologized, grinning broadly at her obvious fear and recovering the parcel of food she had dropped in her instant of panic. "Theodosia worries for you and asked me to come if I could to see you safe in the evenings."

He examined her parcel with shameless curiosity and then started to nibble a crust before she could snatch it back, exclaiming angrily, "Even the poor wretches who live in these hovels will not take what I bring to the hospital!"

He shrugged, falling into step beside her. "What is so little among so many? They will all die, either from their wounds or through the crazy wizardry of Mavurian." He crossed himself.

Eleanor clutched her package tighter. "What do

281

you mean? Dr. Mavurian is about the only doctor who is doing his best to help."

"He is a wizard and a demon and those who are under his care will only live to find their souls possessed by him. The *starets* is right indeed when he says it is better to die than to live in such bondage—and always where Mavurian goes, men die."

"Of course they do. What do you expect when he tends the dying and does his best for those in whom life is but a small flame?"

He shrugged again. "Unless he practices wizardry how would some yet live whom God has plainly called to Himself? Why should he labor among those who can have but days or hours to live unless he desires their souls? What else have they left to give him?"

"He is trying all he knows to cure them!" Eleanor cried, aghast. "All doctors are bound to try all they know even if it seems hopeless."

"Then why, if that is so, Ilena Vassilievna, do all the other doctors in the town stay by their own hearths and comfort themselves with wine?" he demanded unanswerably.

"The army doctors are working with him, and I have often seen Dr. Peschenko," Eleanor said lamely.

"Dr. Peschenko, yes," Akim brooded. "But he is not so filled with guile nor has he gathered in so many souls at Mavurian. The army doctors, that is reasonable, they are under orders and secretly they rest and drink and play their cards for high stakes in contentment when none can see them."

They walked on a way in silence until the graceful domes and thin, lacing shadows of the Church of the Transfiguration were etched against the dim light from the barracks before them.

"Where do these evil thoughts take you, Akim Akimovitch?" asked Eleanor forthrightly as they stood a moment under the protecting walls of the church.

"They take me nowhere, *barishna*," he answered somberly. "Except into bitterness, and fear, and for others, starvation and distress. These things cannot be ignored forever. The doctor is capturing their souls for his master the Devil by giving them Devil's balls, isn't he? This sin is a curse on the land and our *starets* has said that surely the justice of the gracious God will strike him."

Eleanor knew that the wounded were being given potatoes because most of them, being foreigners or Russians from other parts of the Empire, had no objection to eating them, but she was well aware that this was not an explanation which either Akim or the *starets* was likely to accept. She wondered whether there was any entrance to his mind, any way over his prejudices, any appeal which he could comprehend. At least he was more concerned for the welfare of his fellows than anyone else she had met, but so many of the things she took for granted were utterly outside his experience, slanting his mind so that there could be little point of contact except liking between them. Yet he was no fool, no idler, no blank-minded simpleton.

She chose her words carefully. "The Devil's balls are only evil to those who believe them evil; the doctor and the administration, and the wounded men who will die without food, do not believe them evil or a trap of the Devil. To them they are the food of life given by God to save them. To you, thinking them evil, it is for you alone whether you eat or not, but to judge others is a great sin, only God can judge."

Now, has any of that done any good? she wondered desperately, as he pondered her words.

Eventually he said: "Yet if we do not judge, all we can do is to send our enemies to God, who is the judge of all, as you say. The *starets* also says that thus we will do God's will. By such means we will rid the land—our land—of the curse which still lies on it. Better for us all to die than live in slavery with an unquiet conscience. Life is not important, *barishna*, yours or mine or hundreds or thousands of others, we all die soon. How we die is important perhaps, and those we

283

take to judgment when we go. It is all the will of God."
His tone was cold and his face unstirred by any doubt
as he looked across the river at the shrouded city beyond, and he was gone before she could stop him.

I should have called him back, I should have argued,
I should have—but what is the good? she thought miserably, as she trudged across the parade ground and
turned into the hospital building, the familiar smell
of suffering and putrescence heavy and nauseating in
her nostrils. With sudden clarity she saw that nothing
she could say, nothing anyone could say, except perhaps the *starets*, would make any difference to his convictions, which were beyond pressure or argument.

She knelt beside one of the patients whom she had
come to know well in the past weeks. A Frenchman
from Marseilles, he spoke the most extraordinary version of the French language she had ever heard, but he
was gay and whimsical, uncomplaining despite the agonizing injuries to his legs from which she feared he
would never recover. Whatever his pain, he never failed
to kiss her hand or toast her health in his miserable mug
of water, or describe the mouth-watering recipes into
which his rancid gruel could be transformed.

But tonight Marcel did not even open his eyes at
her approach, although he knew she was there, fever
only too obviously burning away his last reserves of
strength. Despite the lateness of the hour, after she
had completed her rounds she came back to kneel beside him and this time his eyes fluttered open. A ghost
of his old smile lit their depths and touched the haggard
lines of suffering on his face. "*C'est à propos, n'est-ce
pas, que mon . . . dernier coup d'oeil . . . une très jolie
. . . embrasse-moi, chérie . . . la dernière . . .*" She bent
and kissed his lips: he tried to smile and hold her close
but he could not and his breathing slowly became shallower and shallower, no single moment at which it was
there and then was not there.

She did not know how long she stayed kneeling on
the cold stones beside him, but eventually their dank

chill obtruded her bodily discomfort on her numb, scattering thoughts and she struggled stiffly to her feet, almost overbalancing on her deadened, clumsy legs, before she felt herself steadied by a hand on her arm.

Berdeyev was standing behind her, but her brain could register no surprise at his presence or wonder how long he had been there. She could remember nothing at all of the many things she had so long sought an opportunity to ask that he do. Then she had been buoyed up by a great, righteous anger and horror that such things as she had seen should be allowed to happen, but now she felt only emptiness; no anger, no horror, no pity, not even contempt any longer for callous authority which made so little effort to help. She was very tired.

She was not aware of anything even when he pulled a blanket over Marcel's sightless eyes and steered her away along the difficult length of the room, steadying her as she stepped over sprawled bodies in every attitude of pain, slumber, and death, until they reached a balcony at the end, overlooking the dimly shadowed parade ground and beyond that the ridge of darkness which marked the course of the Lopàn.

They stood in silence a long time, each busy with their own thoughts: Eleanor striving desperately to make use of this chance to intercede on behalf of the hundreds of men whose fates, perhaps, at this moment depended on her. And I cannot even think how to begin, she thought despairingly, trying to drive her weary mind into coherent thought. What can I say that will make any difference when all these long weeks he has not even come to see what is happening?

Finally the silence was broken by Berdeyev. "You wished to see me, Miss Lovell?"

"Yes," she said baldly, tightening her grip on the searingly cold balustrade as if the pain would somehow clear her brain. "I did not mean to disturb you at this time of night, but I wanted—I mean I tried to see you at your office but you were always out or away or—"

"I thought I knew what you wanted and there is nothing I can do for you."

"I don't want you to do anything for me. It is for these poor men dying here for lack of food and coverings and medicines—everything! You must do something for them! Now you are here, come round this building with me and see then if you can stay in your office all day and do nothing, while here, even if they survive their injuries, they are likely to die of starvation. What will happen in the winter when already they are shivering with cold with only one blanket and gruel or potatoes twice a day?" She forgot herself, her fears and doubts, the anger he was likely to feel at a chit of a girl speaking so impertinently, in the necessity of making him see the urgency of the problem, trying to pierce his smug, Russian disregard for life and suffering. She spoke quickly, almost lightly, her eyes fixed on her hands, unaware of everything except this one chance she had been given of perhaps saving a few of the many lives now only represented by endless anonymous moans and tossing figures, and the prayers of families all over Russia, Britain, and France.

She thought he would never reply, but when he turned toward her she was unprepared for the look on his face. Rage or indifference or blighting sarcasm she had expected, but all she saw was a bleak weariness. "I knew that was what you wanted but I repeat, I can do nothing for you. All that I can do I have done. A few will live, the rest will die. It is war."

"How can you speak like that! It is not war here, these men are dying of neglect and you are doing nothing to remedy it! You are the governor, it is your duty to do all you can for them, even if you haven't the feeling of a human being for men suffering and dying a hundred yards from where you rest at ease. Perhaps if you would come round the hospitals with me you would not sleep so well at nights any longer." In a detached way she was amazed at her own temerity, but nothing seemed important any longer except somehow

286

to force his support even if she could not obtain his understanding for her point of view.

Berdeyev dug his hands into his breeches pockets, his greatcoat falling open to reveal the round-necked Russian shirt he was wearing instead of a tunic. "I am the governor as you say," he agreed, his voice expressionless, "and I do not sleep well at night now. There is no need for you to show me this or any other hospital, I have been treated in one and I know what it is like. I would do only harm by visiting what I cannot remedy: where I am, I am expected to have absolute control. In Russia the peasants do not blame the person in authority for what is wrong if he is not there. If he is there, then he is expected to be able to cure any trouble immediately and they will obey any orders he gives to that end, however fantastic, providing they are absolute, definite, and enforced ruthlessly. To request or sympathize or argue is worse than useless, my authority would be gone overnight."

"But that is absurd. Why, if you would come here regularly the patients would be heartened to think they were not forgotten and the soldiers might be more attentive to their duty."

"No, Ilena." He used her Christian name for the first time. "That is an English point of view, not a Russian. If I were to come here as a habit and walk round sympathizing every least soldier would say to himself: 'Oho, Nicolai Pavl'itch, our master, knows not what to do, he is like the dust of the steppe blown hither and thither by the winds of doubt. Let us therefore leave him to his doubt and his sad looks and find ourselves a comfortable corner to sleep, for why should we carry food and water to men who will surely die when our general himself does not know to what purpose are our orders?' If I want to get anything done I must never show doubt or indecision, or ask or request or attempt to reason, only order without possibility of failure or disobedience."

Eleanor considered his words, she realized he was

287

probably right, he had had a lifetime of command in the Russian army. She was shaken too by her attempts to argue with Akim and uncomfortably reminded of the incident when she had asked the house serfs to burn their clothes after the death of General Traskine to be met only with derision until Madame Traskine's orders had reinforced her own attempt at logic. "In—in that case," she ventured finally, "could you not order some more help and fuel and food and medicines for the wounded so that others could do more to look after them?"

He laughed harshly. "I have no food, or medicines, or help to send and very little fuel either, that is why I did not wish to see you in my office. I knew you were obstinate enough not to be satisfied until I had told you the truth, but if I do I must have your word that you will not tell anyone else." Eleanor nodded and he went on, walking up and down the narrow confines of the balcony, limping more heavily than she remembered from the past. "As you know, the harvest was a very poor one, few potatoes were grown, and virtually no grain is left over from last year thanks to the mad improvidence of our peasantry. I bought and requisitioned sufficient stocks to supply the city and Chuguyev and the garrison through the winter and the Department of State Domains has some for the state peasants. The people on the free steppe will look after themselves and the private landlords will see to their able-bodied serfs even if the rest starve. For the sick and wounded, the supply trains, the reinforcements in transit, and the rest of the peasants I have perhaps a hundred and eighty thousand *poods*[1] of grain and fifty thousand of potatoes, no more. If we have a mild winter it may be just sufficient with what was gathered in September but there is nothing to spare. I am sending what I can to these men here, but I can do no more and by doing that little I am cutting my own troops below what I

[1] About three thousand tons.

would normally consider safe, for on them depends the peace of this province."

"Surely you can get what is necessary from other provinces? How about all these supply wagons coming through for the army, could you not requisition some of those on the plea of necessity?"

He took another turn across the balcony before replying, his shoulders bowed and defeated in the darkness. "It would be a waste of time. What the army is getting is not fit to keep a dog alive; the boots have paper soles, the cloth of the uniforms is so skimped they would fit only dwarfs, the muskets have no locks and the modern weapons no percussion caps. Everything is piled into the wagons anyhow with no proper record and then dispatched from the north and in every town it passes through more equipment disappears. By the time it reaches here about half—the most useless half—remains and almost nothing of value will reach the Crimea. Our armies will see this winter through without food or clothes or boots and with precious little ammunition or weapons they can use. Everybody from the contractors down to the pettiest official in the administration is draining the lifeblood of the army, the only difference between them being, that the higher in rank they are, the more they steal. I spend my days trying to bring some kind of order to what reaches as far as here: I have warehouses full of useless equipment and camps overflowing with reinforcements for whom I have no weapons or uniforms or supplies. And still the fools pester me to mobilize further reserves from this area and to enlist a fresh levy of peasantry!" He halted in the doorway and for the first time the dim light from within fell full on his face, drawn and gray and haggard, long lines of fatigue and pain etched deeply either side of his nose, the faint light picking out the sharp angles of face and jaw.

"I am sorry," Eleanor said simply; there was nothing else she could say, inadequate though the words were.

289

Before the bitter anguish and despair in his voice she was powerless to make any more protests.

He turned to her, speaking with a cold precision beyond exhaustion or anger. "You will win this war, but do not rejoice when defeat comes to us through our own incompetence and not through any failure in the field. We will all be the losers through this madness, for the one irreplaceable we shall have lost will be time, and that no man can give us again. The strains of war have already torn to pieces the very fabric of the state which in the past held everyone so tightly they could not move, but through those holes will now escape all the stability and law we had left and which we are so greatly going to need in the future."

"There is no 'you' and 'we' any longer so far as I am concerned," said Eleanor gently, adding with unusual bitterness: "I do not belong anywhere any longer. I feel only sorrow and pity when I look around me here. Russian, British, and French soldiers are alike when they come to die." She hesitated, stealing a look at his face, drained and half shadowed as he stared across at the domes of the city, chill and withdrawn, piled in silvered, mysterious majesty against the faint moonlight of distance. Finally she ventured: "It may not be such a bad thing in the years to come that change has been forced on Russia. Things could not go on as they were."

"No, things could not go on as they were. It is the tragedy of this reign that changes were not forced before with all the rigor of the law and the power which we had. Now we no longer have the strength or the impetus from above in a government petrified by servility and double-dealing and corruption. The only progress that is successful in Russia is that which has its momentum given to it by our rulers; when it is yielded weakly in the face of clamor from below it is simply accepted as a sign of weakness and abused by government and people alike. Self-government or government by the people, even the aristocracy, has no meaning here yet."

Eleanor remembered with surprise that he was the son of a Decembrist and, presumably, a constitutionalist. "You have no hopes of a constitution or a Parliament here then?"

Berdeyev turned on her, his eyes dark. "When I was sent a draft of peasants for my regiment I did not give them loaded firearms. Neither did I give them unloaded muskets in case it should teach them only contempt for a weapon whose mechanism they could not comprehend. I gave them a long apprenticeship and discipline while they watched others more skilled than they, so that when they themselves were able to accept my trust they would not abuse it and would care for their equipment and take pride in using it aright. Not even the highest in the land here understands the working of a constitution, and the finest set of rules that ever man designed is useless against inexperience and indiscipline."

"But there are some people whom you cannot just liken to army recruits, Dr. Mavurian, for instance, or even Akim Akimovitch if you know him? They should not feel afraid that the slightest expression of opinion will put them in jail."

"You mean that I am a narrow old general whose only experience is in the army?" he said disconcertingly. "Perhaps. But human nature does not change very much and I have seen plenty of that. We can learn, but it cannot be done in a hurry. The years ahead of us are going to be more bitter and difficult than you can possibly realize."

Eleanor laid her hand on his arm. "Yet despair and pessimism will achieve nothing. If what you say is correct, you will have contributed more than you know in giving this province order and an incorrupt administration in such a crisis. Perhaps enough time here at least, in spite of the war and the chaos and the suffering which is all we see at present."

Mechanically he covered her hand with his. "Time is not a very inspiring thing for which to fight," he said bitterly. "And I have not given them an incorrupt administration, every man in the government here is as corrupt and venal as elsewhere."

"You cannot know that!"

"More than that, I can prove it," he responded with a flash of his old ironic manner. "Most of the clerks receive about one hundred rubles[2] a year salary and my civil police director five hundred. Perhaps, if he is fortunate, an ordinary policeman or copyist might receive ten or twenty silver rubles a year. No one is paid sufficient to live and therefore if they are alive at all I have proof that they are corrupt. I cannot condemn them, it is impossible to be honest on such a salary. I am corrupt myself, I can get nothing done if I do not pay bribes like everyone else. Suikevsky and his police would have long since taken over here if I did not pay for some of the support I need, for such energy as there is in our government is used up in fighting each other as you must have realized by now. Come, I will take you home, you should not walk around these lanes alone at night." Abruptly his mood changed, his customary indifferent mask slipped back into place as if it had never been cast aside, and he led the way through the crowded wards hastily as if he wished to escape the memory of what had been said.

On the parade ground they were exposed to the full blast of the wind, for the first time this winter loaded with tiny ice crystals; Eleanor shivered and hugged her cloak tightly round her.

"Would you object to riding in front of me, Miss Lovell? I have not brought a conveyance and it is a long walk to the Traskine house from here." Berdeyev reappeared out of the darkness leading his horse, an ugly, raw-boned brute which Eleanor eyed with some misgiving.

[2]About twenty-five dollars.

292

"It will be quite all right for me to walk, please do not worry. I do it every evening," she replied in confusion.

"I am afraid that I am going to give orders for you not to be admitted to any of the hospitals after four o'clock. It is too dark to be safe for you walking but I am sure that unless I make it impossible for you to come you will continue to do so."

Eleanor laughed. "I am not completely sorry to have the decision taken out of my hands! But I can certainly walk tonight."

"After all the delays this evening it is certainly too late for you to go home. It seems a little childish for me to follow you on horseback since I am unable to walk that distance with my leg," he said impatiently.

She remembered that she had noticed earlier how much more heavily he was limping than when she had seen him last and felt instantly contrite. The physical exertion involved in the amount of work he was doing must be a heavy burden on a man who had already been invalided out of active service. "Of course I didn't mean —I mean I would—" She floundered and then laughed again. "Thank you very much!"

It was pleasant to ride home and not have to struggle through endles potholes and dim, mysterious lanes; even the sedate walk at which Berdeyev kept his mount while he picked his way through the treacherous darkness was invigorating. It was over two years since her last ride.

"It is wonderful to be on horseback again after so long," she said impulsively, the words whipped away by the wind.

"I beg your problem?" He spoke in English for the first time that evening and she repeated her words in the same language, grateful for his effort to speak her own tongue but feeling the strength of her homesickness again as she always did when she thought of England. With the change of language she was suddenly embarrassed at her undignified position and his arm round her waist.

"You have many horses at your own home?" She caught the interest in his voice and wondered at it.

"Well, we have the carriage horses of course and my father has his hack and a couple of hunters, but he would not let me ride those! I'm afraid I was always the naughty one of the family and I used to go off on the fat old pony who was used for the dogcart, but when my brother was at home he used to let me ride his. I missed him very much when he was married." Embarrassment forgotten, her voice was wistful and her thoughts far away, treasuring yet again those brief, happy moments in St. Albyn Park with Christopher although that was something she did not intend to mention.

"You mentioned some months ago that your sister was to be married. Have you then many brothers and sisters?"

"Two sisters and a brother, although they are all married now." She was surprised at this catechism.

"So none of your sisters are governesses?"

"No," said Eleanor flatly, running her hand absently down the horse's neck. "He is a fine animal, isn't he?"

"Yes," he agreed, and fell silent.

They were threading their way through the narrow streets which led to the quayside beyond the Church of the Resurrection before Eleanor twisted round to look at him and said awkwardly: "I'm sorry if I was rude. I didn't mean to be. It is just—just that when I speak of my home I feel—sometimes—that I cannot bear it."

"Why do you not go home, Ilena? It is no place for you here, where you cannot even understand the people you are among."

"I think perhaps no one understands what is happening here."

"No," he agreed soberly. "Perhaps we do not but

294

this is our country. For what it is worth, we must do what we can, but it is not yours. Go home while there is still time."

"I don't belong anywhere any longer," Eleanor repeated, "and how could I go home now, in wartime and with not—not very much money?" She was glad her confusion was covered by the darkness.

"It could be arranged if you wished it, Ilena."

She looked at his impassive face in astonishment and then turned back to the road in front, saying with finality: "I would not be welcome if I went."

"But your parents are alone now with your sisters married, they will be glad to see you."

"No!" she cried fiercely. The horse pricked up his ears and pulled momentarily against the reins.

Berdeyev ran his finger down the scar on his face. He wanted very much to know why this woman, whom he loved in a way he had not thought possible, had been cast out of an apparently affluent family and sent into the depths of Russia as a governess, without a home to go to or more than pocket money to sustain her. He still remembered her pinched, undernourished face when he had encountered her in Petersburg and the pathetic gallantry with which she had defied the disasters overwhelming her. It grieved him now to see the sadness in her eyes, the tightly controlled mouth which was surely made for laughter, and the way in which her hair was turning gray before she was thirty. Already he hated her smug parents and respectable family for what they had done, whatever their reasons.

"What age are you?" he asked abruptly.

"Twenty-four. Why?" She was startled by his tone as well as the unexpectedness of the question.

Good God, twenty-four, he thought savagely. Twenty-two when I saw her in Petersburg, and already she is wary and tired as I am after twenty years' campaigning. He said aloud: "I wanted to know. You are certainly too young to waste the rest of your life here. Go home, even if you have to become a governess there."

"I told you, I cannot go even if I wanted to. I have saved a little, but it would not take me beyond Moscow, and after my time in St. Petersburg I do not feel I can chance being destitute again."

"And I have said that I could arrange it if you wished me to."

"You? Why should you—" She twisted round again and stared at him in slowly dawning wonder as she read her answer in his expression. She studied his face a moment, distant and controlled as always but this time with something there, indefinable yet impossible to misinterpret. She turned away again, her heart shaking as she strove to assimilate what she had seen. Inevitably she remembered that other time, over two years ago now, when she had thought that another man loved her and the betrayal which followed. How very unlikely it was that this strange, reserved man should have any feeling for her: someone probably twenty years her senior, of a different creed, way of life, and nationality. On the face of it, thinking of her own precarious and solitary position in Kharkov, it was more likely that he thought of her, as did so many of the men she encountered now, merely as a risk-free diversion, but somehow she did not think so. Surely he would hardly be so insistent that she should leave Russia if that were the case.

At last she said, with an attempt at lightness, the sound of her voice strange and surprising in her own ears: "You are very anxious for me to leave here, Your Excellency."

But he would not be drawn and replied without any warmth or expression in his tone, "I am thinking of what would be best in your own interests."

Silence fell again, broken only by the heavy splashing of hoofs on the mired road and the faint sounds drifting across the river from the city, until they reached the upper quay leading to the Traskine house and entered the dark cavern of shadow thrown by the crowding buildings.

"I can't go home, so I hope you will not use your governor's authority to make me in the same high-handed way you have stopped me going to the hospital." She smiled at him over her shoulder in an effort to break down his reticence.

"May I know why you cannot?"

"Yes, I suppose so, there is no great secret about it." She paused, wondering whether she herself knew the real reason why she had left, whether even her mother could explain. Finally she said slowly: "I was always the odd one in our family, I never knew why, but I just didn't even seem to think or act as my brother and sisters did. What was serious to them was amusing to me and—I don't know! If anything mattered a lot to me, like the way the shadows fell on the field or something I had read in a book, it seemed silly or irrelevant to them and blasphemous to my mother. Even as a little girl I used to run away for the day, as my father still does when he goes fishing instead of to the office! Of course the more I did it the more I was punished and made to stay in and the more I wanted to break out." She hesitated, frowning, but when Berdeyev offered no comment she continued doubtfully. "My mother is very religious and she grew afraid of the influence I would have on the others and—to her, you see, life is desperately serious, a service dedicated to God, and she saw my—my heedlessness as a terrible and dangerous sin which would destroy me and all I touched and in the end—I think—grew afraid of what I would do. I think perhaps she thought that by coming to Russia I would work out my own expiation, that it would be the right thing for me as well as safer for the others. I hope you are not insulted if I say that she probably thought I would not find anywhere sufficiently testing in England to work out a satisfactory expiation!"

He still did not speak so she drew a deep breath and continued with difficulty. "She—she had a ruler which she used to use to punish me—us, but one day she picked up my father's ebony ruling stick by mistake and—" She flexed her hand thoughtfully. It still ached occasionally, but it was the bitter reminder it gave her of her last months at home which was greater than any physical hurt. It was a relief to talk about it after so long, but she found that she still could not put into words what she had felt when first Christopher, then each of her family in turn had rejected her, had made it clear that she was not worth the effort of helping.

She felt him rein in his horse, realized they were outside the gates of the house and that his hand held hers gently, his fingers running over the ridges still to be felt there. "That was the reason, wasn't it? I wondered about your hand when I saw you on the *Neptune*." He kissed her fingers lightly, his face still and inscrutable in the faint moonlight. Impossible to gauge what he was feeling or how his thoughts were running or at the deep rage which possessed his body and blurred her face before his eyes.

After a moment in which he neither moved nor spoke, childishly piqued, she plunged on. "It was not the only reason. Most of the land at home is owned by the—by one family, and the son of the house was home before entering the army. He wanted to marry me—" She broke off, her eyes clouded and her mind back among the haunting memories of that long-distant summer. She had tried not to let herself think of Christopher, not even to wonder whether he might be in the Crimea and not too far separated any more, but the happiness that had been hers was still vivid in her mind as was the aching loss which had followed, not only of love but of pride, of dreams, of hope. "I gave him every chance to decide for himself, for I knew it would cause a great deal of trouble, for we are not of their world, but he was quite determined." She swallowed painfully. "Somehow his father must have talked him out of it, for I don't think Chris—that he was ever told we intended to marry. He went off into the army and of course all this confirmed my mother in her opinions of me and I didn't care what happened anyway, so I came here and you must see I cannot go home again, there is nothing for me there, nothing."

"No," he said heavily. "Come, Ilena, I will take you inside."

"You—you are not angry with me?" she faltered, upset by his harsh expression and lack of sympathy. Surely if he felt for her at all he would at least offer some reassurance or comfort?

The grim line of his mouth relaxed. "That would be impossible, my dear." He held her lightly a moment as she slid down to the ground, but then turned away toward the house.

She was conscious of disappointment, of chagrin, almost of fear at his unpredictability, his difference from everything she understood, as well as irritation with his silences and the inscrutable control he kept over his every expression and emotion. She was still wondering at her own reactions and trying to sort them into some kind of order when the front door opened and a long line of light stretched across the courtyard toward them.

Twenty

It was the most unfortunate of encounters.

Suikevsky was in the hallway making his final adieux to Madame Traskine, his elegantly manicured hands gracefully emphasizing the depths of his bow, his handsome face mocking as he protested the heights of his devotion.

Both parties to this unexpected meeting were almost equally taken aback, covering their surprise with conventional greeting, but Berdeyev did not miss the swift glance of triumph which passed between Madame Traskine and Suikevsky and he frowned; he was used to ostracism and hostility and was not particularly worried by it, but here the feeling of trouble was so strong as to be tangible.

"But delightful, my dear General, delightful," purred Suikevsky, flourishing his glittering helmet, "and my dear Mademoiselle Ilena too. A charming evening for a stroll, is it not?"

"If you like a full gale and the first snow of winter, why, yes," Berdeyev replied, bowing to his cousin. "Miss Lovell and I encountered each other at the barracks hospital, however, which doubtless you know by repute even if your duties do not take you anywhere so unpleasant."

Suikevsky shuddered affectedly. "Indeed no! Life in the raw I find singularly trying, and there I have no doubt it is very raw, is it not?"

"Those whom your police are at present seeking will doubtless be pleased to hear of your dislike of—er—rawness," observed Berdeyev dryly.

Suikevsky looked pained. "Unhappily, as you know, dear General, one's scruples have to be subordinated to the interests of the state, unfortunate though it may be. You do agree with me of course?"

Madame Traskine and Eleanor stood, tense and silent onlookers as the two men watched each other, their antagonism scarcely disguised any longer. Eleanor glanced distastefully at her employer's avid expression, her lips parted in excitement, anticipation, and pleasure, and then at Suikevsky, his face smiling and suave, dominated by the cold intentness of his eyes. In that instant he looked a very dangerous man.

"I know of no honest scruple which would be a disgrace to the country we serve," said Berdeyev deliberately. His wet clothes and loose Russian shirt contrasted with Suikevsky's exquisitely tailored sky-blue and gold brilliance, and in the bright light of the hallway his face appeared almost bloodless.

Suikevsky's smile broadened as he studied the condition of his adversary. "You look tired, Your Excellency. Are you sure that your injuries permit you to give sufficient attention to your duties in Kharkov?"

"If I am tired it is with my duties and not my injuries, from which I have long since recovered," replied Berdeyev shortly.

"And yet I fear you are being somewhat forgetful, or shall we say that you are allowing fatigue to overrule your judgment and possibly even your sense of —self-preservation?" Suikevsky's tone was as soft as ever.

Berdeyev's eyes narrowed. "Explain yourself, Colonel."

"It is always distasteful to have to listen to these things, Excellency, but I have information that the latest batch of mobilization orders have not yet been issued for this province or for the remaining reserves at Chuguyev."

"Your predilection for gossip has not misled you on this occasion."

"And yet—correct me if I am wrong, I beg you— I understand that instructions have been issued in Petersburg for this to be done?"

"The arm of the Third Section is long, Colonel, and again your information is correct. But you should deliver a reprimand to your informant; I have discretion as to how I implement these orders."

Suikevsky showed polite interest. "And for how long do you propose to exercise your—ah—discretion?"

Berdeyev smiled faintly. "The Third Section is not yet pulling every string in the Ministry of the Interior, Suikevsky. You may comfort yourself with the reflection that during the course of time your curiosity will doubtless be satisfied. At present I have neither the facilities nor the supplies to maintain even the reinforcements already passing through Kharkov. I am sure you will forgive me if I retire now so that you can discuss my shortcomings at your leisure. Your servant, Marya Fedorovna, Miss Lovell."

Eleanor lay awake for hours that night, watching the dark shadows of her whitewashed ceiling gradually fade to an even gray as the weather outside thickened from drifting ice particles to isolated snowflakes and then into the first heavy snowfall of winter. The events, the words, every movement of the evening passed in jumbled review before her open eyes, sometimes hopeful, sometimes mocking, always obscure, and lost in a tangle of surmise. No single fact emerged clearly: she had been sure, for a fleeting moment in the darkness, that she had read love in Berdeyev's eyes, had sensed it in his bearing. She could still feel the touch of his lips on her fingers, but his manner had remained so detached and calm that it was hard not to believe herself mistaken. Within a very few minutes, in the clear light and sudden crisis confronting him in Madame Traskine's hall, he had shown all the signs of a man completely in command of his emotions, bending the full force of his mind to his position and the discomfiture of his enemies.

Even the condition of the wounded, which she felt sure would be rectified if only the authorities could be jolted out of their callous and incompetent indifference, was revealed in all its stark grimness. What could be done was being done and she knew sufficient of the Russian winter by now to realize that the reckoning for this insane war had not yet been met even fractionally. Berdeyev's face, defeated and exhausted already by a losing struggle against the overwhelming weight of indifference, incompetence, and robbery, which was draining the means of bare subsistence from the army before a shot was fired, was a bitter illustration of the odds the Russian people had piled against themselves. She could guess dimly how he felt as he had to watch, powerless in spite of his efforts, the inevitable decimation of men with whom he had doubtless served, through the heedless folly which had committed them to a battlefront a thousand miles from their sources of supply without the most elementary precautions being taken to ensure their survival, let alone victory.

At this stage in her reflections she turned over uneasily, unable to balk her own feelings any longer, confused as they were. It was not her anxiety about the wounded or even her pity for the great silent country around her which was in doubt: in the honesty which comes with the quiet hours of early dawn, she forced herself to face the issue she had been subconsciously avoiding all through the long night. Suppose Berdeyev did love her enough to ask her to become his wife, unlikely as it seemed, what would she reply? What would she do? What would she say if he asked her today, tomorrow, next week? It was impossible not to feel happiness and warmth with the realization that somewhere there was somebody again who cared for her as a person, however slightly; who might feel concern if she were ill or unhappy. But doubt struck very deep, doubt of his motives, of the truth and strength of what she thought she had seen in his face, and above all of the man himself whom, she realized, she scarcely knew and—in the clarity of the moment—did not love. He was the one Russian she had met whom she could and did respect, whose integrity and purpose she believed in, and his attraction for her was undoubtedly enhanced by her solitude, loneliness, and total insecurity. But that was all. She found it impossible to visualize him as a husband and the chill, familiar fear touched her at the thought of his cold certainty of himself, of the unwavering strength of purpose devoid of warmth or emotion which he had exhibited throughout the past difficult year of office, facing a degree of opposition and ostracism which would have defeated a less hard and self-contained personality. It might be dull and depressing and lonely as she was, but at least some of the fear that had ridden her and the bitter hurt which had haunted her every craving for affection was fading, locked out of her mind and heart. Only the emptiness within betokened the gradual withering of all that was spontaneous, loving, and gay in her generous nature.

For I don't think I can stand being hurt again, she thought dismally, and if what happened with Christopher could happen when I loved him, what would it be like with someone whom I don't love and could easily be frightened of? Security and cessation of her uncongenial labors could not be bought at the price of her delicately balanced and hardly won peace of mind.

At this unhappy point in her reflections she fell into an uneasy slumber at last, to awaken two hours later, heavy-eyed and still desperately confused in mind, the impersonal clarity of the previous night as unreal as a half-forgotten dream.

She went about her duties and her visits to the hospitals during the day in a mist of exhaustion and abstraction, half fearing, half hoping to see Berdeyev so that she could test her reactions to him. But as day followed day and then slipped imperceptibly into weeks while still she did not see him, she realized, with what she told herself was relief, that she must have been mistaken and tried to dismiss the matter from her mind.

With the onset of winter, but before the heavy frosts, the roads became impassable and there was a welcome relief from the convoys of sick and wounded from the south although from the north and east, where winter came earlier, jostling supply trains, straggling lines of reinforcements, and long strings of half-broken steppe ponies still poured through the city.

A thin trickle of British and French officer prisoners coming into Kharkov were the first sign that the roads to the south were clearing again. Before, the only fellow countrymen Eleanor had seen were too sick and wasted by privation to be more than so many patients to her, but now she was suddenly excited, wildly excited, as the groups of prisoners arrived and she mixed for the first time in over two and a half years with young men of her own age and country. From them she heard eye-witness accounts of those distant events which were only names in Kharkov, of the charge of the Light Brigade, the confused struggle at Balaclava, the night action at Inkerman, and the long, bitter siege of Sebastopol.

"The Russians can fight if they've a mind to, Miss Lovell," said one of the officers, Alexander Lennox, a cavalryman whose baby face was rendered absurd by a large, bristly mustache of which he was inordinately proud. "But they have no initiative. Put 'em in a spot and tell 'em to fight and they'll stay there till they're dead, but leave something to chance or expect them to cover up a mistake or turn the tide of battle by a sudden bit of daring and they're lost. George Steward here swears their cavalry has the heaviest hands on a horse he ever saw but I don't know; I always heard their Cossacks were murder but we haven't seen any."

"They're all right," observed Steward comfortably, "though I must say one would have thought they would be used to their own beastly climate even if we aren't, instead of which they are dying as fast as we are. Faster in fact."

"There is a lot of disease then?" asked Eleanor quickly.

"Oh, quite a bit, you know, same as always on campaign, but it's chiefly supplies. Everything we need outside Sebastopol packed up one deathtrap of a trail and the wretched horses chewing each other's tails off with hunger."

"And the Russians are the same?"

"I think so." His face wrinkled in puzzlement and the ridiculous mustaches drooped comically. "Can't understand it myself but they seem to have precious little of anything, although except for Sebastopol, where you'd expect them to be short, they are not cut off like we are. We never capture anything worth having from them either and I did hear their ammunition was rationed. If only we had a few more men and supplies and it wasn't the worst weather the Crimea had ever known, it would be the easiest victory we could wish for."

"Too many ifs and buts, old man," chipped in his friend lazily. "Unsound military thinking. You'll never make a general whatever your doting young woman in Scotland may think!" Lennox threw a cushion at him and the argument degenerated into a good-humored scuffle on the floor, so reminiscent of the nursery before John was married that Eleanor felt again the rush of homesickness that increasingly threatened to overwhelm her with the advent of the British prisoners. The free and easy informality and lighthearted chaffing that the half dozen officers brought with them wherever they went in the city was like a breath of youth and zest from the past. For they went everywhere, Kharkov feted them as if they had been returning heroes in their own land, and all the hostesses vied with each other to invite them to balls, soirees, card parties, theatrical entertainments, and any other kind of diversion ingenuity could suggest. There was no question of their being confined or treated as enemies; they were novelty and Kharkov surpassed itself in an effort to extract the utmost enjoyment from the situation and to help them forget any chagrin they might feel at their capture.

Neither the depressing news from the front nor the strict regulations regarding the distribution of food made much difference to the scale of social life in the city. The one, they felt, was none of their affair and the second could easily be circumvented by transporting what was needed from their country estates, heedless of the consequences.

Eleanor felt strangely ignored and remote from these festivities; she was invited to few parties, for the events of last year's ball had not been forgotten, and if she were, however hard she tried she could not join in the lighthearted gaiety when she saw each day men dying from inattention and starvation only a few hundred yards from the brightly lit ballrooms. She also found that, though she longed to be with the British officers every moment of her time just for the joy of hearing their English voices and cheerful banter, she had lost her old spontaneity and they were uneasy and unsure of themselves in her presence. She no longer shared their outlook, and the sorrow of this was to her yet another deep hurt and loneliness.

After a week the first group was moved on to a central depot at Riazan, south of Moscow, but they were soon followed by others and a fresh, lavish round of entertainment was launched at each new arrival. Some Eleanor saw and welcomed; many were a faceless scarlet and blue relief from the endless green and gray of the Russian troops, no more: come and gone like a faint beckoning call from England, reminding her of what she had missed and underlining all she could never now have.

She saw little of Berdeyev either, sometimes a glimpse of his back as he inspected the remounts in Mikhailovskaya Square or a distant bow as he rode on his way to check more of the supply wagons parked in the cattle market, their pathetic, useless, half-empty loads a searing daily reminder of the rapacious hands and light-fingered peculation that bedeviled their route south and ruined the manufacture of the little they did bring. Cardboard boots, thin cotton greatcoats, inadequately salted and rotten meat, bullets already cracked, and powder incombustible at the touch of a match littered the supply areas of the city with endless rubbish dumps. What little was worth further transport to the Crimea was collected and reloaded into carts and sledges, to which were harnessed all the fit horses and oxen taken from the other abandoned transport. Even these would probably be sold off by their drivers, the governors of other provinces, or the army supply authorities themselves long before they reached the front, but it was the best that could be done.

All through those long weeks Berdeyev held to his resolve not to mobilize any further reserves or call up another levy from the province. Only he knew, and

Suikevsky guessed, the endless series of threats, orders, and demands from Petersburg which bedeviled his existence and exacerbated his temper. He doubted whether his careful reports explaining his reasons were ever read; orders had been laid down, so let it be done, regardless of cost, of futility, of riot, rebellion, or starvation. He knew as a soldier the utter uselessness of sending untrained, unequipped, doubtfully officered peasants to a front five hundred frozen miles away to fight against trained, professional adversaries, whatever deficiencies those adversaries themselves were suffering. He also knew the stark peril of denuding an already underfed and disaffected countryside of the few trained men he still retained under his command, then gathering together and arming the fittest peasants in the area. In spite of all his efforts, he was also well aware that the time for which he could refuse to carry out the very strict orders he had by now received was limited. A month, six weeks perhaps, would see him replaced, possibly facing exile or worse, if he did not comply. The few priceless supplies he was managing to conserve for the army, the complex organization he had built up to protect the province from the worst effects of the famine already raging elsewhere, the bare minimum he had been able to do to ensure life to the strongest of the wounded, all this would be swept away and his place taken by another of the endless procession of hungry-pocketed, vapid-headed nonentities produced in such quantities by official Russia.

* * *

Sundays were the one day in the week when Eleanor did not visit the hospitals in the morning; instead she attended morning service and afterward went to lunch with the Braillards as she had always done. Mrs. Braillard kept open house for the British officers and Sunday lunch there was an occasion to which Eleanor looked forward all week.

It was on the last Sunday in February, a bright and bitter day which pulsed life through the most sluggish veins, that Eleanor walked into the Braillards' parlor as usual and saw Christopher across the room, shabby in battle-worn remnants of the blue and gold of the Light Dragoons, but as debonair, as disturbing as she remembered him. She was instantly aware of him and his every movement, standing frozen in the doorway when he looked up, laughing from what he was saying, and met her horror-stricken gaze.

For a terrible moment she thought he had not recognized her, then he pushed his way through the chattering group by the stove and came over to her, a wide welcoming smile on his face. "Well! If it isn't Nell Lovell! I wondered whether I should see you on my way through Russia." He squeezed her hands and laughed at her in the way she remembered so well. "You are certainly not the buxom country girl I knew, what has Russia been doing to you?"

But even under this unintended insult Eleanor stood mute, unable to penetrate the shock which grasped her tongue, horrified at his presence and to find her love, which she had hoped was forgotten and over, was still alive and agonizingly real. Eventually she managed to say stupidly: "I—I am quite well, thank you."

"That's a fine welcome for a man after nearly three years! What have you been doing? Tell me all your news and how you like it here."

It is as if he had forgotten all about us, she thought numbly. It really meant nothing to him, nothing at all. He would say the same if he met one of the vicar's daughters in London. Unresisting, she allowed herself to be drawn over to the stove and introduced to a fresh group of prisoners, all, she gathered, like Christopher, survivors from the heroic action of the Light Brigade at Balaclava, spoken of with awe and mystification even in Russia.

"May I introduce to you Lieutenants Macreary and Somers? This is Nell Lovell, whose family lives very

309

close to us in Sussex, we've known each other since I was in short coats." Christopher grinned.

That we did not! thought Eleanor indignantly, mechanically acknowledging the bows of the men. I only ever spoke to you about twice before that year; the timber merchant's daughter and the heir to all the St. Albyns met at church and Open Days and that was all. I wonder whether he has convinced himself that it was truly nothing but a flirtation to pass the summer, or is he as ill at ease as I underneath?

Ill at ease he might be, but if so he hid it very well and even Mr. Braillard emerged from his usual abstraction to smile at his outrageous sallies and extravagant wooing of Mrs. Braillard. He had grown, Eleanor decided, watching him covertly while she ate her untasted food; he was more sure of himself without abating in the least the gaiety and ready laughter she had loved so much—did still so painfully and unexpectedly love. His drooping cavalry mustache was still thin and half grown, his fair hair and tattered uniform emphasized his youth, but his bearing was now that of a man who has found his strength and is pleased with it.

Immediately the endless meal was over Eleanor made her escape but as she walked down the stairs to let herself out of the house she found Christopher waiting for her at the door.

"You are off in a great hurry," he said, smiling. "I thought I would walk home with you if you didn't mind."

"I'm not going home." She spoke as coldly as she was able. "I'm going round the hospitals in the town."

He grimaced. "Not much in my line, I fancy, but I'll come with you anyway."

"You needn't trouble."

"But I want to! Come, Nell, you never used to be as forbidding as this with me, what's the matter?" He followed her out of the house.

"What's the matter?" she echoed chokingly. "Do you really remember us as just old family friends and

310

nothing more? Is that really how you remember that last summer I was at Mayhurst?"

He slipped his arm through hers. "No, of course not, but I can't very well kiss you in the street or in that extraordinary old woman's parlor! How did you think I should introduce you to my friends—the girl I loved for a few months and then like a fool parted from and thought I'd lost forever?"

"No, because it wouldn't be true," she said sadly. "Be honest with yourself and with me this time, Christopher. I'm not a girl any longer."

"I think perhaps it is true," he said, glancing at her out of the corners of his eyes, puzzled at his own feelings and speaking them aloud. "I have thought of you often, Nell."

"Yet you hardly recognized me when I came into the room this morning," she said tartly, but her heart was beating wildly, the old spell of love and joy was on her again, bubbling in happiness through every chink in the protective armor her hurt and disillusion had built against him.

"I will recognize you next time and go down on my knees to you wherever it may be, declaiming *mea culpa* at the top of my voice!" he promised, and abruptly they both burst into laughter, almost hysterical on her part. It left her cleared and free of resentment and unhappiness at last, rejoicing in the blue sky, crackling clear air, and the presence of the man she loved again at her side. Together they pushed their way through the jostling, gesticulating throng in the Bazaar toward the small central building which housed one of the temporary hospitals.

"I say, Nell, don't go in there!" he exclaimed, wrinkling his nose at the terrible smell of human suffering and putrefaction greeting them at its entrance. "It is not at all the thing for you."

"I must go; they look forward so much to my coming."

"What can you do? You know nothing of wounds

or sickness, and it isn't right for a lady to go into such a place."

"It wouldn't be right if I didn't go, and I have learned a great deal about wounds and sickness lately. I used to help carry food and water to them but there is less to do now the fighting has died down for the winter. But there are still many little things I can do which make so much difference to them, especially the British a long way from home. Soon they will be able to close this building and others too, but it has been terrible; I'll never forget it."

He eyed her uneasily. "Why don't you forget it for one day if they are getting better? It looks fun to explore the Bazaar here and it's much too good a day to go moping round hospitals."

She could not explain how she felt, how her own supreme happiness made it impossible to ignore the claims of others on her, especially these pitiful crippled wrecks, to many of whom her visits were a life line of sanity to which they looked forward through agonized night and endless day. "No, Christopher, I must go. You explore the Bazaar. There's nothing for you to do anyway."

He looked relieved. "All right then, if you are sure there is nothing I can do. Should I meet you here later?"

"I have to go to the other hospitals after this one, it will take me all afternoon." She watched the struggle on his face with sadness. But he had changed; this time self-interest was defeated and he took her hand, smiling. "Lead on, my lady. If that is the case, then I'm coming with you, although I have to report back with the others in a couple of hours. The Russians are very good to us but they do like to know we are still here occasionally. Will I be seeing you tomorrow? We are all invited to a party; it would be splendid to have our first dance together there."

"It would be lovely," she said wistfully.

"That's agreed then. What time should I call for you and where?"

"I can't just go to any party!" she expostulated, secretly delighted by his eagerness. "I have to work and already I take many more hours off than I am entitled to for my hospital visits."

"Oh, stuff! Any employer would let you go just once with an old friend from home."

"I could ask," she said doubtfully, "but I am not invited and I don't suppose I will be. I am only a governess here after all."

He laughed. "You could always manage to do anything you really set your mind on! You just ask and see if I'm not right." He kissed her cheek lightly, carelessly.

Even after he had had to go, all the way round the endless crowded floors of the hospitals, all the long, frozen ruts she had to traverse and the steps she had to climb that afternoon, Eleanor was speculating on her chances of going to the party, hugging her re-awakened love and happiness to herself. She did not even wonder at what was happening to her and for the first time she ministered to the wounded mechanically, her thoughts not with them. She realized dimly that, at the back of her mind, she had never quite lost the belief that somewhere she and Christopher would find each other again, that the link between them was simply too strong to be broken by the chances of birth and events.

As often happens when complicated plans are laid to achieve a simple objective, none of the various approaches she had carefully rehearsed to gain permission to go to the party were needed. On her return that evening she encountered Madame Traskine in the hall and before Eleanor could do more than curtsy she said: "Oh, Ilena Vassilievna, I was hoping to see you before I went out. I shall be late tonight and do not wish to be disturbed until midday tomorrow."

"Yes, madame."

"Madame Vershinina is holding a select evening

gathering tomorrow for the English officers and has invited you to accompany me. It is very kind of her to overlook your conduct last year and I trust you will not disgrace me while you are there."

"No, madame, and thank you," Eleanor said meekly, curtsying again, and all that evening, as she played with Micha and Sacha and then put them to bed, she could hardly stop herself from singing.

The following evening her happiness was still a great, heady bubble bearing her along. She knew that the blue dress given her by Madame Traskine the previous year became her, even without the jewelry customarily worn by Russian girls, and the fact that the sharp-eyed hostesses of Kharkov would recognize it in a moment mattered not at all with Christopher. She felt that nothing except themselves mattered any more, and as the Traskine carriage jolted them to the reception over the icy ruts of early spring, Madame Traskine was both startled and puzzled by her governess' glowing beauty: gone were the shadowed eyes, guarded expression, and tensed wariness of past months.

Madame Vershinina lived on the Soumskaya, immediately opposite the Provincial Government building, but as they went by and looked across to see the lights there still burning brightly, Eleanor no longer had a thought to spare for Berdeyev and the problems besetting him.

Twenty-One

Inside the Provincial Government building, Berdeyev was clearing up some last-minute business before himself leaving for Madame Vershinina's. Although the

314

hostility he had at first encountered had now mostly reverted, except among his cousin's private clique, to the eager subservience with which provincial governors and their valuable patronage were more normally treated, he did not particularly enjoy such occasions but found them useful for keeping in touch with gossip, opinion, and likely new sources of trouble.

"There's a rather unusual request here, sir." Volodya came in with a sheet of paper in his hand.

"What is it?"

"A message from the Gendarmerie asking you to call in to give a character reference for someone being examined on suspicion of treason."

Berdeyev looked up at once, all his instincts alert. "What name?"

Volodya looked down at the paper. "Yuri Anton'itch Spevashev. Senior lieutenant, 3rd Don Cossacks."

Berdeyev frowned in an effort of memory; the name meant nothing to him. "Is that all?"

"Yes, Excellency. It just says he was arrested entering the city this morning on suspicion of treason and has claimed acquaintance with you. The Gendarmerie would be grateful"—Volodya's tone was skeptical—"for your help in vouching for his identity."

Berdeyev thought about it in silence. It certainly seemed very odd and anything to do with Suikevsky was suspect. Vouching for someone under suspicion of treason could be a dangerous matter; on the other hand if it was some boy in difficulties with whom he had a slight acquaintance—try as he would, he could not put a face to that name. Finally he said: "I am certainly not going to the Gendarmerie. If the Third Section is in need of my co-operation, then Suikevsky had better send the young man round here for identification. Tell him I am going out soon."

When Volodya had left Berdeyev returned to his papers but he was unable to concentrate. He wondered whether Suikevsky would come himself—would it tell him anything if he did? Uneasily he got to his feet, having to steady himself on the desk as he did so. Recently his leg had become too painful to ignore any longer and he had been attempting, unobtrusively, to rest it as much as possible, a curtailment of his activities which had mercifully coincided with a temporary reduction in the seriousness of the problems facing him.

Late January and early February was the best time for travel; the winter was not excessively cold yet had been cold enough to reduce the fighting in the Crimea to a minimum. Unfortunately this brief lull was now nearly over: a spring campaign was in the making and mobilization orders were flooding in regardless of his protests. Food was scarce and with the increase in military activity becoming scarcer, interdepartmental struggles in Petersburg as in Kharkov were growing daily more bitter as the dimensions of the defeat which awaited the Russian Empire became more apparent, and the search for scapegoats rather than solutions became everyone's most urgent objective.

"Colonel Suikevsky is coming himself, sir." Volodya returned as Berdeyev was changing for the Vershinins' party.

"Did you gather any more of what it is all about?"

"No, Excellency, except that there was some fracas in the fellow's unit this morning while it was camped to the north of the city, but if I rightly understood what was said, then I don't think he was there at the time. It sounded to me as if any charge there might be should have rested with the military authorities for negligence or absence without leave."

"Ah, General, I am glad to have caught you before you went out on more of your ceaseless activities. I am afraid we need your help in a trifling difficulty which has occurred." Suikevsky was as urbane as ever.

"Anything I can do, of course," responded Berdeyev noncommittally. "But I cannot recall any officer of the name you mentioned."

"Not many are anxious to do so where a charge of

316

treason is concerned." Suikevsky was unable to resist the jibe, his good fortune that morning still a source of pleasure to him. "He says that he worked with you in the Department of the Inspector General of Cavalry in Petersburg two years ago."

Berdeyev hastily ran through the rows of junior faces he had briefly known during his months in Petersburg, but his mind obstinately refused to yield up any information at all. He shook his head.

Suikevsky waited, brows raised, a look of pained surprise on his face. "How strange. Yet, according to Spevashev, you chose him for some private duties of your own, so that you would be bound to remember him." He clicked his fingers and two gendarmes brought in a tall young man, wearing a look of bewildered anger.

"Yes, of course," Berdeyev said at once, cursing his own stupidity. "I remember him now perfectly. He was in the Inspector General's department at the time you state, where he proved himself a conscientious and reliable officer."

"Ah." Suikevsky bowed. "Thank you, Excellency. It seemed strange to me that he should so confidently claim acquaintance when falsehood could be easily exposed."

Berdeyev ignored him, turning instead to Spevashev. "I am sorry not to have been able to vouch for you at once. My memory, it seems, is not as good for names as it is for faces. What is the trouble?" He had an uneasy feeling that Spevashev might be in trouble because he had claimed his acquaintance and not in spite of it.

"I don't know, sir!" the boy burst out angrily. "I came into the town and inquired for the direction of a friend I wished to call on. I was whisked into the Gendarmerie, made to wait a couple of hours, and then told there had been a mutiny in my squadron of Cossacks!"

"Who had been jaunting round the country on your

317

private affairs," murmured Suikevsky.

"They had not!" He turned to Berdeyev again. "Sir, I swear I was told in Moscow to find my own way to Kherson with my squadron. It seemed sensible enough, and not much farther, to come by way of Kharkov rather than the usual route from Kursk to Poltava, there was nothing wrong in that. My men were all bivouacked when I left this morning, under orders to move round to the west of the city where I would join them this afternoon. God knows where they are now."

Berdeyev turned to Suikevsky, the warning bells ringing now, loud and long in his mind. "Would you be good enough to explain, Colonel, precisely what did happen, or is this a matter only for the secret police?"

"Certainly I will explain—"

"In that case," Berdeyev interrupted icily, "as it is not apparently a matter private to the Third Section in which I am unable to interfere, will you also explain why such a trivial complaint as this appears to be has not simply been reported to the military authorities?"

Suikevsky hesitated, aware of having been lured into error.

"Well, Colonel?"

"It is not the trivial matter you seem to imagine, General. Who was it you intended to call on, Lieutenant?" He rounded on Spevashev.

"I have told you, Ilena Lovell, the English governess, there is no secret about it." Spevashev was looking sulky now and a little frightened, wondering what he had stumbled into.

Berdeyev tensed but said nothing when Suikevsky glanced at him before asking, roughly now: "Nothing secret when a serving officer brings his unit many versts out of their way to the battlefield in order to visit an enemy alien? Do you think that is creditable conduct? Answer me!"

"No, sir." Spevashev spoke reluctantly though, and added stubbornly: "It was not far out of my way and a faster route for cavalry. I only wished to call on Ilena Vassilievna, as I had said I would two years ago if ever I was in this area. There was nothing whatever treasonable in my intentions."

"You do not think your actions are such as to make that very difficult to believe? You were a staff officer in St. Petersburg, with information to sell, no doubt, when you met this English girl. You did not see her again until war broke out against her country but then you immediately went to immense trouble to visit her, making sure at the same time that the men entrusted to your command will be missing from the field of battle at a time when every man is needed urgently?"

Spevashev's face paled. "It was not like that at all! I met her in St. Petersburg for two or three days and promised to call if I was ever posted down here. Of course I never discussed military matters with her, why should I?"

"Why should you not?"

"Because she would not be interested!"

"Ah. So you did discuss them and she pretended to a lack of interest?"

Berdeyev knew he could no longer stand on the side lines, for any protests Spevashev made would only bog him deeper in the mire of counteraccusation. It was a technique the secret police delighted in, for anything the victim said could be twisted and made to count against him. Somehow Spevashev must be got off the hook Suikevsky had baited before he implicated them all in a fanciful tissue of half-truths which could be made to prove almost anything. He sat down, pretending to more ease than he felt. "At what time did you enter the city, Spevashev?"

"About seven o'clock this morning, Excellency." He seemed clear and steady enough in his answers.

"What did you do then?"

"Inquired at the entry barrier for the address of Ilena Vassilievna."

"Who did you ask?"

319

"The sentry on duty. He did not know and called up a gendarme who was at the post nearby."

"And then?"

Spevashev hesitated, frowning. "It was very queer. He looked at me, repeated the name two or three times, and then took some papers out of his pocket. I thought he was looking up her address or something, but instead when he found whatever he was looking for he called up two of his fellows and brought me to the Gendarmerie."

Berdeyev turned to Suikevsky. "What was he looking up, Colonel?"

It was Suikevsky's turn to hesitate. "Ilena Vassilievna's name," he said finally. "As an enemy alien, all my men have routine instructions to watch her contacts and report anything suspicious to me. We are at war with England, you know, Excellency."

"Yes, I did know," Berdeyev replied gravely. "What happened next?"

Spevashev shook his head. "I don't know, sir, I was questioned for hours. I am sorry if I have caused you trouble but I knew you were governor here and I thought—"

Suikevsky interrupted, quick as a whip. "You knew he was governor and it was he who introduced you to Ilena Vassilievna, wasn't it?"

Spevashev shifted uncomfortably.

"Wasn't it?"

"There is nothing of treason in that." Berdeyev sounded amused. "I asked Lieutenant Spevashev to escort Miss Lovell to Madame Traskine for an interview for the position she now holds."

Suikevsky hooked his fingers into his belt. "Now why should you do that?"

"It does not seem to me an affair of sufficient importance to trouble the secret police. My cousin required a governess who would come all this way; I had met one on the ship from England. As you can imagine, I was hardly likely to give myself the trouble

320

of escorting governesses round St. Petersburg, so I chose Lieutenant Spevashev because I was confident he could be trusted to behave in an honorable and pleasant way to a guest in our country." God forgive me for that, he thought, remembering the humiliating jealousy he had felt when choosing this boy as an escort for Ilena, so much more suitable than himself in every way.

Suikevsky looked skeptical. "You do not think it strange that two and a half years later here you all are, in Kharkov, with mutiny being caused by this young man's infatuation from so very long ago?"

Berdeyev ignored him again. Protestations were useless, arguments were useless; those who spent a lifetime with their movements watched by the secret police, as he had, soon learned that. "I wish to know about this mutiny if you please; this is certainly a military matter which requires to be dealt with."

Spevashev shrugged. "I know nothing about it. They are good lads in my squadron. We have had a rugged journey south with precious little food for men or horses, losing about twenty out of the hundred, but that is less than most and better than if we had gone the direct route where there would have been even less fodder or rations." He glanced angrily at Suikevsky.

"What happened then, Colonel?" Berdeyev turned to Suikevsky as if he were a subaltern of very questionable value.

Suikevsky nodded at one of his gendarmes and the man stepped forward, reciting in a high nasal monotone: "I was on duty at 9:00 A.M. this morning at the north barrier when I heard a disturbance from the unit assembling ready to move off. I went to investigate and found that three men had been found hiding in a hut, in an attempt to avoid marching with their unit"—he glanced at his notebook—"J squadron, 3rd Guards Regiment of Don Cossacks. There was some disorder as there was only a cornet in charge and he seemed uncertain what to do—"

"What have you to say to that, Lieutenant?" Suikevsky interrupted. "I understand your other officer was one of the casualties of the journey south."

Spevashev drew himself up. "I much regret it. I neither expected nor foresaw any trouble if I was away a few hours."

"And?"

"Colonel, could we leave these pleasantries for later? I wish to hear what happened that your police allege amounted to mutiny," Berdeyev interposed again.

Suikevsky shot him an angry look but nodded to his gendarme. There were some disadvantages in dealing with the son of a convicted Decembrist; he at least was only too well acquainted with the habits of the secret police.

"After some discussion the three men were charged with desertion—"

"Whose discussion?" This time it was Berdeyev who interrupted.

The man hesitated. "The sergeant wanted it."

"The squadron sergeant urged the cornet to charge these men with desertion?" Berdeyev's disbelief was obvious. No unit which had lost twenty men out of a hundred traveling halfway to battle would be anxious to lose three more if it could possibly be avoided. Sergeants were practical men.

"He agreed there was no alternative."

"Agreed with whom?"

"With the cornet."

"But we have already heard that the cornet did not know what to do. Now you say he made a suggestion with which the sergeant agreed?"

"There were various suggestions. That was the one the sergeant agreed with."

"Do you mean to tell me that there was a general discussion as to penalties?"

The man looked increasingly uncomfortable. "Yes, sir."

"Where?"

"Well, sir . . . there, near the gate."

"In the open street, in front of the whole unit?" Berdeyev turned to Suikevsky. "I do not believe a word of this man's evidence. However slack and inexperienced the cornet, no squadron sergeant of Cossack Guards would allow such a thing to happen even if he had to march the men out of earshot himself."

Suikevsky looked as if he could gladly murder the gendarme, later he probably would. "There was no need. I told the cornet his duty as he seemed unable to carry it out himself."

"You were there? That seems an unlikely coincidence."

"Lieutenant Spevashev was already under arrest. My men knew of my interest in this unit and once there was trouble they sent at once for me." Suikevsky's face twitched with annoyance at being himself cross-questioned but he could hardly leave matters as they were if he intended to press charges.

"And you then instructed the cornet to charge these men with desertion?"

"It was the correct charge. He was an inexperienced officer and intended to carry out a summary flogging and then forget the whole matter. I am interested to find a general who also apparently thinks that slackness in fighting troops should be encouraged."

The muscles of Berdeyev's face contracted but again he did not argue. "I understand there was also some question of mutiny?"

Suikevsky's voice shook. "I am not your junior officer or answerable to you!" Frustrated rage at last began to shred his accustomed malign calm.

"Mutiny and desertion are both military charges and so outside the competence of the secret police," Berdeyev pointed out. "Lieutenant Spevashev also is subject to military discipline and nothing we have heard so far could possibly substantiate a charge of treason offered in a military court, whatever might be the case with the Third Section. Such a court might well take

323

a serious view of interference by the secret police in military matters once the cornet in charge apparently had decided on the action he wished to take."

"We will see," spat back Suikevsky, thinking of the many generals on whom his department could rely if necessary.

"If you wish to prefer a formal charge, of course, but I certainly could not agree to an officer in the Tsar's own Guards being detained without such a charge being made and substantiated. Where the case is such a serious one, the trial must then of course take place as soon as possible, since we are at war and the lieutenant's unit without officers of experience. As Kharkov is a main supply depot and I am a military and not a civilian general, I have the over-all military command here now and can conduct such a court if you wish."

Suikevsky had not known it. A vital piece of information like that should certainly have been his long since, for provincial governors were not customarily military commanders as well, although it had become obvious that in wartime Kharkov the two functions had inevitably become blurred. In Kherson and Tauride provinces to the south the civilian governors had had military governors-general appointed over their heads and it was dismaying evidence of trust to find that Berdeyev should have been given such an exceptional position. It was becoming clear that this opportunity for attack, so unexpectedly presented by Spevashev's fortuitous appearance, was now likely to prove unrewarding. If Berdeyev was vulnerable Suikevsky had already established that it was not on his military record or professional competence. Besides, as Suikevsky was well aware, the army was the one institution normally strong enough to defend itself against the Third Section and would certainly resent interference in a matter which Berdeyev had astutely twisted into one of military discipline.

All these thoughts raced through his head as he sought for an avenue of tactical retreat. At last he said reluctantly, "The discipline of the unit was poor and it seemed important to make a stand before real damage was done to morale. If I have interfered in the army's concerns, it was only because at the moment His Majesty's interests seemed to demand it."

Berdeyev did not relax but he could feel the sigh that ran round the room. "The mutiny was an attitude and not an action then?"

"Certainly not!" Suikevsky was a resilient opponent and his retreat was only tactical. "One of the men charged struck the cornet in the face."

"My God, I don't believe it!" Spevashev sounded quite incredulous. "None of my men would do that, they all like Cornet Kotlas and they are old soldiers, not raw recruits."

"Nevertheless that was what happened." Even Suikevsky sounded slightly puzzled. "The whole squadron saw it; there was no question over the charge that time." He was on solid ground on this occasion and he knew it.

"So this is the substance of the charge?" Berdeyev looked round the room, at Suikevsky hunched with resentment but vindictive and even more dangerous than before, at Spevashev, who had a look of distant worry in his eyes as if he were considering the men in his squadron one by one, at Volodya grinning at Suikevsky's discomfiture, at the open terror of Suikevsky's gendarme and the greedy curiosity of the other various underlings hanging onto the edges of the scene. "Lieutenant Spevashev was certainly unwise in taking a few hours' leave for a personal visit but I find no other cause for censure. The men in his charge, who unfortunately took advantage of this, will pay the price." His eyes met Spevashev's and he could see the shame there: the penalty for desertion was running the gantlet of the whole regiment, perhaps two thousand blows, which would probably kill or at least reduce a man to a cripple for life; for mutiny the sentence was death. "As Colonel Suikevsky has reminded us, the most important thing is to get all units to the battlefield as soon as possible, so I intend to send the papers in this case to the Kherson Military Command, thus enabling Lieutenant Spevashev to proceed to the Crimea at once with his men, who should not be left under the sole command of a cornet. I believe that his conscience may find some easement in carrying out his duties correctly and courageously, but any specific penalties will be for the military authorities there."

Spevashev closed his eyes. He was a good officer and Berdeyev knew he would blame himself to the end of his life for the mutilation or death of his three men. The cornet seemed to have acted sensibly enough, but no boy of eighteen could be expected to stand against a colonel of Gendarmerie looking for trouble and it was now too late: no sentence for mutiny or desertion could be successfully challenged. He added gently, "Do not blame yourself too much, Yuri Anton'itch, the only expiation for you now is not to fail your men in battle, when they will rely on you for everything."

Spevashev gulped and nodded, unable to speak.

Berdeyev turned to Suikevsky. "Does that satisfy you, Colonel? You can add any complaint your department has to the report I shall send to Kherson."

Suikevsky waved the gesture aside, his composure restored. "Certainly, General, certainly. If you are satisfied with this young man, then I must be too. There are certain oddities in his story which I should have liked further explained but I am sure we must bow to the needs of war."

As he walked over to the Vershinins' party Suikevsky's mind was fixed on the one point in Spevashev's story which he could investigate further without risk. Ilena Vassilievna was not protected by the mighty power of the army, the governor would not be able to plead military necessity or exercise military discipline, or even have the right to inquire into police questioning, in her case. He had waited a long time for the right moment but he now decided that he would wait no

326

longer. Perhaps he would not achieve much by arrest-
ing the Lovell woman, but for Suikevsky the pleasure
of watching his enemy defeated on even a trivial issue
was now enough to justify anything. But he found that
after this evening he agreed with Marya Fedorovna:
he did not think that to Berdeyev this would be a
trivial issue.

Twenty-Two

When Eleanor arrived at the Vershinins' she found
Christopher waiting for her immediately inside the door.
She introduced him to Madame Traskine, who looked
from one to the other with instant understanding.

When Suikevsky came in later she went over to him
at once. "Piotr Dmitr'itch, if you wish to interview
Ilena and through her our friend as we discussed, you
can delay no longer," she said without preamble. "There
is an English officer here whom she knows and who
means much to her."

Suikevsky followed the direction of her eyes and
raised his brows. "As always in such matters, my dear
Marya Fedorovna, no doubt you are right. I am about
to do so for quite other reasons." The anger and
humiliation which had shaken him over since he left
Berdeyev's office was still seething through his mind,
perilously close to the surface, and even Marya Fedorovna was an unbearable irritant. God help anyone his
gendarmes brought in for questioning that night. "I am
going now," he said abruptly. "I will have her arrested
tomorrow on her return from the hospitals. When she
fails to return to your house you are to institute an
inquiry and then inform the governor as if genuinely

puzzled by her disappearance. He has his informants in my office just as I have in his, so it will not take him long to find out where she is, but we do not wish him to suspect any sort of trap. We must trust meanwhile that he does not see her with that half-dressed son of a dog." He nodded at St. Albyn.

There was some justification for his epithet since Christopher had borrowed a tunic considerably too large for him from a friend and a pair of gray breeches piped with red from one of the Russian garrison.

"I nearly didn't come when I saw what a figure I made," he said ruefully to Eleanor. "But it was this or a hussar pelisse and white ducks. I hope you don't mind too much."

"Anything would look all right to me. I don't know what I would have done if you hadn't come." She was beyond subterfuge.

He held her wrist, swinging her hand from side to side. "You've forgiven me, haven't you? I wondered yesterday if you ever would."

She smiled up at him. "When you look at me like that I cannot find anything to forgive. I have been telling myself all these long years that I had forgotten you, never realizing that by doing so I was remembering all too well."

He laughed, flattered that after thirty-two months of time and two thousand miles of distance her love for him should be as strong as ever. But, by God, he thought, I have injured her once, I must not do it again. One evening of fun here and that must be all, I like her too well to wish to see her again as she was that day we said good-by at Abbotsfield.

He saw too her unfashionable dress and graying hair, noticing the lines of strain and tiredness on her face for the first time. She is like a stranger, he thought. Aloud he said, "You speak like a little foreigner now. It sounds as if you were reading your sentences out of an English grammar."

She flinched as if he had struck her, as much with

328

the way he had ignored her shy avowal of love as at his clumsy exposure of her alienation from her own country. "I've hardly spoken English since I left home until the prisoners started coming through," she said defensively.

"How do you find it on your own?" he asked curiously.

Her pride would not let her tell him the truth; to appeal to pity is very repugnant to love. "I—I find it all right, but lonely sometimes. It is lovely to hear English spoken again, the only person except Mrs. Braillard who ever uses it with me is the governor."

"I haven't met him, have I? What is he like?" He was glad to find the conversation taking a less personal turn.

What is he like? she wondered. She said slowly, "He has been very kind to me, but he is too strict and competent to be popular in the city." She had a sudden indefinable feeling of guilt when she thought of him and, as if in tune with her thoughts, saw him greeting Madame Vershinina. "There he is over there, just come in."

Christopher laughed unkindly. "He looks about half the minimum size allowed in my regiment and shaven ready for his winding sheet to boot! Shall we dance this one?"

She was irrationally angry with him for his laughter and mocking words. He took her silence for consent and they were soon whirling round the floor, her resentment forgotten in the pure joy of dancing again, of being escorted to a social occasion and free from the risk of drunken importunacy for the first time in two and a half years.

She sparkled with effort and pleasure and when at the final chord she curtsied to him laughing, he felt his breath catch in his throat as he stood looking down at her, a strange expression in his eyes. She was not strained or unfamiliar to him any more but surprisingly precious. "D'you know, Nell, you are beautiful tonight?" he said slowly.

Her smile faded. "You sound surprised."

"Well, when I saw you yesterday I was a bit shocked, you know. You seemed almost like another person, hard and—and well, older than I remember somehow," he replied disastrously.

"I am harder and older than anything you could remember. Life has not always been easy and I have seen many terrible things since I left Mayhurst." She looked at the floor, blinking back her tears.

He touched her arm. "Don't cry, Nell, I hate to see you cry. That was yesterday, today you are as I always remembered you, gay and laughing and beautiful. Don't spoil it."

"Oh no, I mustn't spoil your evening, must I?" she said bitterly.

"I didn't mean that, you know I didn't!" His brow knitted. "I don't understand you, whatever I say seems to be wrong. As well as not speaking like an English-woman, you don't seem to think like one any longer. I think you should leave here and come home before it is too late."

"How can I leave here? I have begun to wonder these past months whether I belong anywhere any longer, and meeting you and the other English officers has shown me that I don't. I feel as strange with you as you and the others feel with me."

"I don't feel strange with you, Nell, not any more." He tried to put conviction into his voice but the brief moment, when he had looked at her and been startled by his own feelings, was already fading.

She squeezed his arm; Christopher brought so much of the past with him that he shattered at a touch the peace of mind she had thought she valued so much. But in a way it was a liberating process: she was living again and the world around took on a new zest. "Christopher darling! But, whatever happens, I am never going back to Abbotsfield."

"You would soon settle down there again, you are

older now, your mother could not treat you as she did before."

Or your father either, she thought, her heart thumping. "No, I could never settle there. I would be poor Eleanor now—or perhaps Aunt Eleanor whom we can't really introduce to you because she is a little strange in her ways, poor thing. No! A thousand times no!" She could visualize it all so clearly: she would be a shadow on the staircase, a ghost sitting at the table, given charity in her parents' house and then, grudgingly, by John and her sisters for all the meaningless years of her life; seeing the children shielded from her influence, cut off from life passing her by so closely. Her mouth set in a straight hard line below unnaturally bright eyes: better by far to be a governess all her days.

Christopher eyed her uneasily. She no longer looked beautiful. He was worried and slightly repelled by her expression and began to wonder how he was going to extricate himself from a situation which was clearly fraught with all kinds of future difficulties. Across the room there was a particularly attractive young lady who was already dimpling prettily at his stolen glances, the softness of her young figure revealed by a low-cut muslin dress. Her uncomplicated coquetry drew him, yet he was genuinely sorry for Eleanor and did not wish to hurt her. Her intensity disconcerted him also, for he recalled her as a carefree, lighthearted companion, but she had a power over him that he could not deny, which quickened his blood and remained in his memory when he could no longer recall the names of lovelier, more yielding belles. All over again he was beginning to resent the strength of her hold over him, as he had done before, when his feeling for her had nearly led him to disaster. Then he had hurt her deeply in his efforts to cut loose, clamping down tightly on the other half of his mind and body which yearned to comfort the hurt he had caused. Now that avenue of escape was closed by the injustice he had already placed between them, by the astonishing, apparently enduring strength of the ties which, in spite of everything, still bound them.

"Shall—shall we dance again?" he said eventually. "Come, Nell, don't look so tragic, I can't make you go back to Mayhurst if you don't want to go. I only thought it might be the best thing for you."

She smiled back at him but shook her head, her pleasure in the evening dimmed. She could see too clearly his indecision and had intercepted his glance at Madame Bezborokova's insipid daughter.

"Come on, Nell! If you don't want to go home there is nothing to be in the dumps about because you can't! Let's have a good time while we can and leave tomorrow to worry for itself. After Balaclava I don't feel like worrying about the future ever again, that was bad enough to last forever." He looked at her whimsically. "Smile at me, Nell, I don't like you to be angry with me and if I've said anything to annoy you I apologize. I can't say more than that, can I?" He cocked his head at her and pursed his lips, all the old irrepressible fun she had loved so much showing in his laughing blue eyes, so that she could not help smiling back at him. "That's what I like to see!" He bent quickly and kissed her lightly on the lips. "No more gloomy faces for the rest of the evening! What are you laughing at?"

"You," said Eleanor with devastating frankness. "As long as everyone is smiling and gay, everything must be all right. Never mind, perhaps you are right." But she was really thinking how strange it was that a kiss, which an hour ago would have left her in ecstasy, should now not only give her no pleasure, but no sadness either. In a few idle sentences, with the timbre of his voice, the facile laughter which came so easily to him, he had forced her outside herself and her emotions at last. She felt as if her mind was standing coldly and accusingly beside her, forcing her, truly and conscientiously, to look at Christopher for the first time—and to look at herself too, a misfit in her shadowed home,

332

eager to seize any means of escape. She felt nothing for him any longer, not even emptiness where her love had been. She was free.

When he came up to them she introduced Berdeyev to Christopher without a qualm, only glad to have the opportunity of showing St. Albyn the shallowness of his first impression. She stood a little aside from the two men, comparing them in the new-found clarity of her mind and aware again, with a sudden strange pricking of anxiety, of how worn and driven Berdeyev looked. But his intellect was unimpaired and she could feel his interest when Christopher said that he had known Eleanor in England.

"You lived close to Miss Lovell?" he inquired.

"Oh, yes, more or less next door, as you might say!" grinned Christopher.

Berdeyev shot him a penetrating look and said smoothly, "Your family are considerable landowners in the district, I understand?"

Christopher look surprised. "Well, as a matter of fact, we are. How did you know?"

Eleanor intervened hastily, entering the conversation for the first time. "There are several big landowners in the area, aren't there, Christopher? I've been trying to describe Sussex to His Excellency, but it is sometimes very difficult, things are so very different from the way they are here." She laughed nervously.

"They certainly are," Christopher agreed fervently.

Berdeyev looked from one to the other and was not deceived. "It must be very pleasant for you both to meet again after so long," he said politely. "I trust that you find old—ah—comradeship revives easily under such unusual circumstances?" Spevashev had been safely dispatched out of the city under Volodya's care; looking at Ilena and encountering in one day these two young men who were her natural companions and sweethearts made him feel every one of his forty years.

"Naturally we are delighted to see each other again," replied Christopher stiffly. "Although I don't mind tell-

333

ing you, sir, I was horrified when I heard she had come to Russia."

"I am not surprised," agreed Berdeyev. "But you must at least be glad now?"

"Well yes, of course I must be! But to be a governess and a kind of maid around the hospitals does not seem to me at all the sort of thing for a lady to do."

Berdeyev looked at Eleanor's crimson face. "And did you tell her so?"

"Yes, by Jove, but it didn't do any good! I have been telling her she should come home."

"You astonish me." Eleanor saw a muscle quiver in his cheek. "But you are undoubtedly right about her going home. I have said the same thing." He turned to Eleanor and bowed gravely. "I must not disturb your charming reunion any longer, but I have been delighted to make Lieutenant St. Albyn's acquaintance."

Christopher eyed his retreating back resentfully. "What an odd sort of man. You know, Nell, you really would do much better to come home while there is still time. Never saw such a country in my life and before you know where you are you'll be the same."

She laughed and slipped her arm through his. "Truly I don't wish to go, there is nothing for me in England any more. Let's dance again, I feel I can't waste a moment of such an opportunity!"

Twenty-Three

The edge of night was melting from the brightening light of day as Eleanor let herself silently out of the house the next morning and hurried on her way to visit the hospitals. Ever since Berdeyev had made it impossible for her to visit in the evening, her morning journey had had to start at first light if everyone was to be fitted in at least once or twice a week. Even so Madame Traskine had recently become restive at her long absences from Micha and Sacha, about which Eleanor herself already felt sufficiently guilty. Only the reduction in numbers of the wounded, which had resulted in two of the emergency hospitals being shut, had staved off real trouble between them and Eleanor felt sure it was only a matter of time before all but her Sunday visits were stopped.

It was only about ten o'clock when she started on the long walk back from the barracks to the Traskine house, which in the daylight she thoroughly enjoyed. She reveled in the crisp, clear air and, as she often did, paused on the ramshackle bridge over the marsh stream to gaze at the piled dómes and crazy, endearing fretwork of jumbled buildings crowding University hill across the river. Silver and gold, burnished by the early morning sun, tinted blue by the sky, white by the snow, and green by the painted roofs around, a burning unbearable fire shone from cupolas and spires and layered pinnacles, thrusting into the sky and floating with majestic ease above the everyday cares of the city.

She drew aside automatically when she heard the high-pitched whine of an approaching sledge, but as it came abreast of her it stopped and a man jumped out, dressed in heavy furs and a round fur hat, on the front of which she recognized the silver badge of the State Gendarmerie.

"Mademoiselle Lovell?" he asked, speaking in French.

"Yes," she answered, surprised.

"Will you come with me, please." He stood aside for her to enter the *izvochtchik*.

She stared at him. "Certainly not! I am on my way home. I am Madame Traskine's governess."

"I know that," he said impatiently. "I am from the

335

State Gendarmerie and have orders to bring you to headquarters for questioning."

"But—but you . . . I can't come just like that! What have I done? There must be some mistake."

"It is not for me to say, mademoiselle. I have my orders and will carry them out." He took a step toward her and she realized the futility of arguing. He had his orders, no protest, no refusal would make the slightest difference. If necessary he would pick her up and carry her to police headquarters.

"Very well, I will come with you, but will you please drive round by Madame Traskine's? Then I can tell her what has happened."

He climbed in beside her, shouting to the driver. "I am sorry, but that is impossible. She will be informed in due course no doubt, but I have already wasted time searching for you."

During the short drive across the river and through the center of the city Eleanor looked round her desperately, hoping to see someone she knew to whom she could indicate her plight, in the comfortable knowledge that such a choice piece of gossip would surely be in the possession of everyone within a few hours.

But although she had herself been up for a considerable time it was not yet the fashionable hour for breakfast, and the streets were deserted except for soldiers, carters from the country, and merchants' apprentices running errands and delivering goods, blind and indifferent to everything except their own affairs.

She had often seen the Gendarmerie Building from the outside, an ornate slice cut from the hideous, over-decorated block housing the Department of State Domains. Many of the peasants crossed themselves surreptitiously as they passed and even Madame Traskine's friends preferred to walk to the Nobles' Club through the winding streets of the old city rather than pass its doors. Eleanor had been inclined to regard their exaggerated fears with a certain amount of skepticism but during the past months she had become very much

336

aware of the great difference between the State Gendarmerie under Suikevsky, responsible to no man but the Tsar, and the city and rural police controlled by the provincial authorities and employed on normal civil and criminal operations.

There was nothing frightening about the building itself, dark, dusty, and oppressively hot, but a brooding silence lay over the atmosphere as grime lay over the florid, tasteless furniture. She was shown a bleak waiting room containing a vast table, a heavily carved chair, and nothing else at all, not even a carpet or a magazine, and curtly told to wait. After half an hour of restless fidgeting she was beginning to feel extremely nervous; after an hour and then two hours, she was not far from panic.

Once she opened the door, wondering whether she had been forgotten and could leave before anyone noticed her absence. Across the hall two armed gendarmes were talking idly, plainly in no casual meeting but posted there on duty. They broke off their conversation abruptly on hearing the latch click, one made a comment, and they both laughed, their eyes running over her figure impertinently until she retreated hastily, cheeks flaming.

The long waiting minutes stretched into a blur of time; she had no means of telling how long she had been confined in this weighted stillness. The outer of the double windows was so thickly encrusted with frost that she could see nothing through it and the building might have been inhabited by ghosts, so uncannily still was it. In spite of the heat she began to shiver, her mind a prey to fears which were none the less terrifying because she told herself they were baseless.

She was also extremely hungry, having eaten nothing since the previous evening, and in an effort to forget this she began to pace the bare boards, wondering suddenly how long it would be before Madame Traskine discovered what had happened to her. Perhaps it would become a joke between her and Suikevsky, her conscience salved by the reflection that a short stay in the Gendarmerie was only to be expected by an enemy in time of war.

And Berdeyev? Eleanor knew in her heart that if he heard of her predicament he would surely try to obtain her release, but more and more as the weary hours passed the hope withered that he would be able to prevent her remaining for the night. For she was only too miserably aware that he might easily have left that morning for another part of the province: his responsibilities covered over fifteen thousand square miles of territory divided into sixty police districts and thousands of communes, estates, and settlements of all kinds. But she could not allow panic to chip at her composure, or silence to feed the fantasies of fear which could so easily grow in such an atmosphere. Standing there, very alone and very quiet, she thought deliberately of the hills of home, of the light on the stippled fields of Nipocritiy, of the wind on her cheeks and the ice crystals in the air, then suddenly and painfully of the moment four months ago when she had ridden home in front of Berdeyev and imagined briefly a human contact which time had since disproved. She edged her mind away from that too, there was so much forbidding ground where her thoughts must not stray.

Slowly, minute by minute, fraction by fraction, the most difficult defenses of all began to be erected, the solitary defenses of the spirit manned by resolution, by prayer, by the tripwire of obstinacy when these are the only resources left to draw on.

. . .

His Excellency the Governor of the Province of Kharkov, General Count Nicolai Pavl'itch Berdeyev, slowly reread Madame Traskine's note and then raised his eyes to a flustered Didi standing before his desk.

"You say that one of the house serfs returning from

338

market saw the *barishna* being taken to Gendarmerie headquarters?"

"Yes, *barin*, Ivan Stepan'itch, a good lad and not one to let his imagination deceive his eyes. He ran home directly to tell us in the *izba* and I told the *barina*, but she already knew and had written this note to you."

Berdeyev became suddenly intent. "She already knew that the *barishna* had been arrested?"

Didi shrugged. "She told me that Ilena Vassilievna was late home and was not surprised when I told her Ivan Stepan'itch's tidings. She was already worried and, as I said, had written you that message."

"She had already written this." Berdeyev read the note again, aware of some element of falsity and deliberation in the wording. He drew his watch from his pocket and then asked abruptly, "At what time does Ilena Vassilievna usually leave and return to the house?"

"Early, very early, *barin*. Before we are awake or the first fronds of dawn stir the sky."

"And she returns?"

Didi reflected, rather enjoying the importance of the moment. "After I have served the *barina* and the young *barin* with their morning meats. Theodosia saves what she may for the *barishna* but indeed she eats little and—"

"Enough! Has the *barina* received any callers this morning?"

Didi stared. "I left immediately, *barin*, with this letter. At this time the *barina* is still in her room and would receive no one."

"I see. Tell me, Didi, how did the *barina* know that Ilena Vassilievna had not returned? Does she go to her room to receive orders for the day or to take the young *barin* to see her?"

Didi scratched his beard thoughtfully. "No, *barin*, the *barina* would sleep late, having returned but a few hours earlier from a festivity in the city. But this morning she rang early to ask Theodosia if the *barishna* had

339

returned; when she heard that she had not, the *barina* asked for materials that she might write a letter to you."

"Did Theodosia explain that Ilena Vassilievna seldom returned so early?"

"*Barin*, I do not know, but she was much surprised at the *barina*'s anxiety."

Berdeyev leaned back in his chair, only one link missing in his chain of supposition. "Did she ask at any time this morning whether there had been a caller for her?"

Didi nodded. "Yes, *barin*. It is very strange, for who could she expect to call so early in the morning?"

It was clear enough now, and he realized that after Suikevsky's humiliation of the night before he ought to have foreseen it. He had not because it had not occurred to him that Suikevsky would know that a blow against Ilena would be a blow against himself. Spevashev's foolishness yesterday had certainly given Suikevsky ample excuse, if excuse he sought, to question Ilena as a possible witness, or accessory, or whatever else he chose to make her.

Berdeyev pushed back his chair and limped over to the window, hoared and rimed with frost, the dim length of the Soumskaya only faintly etched in its patterned luminescence. He leaned his hands on the sill, feeling tiredness like a physical sickness clogging his thoughts. He looked at his watch again; it was not yet eleven o'clock. There was no escaping the fact that less than an hour after Ilena's earliest time for returning to the house Marya Fedorovna had been sufficiently worried about her lateness to write to inform him of it. This immediately put a more serious complexion on the whole affair, for if there was collusion, then Ilena's detention must be part of a deliberate plan, the letter a calculated first move to bring him into the game. Anxiety, or perhaps conscience, had made Marya commit the mistake of warning him prematurely but, he thought acidly, Suikevsky is not such a fool. He has not yet sent to tell her to dispatch her note in case I should suspect. And even if she had sufficient sense, or fear of Suikevsky, not to send it off until she should hear from him, had not Ivan Stepan'itch given her the excuse she needed. She does not like the part she has to play as well as she thought she would.

"Wait here till I return," he ordered Didi abruptly and went out, calling for Ivan Ivan'itch, his servant through many years, whose bearded presence on the *Neptune* had so much impressed Eleanor.

"Listen, Ivan. I have one of Marya Fedorovna's serfs in my office. I do not wish him to speak to anyone for the rest of the day." Berdeyev had no desire that Didi should report the drift of his questions to his mistress. If trap there was, then the longer his awareness of the fact was kept secret the better.

"As you order, *barin*." Ivan was imperturbable as always.

Having given a protesting Didi into his care, Berdeyev sat for a time in deep thought: long ago his brother officers had teased him about his habit of thinking his way thoroughly through any problem, but he had seldom found the time wasted. Occasionally he fell to pacing the room, but the pain in his leg denied him the movement with which he was used to match his thoughts through many years of open-air campaigning.

He dug his hands into his breeches pockets and closed his eyes. It was clear, he reflected grimly, returning to his earlier train of thought, that Spevashev might have given them their excuse but this was something which bore all the hallmarks of long planning, and something moreover that had nothing to do with Ilena. Arranged between his cousin and Suikevsky, it was directed solely against himself, their hatred of him being the only subject which such an unlikely pair could be relied on to agree on for any length of time. A pretty, spiteful, woman's intrigue, he felt sure, of which Suikevsky had taken advantage. They were obviously perfectly aware of his love for Ilena, a thought which made him stir un-

341

comfortably before he thrust it away, and were gambling that he would try to obtain her release regardless of the consequences or the limitations of his own power. Having reached this point, he frowned to himself and walked restlessly over to the window again; it was far from clear what they hoped to gain from such an attempt on his part. A reprimand? Some further attempt to fasten treasonable intentions on him? Hardly. Without Spevashev or indeed any evidence whatsoever, the army and the Ministry of the Interior would certainly value his work here too highly for such an attempt to have any real chance of success at this stage in the war, even if the Tsar himself was always willing to listen to the Third Section. Just pure malice? That, he felt, was nearer the mark where Suikevsky was concerned. They must know that he would not wait the six weeks or more which might easily elapse before he could obtain Ilena's release through the normal channels in St. Petersburg. It was unlikely Suikevsky would hold her so long anyway once he saw his plan had failed. If he only waited, Ilena was bound to be released; with English prisoners in the city, even the Third Section could not approve her detention. But of that he was not capable: going his way in peace while his love remained the sport of every ribaldry and indignity, and Suikevsky knew it. He obviously intended to exploit this knowledge ruthlessly to restore the influence of the State Gendarmerie in Kharkov to its former all-pervading importance. To Marya would go revenge alone, and he did not doubt her pleasure in that, even if the government's grip on her lands was now too strong to be broken.

Berdeyev was shaken, not just by his personal predicament, but by the malicious, small-minded, wasteful stupidity of it all. The situation in Kharkov was only one variant of the unremitting struggle fought between the various factions in the imperial bureaucracy, and that grown men with heavy responsibilities should be so squandering their energies at such a crucial time revealed the depths of the pit in which Russia was doomed to struggle.

He was pacing again, oblivious to pain until it would no longer be denied, and he leaned against the wall suddenly, swearing with the agony of it. He passed his hand wearily across his forehead, wondering savagely why this had to happen when he was already exhausted and, by the tidings which had come for him late last night by special courier from the Tsar, condemned to carry out a policy which he had long been certain could only bring more disaster in its wake.

With the thought, the confusion in his mind clarified suddenly. Suikevsky must have seen that an attempt to help an enemy, trivial in itself, could be used to highlight the far more serious matter of his failure to mobilize. But what Suikevsky did not yet know ... . When Volodya came into the room a few minutes later he found his general still leaning against the wall, staring unseeingly before him.

"I beg your pardon, Excellency, I will return later." Confused, he made as if to withdraw.

Berdeyev roused himself, moved heavily over to his desk, and sat down. "No, I want you. You have heard that Ilena Vassilievna has been arrested?"

"Yes, Excellency. I am very sorry." Volodya looked at him compassionately and Berdeyev reflected wryly that he must have made his feelings a good deal more conspicuous than he had thought.

Abruptly he asked, "With the best horse in my stables, how long will it take you to reach Chuguyev and return here?"

Volodya blinked at the change of subject. "About seven hours, Excellency, the roads are quite good for this season."

"Very well then. I want you to leave at once with movement orders for the remaining units at Chuguyev and also decrees mobilizing eight in a thousand souls for the entire province except this city. Give these to the commandant there and tell him to have them en-

343

forced forthwith. He is to retain enough men at Chuguyev to carry this out and also the best squadron of regular cavalry and a company of base troops to keep the peace—if he can—at Chuguyev. I shall expect to see his advance units in Kharkov tomorrow afternoon ready for inspection but I realize it will be several days before the rest can be moved."

"Yes, Excellency. You are mobilizing at last, then?"

"I no longer have any choice." Berdeyev was not quite able to keep the anger out of his voice. "I received personal orders from the Tsar himself last night; those I cannot disobey whatever the consequences." Yet perhaps I should disobey, he thought, and follow what I believe to be right regardless of the consequences, regardless that it would do no good and someone else would blindly carry it out in my place and undo all I have tried to build here. Perhaps. But I cannot do it; the Tsar I cannot disobey.

He roused himself from his uneasy reflections and continued slowly: "Wait at Chuguyev until the messengers have been sent out with the mobilization orders and then return to me here. Explain to the commandant that I am expecting you back within seven hours but that you may not leave until you have seen the messengers go. Be sure you get a dated receipt for these orders from the commandant."

"Yes, Excellency," repeated Volodya, mystified.

"And, Volodya—do not tell anyone your mission or appear to be in a hurry until you have left the city behind. I do not want our friends at the Gendarmerie to know anything is afoot."

There was nothing more he could do until Volodya returned, and for the rest of the long day Berdeyev carried out his normal program, refraining even from checking with his paid spy in Suikevsky's headquarters whether Ilena was indeed there. Suikevsky and his cousin were both worried by these tactics, and both took care to encounter him on his way to a session at the Judicial Tribunal across the square, but for neither would he stop or give more than a distant bow in passing. Through many difficult years forced into a complete mastery of himself, his manner and expression still betrayed nothing of the driving worry which gripped him, but as he went through the endless dreary papers of the province's legal affairs it was impossible to force a meaning into the words shuffling in front of his eyes. Whatever risks he took or pledges he gave, it was not going to be easy to free Ilena, for every move he made would only impress Suikevsky further with the value of the pawn he held.

The Tribunal Building was stuffily hot, the atmosphere fetid and dusty with the burrowing bureaucracy of generations: every witness in every case coming before the judges for trial had his evidence laboriously taken down in longhand and the verdict depended on these written depositions, copiously annotated with points of law and precedent by snuffling, semiliterate clerks. No judge saw the accused or cross-examined a witness, most of whom were beaten up by the police as a matter of routine before giving their evidence and then locked away in the filthy, overcrowded, disease-ridden jail while their evidence was sifted, shuttled in a leisurely fashion through the various departments concerned, and a verdict eventually given, often years later.

The provincial governor had to countersign the more serious of these judgments but by the time they reached him Berdeyev generally found them so obscure, confused, and dog-eared that critical assessment was impossible and any query simply kept everyone concerned in jail for more weary months. However reluctantly, he had had to content himself with clearing out most of the hundreds of prisoners left over from Traskine's day and putting some kind of motive force behind the machinery of justice. The average stay for a witness in Kharkov prison had been cut down to about six months, almost a record for the Empire, and, to their hurt astonishment, he had also curbed some of the worst excesses of his own police. Nevertheless, he was well aware that the whole system was too rotten to be capable of real improvement, so it was scarcely surprising that he found it difficult to keep his mind on papers which he knew to be fraudulently put together, corruptly judged, and full of faked evidence.

It was the final dossier which jolted him into awareness. "Stepàn Karajevitch Domovoye—Corporal, 3rd Guards Regiment of Don Cossacks, on a charge of mutiny." He stared at the heading stupidly and then realized that of course this must be the man from yesterday's fracas at the north gate. On a capital charge like mutiny the wheels of justice turned very rapidly indeed, for no mitigation was ever allowed, and with a military crime the original file would come to him in his capacity of garrison commander.

He glanced hastily through the papers: garbled rubbish as usual, but here at least he was to some extent his own master and he called over one of the clerks. "Is this man in the cells here?"

The man rolled his eyes and grinned stupidly, probably too nervous to speak, dreaming already of the stories he would tell of speaking to an excellency. It took several minutes to elicit the information that Domovoye was not there but held in the guardhouse of the barracks. Berdeyev hesitated; it was a damned nuisance to have to go right over there; for him it involved ordering a horse and being away an hour or more listening to the man's evidence. If he took an *izvochtchik* or ordered him brought to his office there was the certainty that Suikevsky would hear of it and remember this piece of flotsam so utterly destroyed by a chance involvement in affairs of which he knew nothing. Even to himself Berdeyev would not admit that he had any hope at all that something could be done for Domovoye, but any revival of interest from the Gendarmerie would certainly be fatal.

After looking through the useless file again he decided to go; he could do nothing for Ilena until Volodya

346

returned and a man should not be condemned to death without his even making the effort to go across the town. The guardroom was thrown into confusion by his arrival, only the prisoner seemed quite unconcerned, watching the bustle with the detached boredom of an onlooker. Short, bandy legs, small eyes set in a face wrinkled like the banks of an eroded ravine, cheekbones slewed onto a flat bone structure, Berdeyev noted, and recognized a true Cossack of the blood, coming from the wide plains and not half domesticated like his brothers in the settled areas. Even his name confirmed this, a mere Russianized nickname, Stepàn Domovoye, Stephen the Hobgoblin, and he looked it.

Even with all his knowledge of soldiers Berdeyev found questioning the man difficult. With Spevashev yesterday, Didi this morning, and now Domovoye, he seemed to have been probing recalcitrant witnesses about dubious plots for so long that his mind jibbed sullenly at the new effort he must now make. The man's disinterest was disturbing too: he knew he was to be shot, probably within a day or two, but he was not just pretending indifference. He gave the impression of accepting an invitation to death of his own free will.

It was impossible to know the right questions to ask when Domovoye would give him no help at all, but piece by piece small splinters of the story began to emerge: a pathetic, irrelevant series of trifling events brought into sudden focus. Domovoye and the other men of his squadron had been hungry and very tired when they arrived at Kharkov, thankful for the chance of a warm night's sleep in some huts just outside the city.

"So when your squadron assembled the next day you decided to stay behind?" Berdeyev prompted as the man's descriptive powers petered out yet again.

He looked offended. "Of course not, sir."

"But you were not on parade," Berdeyev persisted.

"No, sir."

"Why not?"

Domovoye glanced around the bleak barrack room, at the tattered notices and racks of weapons, the two impassive guards at his side. After a long pause he shook his head. He had already admitted that he had struck the cornet and Berdeyev wondered wearily whether it was worth the effort of probing any further into what had driven him into doing such an extraordinary thing. Nevertheless he tried once more. "When you were found in the huts and brought before Cornet Kotlas, what did he charge you with?"

"Loss of equipment, sir."

"Loss of equipment?"

"Yes, sir."

Now that is a surprise, thought Berdeyev. "What had you lost?"

"My overcoat, sir."

"And the other men?"

"Their overcoats, sir."

Berdeyev ran his finger down the scar on his face. How much simpler it would be if only the man would tell him plainly what had happened. He thought over his own distant memories of night bivouacs when he had commanded squadrons of cavalry: carbines piled and guarded, lances used as framework for tents and picket lines, swords laid ready for emergency beside tack and blanket, overcoats rolled and placed in a circle as pillows. Accidental loss was impossible. "Were there peasants in the huts you were using?"

"Yes, sir."

"Did they take the coats?" A squadron of hungry Cossacks could not have been a welcome addition to poor peasant households.

The man hesitated and then said sullenly, "The coats were found."

"Brought out to you, do you mean, when the peasants saw you were in serious trouble?" A nod but Berdeyev knew this part was not quite right. He passed his hands over his face, a nervy gesture he sometimes now noticed and despised in himself. What was happening

348

to Ilena while he was fooling around here with this oaf of a corporal? Suddenly some sympathy of ideas made him certain of one thing in all this evasion. "A girl took them?" No reply. "You slept with a woman that night?"

"Yes, sir."

"She stole your coats—why?"

Nothing, not a blink, nothing at all.

There could be only one thing in such a content which would so shame a Cossack that he preferred to die rather than speak of it. Berdeyev mused aloud. "You found a woman in the hut, shared her among you. You passed the night in contentment? Answer me!"

"No, sir." Automatic reflex to command.

"You were tired and underfed and she was not." Statement of fact remembered from days of army rations and the half-savage women of the steppe.

The man looked away, humiliated even to think of it, but Berdeyev knew now. "She was lusty and shamed you with her jests. Then she stole your coats and led the three of you a merry dance to provoke you into taking her again before you left."

It was another statement and not a question but this time Domovoye answered. "She said she expected better things of Cossacks, that we were weaklings when the three of us could not give one wench a good night's bedding." His face reddened with remembered anger.

It was ludicrous: three men frantically following some peasant girl in and out of huts searching for their coats, infuriated by her jests, probably tantalized by coarse provocation, determined after a night's rest to show her Cossack virility; then haled outside to find the squadron assembled and themselves charged with desertion. No, loss of equipment; Berdeyev was beginning to have confidence in the judgment of Cornet Kotlas.

"The charge of loss of equipment was changed to desertion later?"

"Yes, sir." He was willing enough to talk now.

"Some officer came along and told Cornet Kotlas and Sergeant Chenidze that it should be desertion, threatend them with all kinds of trouble if it wasn't."

Suikevsky manufacturing his case against Spevashev through Ilena to himself. "And the cornet agreed?"

"He had no choice, sir. This swell spouted all kinds of regulations at him, properly made our heads ring. 'Twasn't his fault." No malice there.

"But you have ended up in front of me on a charge of mutiny for striking Cornet Kotlas?"

"Yes, sir."

Berdeyev stood up and put on his cap; formality alone might jerk out the last necessary explanation. "Corporal Domovoye, you are charged with the most serious crime a soldier can know, a disgrace to your kin and to your regiment. Think very carefully before you answer, I want nothing but the absolute truth. What made you strike Cornet Kotlas in front of your squadron and an independent witness of the police?"

Domovoye was deathly pale, but now he had confessed the shame of his manhood he replied, hesitantly but readily enough. "It was for my kin, sir. The gauntlet and the lash. I couldn't stand the dishonor and neither could they. To be shot is a man's death, but the flogging for desertion, that is the way of a pig led to the slaughterhouse."

Berdeyev stared at the man, in no doubt that this was the truth. His first impression of Domovoye's bearing had not been so very wrong: he had invited death as the alternative to the degradation of the lash. What bitter, brutal, bloody waste. God help us, he thought, for truly we need it. Every possible thing we waste and twist and make unusable: waste our time with criminal feuds, our land with insane beliefs, our men by treating them like animals. Three men's lives smashed in a couple of minutes by a stupid bitch and a worthless policeman. This one somehow I will save. He smiled grimly to himself: a life for the Tsar. He did not think it was a joke Nicholas I was likely to appreciate.

It would have to be done carefully though. The mutiny was clear and unprovoked, discipline must be maintained. Just as important, Suikevsky must be left no lever for later use against himself and the Administration. Berdeyev took off his cap again and walked over to the grimy window, considering. At last, his mind made up, he sat down and signed the sentence in front of him: to be shot. The man's eyes followed every movement but he remained stiffly at attention and said nothing. "Stepàn Karajevitch Domovoye, you are sentenced to be shot for mutiny occurring on the twenty-first day of February 1855 in this command of Kharkov. There were others involved in this incident"—he glanced down at the papers—"Troopers Morozov and Serdyuk, who are still facing charges of desertion. I am therefore temporarily suspending the execution of your sentence and sending you to the cells at Chuguyev in case you might be required as a witness by the Kherson command or the police." He could not possibly say that some opportunity to commute the sentence might occur during the next few months, could not help leaving the man on the rack of uncertainty; it was the best he could do. If, somewhere, Russian arms could scrape up a victory in the coming campaign the celebrations which would certainly be ordered to publicize such a change of fortune could be used as an excuse for unobtrusive clemency, the reference to the police a possible additional protection if he should ever be asked to account for his actions.

As he rode slowly back to his office he was glad that he had at last taken the time to understand the pride of Corporal Domovoye. For a moment the murkiness of trickery had been lightened by the little man's simple dignity and resolve.

Twenty-Four

Volodya returned in seven and three quarter hours, mud-stained and cheerful, laughing at the consternation on the commandant's face when he was informed that his advance units were expected in Kharkov the following day.

"I'm afraid your horse is going to take some time to recover, Excellency. I left him at Chuguyev, but they are all so upset it may be hours before he is tended."

"I will send Ivan over for him tomorrow. No one remarked on your leaving or returning to the city?"

"I gave a comely peasant girl a lift before me the last two versts into town. Even I could hardly suspect myself of ulterior motive in assisting anyone so beautiful!" He kissed his fingers gracefully.

Berdeyev dropped his hand lightly on his shoulder—he was fond of this youth who had supported him unswervingly and lightheartedly through the past difficult months—and then turned away, saying dryly, "One day you will find yourself entertaining the father and brothers of one of your beautiful peasant girls. Go and get some rest now, I shall not need you again tonight."

"Is there nothing further I can do, Excellency? I'm not tired." Volodya, who had also become genuinely attached to Berdeyev, only just stopped himself from saying that it was he who needed rest.

"No. At least—see if you can find that rat we pay to tell us what goes on at the Gendarmerie and obtain direction from him as to where exactly in the building is Suikevsky's office. I have no wish to be kept indefinitely in some waiting room while he gloats through a keyhole." As he spoke Berdeyev was putting on his full-dress tunic and buckling his heavy sword belt, neither of which he usually wore, disliking their stifling discomfort. On this occasion, however, he felt that the full panoply of his office might be an advantage.

"He says that Suikevsky is on the second floor, the last door on the right overlooking the Church of St. Nicholas," reported Volodya, returning to the room.

Berdeyev grimaced. His own office was on the ground floor, owing to his difficulty in climbing stairs, but it could not be helped. He caught sight of the eager speculation in Volodya's eyes and after a slight hesitation said: "I am going to cheat Suikevsky if I can. The less you know of such matters the safer for you, otherwise I would tell you more. I will return here as soon as possible."

Volodya smiled. "Good luck, Excellency. I'll wait for you in case there is anything I can do." As Berdeyev left the room he called after him: "Give the *braht klopy*[1] a kick from me too, Excellency!"

Suikevsky was alone in his office, moodily caressing the backs of his hands, when he raised his head and saw Berdeyev standing in the doorway. At once the doubts which had assailed him all day vanished and there was triumph in his voice as utter certainty took its place. "Your Excellency wishes to see me?"

"Not in the least. Unhappily circumstances make it inevitable."

Suikevsky started forward in his chair. "By the living God, I will make you pay for that! It is unwise to insult those from whom you seek a favor."

"Would it make matters any simpler if I called you a cowardly, mischief-making little cur who makes war on women because the world of men is too difficult for him?"

But Suikevsky had recovered his equanimity, recalling that, whatever Berdeyev chose to say, this time it

[1]Brother of bugs.

was he who came as a suppliant and from whom a reckoning could be exacted for every slight and insult treasured up over the past months. He smiled thinly. "Am I to understand that the great believer in peace is at last offering a duel?"

"You are not. I am particular with whom I fight."

This time Berdeyev achieved more success in his deliberate attempt to provoke Suikevsky beyond reason or prudence, and when he spoke again the smugness of easy victory was replaced by anger. "I will see you dismissed and broken no matter what friends you have in Petersburg! His Majesty is always interested in the Third Section's reports on Decembrist families! And then that woman downstairs turned over the Turkish border at the remotest village I can find."

"Whatever the consequences to yourself?" inquired Berdeyev, faint interest showing in his tone. By all means Suikevsky must be encouraged in any belief he might have of his enemy's influence in St.Petersburg. He added gently, "But then you have not the least chance, as things are, of seeing me dismissed or broken, have you? Quite the contrary, if you exceed your authority and deport an Englishwoman to Turkey without informing Petersburg, especially when there are English prisoners here to report what you have done."

Suikevsky relaxed, stroking his hands again. "I do not think you will let it come to that, my dear General."

"I will not," agreed Berdeyev, and Suikevsky was conscious again of certainty and triumph, as all-effacing as his previous rage, of which it was yet part.

He leaned forward eagerly. "I will release Ilena Vassilievna on condition that you marry her and so become responsible for her behavior. It is what you wish, I am doing you a favor!" To marry an enemy in time of war—his tongue ran over his lips at the thought of the disgrace that would bring to a man in Berdeyev's position of authority.

"I do not strike bargains with the lives and affections of others," said Berdeyev coldly. A spiteful, petty woman's intrigue as he had thought, everything reeked of female malice. Suikevsky had not even had the common ingenuity to think of a subterfuge of his own.

"Yet without a bargain the woman stays here, in the cells, and not any longer in a comfortable waiting room as she has been all day. My information is that you are about to be dismissed for disregarding your orders to mobilize more fully here, so what can it matter to you if you make a bargain with us before you go?"

It would certainly matter to the province and to the incoming governor, Berdeyev reflected, but Suikevsky would hardly expect him to take that into account. "It may not matter to me but it undoubtedly matters to you whether I am merely replaced by my superiors or disgraced through your agency. But I find I am now too weary to care overmuch precisely how my dismissal is achieved: I am therefore willing to see that you obtain the credit for it that you crave in return for your signed statement that you regret the arrest of Miss Lovell, which you carried out to satisfy the domestic malice of Marya Fedorovna Traskine, and for no other reason."

Suikevsky stared at him in silence, trying to read meaning into what had been said. He had never himself set much store by Marya's notion of forcing a marriage as a condition of release: the trouble the Third Section could cause was too obvious. Yet the governor was offering a bargain and after the skill and caution he had shown in defeating all previous attempts on his position this could only mean that he already knew, as Suikevsky suspected, that his days as governor were so closely numbered that it mattered no longer by whose agency the final blow came. When he is a private citizen, thought Suikevsky, his stomach twisted by an ecstasy of hate, there are many known to the police who would kill or maim for a hundred rubles. Had he been thinking with his accustomed clarity he might have paused to wonder whether gifts from an enemy might not prove dangerous, but as it was excitement unsteadied his voice and he leaned forward eagerly. "What do you propose?"

Berdeyev replied slowly, disliking the dirty business he was engaged on, hating himself almost as much as the man opposite, surprising himself with the thought: If it were not for the little I can achieve here, I would be glad to resign and return to the freedom, the honesty, the simplicity of the East. "If I am dismissed, it will be for failure to mobilize as you have said. This can prove my efficiency or my disloyalty, I no longer care which." He smiled suddenly. "Many other governors are inefficient, but if you can prove it was my disloyalty, then it would be to your great credit, for discovering disloyalty is the true function of the Third Section, is it not?" He paused, thinking for a moment of the high ideals expressed in the oath of a Third Section officer: his duty to see that all the Tsar's domains were ruled in justice and honesty, His Majesty's commands carried out *without fear or favor . . . and to the credit of His Majesty . . . to seek out and destroy all to the discredit of His Majesty's service. . . .*" Well, the "seek out and destroy" part was fulfilled anyway. He added with a sudden vehemence he had not intended: "No one will believe that I have ignored my orders because I love my country more than I care for the dictates of the state, you will be safe enough."

Suikevsky sneered. "That will sound attractive when the officials of the state come to question you."

"Quite so, but here we have no witnesses and your hatred is too well understood for your word to be accepted. There is no province in the Empire where the governor and the colonel of Gendarmerie are not trying to usurp each other's authority or plot each other's downfall, to the exclusion of other more important matters. In return for your statement about the reasons for Miss Lovell's arrest I will write a letter declaring my unalterable conviction that further mobilization is wrong and that I will not carry out any more orders I may receive to levy souls from this area

356

or muster any more from Chuguyev. Shall we say that His Majesty will have to lower himself to give me my orders personally before I will move?"

Suikevsky dropped his quill. "You will write that?"

"You have my word."

"As if I would take that! You write it here and now, then you can have your wench and good riddance. I wish you much pleasure of her," he added viciously. "Something with a bit more fire would be my choice."

"I have always understood the choice of the Gendarmerie to be limited to those who exchange their company for money," agreed Berdeyev. "Now sign that declaration and keep any further personal observations to yourself."

"No, by God! Only after you have written your letter."

Berdeyev put down the pen. "Certainly not. You know that you can trust me to write what I have said."

Suikevsky lurched to his feet with an obscene curse but all remnants of prudence had not yet escaped him. "You know I cannot write that I used the powers of the Third Section at a woman's whim!"

"Yes, I know," said Berdeyev grimly. "And I should not write what I said I would either. If you are set on this course it is a gamble we both have to take. Once you have freed Miss Lovell I would look very foolish if I tried to use such a paltry matter against you. So long as she is free you can be accused of very little of substance."

Suikevsky attempted to think clearly about the alternatives before him, but the risk he would have to run was really negligible. No complaint a discredited governor chose to make would be listened to seriously and he had anyway no interest in keeping this tiresome Englishwoman locked up once she had served his purpose. The failure to mobilize now Russia's armies were everywhere facing disaster was Berdeyev's vulnerable point, for here neither the Ministry of the Interior nor the army would support him when it was their policies he was disobeying and criticizing. After a long moment of incoherent consideration he reached blindly for the quill and dashed off a few words, his eyes still so blurred with rage that he could scarcely see the paper.

Berdeyev read it through deliberately before folding it away in his tunic pocket, then drew a sheet of paper toward him and began to write, hesitating irritatingly from time to time under Suikevsky's devouring gaze. Suikevsky thought he would never finish. So impatient was he that his hands snatched at the letter as soon as Berdeyev signed his name carelessly at the bottom and before his brain had even grasped that it was done.

"Who is this written to?" he asked suspiciously.

"To the commandant at Chuguyev; even the Third Section could not be such fools as to believe I would write a letter of that nature to a colonel of their Gendarmerie. It is touching to see their officers retaining so much faith in human nature that they expect such confidences."

Suikevsky's smile was ugly. "You may sneer now, but when this reaches Petersburg and I tell them also of your demands and threats to me to release an enemy, you are a fool to believe it will only mean your dismissal."

Berdeyev walked over to the door. "That may be," he agreed coolly. "I find this conversation singularly repetitive and disagreeable, however. I would be grateful if you would request one of your—er—menials to escort Miss Lovell to the hall, where I will await her in more congenial surroundings."

As the door closed behind him Suikevsky wiped the sweat from his brow. He found the governor's confident condescension singularly unnerving and before sending Odzanov to release the Englishwoman he had to glance again at the paper he held in his hand for reassurance. The words, unequivocal and damning, leaped at him from the page: ". . . wholly opposed to further mobilization . . . danger to the countryside . . . misconceived orders . . . finally, on this date, the nineteenth February

358

1855, must decline to put any further instructions or orders . . . on this subject into effect . . . inform His Majesty of my refusal and demand his personal intervention." Demand indeed! From the son of an unforgiven Decembrist such arrogance to the Tsar would indeed be more fatal than flat disobedience. This must be victory, complete and final. With the hostility of the Third Section to reinforce the Tsar's outrage, mere dismissal would never be sufficient: he began to dream of the outstandingly zealous ways in which he could have discovered such a letter, to the credit of himself and his service. He was possessed by a physical ecstasy of triumph, for what had started fifteen months ago as mere professional antagonism had grown, almost unperceived, into an unreasoning personal hatred, fanned into sudden incandescence by the fiasco over Spevashev and now again by an offhand contempt to which not even the humblest member of the Third Section was accustomed.

On the other side of the door Berdeyev closed his eyes a moment before proceeding slowly down the stairs. The risks he had run by his deliberate provocation of a man who for years had seen nothing but obsequious heads and cringing backs had proved justified, but in retrospect the memory turned him cold. Instead of striking his bargain with a level-headed, cautious policeman, it had been with a man driven outside his normal habits of thought and prescience by hatred, who could see only what he wanted to see in the letter—above all, the date of two days earlier, so that it was established that the letter preceded Berdeyev's acknowledgment of, and obedience to, a personal order from the Tsar. Already the orders for a full levy of eight in a thousand were being posted, the first units moving from Chuguyev, already the Chuguyev commandant's receipt for his orders had been forwarded to St. Petersburg together with copies of the provincial mobilization orders.

The Tsar's order had been direct and explicit, allowing no further equivocation; Berdeyev's letter left with Suikevsky had acknowledged, however crudely, that this was the intervention he sought and which only the quality of his administration at Kharkov had given him. He was in little doubt that it was the army command who had represented to the Tsar the extreme unwisdom of replacing the governor of Kharkov at the very moment when the spring campaign was about to open. It did not mean that he had the confidence of the Tsar, it was more likely that the Emperor's antagonism was increased by the distasteful necessity of retaining him for the time being. But now the Tsar had intervened and been obeyed without question, the Autocrat of all Russia would never admit that he could have been wrong to act personally in such a matter; therefore anything Berdeyev might have written demanding such intervention would be unusable by the Third Section. Like other methods of government, autocracy too was open to manipulation.

All these considerations ought to have been weighed by Suikevsky. If his spy system was as good as he imagined he should have known about the Tsar's letter whatever time of night it arrived, but Suikevsky, although an intelligent man, was not a very profound one. Just as he had not noticed the unselfish ambitions of his youth being corrupted by the daily bureaucratic struggle for recognition and promotion, so, for all his networks of spies and schemes, he still failed to make allowances for the unexpected, for human failings and aspirations.

Berdeyev had spoken to Suikevsky at any length only two or three times before that day, yet he had staked everything on his estimate of Suikevsky's character, on the belief that he would be unable to put himself inside his enemy's mind in a sudden crisis of decision. As he walked downstairs, his thoughts went back to a similar occasion when he had based a dangerous night attack on his estimate of the likely reactions of a Kazakh chief whom he had met only once at a parley, and how his success then had left him as weak and drained as it did now, haunted by the memory of outrageous risks run. Then he had been proud of his judgment and the victory he had snatched, now he felt ashamed and smirched by the deceit he had practiced and there was no triumph in him.

. . .

Eleanor had been sitting in the dark for what seemed like an endless space of time; the feeling of abandonment, the sense that the world already hurried over the place in life which she had once occupied, had become almost overwhelming as the hours passed and darkness fell: it was as if she were already dead.

It was difficult to concentrate her mind in such silence, to feel it worthwhile to make the enormous effort necessary to hold onto the shreds of her composure. She felt alarmingly weak after nearly twenty-four hours without food but somehow in the solitary depths panic was held at bay and she discovered a strength and determination she had not known she possessed. When Odzanov eventually came for her she was able to face him in silence, and with what she hoped was dignity, although she could feel the twitching of her knees, the betraying tremble of her skirts.

"You have no protests or demands to make?" Odzanov regarded her silent figure derisively.

"None that you are not aware of yourself without my needing to repeat them," she replied quietly. "If you cannot think of anything on which to question me I must ask you to let me go home now."

He laughed, a shade uncomfortably, she thought. "So you shall! By the great generosity of our colonel and as a concession to your youth, I have come to tell you that you may leave."

She was gratified to see how piqued he was by her silence, conscious of pleasure that she had managed to hide the overwhelming relief she felt, that she was

361

able to follow him out of the room without faltering on her treacherous legs. There was no trace in his manner of the friendliness he had shown at the ball the previous year, nor did he betray by a single gesture that they had been acquaintances, exchanged jokes, played cards together at Madame Traskine's. Instead he said viciously, "Remember in the future to behave with discretion lest your next stay here be more uncomfortable. Remember too the leniency of His Majesty's Gendarmerie, for such good fortune does not come twice."

She was spared the necessity of answering by Berdeyev's voice saying caustically, "Calm yourself, Lieutenant, we are all agreed that Miss Lovell is not a dangerous criminal." He limped forward and offered his arm, adding mockingly, "It is you who should be more careful over your choice of friends, otherwise one day you might be put to the disagreeable necessity of acknowledging one when it does not suit you."

Their last sight of Odzanov, as they went out into the biting, refreshing, liberating air outside, was of his face livid with fury in the faint light of the hallway.

"I am afraid the night watch of gendarmes are going to have an uncomfortable time after that remark," said Eleanor shakily, unable to voice the many more important things jostling to be said between them.

Berdeyev grunted. He would not look at her, it was almost as if he were a stranger. "Would you mind returning with me to the Government building while I order an *izvochtchik* to take you home?"

"No, of course not." She glanced up at his face, puzzled and distressed by his expression of distaste, as if he were blaming her for what had occurred. They crossed the road in silence and were mounting the steps into the Government building before she felt able to continue: "I haven't said how grateful I am to you for getting me out of that place. I'm sure, in spite of what Odzanov said, it was your doing and not their leniency."

"There is no need for gratitude," he replied curtly.

"It is rather I who should apologize to you that such things happen in my country."

"I thought I was there forever, until everyone had quite forgotten my existence," she confessed. "Though I knew you would try to help me if you could. How did you manage it, sir?"

"I cheated him," he said shortly, hating the sound of his words.

Seeing the forbidding expression on his face, she asked no more of the questions on the tip of her tongue. Although the full intricacy of Kharkov official politics was unknown to her, she had had a long day in which there had been nothing else to do but think and she also had realized that, since she had not even been questioned, the only reasonable explanation for her arrest was that Berdeyev, and not she, was the intended victim. If she had known that he would surely help her if he could, so too had others, and they had used this knowledge to force his hand through her. She could appreciate his resentment at this but was hurt to find it was she he appeared to blame. Her profound relief at finding herself free again turned to upset and bewilderment by the hatred she sensed in him, against her or against what he had had to do: she did not know which or understand his attitude.

He held open the door to a cheerless waiting room, almost exactly similar to the one at police headquarters except that here there were two chairs instead of one and a dingy, guttering candelabrum illuminated the gloom. "Would you mind waiting here a few minutes while I make some arrangements?"

She was chilled by the impersonality of his tone. "Certainly, Excellency. Er—General?"

"Yes?" He halted impatiently by the door.

"Did they get what they wanted or will this happen again, do you think?"

He stared at her appalled, realizing that of course she must guess the true reason for her arrest. He passed his hand over his eyes, wishing he were not so very weary of it all, and then said slowly: "I have done what I can to ensure it will not happen again but I cannot be certain; for your own sake you should not delay your departure from here any longer. Whatever your fears of returning home, they are less deadly than for you to stay here now."

"But I do not wish to leave," she said quietly, smiling at him.

He went out without a word, leaving the smile dying on her lips.

Volodya jumped up from his desk as Berdeyev entered. "What luck, sir?"

He slumped into a chair. "She is in the waiting room. Be a good fellow and see her home for me."

"Yes, of course, Excellency, but are you all right? Can I get you something?" Volodya hovered anxiously, looking in concern at his general's face, almost transparent and vulnerable suddenly with the sweeping away of a guard he had never before seen lowered.

"No, I'm all right, just tired." The words were slurred, as if he had been drinking. "Very tired. Twenty years since my commission and never until this day have I broken the oath I took then, or given my word on anything I knew to be trickery. And now I can only exploit what I have won and pretend that what I have lost was nothing." He opened his eyes and blinked at Volodya as if he had not known he was there and then said in an altered tone: "Send my compliments to Colonel Suikevsky, together with a copy of the Tsar's personal letter to me ordering mobilization, also my acknowledgment, and attach a note drawing his attention to the date. Send copies of the movement and mobilization orders I have issued and the receipt you obtained from the commandant at Chuguyev. Invite his presence at the parade ground tomorrow to inspect the advance units of the cavalry reserve we are expecting. Send a messenger, do not go yourself lest his rage recoil on you."

Eleanor, wondering whether she had again been for-

364

gotten but this time more hurtfully, looked up in surprise when Volodya at last came into the room.

"His Excellency has asked me to escort you home, mademoiselle. Vladimir Serg'itch Ryzhov at your service."

"Is His Excellency free for a moment? I have not really thanked him properly for obtaining my release from that horrible place." Her upset and mystification at Berdeyev's offhand behavior were almost unbearable.

Volodya looked uncomfortable. "He is very tired, mademoiselle, and begs you to hold him excused."

She accompanied him without further protest, which she recognized as being useless.

"I have ordered an *izvochtchik*, I expect you are tired after such a disturbing day," said Volodya formally.

"Disturbing?" His understatement struck her as exquisitely funny and she laughed irresistibly. "I suppose you might call it that! I am not so much tired as hungry, I shall have to enlist Theodosia's services to find something to eat as soon as I get in."

He was shocked. "Haven't you had anything to eat all day? I expect the guards ate what was intended for you and no one any the wiser. I should be very pleased to take you to a little place I know in the Skripnitskaya if you didn't mind it being rather rough. I'll take good care of you but I don't know of anywhere else more respectable where we could eat now."

She looked up at his pleasant face and engaging smile before making up her mind. "Thank you very much, I'd love to come if your friends won't be too shocked at me."

"Who cares about that! You're hungry and so am I; I've been to Chuguyev and back today. When I became a governor's aide I expected to spend the night dancing and the days in a little gentle card playing, instead of which I find myself wearing out all the mud tracks of the province."

Volodya proved himself an easy and entertaining companion; the *izvochtchik* drove them round to the

Skripnitskaya and settled down with the stoicism of his kind to a long cold wait, while they dived down into a smoky and cheerfully noisy room just below the level of the street.

It was a side of Russia Eleanor had never seen, full of lively song and dance, argument and commotion. Most of the clientele was made up of young officers, many well known to Volodya, who accepted her presence without surprise. He introduced her with easy informality and squeezed her into a place at a long crowded bench, loaded with all kinds of *zakuski* and cheeses served with round flat discs of bread. As elsewhere in the city, there was not much sign of the shortages threatening many of the less fortunate members of the population.

"You are a lucky dog, Volodya, how many times a day do you have a different girl?" called one of the men across the table. "I saw you with as pretty an armful as ever I should wish, riding into town this afternoon!"

"As many as I can! A moment off and I'm scouring the district to see what you fellows have left," retorted Volodya gaily, pouring wine for both of them.

"You will be in trouble one day with your old martinet if he finds out how you spend your time!"

Eleanor opened her mouth to say something about Volodya going to Chuguyev, but caught a warning glance he shot at her and changed it into a teasing remark about the preference of the army for dancing to marching.

"Now is that fair or reasonable, Ilena Vassilievna, when I myself spent the last week showing a bunch of plowboys which is the right end of a musket that was old in Napoleon's time?" protested another of the men, laughing. "It is Volodya here who rides around as if he were governor himself and elbows us away from all the prettiest ladies."

"It is not my fault if you clodhopping infantrymen lack the address to stop even the ugliest girl from yawning after five minutes of your company," protested

Volodya, grinning. "*Holà* there! A dance for the lady!"
He beckoned across the room to some musicians and
they struck up a fierce, lively rhythm which set everyone
shouting and tapping the table, restraint thrown to the
winds. Some gypsy dancers came in, flirting and dancing
between the long tables, jingling the coins round their
necks and flicking gold earrings past the young men's
eyes. Everyone joined in the wild, rousing choruses,
the passionate thrum of the guitars rising higher and
higher, faster and faster, until everything but the joy
and excitement of the moment vanished.

When the song crashed to its end everyone cheered
and shouted until the most striking dancer of them all
jumped on a table and began to sing:

> "My land of love,
> My empty land . . .
> The land where men may roam,
> Where the space within us fills with love
> For my land, my empty land . . ."

The chorus this time was soft and lilting, the deep
bass of the men harmonizing plaintively until a picture
of the endless plains of Russia, the life of gypsy freedom and sparkling campfires, was conjured up before
the mind's eye, until everyone was swept by the same
profound sensation and it was as if the rolling Russian
earth itself was invading their festive cellar. The brief
emotion and melancholy did not seem out of place, nor
was it incongruous when it, in its turn, was swept away
again by some flashing Cossack dances from two of
Volodya's friends.

It was a wonderful evening and by the time Eleanor
let herself into the hall of the Traskine house she had
almost forgotten the events of a day which she had
thought could never be erased from her mind. The
magnificent, untrammeled good spirits, the dash and
easy camaraderie she had experienced with Volodya and
his friends, had given her a glimpse of a Russia totally

at variance with all she had so far seen. Until now she had been conscious above all of apathetic hopelessness and poverty overlaid by a superficial social whirl which forever failed to keep a bottomless boredom at bay. Now she had seen the almost untapped resources of energy and vigor which Russia also possessed but which were being allowed so senselessly to run to waste: poisoned by corruption, tied down by regulations and destroyed by the gray monotony of a life without opportunity.

These reflections fled before the simple, tearful joy with which Theodosia met her, hands shaking as she kissed her fingers and lifted her cloak tenderly from her shoulders.

"What happened to you, Ilena? We have all been so worried about you." Madame Traskine swept across the hall and embraced her dramatically. "We heard you were arrested."

"I was, but the governor arranged for my release." Explanation seemed impossible and weariness at last almost crushed her.

Madame Traskine clasped her hands and demanded eagerly, "How did he manage that? What did he agree with Suikevsky?"

Eleanor stared at her in slowly dawning comprehension. She understood then that Madame Traskine also had known why she was arrested, had possibly even helped to arrange it. She said guardedly: "I don't think he arranged anything. I suppose he convinced the police that they had nothing against me."

"I'm sure I hope he succeeded and you won't find yourself arrested again," retorted Madame Traskine. "You will be giving our household a bad name."

"I hope not, madame. But I think perhaps you know, as do I, that they have no cause to arrest me. It is not I whom they seek to harm." She looked at her steadily and after a moment it was Madame Traskine's eyes which fell and she turned away into her room, slamming the door behind her.

Twenty-Five

Christopher St. Albyn was lying full length on his bed in the building used to house Allied officer prisoners in the Alexandrovskaya, smoking and thinking idly of the pleasures he was missing in London. This spring his mother was launching his sister into society and his father had taken a house in Berkeley Square for the season. They had all been disappointed when he left with his regiment, and his mother, he knew, had died a thousand vicarious deaths for him the past year.

I hope she knows by now I'm all right, he thought, shouting, "Come in!" to a knock on the door.

"Lieutenant St. Albyn?" Christopher nodded. "I am Vladimir Serg'itch Ryzhov, aide-de-camp to the governor. He has sent me to ask if you would be good enough to come to the Government building."

"Me? Why?" Christopher swung his legs off the bed.

"He wishes to speak with you, monsieur, I do not know why."

Christopher lounged to his feet and yawned. "Oh, very well then! Seems queer to me though, I hardly know the fellow."

Volodya flushed angrily at his tone and said coldly in his stilted French: "I will await monsieur below. I have brought an *izvochtchik* for your conveyance as soon as possible."

Berdeyev was signing another long series of mobilization proclamations, his lips tightly compressed with distaste, when Christopher was shown into his office half an hour later.

He looked up and studied Christopher until he felt

369

quite uncomfortable, before rising and greeting him in English. "Good morning, Lieutenant, I am sorry to have disturbed you so early." He handed the sheaf of papers to Volodya before he went out, closing the door behind him.

"That's all right, sir, I was only still in bed because there is nothing else to do. I'm getting devilish bored here, I don't mind telling you, though of course everyone has been most kind," he added hastily.

"It is a strange winter; it has started to thaw already and the roads are blocked in places, otherwise you would be leaving for Riazan tomorrow."

I am sure he did not bring me here to talk about the weather, thought Christopher, mystified, saying aloud, "Indeed, sir?"

Berdeyev smiled slightly, reading his thoughts. "I did not request you to come here to talk about that, however, but to ask you a personal question."

"Indeed, sir?" repeated Christopher warily.

Berdeyev resisted a temptation to walk around the room and tilted his chair instead. "I believe you knew Miss Lovell quite well at her own home?" Christopher nodded. "I also believe that she came to Russia chiefly because of you?"

Christopher jumped to his feet furiously. "Did she tell you that?"

"I have learned some of her history, and it was not difficult to guess the rest when I saw you together the other night."

"It was nothing to do with me! That tiger of a mother of hers made her come. If I had known anything about it I would have told her it wasn't a good idea, not that it is anything to do with me or you either."

Berdeyev ignored this. "Yet I am right in thinking that you could have stopped her if you had wished?"

"No! Look, what is all this? Nell is nothing but an acquaintance from home to me, or I to her!"

Berdeyev brought his chair legs down to the floor

with a snap and stood up, his head reaching perhaps to St. Albyn's chin. "You really believe that?"

Christopher looked away and muttered sullenly, "I could not help it if she became fond of me; it was just fun and I did not realize she was serious until—"

"So it was just fun, was it?" Berdeyev broke in, his tone icy and his hands thrust deep in his pockets, as if he were afraid of what he would do if they were free. "Happily your conduct is not my affair, but Miss Lovell's position here is. Because of her family and your fun, she is isolated in an enemy country over two thousand versts from home. Yesterday she was arrested through no fault of her own, and although she is now at liberty, I cannot say how long that will last."

"Nell arrested? By God, that's rich. I would give a monkey to see her mother's face when I tell her that her eldest daughter has been in jail!"

Berdeyev turned away and stared out of the window. When he spoke again his voice was very quiet. "This is not a game, Lieutenant, it could be very serious for her. I should not otherwise ask for your help."

"Ask my help? What can I do?"

"You can marry her."

There was a stunned silence before Christopher laughed disbelievingly. "Are you mad? I haven't seen her for nearly three years. Even if I wanted to I couldn't; my family would just about disinherit me for such a thing."

"I am not mad. I am asking you to right a great wrong you did and which you know you did, whatever you may say. She must leave here at once and she cannot and will not go alone. I do not believe your family would think the worse of you for such an act."

"If I married a chit from the sawmill, with me my father's sole heir? Especially someone my father thought was one of old Lovell's by-blows—he told me so when he heard I was fond of Nell. He also said it would have been better if Mrs. Lovell hadn't demonstrated her Christian duty by taking Nell in, because it only made

371

her more set on proving how unfit her sacrifice was forever after. Devilish knowing man, my father, wouldn't be surprised if he was right, he hears everything that happens around home."

"So that was why—" said Berdeyev slowly. He pulled himself together. "What I am trying to impress on you is that I cannot guarantee Miss Lovell's further immunity from arrest. I have some safeguards, yes; but if the police decide to deport her, in the last resort I could not stop them in time. She might be put over the Turkish border unprotected, many miles from help. Whatever excuses you may think you have for this situation, I felt that, as a gentleman, you might do what you could to rectify it."

"I've told you it is nothing to do with me and I couldn't marry her! Good God, she can't have done anything wrong, why should the police deport her? She is English after all."

Berdeyev's face changed. "She is English but after this conversation with you it does no appear to me such a privilege as it did. Our police, like you, are not interested in responsibility, or blame, or in the difference between right and wrong, but only in serving their own selfish ends. I hope that when you marry some lady of noble birth you will perhaps remember the murder you were willing to commit to achieve your ambitions."

Christopher took a hasty step forward, eyes blazing and fists clenched, but Berdeyev turned his back on him, saying contemptuously, "To start a brawl will not change the guilt you will feel for the rest of your life. It will merely give me an infinite pleasure I have so far succeeded in denying myself."

Christopher eyed his back smolderingly, baffled by his cool disregard and lashing tongue. Now he recollected himself, all his training restrained him from striking a man twenty years his senior and a general into the bargain. He cast about in his mind for the most offensive thing he could say. "Of course I might expect that a cripple would take advantage of his condition, knowing I couldn't take action against him whatever lies he spread." He was half sobbing with rage and flung out of the room without a backward glance, almost sprawling down the steps in his haste to get away.

He returned to his room still seething with anger, thankful that none of his fellow officers were in the building to offer commiseration or ask awkward questions. Eleanor's perfidy in discussing his affairs with nameless foreigners, Berdeyev's gross insults, and his own faint sense of guilt fermented together in his mind, but eventually it was his own sense of guilt and injury which emerged most clearly. He did not recognize that he was in any way responsible for Eleanor's coming to Russia or for her present difficulties with the police, which he neither understood nor wholly believed, but he acknowledged that her long-standing and undoubted attachment to himself did imply certain obligations on his part, nebulous though these might be. He found, too, that he was surprisingly unwilling to leave her unsupported if she truly was in trouble. But above all his own pride had received a blow from which it would not easily recover without some drastic action on his part. His immediate reaction had been to knock Berdeyev down, but this was denied him, as, by his own innate honesty, was an absolute conviction of the uprightness of his own conduct.

He ran over the conversation again and again in his mind and as he calmed somewhat, the conviction slowly grew that in those very reasons he had given for not marrying Eleanor lay the grand gesture he sought. It would be a truly splendid sacrifice to marry her in spite of everything, not ashamed, but proud of his magnanimity in giving up his advantages and expectations for his gentleman's scruples. Such an action could not fail to redound to his credit when it became known and it was pleasant also to think of the love and gratitude of Eleanor herself. The more he reflected, the more inevitable and alluring did this solution become and he was quite restored to his normal sunny humor by the time his friends returned.

He could not wait to give Eleanor the realization of all her dreams and when she did not appear at any of the various entertainments offered that evening in Kharkov, he went round to Madame Traskine's, whose direction he discovered without difficulty.

Fortunately Madame Traskine herself was out, attending a performance by Count Golitsyn's celebrated theatrical company, which was entirely made up of talented serfs, and Theodosia's excitement and curiosity knew no bounds when she showed him into the drawing room and ran to find Eleanor. She discovered her bathing Sacha while playing a complicated guessing game with Micha, all three laughing and wet from head to foot. She took Theodosia's news with maddening calm and it was nearly half an hour before she came into the drawing room.

"Wherever have you been? I've been here for hours, wondering what had happened to you!" Christopher exclaimed irritably.

"I'm sorry, but I was in the middle of putting the children to bed and couldn't leave them," she replied calmly.

"Well, of all the—! Here am I rushing round to see you in the middle of a devilish good evening's entertainment and you won't even see me because you are putting the children to bed."

She smiled and moved over to the stove. "It was very kind of you to come. Is this to say good-by? I heard the prisoners were being moved on again soon."

"No, it isn't!" he retorted, nettled. "Upon my word, Nell, you've grown mighty casual all of a sudden."

He looked so put out, like a sulky schoolboy angered to find that his elders do not crave his company, that she relented. "Of course I am delighted to see you, it is wonderful for you to take the trouble to come round. Would you like anything to eat now you are here?"

"No. Nell—" He grasped her hand. "I'm going to

marry you!" He had never intended to blurt it out like that but after the intensity of his emotions during the day he was thrown off balance by such a cool reception and the words tumbled out before he could check them.

She stared at him, dumbfounded. "You are what?"

"I want to marry you! Darling Nell, I—" He pulled her toward him, his hands hard and demanding as she struggled to free herself.

"Christopher, no! Please, no!" Her words were stifled by his lips and everything dissolved before his insistence until her words penetrated his mind and he released her as if she had been charged.

"What do you mean, no?"

She turned away and walked unsteadily over to the window and laid her forehead on the icy glass. "I mean no."

"But don't you want to marry me?" he cried, amazed.

She smiled faintly and countered, "You don't want to marry me, do you?"

"That's different! Besides, I've just asked you to marry me, what more can you want?"

"Nothing at all. It is very generous of you to ask me and I do thank you for it. I shall always remember the honor you did me." She listened to her own stilted words with detached amazement. The perfect way to decline an offer of marriage, I wonder where I learned to be so stately?

"I was beginning to wonder whether you understood what I'd said," he observed, faintly gratified and wondering whether perhaps she found the honor rather overwhelming at first. "I mean it, Nell, I'm not just funning. We can be married here and then you would come with me when we are moved north. I expect it could be arranged and I can't leave you here."

"Is that why you asked me? It is a wonderful thought, Christopher my dear, so very generous and like you."

"Well, I thought so too," he confessed, "but to tell the truth, Nell, I really like the idea now. I think we will

375

deal together very well and when I explain to my parents how it was they will quite understand, so you need not fear any unpleasantness there."

A low laugh shook her. "Christopher, what a way to propose! Of course I couldn't accept such an offer."

He stepped back a pace, astonished. "You mean you won't marry me? But that's fantastic, Nell, you must!"

"It is you who are fantastic! Though whatever you had said, I wouldn't have married you, even if you loved me, which you don't."

"You've always loved me and wanted to marry me." He sounded aggrieved. "Why, just the other night—"

She broke in hastily. "It was the other night I realized that, just as you have grown and changed, so too have I. Whatever happens, I'll always remember you now with affection, and the memories we have between us are pleasant and not bitter any more. I am not the wife for you, we should be miserable in a few weeks, but I shall treasure the thought that, for my sake, you asked me to marry you."

He still could not believe her refusal, that she could spurn his sacrifice without qualm or difficulty was galling, but that she should laugh at him and openly prefer to remain an obscure governess to being his wife was insufferable. His face was flushed with anger as he repeated doggedly: "You must marry me, you are not safe here. You may be rearrested at any time."

"How do you know anything about it?"

"The governor told me, though why he can't stop them if he is so concerned about you, I can't imagine. So you see, Nell, you must come with me. Good God, you couldn't prefer being a governess in a devilish uncivilized hole like this to being my wife!" The resentment in his tone was obvious and it was plain that any hurt he had suffered was to his pride and not his heart.

Eleanor considered him objectively, noting the long, willful lines round his mouth, his restless, dissatisfied expression, and wondered why she had ever loved him.

She probed cautiously. "You have seen the governor today, then?"

"Yes, and if he hadn't taken advantage of being a damned cripple I'd have shown him what an English gentleman does with such lying accusations." He was too absorbed in his humiliations to heed what he was saying.

"He isn't a cripple! And if you had tried to fight him I've no doubt he would have dealt with you as you deserved."

He eyed her in astonishment. "All right, so he isn't a cripple except for hardly being able to walk round his own office! He seemed mighty concerned about you though. I should be careful if I were you, Nell. I wouldn't be surprised if he didn't have his own eye on you and he's the queerest customer I ever came across."

"What a horrible thing to say! I can see now that I was quite wrong in thinking it was your chivalry which made you propose to me. It was the governor who shamed you into it as I might have known."

"Lord, Nell, you don't like the fellow yourself, do you?" He was flabbergasted as he saw the color steal into her cheeks.

"I don't know," she said softly, and then laughed suddenly. "Enough anyway not to be tempted by your flattering offer."

To prefer a shaved scarecrow like that to him! It was the last straw and Christopher snatched up his shako furiously. "If that is how you feel there is nothing more to be said! But if you take my advice you'll tread warily; he's not the sort of fellow I'd like my worst enemy to trust and you, being alone here, are just the sort of woman a cursed queer character like that would take advantage of."

"You should know all about that," replied Eleanor acidly.

He jerked the door open savagely. "Never say I haven't done what I could to save you from your folly! If you think toting a girl round the town trying to find someone to marry her is a sign of love, you must be out of your mind like everyone else in this damned country!"

The door slammed behind him, leaving Eleanor to reflections which were by no means tranquil. She felt only relief at Christopher's departure from both the room and her life; it was natural and inevitable and she hardly gave it a thought. She realized well enough that Berdeyev's endeavors to protect her by shaming Christopher, whom he plainly thought she still loved, into marrying her could be signs of a love far more profound than any which entered into St. Albyn's calculation. But so long as that was the only way in which he would permit his interest to manifest itself to her, her own confusion was likely to remain unresolved. The deep hurt he had inflicted by his attitude the night before was still too sore and recent for her to feel able to count on anything where he was concerned.

Twenty-Six

Suikevsky's rage when he realized how he had been tricked was reported to be terrible. Although no one but he and the governor knew of the details of what had passed between them, it was plain to the most uninformed onlooker who had won the encounter. Berdeyev's military authority, which became a matter of common knowledge once the increased tempo of mobilization put additional strains on the provincial and garrison administrations, was also accepted as a sign that in Kharkov at least the State Gendarmerie would have to take third place to the Ministry of the Interior and the army so long as the war lasted.

Suikevsky knew this too, for if the Tsar, against his own inclinations, had decided that it was temporarily undesirable to relieve the governor of Kharkov of his duties, then the Third Section had no choice but to agree with that decision. But the Third Section was always prepared to wait if necessary: more favorable circumstances would recur. The war would not last forever, scapegoats would be needed for the defeat which was now certain, the provincial administration was so weak and stretched and tested under the extremely difficult circumstances of spring 1855 that failure and disaster of some kind were almost inevitable and could be discreetly furthered.

From all corners of the province recruits were being brought in under escort, sullen, dazed, and openly tearful at the fate which had overtaken them, the most fearful fate of all in the eyes of the Russian peasant. Already the remaining infantry battalion of the garrison had marched away to the south, accompanied by the cavalry units from Chuguyev. The garrison of Kharkov Province was now reduced to around two hundred men in addition to those officers and sergeants who were blasphemously attempting to instruct the mass of raw levies delivered to them in the rudiments of military life and discipline.

Berdeyev, fearful of the effects of this rabble on his remaining trained men, had billeted them on the Customs House, clearing the barracks for the levies except for a few wounded still concentrated in one building there. From the Customs House the pitifully reduced garrison would be able to keep some kind of a watch on the barracks and also be a measure of protection to the remaining food stocks in the Cattle Market, though what a hundred men could do against the thousands of levies was far from clear. The other hundred garrison troops Berdeyev divided between Chuguyev and roving patrols of the province, to bring in the required recruits and give the greatest impression of armed strength he could contrive. A riot in the city might be faced down but a rising spreading over the countryside would be uncontrollable with the forces at his disposal.

Spring came mercifully early that year. As if by divine intervention, the day the last of the reserve stocks of grain were broached, the warm winds began to blow, the snow melted, the ice showed the first streaks of darkness on the rivers, and by the middle of March the nightingales were soaring on the soft air. The streets of the city turned into their accustomed knee-deep black paste, impassable and strangely silent without the endless columns of soldiers and supply trains which had grown so familiar during the past year and were now bogged down in the clinging glue that was the main road to the north. Everywhere there was an atmosphere of waiting, all felt uneasy about the undisciplined hordes confined just across the river, the new campaigning season was about to open in the Crimea, and no one could remain ignorant of the disasters it was likely to bring.

After careful consideration, Suikevsky had decided that the most damaging action he could safely take against Berdeyev was to find trivial excuses for interrogating and detaining, usually only for a few hours, anyone whom he could see co-operating with the governor. The Third Section needed no excuses for the arrest, detention, or interrogation of anyone, and in the prevalent muttering discontent a stepping up of activity could only reflect credit on the Gendarmerie. For the moment Suikevsky judged it wise to leave Ilena Vassilievna alone even if few others were spared: if she were arrested the paper he had signed could certainly cause him trouble even if it failed to help her.

One of the first victims was Volodya. Suikevsky had obviously seen the regard which existed between him and Berdeyev and sent round to his rooms one evening. Fortunately, being young, disrespectful, and active, while the two policemen sent to arrest him were both fat and stupid, he escaped by way of the window and raced up the street to the University Gardens where he had left Berdeyev a few minutes previously, giving orders for new training grounds to be roped off among the stunted bushes. When he pantingly explained what had happened, Berdeyev dismounted quickly and drew him away from the curiosity of the other officers around them.

"Take my horse and go at once. It is because of me you are in trouble and not through any fault of yours."

"I can't leave you, Excellency," protested Volodya, looking at the older man with affection.

"Don't be a fool, if you are arrested now there is nothing I can do for you. I will not be able to trick Suikevsky again and it might be months before I could obtain your release from Petersburg." He clapped him on the shoulder. "Up with you now! I will try to straighten things out for you here, though once you have left I do not think you will hear any more of it. Go to my good friend General Lyzin of the 2nd Division in the Crimea, he will give you an appointment, and meanwhile I will have you officially transferred so there will be no difficulty in the future. Have you any money?"

Volodya started to protest but there was a shout behind him and he saw some sky-blue figures running down the street toward them. Berdeyev put some notes in his hand and said quietly, "Take care, my son, for that is how you have come to be to me these last months."

Volodya saluted, tears pricking his eyelids, and then spurred away.

Berdeyev walked slowly back to his office, having blandly expressed astonishment that the police should have wished to interview his aide, and apologized gracefully for any inconvenience he might have caused by sending Lieutenant Ryzhov away on an urgent and prolonged errand. He found that he missed Volodya sorely; he was virtually the only person he had been able to trust to carry out his instructions faithfully and

Gatchukov, whom he had to appoint in his place, lacked both Volodya's good humor and his sympathetic understanding. He carried out his duties adequately but that was all, and enmity, though never expressed, was seldom far below the surface.

Although Berdeyev had judged it best to make no announcement, the official inquiry into the finances of Kharkov Province had ground to its almost inevitable end. Traskine had never supervised the treasurer or his accounts, had himself taken whatever was easily available, and most of the administration had followed his example. This much was clear, but in the absence of proper accounts and with everyone implicated, blame could only be distributed wholesale. In the confusion and demoralization which had reigned unchecked for years, the Gendarmerie had been able to manipulate the administration as they chose, and this at least Berdeyev had succeeded in limiting, chiefly by massive transfers of staff so the subtle processes of police blackmail would now have to be built up all over again. With Gatchukov now on his staff, it was impossible to keep the failure of the financial commission from him, and within a week Berdeyev was able to watch, with a certain sour amusement, the transfer of his attentions from Ilena to Marya Fedorovna. That at least was a gain, for Nipocritiy was unlikely to prove profitable, however won, and he had detested seeing Ilena fighting off Gatchukov's unwelcome attentions unaided.

As Suikevsky's campaign unfolded, all those who had shown themselves in any way sympathetic to or even tolerant of the governor found themselves under ceaseless surveillance and harassment. Finally, in desperation, Berdeyev dispatched Ivan to St. Petersburg with a personal letter to Count Orlov, head of the Third Section and a pleasant, lazy aristocrat who took considerable care not to discover the outrages committed by the department under his nominal authority. This was chiefly an excuse to send Ivan beyond Suikevsky's grasp before he too should be arrested and he was not hopeful that it would achieve positive results. This time Suikevsky had chosen his course of action skillfully and it was extremely difficult to find grounds for complaint which would sound convincing in far-off St. Petersburg where Suikevsky's application to his duties would be considered a matter for congratulation rather than reprimand.

Christopher came to see him before he left for Riazan, determined that at least one person should know of the sacrifice he had offered.

Gatchukov showed him in and would have lingered had he not been ordered curtly from the room, Berdeyev reflecting irritably that Volodya would have gone without being asked.

"I am sorry if I am disturbing you, but we are leaving today," said Christopher formally.

"I know, the roads are still bad but the sooner you have all left here the better."

Christopher looked at him curiously, noting the tense, fine-drawn lines of his face. He had picked up a certain amount of gossip while he had been in Kharkov, for Eleanor's rejection had made him both more perceptive and perhaps more understanding than he otherwise might have been. "Things are a bit tight, aren't they, sir? Not that it is any of my business," he added hurriedly when Berdeyev made no comment. "I—I just wanted you to know that I did ask Eleanor to marry me."

Berdeyev became absolutely still. "Yes, Lieutenant?"

"She wouldn't have me, sir. She said she wanted to stay here."

"Dear God, why?" The creeping threat to everyone who assisted him, or on whom he was forced to rely, had sapped his nerves as nothing else could have done and his sudden unreasoning pleasure was swamped in a flood of apprehension.

"She—she said she didn't love me any more or wish to return to England even as my wife." The anger and hurt pride were raw in his voice still.

383

There was a long silence and when Berdeyev looked up at last his face was unreadable again. "There is nothing more to be done then. I apologize for anything I may have said at our last meeting and hope that the remainder of your stay in my country may be pleasant."

Christopher rose to his feet awkwardly. "I am sorry. I mean, I hope we meet again one day under—under happier circumstances."

"I hope so indeed. Good-by, Lieutenant."

"Good-by, sir." He hesitated at the door and then turned back. "Forgive me, sir, it's none of my business except that perhaps I have discovered I am fonder of Nell than I had thought—" He broke off uncomfortably.

"Yes?"

"I—er—wanted to tell you the real reason I think Nell will not marry me, for it's a devilish good offer after all!"

Berdeyev smiled faintly. "And what is that?"

"I think she is—is very fond of you!" he blurted and then colored scarlet as if he had been dipped in boiling water. "I beg your pardon, but I have known her fairly well and I would not like her to—er—"

"Waste her life," finished Berdeyev coolly. "I know, that is another reason why I wished her to leave but if she will not go I cannot force her."

"I wanted to say too that very likely there is no truth in that old scandal I told you about her being . . . well, one of old Lovell's by-blows. I've never heard anyone else mention it if you were thinking—I mean I wondered why—" Christopher floundered and then broke off; he could not ask this self-contained foreigner his intentions as if he were Eleanor's father.

But Berdeyev read his thoughts again and turned away from the window where he had been studying the silent street. "Why don't I marry her myself was what you wanted to say, was it not?"

Christopher disclaimed hastily. "Not my affair at all, sir! Only, having known Nell so well, you see—"

384

Berdeyev had no desire to account for his actions to this unlicked cub and felt an almost physical revulsion from exposing any part of feelings upon which he could not allow even his own mind to dwell. But St. Albyn would be returning to England, to Ilena's home there, and God knew what rumors he might not spread, what hurtful letters Ilena's family might not send when they heard his gossip. He must somehow enlist his sympathy, must try to offer some sort of explanation for Ilena's difficulties with the police, explain his own position so that at least the stories the boy told at home would not revive any speculation there might once have been about Ilena's birth.

"There is nothing I desire more, supposing she wished it but unfortunately it is impossible," he said finally. His voice sounded unemotional as ever but it required the most savage effort of will to continue. "As you have probably found out, there is a feud here between the police authorities and the provincial administration which makes my position less powerful than perhaps appears. I have an undertaking from the police that they have no complaint to make against Miss Lovell, but now she is involved in our private squabbles it is very doubtful how much value that would have if it suited their ends to arrest her. Her only chance is to have no contact with me and to rely on her British nationality, which is greater protection than any I could give her even if we are at war. In any event, in my position, I could not marry an enemy subject in time of war. Even if these objections were removed, my position here is much too precarious to allow me to support a wife in the security I should wish, I am more than fifteen years older than Ilena and I am, as you said yourself, a cripple."

Christopher glanced involuntarily at his leg. "I'm sorry I said that, sir, but at the time I was too angry to care."

"You need not be, it is the truth." He extended his hand. "Adieu, Lieutenant."

Long after St. Albyn had left Berdeyev sat in deep thought. He had been more shaken than he could remember by Christopher's revelations, and then by the need to put forward, clearly and coldly, all that prevented him from achieving his heart's desire. He had known that Ilena liked him but that she should refuse a brilliant match and triumphant return to her homeland, which she had left in such loneliness and despair, could only be explained if he acknowledged that she loved him even as he loved her.

Yet instead of feeling overjoyed, it was the last cruel stroke almost beyond his strength to bear. He could not even speak to her or seek to lessen her hurt by explaining the insuperable nature of the barriers between them, so closely had Suikevsky succeeded in isolating him. Only the other day Vershinin had cracked a casual joke with him at a reception and the following morning found himself with questions to answer at the Gendarmerie. Of course they had been about something different, but everyone knew the true reason and hardly now dared to do so much as glance in his direction.

He dropped his head in his hands and for the first time let the deep tide of despair wash over him. How long could he hold out almost singlehanded against the immense odds mounting daily, struggling against a situation which demanded the wholehearted attention and co-operation of his entire administration? Even his own efforts were less effective than they had been as he felt himself distracted and torn by Suikevsky's steady, grinding campaign, wearing away his resistance and energy, throttling co-operation before it was born. During sixteen months in Kharkov, Ilena, his country, his work, Volodya, and Ivan alone had had any real meaning for him, and one by one he had lost or been defeated in them all. His defeat and his exhaustion lay heavy and sour upon him.

There was a slight movement at the door and when he jerked upright he saw Gatchukov looking down at him with triumph in his eyes.

Twenty-Seven

The remaining overflow of wounded, now reduced to a mere two or three hundred, were concentrated at the barracks hospital. Most of these were permanently disabled or too wasted or old to have the strength to recover from their privations; consequently the death rate remained alarmingly high. There was also the occasional case, deposited like unwanted rubbish from the passing supply convoys now flowing south again, who had fallen sick or been injured on the journey from distant depots to the north or east.

Eleanor still visited the hospital, her task infinitely eased by having them concentrated in one place, but not as frequently as before, since Madame Traskine had made it clear that one or possibly two excursions a week was the maximum she would allow. Perhaps unconsciously, Eleanor discounted any further risk of arrest or dismissal from Madame Traskine's service: she was not in a position to hear more than occasional gossip and speculation about Berdeyev's continuing difficulties with Suikevsky and was serenely confident in his ability to circumvent any future attempts to harm her. Even so, she was disappointed and hurt by his failure even to inquire after her well-being following her release from police custody. As week followed week without so much as a glimpse of him she became depressed and irritable but still unable to believe that what she and Suikevsky, Madame Traskine, and Christopher had all guessed was not true. Her own dawning love began to wither under excessive introspection as she vainly sought an outlet from the stultifying impasse which afflicted her.

With the coming of spring the long walk to the barracks was intensely enjoyable; the difficult part of Eleanor's journey now lay at its end when she had to force her way through the crowds of levies in the parade square and barracks block itself. Virtually no discipline could be enforced on these masses of peasants and those in whom hard work had briefly instilled a rudimentary understanding of what their officers and N.C.O.s were striving to teach were swamped by the fresh intakes arriving daily, scattered and lost without trace in the shifting throng filling every corner and for whom there were no instructors available. The new-comers were nearly always half starved, sullen, and resentful of the evil chance which had wrenched them from their homes without warning or mercy. While they were fed after a fashion, neither uniforms nor equipment existed with which they could be issued and the little that could be scraped together disappeared without trace into the featureless mob. The levies were contained in the barracks by armed guards on the gates, but the last ice had not yet vanished from the Lopàn and many of the braver spirits risked the perilous cross-ing and disappeared forever when the drifting floes wedged occasionally into a perilous ice bridge.

It was almost exactly what Berdeyev had feared would happen once large-scale mobilization was em-barked on, for he had no choice but to order that the best of the recruits should be confined in a small section of their own and the efforts of the instructing officers and N.C.O.s concentrated on at least turning these few into the semblance of soldiers. As a result the over-whelming majority were left in emaciated idleness day after day under increasingly appalling conditions, un-able to see any reason for, or any end to, their im-prisonment.

Their rough, unkempt bodies and mounting violence became a daily nightmare through which Eleanor had to force her way to the hospital, her tightly compressed lips and aloof bearing attempting to deny her inward fear. She could sense each time she went an increase in tension and the few inadequate guards at the main entrance now stood outside heavily barred gates nervously fingering their weapons.

Fortunately for her, Akim Akimovitch was one of the many who had been swept into the all-embracing net of the levy, and he usually met her inside the gate to escort her, with natural courtesy, to the hospital. Under the influence of his good-natured banter most of the men accepted her presence and were pathetically grateful for the few small presents and pieces of news she brought from the outside world, kissing her hands and weeping unashamedly when she gave them a token from their families or brought a reply to their messages to friends in the city. There were a few, however, who, usually drunk and half mad from the frightening spirits distilled secretly in the barracks cellars, sometimes turned her progress into a series of fights, terrifying in their primitive savagery, as those who had come to regard her as an almost sacred link with the outside world took battle on her behalf, enjoying the momentary relief from the unbearable monotony of the day.

"It is very bad today, *barishna*," said the sergeant of the guard as he unlocked the postern door for her on a particularly beautiful morning at the end of March. "All morning that friend of yours has been inciting them until he has them howling like the wolves that inhabit the forest around my home. You should not go in today."

"It seems quiet enough now," she said uneasily.

He shook his head. "That is a sign of much danger. I have sent to warn the garrison at the Customs House but they will not believe me. We have five more men on duty here but five men . . ." He shrugged. "It is nothing against so many."

Eleanor looked at his square peasant's face, enduring and fatalistic like so many she had known, but dis-

389

ciplined and reliable, one of the best products of the Russian army.

"I'll be all right, Akim will be waiting for me."

The sergeant shook his head again. "He is one of the ringleaders. I think he will be too busy to wait today and if he is not there I cannot let you through. I dare not send one of my men and I have the governor's orders not to let you go unescorted."

Eleanor felt a warm glow of pleasure at this unknown solicitude for her, but said lightly: "Any trouble there is always dies when the rations arrive, which is why I try to come at this time."

"Today it is the rations which may provoke the trouble. Your friend is leading this pack of *duraki*[1] in a campaign from which there is no retreat, for this day the rations are only potatoes now the grain is all finished, and he tells them that to eat means death and more than death." The sergeant screwed his face up in contempt for the ignorant beliefs of backward provincial sectarians, for he was a Great Russian from east of Moscow. "Either he must eat his words and the potatoes or find his followers different food, there is no other way." He swung the gate open and accompanied her into the courtyard, deceptively quiet and still, his musket at the ready and his finger on the trigger.

"There's Akim, I knew he would come!" cried Eleanor, adding softly to the sergeant, "I will speak to him and try to rid him of this madness if I can."

He nodded but spat as he turned back to the gate. "It is not within any man's power, *barishna*, or any woman's either."

She knew that he was right as soon as she saw Akim's face, uplifted and in some new way truly beautiful, fined down by conviction, illuminated by the feel and substance of power and secured by faith in what he did. When they were out of sight of the gate he slipped a modern English rifle out from under his tattered great-

[1]Fools.

coat, his fingers on the oiled barrel and heavy, rusted bayonet like those of a man on the skin of the woman he loved, mesmeric, caressing.

"Where did you get that?" demanded Eleanor as they walked across the strangely quiet parade ground between knots of silent, watchful men.

He did not appear to hear her, his eyes were all for those around him. He whispered, almost to himself: "The *starets* has sent to me, at last I am chosen to show the will of God, to blot out the curse of the Devil forever from our land and those also who would gather our souls to barter with him for his evil fruits."

"What are you saying? Where did you get that gun?"

His glance slid over her, his eyes no longer seemed to belong to someone she knew. He did not notice her presence at all, it was as if his body were carrying out his regular duty of taking her to the hospital without his mind being released from the blinding vision which held it to the exclusion of all else. When she repeated her question yet again in an attempt to break through to him, he only replied, in a curious rhythmic chant and addressing the men around rather than answering her question. "It is the hand of God, telling of destiny and justice, it comes with the swiftness of an eagle from heaven to shrivel the Devil and all his works from among us. Too long have we lain in his lust and followed his wickedness, sinning against the holy soil of our land and delivering our souls to be a barter of the Devil. Purge your sins, my brothers, purge your sins! God's sentence rests upon those who trade with the Devil: for your souls and your land His sentence must be carried out or His curse rests upon us! Purge your sins in the blood of the Devil and his followers—" His voice rose from a chanting, almost personal declaration of faith to a confident roar and then almost to a scream, his eyes tightly closed with the ecstasy of it and the rifle held above his head as if it were a sacred crozier.

The men around him murmured and one of them started haranguing the others around him, thumping the ground and pointing at the rifle. More joined in, their faces fervent, acceptance and passivity banished by excitement, shouting what appeared to be an affirmation of faith. "Follow the judgment of God! Death to the Devil and his agents!" Those in the foremost ranks sought to touch the rifle that it might give them the protection only conferred by a relic of exceptional power.

The crowd was developing into a struggling, avid, predatory, half-hypnotized mob in danger of squandering their ardor in bloodshed among themselves, when Akim proved himself to be a leader before he was a visionary.

"Silence, my brothers! God is not to be served in words but in deeds! Go, all of you. Seek those who will join our crusade and bring them to me that we may execute judgment upon the curse which afflicts our land, and feed again on the food which God gave us, destroying forever the Devil's balls as the scorpion is trampled by the wild horse!"

There was a wild shout of assent and the mob, like the pollen of an overripe flower, scattered and disappeared, leaving no sign of its passing except a steadily rising animal roar in the wake of their chasing feet. Eleanor was left standing, limp and numb, in an emptiness so complete it was difficult to grasp the truth of what she had seen only a moment before.

Abruptly, she too turned and ran as fast as her hampering skirts would allow to the hospital block. She had remembered all her arguments with Akim over the last few weeks in which she had been quite unable to shake his belief that Dr. Mavurian robbed those he tended of their souls, so that he might trade them for favor with the Devil. Nothing she could say had made any impression on him and in complete vindication of his beliefs he had pointed to the feebleness and lack of progress of those remaining under care in the hospital.

She ran breathlessly up the steep stairs and then

stopped dead when she saw Mavurian bending over one of the patients, a boy who yesterday had fallen from a gun limber and had his leg crushed. "Doctor! I hoped you were not here today! You must go immediately, have you heard the—"

He straightened up slowly and unclipped his pince-nez, a small man alone and afraid. "Yes, Ilena Vassilievna, I have heard what they say. Now it is almost true, for the men here have heard also and when they are well enough to understand they cower away from me. I can do nothing for them."

"B-but, Doctor, you—you must go at once!" she stammered. "I have heard Akim outside, they'll kill you if you stay, soon they will not know what they are doing!"

He smiled, trying to control the trembling of his lips, and wiped his pince-nez as carefully as if he had dropped it in the mud. "I should not get ten paces without being seen. If I stay here, away from sight, they may forget me or hesitate to come into the hospital or reinforcements may arrive. Meanwhile I have a task to do or this boy will not see the week out." He bent over the tossing figure on the floor again, but his fingers trembled so greatly that he could not unwrap the bandages, fumbling with the simple knots that held them. From outside came an angry, menacing shout and then silence dropped again as somebody spoke. Akim again, Eleanor supposed savagely as she stepped forward and took the bandage from Mavurian's hands.

She looked up at his face and saw that he was weeping softly. Not, she realized, with fear but with anguish, the bitter, frustrated anguish of a man who has given of his best and has seen it turn into corruption before his eyes. She wound the roll carefully. "Why did you come here today?"

He blinked at her and said, half angrily, "I had to come. If I had not I would never find the courage to walk the streets again. I would be admitting that what I tried to do all these years was a fraud as these ignorant peasants say. So long as anyone needs my services I must go; when I don't believe that any longer I will believe in nothing and will have sold my own soul to the Devil also." He bent down blindly and started to pick the dressings off the soldier's leg and then deftly, his hands still obeying a lifetime's discipline, washed, tended, splinted, and rebandaged it, Eleanor mutely handing him what he required and marveling at the indomitable spirit behind his ashen, twitching face, misted glasses, and absurd, scraggy beard, quivering as he clenched his teeth in an effort at control.

When he had done he sat down numbly, the mainspring which had driven his hands about their accustomed tasks run down, leaving only the shattered case of a man watching his fate approach.

"I will go and get the guard. They will escort you to safety," Eleanor said at length.

"It will be no use, I have felt that this would come for many months."

She was unreasonably annoyed to see in him the same fatalism which so often stultified all action in Russia. "Why should you be murdered by a stupid prejudice when you are the only doctor in the province who is any use at all? You must try to escape, for those who need you if not for yourself."

He smiled sadly. "Ah, Ilena, how little still you understand us. Without their belief in my powers I am no use to them or to myself. I have sinned against their beliefs, which perhaps is worse than sinning against my own. I accuse myself of this and am willing to die."

"Oh, nonsense! It's all rubbish and you know it! As a doctor you had to do everything you could to save life and it is not your fault if your patients and their holy man hate potatoes and decide that you are somehow in league with the Devil."

But he would not be comforted. It was almost as if he welcomed the judgment of others on doubts which had proved too hard for his own. Even in a qualified, educated man the communal spirit was still so strong that when he was condemned by the community his only reaction was to look for the fault in himself.

Eleanor did not continue the argument but hastily flung on her cloak and tied her bonnet strings.

"Where are you going?"

"I told you, to get the guard to escort you to safety."

"It is no good, they will not come into the barracks, they are too few."

"Then I shall have to go to the Customs House to—"

"Why should they believe anything you tell them? It looks no more disorderly here than it has looked for weeks."

She saw the force of this, remembering the sergeant at the gate had told her how his warning had been ignored. "In that case I will have to go to the governor and tell him what is happening so he can do what is necessary. It is no good just sitting here waiting for something to happen."

"You will be hurt, perhaps killed, Ilena, they will never let you through."

"I think they will, they have no grudge against me and they are used to seeing me around. Anyway they have many more important matters on their hands at the moment."

Mavurian shrugged; he was not really much interested. To waste one's energy in attempting to bend an obviously implacable fate verged on the blasphemous as well as being fruitless.

Outside, the parade ground was very quiet, the only sign of tension a growing throng of men by the riverbank listening in ominous silence to Akim, who was standing on one of the summer bollards, still holding his rifle like a standard of faith.

Eleanor slipped round the side of the building out of their sight and gained the shelter of the main barracks block without difficulty. But in the courtyard by the entrance there was another small knot of men talking and gesticulating excitedly, some holding iron bars and balks of wood driven with nails, two or three with rusty swords and one proudly guarding a very old musket from the envy of his fellows. She hesitated and then advanced boldly toward them, her mouth uncomfortably dry and her heart thudding unpleasantly in her ears.

- For a moment she thought they were going to let her through, uncertain and nonplused by her air of confidence, but when she was within a few yards of the gate one of them barred her way.

"Where are you going like a horse to his stable with his eyes closed? No one leaves until we all do, unless your spirit wishes to go alone, leaving your body here with us." He fingered the long artillery rammer he held and the others laughed.

"I am a friend of Akim Akimovitch, he has escorted me here in safety these many days. He will be very angry if his wishes are not carried out because today he is too busy to come." She replied calmly, making herself meet his eyes without flinching.

After a moment he looked away, a giant of a man but slow and clumsy, unable to entertain more than one idea at a time.

"Akim told us to stay here and stop anyone trying to get out, we all goes together. So we stop anyone going out, even you," he said stubbornly, but he was staring at the ground, confused and troubled, and she took heart.

"It is easy when many matters weigh on the mind for one of little importance to slip by unnoticed. Akim did not remember that I was still in the hospital, otherwise he would surely have given orders for you to take his place this day and escort me out in safety."

But her unfortunate reference to the hospital proved her undoing. "It is the hospital we seek to purge of our sins and send the Devil to heaven for judgment!" He advanced on her menacingly, his rammer cocked until the point rested against her throat. She tried to hold her ground and keep her eyes on his face but the blank lust to kill she saw there stiffened her mouth so that no words would form on her wooden tongue.

Dimly she heard the men arguing. "It is true she is a friend of Akim's, he will be angered—"

"She eats the Devil's balls, we must purge—"

"Akim himself has said that all who aid that Devil's-spawn doctor must—"

"—she has been our friend and has brought us many things."

"—let us keep her until we have executed God's judgment on the Devil and his works, then if Akim says she too must go to God, it is work for another day—"

"And I say kill now, what is one when there is doubt?"

There was a growl of agreement and the argument waxed hotter, the giant with the rammer urging his eagerness with wild sweeps of his ungainly weapon, and it was not long before Eleanor was almost ignored as she crouched back against the angle of the wall. The clamor rose higher and higher and the man with the musket leaned it carefully against the wall before it should be harmed in the inevitable fight.

Eleanor looked surreptitiously toward the gate, weighing her chances of reaching it unseen. The postern through which she had been admitted was some thirty paces away to her right but, as she well knew, it was double-locked and barred: long before she could convince the guard of her identity she would be stopped and this time there would be no mercy for her. The noise beside her rose to a new crescendo, it would not be long before others were attracted by the sound. She glanced again longingly at the gate and then tensed disbelievingly.

The postern was ajar.

Even as she watched, it opened a fraction more, unseen by her jailers, two of whom were already fighting, one wielding the leg of a table with a vicious-looking spike driven through the end.

Very cautiously, she saw a hand appear and then the face of the sergeant of the guard. He beckoned her urgently, but even as she hesitated there was a terrible scream beside her and she saw one of the men pinned to the ground by the spiked table leg like a butterfly on a cork, thrashing his limbs in agony and crying out in a horrible high-pitched monotone. For a moment she thought she was going to faint, the acrid revulsion of absolute horror rose in her throat, the sky darkened, and the hard roughness of the wall was heavy against her shoulders. Dimly she heard running footsteps and hands on her arm and then she too was running, stumbling, sitting on the blessed ground outside the gate with someone holding a glass to her lips. Involuntarily she drank and in the exploding fire inside her mouth and brain her faintness fled and she was shamefully, mercifully sick, there in the gutter before the curious eyes of half a dozen soldiers.

It was several minutes before she recovered sufficiently to stagger to her feet, almost in tears from weakness and shame.

The sergeant steadied her. "Careful, *barishna*, you should rest until you are well." He held out another glass of vodka to her.

She shook her head, trembling violently and pressing her handkerchief to her face in an endeavor to avoid their gaze. Suddenly she remembered why she was here and in the shock of recollection her own feelings and pitiable, insignificant embarrassment disappeared.

"I've come from the hospital! Dr. Mavurian is there —I think they will kill him if you don't get him out," she gasped, her voice thick and unreliable.

The sergeant nodded. "I warned him this morning not to go."

"Can you send a detachment in to escort him to safety? They are talking of—" She shuddered. "Soon it will be more than talk, there is so little time."

"I know, *barishna*, but I cannot risk my men in there. I could only spare three or four and they would be swamped long before they could reach him. I must keep my men together here, for I have the governor's orders

398

that whatever happens I must always hold the gate."

"Yet you opened the gate for me."

"Those sons of corruption were occupied with their own affairs for that moment and I could see that the *barishna* had no strength to run on her own."

"You came in after me?"

"Yes, *barishna*, but there was no danger if I was quick. I failed in my duty by admitting you this morning, the wrath of the governor would have been terrible if you had come to harm this day."

"It was a wonderful thing for you to do!" she said warmly, and he shuffled his feet and spat, looking away in embarrassment down the empty road toward the bridge. She added, more practically: "I must get some help for the doctor. Does the governor know what is happening here?"

"I do not know, *barishna*, I have sent messengers to the Customs House asking for further reinforcements, but most of the men they have are needed on the other side in case the ice is strong enough to bear those who would escape by the river. I think they do not entirely believe me when I say it is serious here now, for the messenger told me that they watched the parade ground from across the river but no man stirred or disturbed the quiet while they watched so they said I was but an old woman with bad dreams in the night."

"Well, I can tell them it is serious all right," Eleanor said grimly. "Have you a horse I could borrow so I can ride directly to the governor?"

He looked doubtful. "Not fit for you, *barishna*. There is my messenger's mount, which is a wild and dangerous animal with only a Cossack saddle, or the supply pony, which has no saddle at all." He indicated a sad-looking beast covered in mud, hanging its head dejectedly in one corner of the guardhouse.

By this time Eleanor was so well used to the deceptively run-down appearance of most Russian horses that she was not unduly cast down. "He will have to do then, it would take me half an hour to walk. Have you some sacks or anything for me to sit on?"

The pack pony was willing enough but his gait had a curious three-legged hop in it, peculiarly disconcerting to someone perched precariously sidesaddle on a pile of sacks. She took no notice of the laughter, pointed fingers, and shouted remarks that followed her through the bustling streets of the city, but the journey seemed endless: George, as she had christened him, utterly refused to adjust his accustomed pace to the circumstances whatever her blandishments.

When at last they reached the Government building she slid off his back with a sigh of relief and ran up the steps past the startled sentry, never thinking of the disheveled figure she must present. When she demanded to speak to the governor the clerk in the hall merely goggled at her, his stupid face agape with astonishment.

"Which is his room then?" she demanded impatiently.

He shook his head dumbly, but his frightened glance strayed to a passage at the end of the hall.

"Is it along there?"

He nodded and gulped. "Y-yes, but you mustn't—"

She did not wait for any further protests, her urgency driving through all the canons of conduct so painstakingly instilled into her over the years. The memory of the horror in the courtyard at the barracks was so vivid that the need to prevent the eruption of such uncontrolled savagery into the city overrode all other considerations.

The corridor was long and dark, flanked by doors on both sides, and she hesitated a moment irresolute, until she saw that one of them was ajar and recognized Gatchukov standing in the entrance.

"Excuse me, Captain," she began, and then when he swung round toward her she saw Berdeyev seated at his desk beyond. Unceremoniously she thrust past Gatchukov. "Oh, I'm so glad to have found you!"

Berdeyev rose slowly to his feet. "What can I do for you, Miss Lovell?" he said heavily. For once his control faltered, dismay and shock at her imprudence showing clearly in his face.

Gatchukov chuckled and Eleanor glanced from one to the other, sensing at once the tension in the room, then all was forgotten again as she turned back to Berdeyev. "I have come from the barracks to warn you. The sergeant of the guard sent a messenger to the Customs House but they do not believe there is anything the matter because everything looked quiet, but indeed there is! You must believe me. Dr. Mavurian is there and I think they will kill him unless he is escorted out and the sergeant dares not risk his men."

"Women's rumors!" scoffed Gatchukov. "If all is quiet, then all is well; it is only vodka that will make that rabble dangerous."

"Be silent!" snapped Berdeyev. "Why wasn't I told of this message?"

Gatchukov shrugged insolently. "It was not necessary. The officer rode on to the quayside and told me he could see nothing amiss across the river."

Eleanor made herself speak calmly. "It is not true. I have been in there and but for the bravery of the sergeant would not be here now. It is the quiet that is dangerous, this is not something to be angered over and then forgotten in a moment, but real determination. Akim Akimovitch has got them all following him, although I think for most of them potatoes are only a symbol of their grievances, for each a different one. I do not think anything will stop them now until they have destroyed the stocks of potatoes and killed Mavurian— I know it sounds silly and childish but it is not, not this time!"

"Akim Akimovitch is their leader?" asked Berdeyev, looking round for his cap as he buckled on his sword belt.

"Yes, but it—it is almost as if they were all run mad. I saw—" She shivered and clenched her fingers.

He touched her shoulder and smiled briefly. "Do not worry, Ilena, I will go and see what is to be done.

401

You should perhaps stay here for the moment, it might not be safe for you to go home until this is settled." If it is settled, he thought, turning to Gatchukov. "Go at once to the Customs House and order another ten men to join the guard at the main gate of the barracks, the remainder to reinforce the positions on the quayside facing the barracks and stop any attempt to cross over on the ice. They know; I have discussed it with them several times. Picked sharpshooters in the windows of the quayside buildings and ten men as rear guard at the entrance to the Customs House in case anything goes wrong."

Gatchukov shrugged, turned to go, and then stopped dead. Clearly through the open window came the distant crackle of shots.

Roughly Berdeyev pushed him out of the way, striding as fast as his leg would carry him down the passage. "My horse, *skorei!* Quick!" he called to the bewildered clerk. He rounded on Gatchukov in the entrance to the building. "Go at once to the main gate yourself and stay there. Whatever happens, it must not be forced, it must not be forced. If it is for any reason, retreat to the marsh bridge and hold that."

"And you, Excellency, shall I tell them reinforcements are coming?" With the necessity for action all Gatchukov's spite had vanished, diverted into more urgent channels until such a time as he would be free to scheme again.

"Probably not, you know the numbers of the garrison as well as I do and if there has been a breakout over the ice everyone will be needed on the west bank. Quick as you can now!"

Gatchukov saluted and ran off, tipping a passing merchant off his horse and commandeering it in a flurry of hoofs.

Berdeyev remained sunk in thought a moment, stooped and lonely in the bright spring sunshine, and then slowly unbuckled his sword belt again.

"What are you going to do?"

He started, her presence forgotten in his abstraction, and then turned away to throw his sword into a corner. "Talk to them. If there has been a serious breakout a sword will not help me now, any more than a hundred soldiers will be able to hold back thousands of berserk peasants, unarmed though they are."

"Akim is armed and they all have bars or bayonets or something! They'll kill you, you mustn't—they will not listen and you will die for nothing, one man could not stop them now!" she stammered, a great terror springing from the vulnerability of her love for him.

"If I cannot, nothing else will, although many will die in the attempt. The little opposition the garrison can offer will only serve to inflame them further and then God knows where it will end with the countryside swept bare of troops."

"But you can't! You warned them what would happen, it isn't your fault!"

"I warned them, but the responsibility is still mine." A trooper came running round the side of the building leading a horse to the sound of a fresh outburst of firing from across the river.

Berdeyev bent and kissed her gently on the mouth. She felt the hard grip of his hands on her shoulders, his voice saying huskily in English: "My love and my darling!" and then he was gone, away down the steps, mounting clumsily hunched against the hamper of his leg, then lost in a swirl of dust as he rounded the corner into Sergeievskaya Square.

Eleanor stared blindly after him, her hand to her lips, while in the distance the sound of firing faded into single shots again. Faintly interspersed she could hear now a continual thin howling like the hunting wolf pack they had heard at one of the staging posts in the central forests on her journey south so long ago. The sound then had rested for days in the fabric of her mind as they sped through the dark, enclosing trees and now she felt as if she were entering just such another claustrophobic tunnel of horror, losing all the sudden

403

promise of the future in the moment of its achievement.

Unseeingly she bent down and picked up Berdeyev's sword belt, and then stood half dazed, there where he had left her, turning the heavy leather slings over and over in her hands.

With the first rattle of shots the streets had cleared, all movement expunged from the dusty surface as the whirling autumn leaves are submerged, it seems forever, in the first drifting snow of winter. Only George the pack pony stood patiently in the solitude, chewing contentedly at an osier basket abandoned beside him.

George! Of course, she thought thankfully, knowing she could never bear to stay tamely in the city waiting in dread to hear a fourth-hand version of Berdeyev's death, even the thought of which resolved at last her troubled hesitations of the past weeks and made her realize how unbearable, how irreparable, would be her loss. She had no illusions over the havoc which would be spread by the simple, kindly men she had come to know at the barracks once they burst out of all control and sealed their victory with blood: in this mood mere words would never stop them. She just knew that she would sooner be there, whatever happened, rather than waiting endlessly in ignorance and slender safety.

George stood like a rock while she scrambled awkwardly onto his back, indifferently continuing to eat his basket even when she tried to urge him down the street. She was almost sobbing from strain and frustration when the last piece disappeared down his throat and he at length consented to move slowly into the square. Under her frantic kicks and cries of encouragement, which echoed round the empty façades of the pompous, overdecorated buildings, he broke into a heavy lumbering trot and then, probably for the first time since he had entered the army supply services, a jerking, uneven, perilous canter. Almost unseated a dozen times, tossed onto his neck, clinging desperately against being pitched sideways off his back, Eleanor strove grimly for control but, once having started,

George was not to be lightly stopped and he clattered down the quay and over the bridge into the Bazaar like the good army horse he was, making straight for the sound of the firing.

At the corner of the Ekaterinskaya she at last managed to bring him, quivering, to a halt, his pathetic, half-starved frame blowing and trembling with exertion, the scattered firing suddenly very loud and close at hand. Gently she urged him on again, hugging the shadow of the buildings and feeling very conspicuous in the brooding silence rendered only more intense by the occasional shot.

From the next corner she caught a glimpse of the Customs House, enveloped in a faint smoke haze. The following moment she was in a millrace of running soldiers, clinging precariously to the makeshift reins as George bolted irresistibly in the contagion of their flight, bearing her back the way she had come and depositing her like worthless salvage between the grotesquely ornamented pillars which formed a kind of breakwater at the city end of University Bridge.

At a quick order from their officer the men scattered into buildings and doorways on the quayside behind her. In their urgency no one seemed to have noticed the temporary presence among them of a woman and a pony. Nervously she shrank back into the slender cavity formed by the pillars with the parapet and angle of the bridge they embellished, realizing that if they were to attempt to hold the bridge her position was in the direct field of fire, although what good such an attempt could do was obscure when there were three other bridges into the city on the western side alone.

Cautiously she slid from the pony and backed George farther into the recess, tying his reins round the outstretched arm of a portly, smirking cupid, and then peered out, marking again the faint haze and ominous silence mantling the other bank. There were several large ice floes drifting down the river but here there was no question of being able to cross on the ice as there was lower down after the confluence with the Kharkov. There the river narrowed and ran between quite steep banks and the ice still occasionally jammed together in a series of semi-solid ridges which were briefly passable until the weight of the current caused them to break up with a crash, to form another perilous pattern of steppingstones sometimes minutes, sometimes hours, later.

The sound of another scatter of firing drifted across on the still air, interrupting for a moment the song of a bevy of chaffinches fluttering and calling around the burnished fire of the cathedral domes. In spite of the bright spring sunshine Eleanor felt as if one of the ice floes grinding under the bridge had touched her spine, each shot in her imagination directed only at the one she loved.

As if in immediate contradiction of her fears she heard a shout from the officer behind her and, turning, saw Berdeyev trotting up the quay from the south toward them. A great weakness of thanksgiving filled her and when she had recovered all the inadvisability of showing herself was again remembered: he would certainly be extremely angry with her for coming and would send her away at once, annoyed and distracted by the inevitable comments of his men. Yet if he were to die in the fragile crystal beauty of this perfect spring day, then she would wish to be here also and not huddled away in the illusory security of the city.

"I thought you were surely dead or captured, Excellency," called the officer.

"Not I," replied Berdeyev, drawing rein not twenty paces from her hiding place. "Only somewhat wet and cold."

"You never crossed on the ice, it's only below the Kharkov that it is piled thick enough!"

"No, Kaspar here swam. The ice was more trouble than the water." Indeed his mount was streaming with water and shivering uncontrollably and she could see that Berdeyev himself was wet to the waist but he appeared more cheerful and unworried than he had for many months. Now with the moment of action his frustrations and anxieties were forgotten and the cool, trained brain of a professional soldier cast aside all irrelevance. "You evacuated your men successfully and gave my orders to the Customs House, Kirsel?"

"Yes, Excellency," Kirsel replied. "Four men are missing, six killed or wounded, and Sergeant Kirimayev with twenty men is detached to block further approach to the Bazaar and other bridges."

"You told him to keep his men concealed and give the impression of being pushed back from the approaches to this bridge?"

"Yes, General."

The two men fell silent, staring back across the river where the sounds of shooting from the direction of the Customs House were becoming almost continuous.

"Will they never give up trying to storm that fortress when the rest of the city lies open to them?" exclaimed Kirsel fretfully at length.

"In their first fighting madness they are blind and deaf, it will take a repulse there and the open space of the quays and this bridge to bring any thought or sense into their minds," replied Berdeyev. "I have seen it before, where men are inhuman in their bravery while actually fighting, however hopeless their task. In the open and silence they are nervous and panicky as children in the dark."

"They are taking a long time to realize their madness and leave the Customs House in peace and plunder at their will."

"No one, not even a peasant armed with a rusty sword, likes to leave the enemy unreduced in his rear. Tell your men that when they do come no one is to fire until you give the order. Anyone who does will be flogged without mercy tomorrow." They exchanged a rueful smile, knowing that tomorrow was something which might well concern none of them.

"Yes, Excellency." The captain walked away and

Eleanor, through a hole in the ornamentation of the pillar, saw Berdeyev, left alone for a moment, slowly press his hand to his neck and stretch, like a man forcing himself to relax. Then he cocked one leg over the saddle and gazed about him, at the startling white of the ice floes against the muddy depths of the river, the rich blackness of the soil in the roadway, the strong blue sweep of the infinite sky, the silent, watchful, glittering domes, aloof but sentient with life above his head, as a man taking a last farewell of his beloved will look deep into her eyes, striving to commit every fleeting expression to memory. Then he slowly crossed himself, Orthodox fashion.

Eleanor cried out to him, to hold him from what he meant to do, to beg and pray him not to try, her limbs heavy and unmoving, her eyes closed, astonished to find she had neither moved nor spoken, that her desperate heartbroken pleadings were within herself alone. In this he would not listen to her and as her last gift she could not give him her weakness.

"It is as you ordered, Excellency," broke in Kirsel's voice. "They are good men as you wished, mostly sergeants from the training detachment, and they will not fire too early. When do you wish me to give the order?"

"When Sergeant Kirimayev and his men are pushed back from the western end of this bridge, I expect that Akim Akimovitch will lead his followers directly across the bridge here. It would be a long task to drive even a few determined defenders out of that rabbit warren in the Bazaar and we will hope that he does not realize just how few they are. Without firearms his rabble will have no stomach for such a task after the mauling the poor devils must have taken at the Customs House. Besides, if he doesn't lead them here they will surely come without him, and I think he is clever enough to know that then his authority will be gone, lost in a thousand looting fragments all over the city.

"I expect them to come slowly, fearful of the open after the hand-to-hand savagery over there. If just a few come at first, let them through without revealing yourselves, they will disappear into the city. When Akim and the main body cross I will speak with them on the bridge and try to get them to return to the barracks peaceably—"

"Excellency, you can't! It is madness, they will certainly kill you!" Kirsel's horror was a ludicrous echo of Eleanor's own.

"If that should be, it is as God wills. After such excitement as that they will surely come in a mass over the bridge: wait until the leaders reach that pillar there and then order rapid fire. They will have no cover and it may be sufficient to cause a panic with Kirimayev firing into their rear as well. If you drive them off the bridge keep your men under cover, never let them see how few you are, and try in the dark later to cross and wheel left, linking with the Customs House, and hold them against the riverbank so it is easy for them to return home or to the barracks when they are hungry or tired."

There was dead silence. Over the river the firing had ceased and Kirsel was tracing a design on the ground with his saber while he summoned up his courage for a protest. At length he said desperately, "Please consider, Excellency! What you propose will do no good and only lead to your own death. Once you are killed we are all lost and those swine across there will never surrender. We have a chance of stopping them here and teaching a lesson the province will never forget."

"And if we do not stop them? No, Captain, I am giving you the harder task. I would not wish to be part of such a massacre of my fellow countrymen as that will be, whoever triumphs. It is my duty to try to stop such a terrible thing if I can whatever the cost, and yours to oppose it with all the force at your command if I fail." He listened a moment. "They are coming now, wait under cover where you can see me and remember, whatever happens, don't fire too soon."

Kirsel saluted. "May God be with you, Excellency."

Berdeyev grunted noncommittally and wheeled his horse to the other side of the pillared recess in which Eleanor was crouching. She could see his back and the lower part of his face framed in the clumsy carvings and she ached to touch him, to comfort him as she saw a thin trickle of sweat running down his jaw and the way his hand trembled when he impatiently brushed it away. Whatever course of action logic and determination have decided on, it is hard to wait quietly under the indifferent sun to meet the face of death. But without doubt it is harder still to watch one loved beyond bearing tense in such a vigil, unable to protest or stay the inexorable passing of the minutes.

She was almost glad when the shots broke out again, much closer this time. Peering back across the bridge, she saw some figures on the distant quay, stopping to fire another volley and then running across the end of the bridge and diving into the comparative safety of the approaches to the Bazaar with its maze of hovels and shacks. She just found time to wonder irrelevantly at the complete desertion of everything in the city; for all the signs there were of any inhabitants, the scene might have been taking place on a deserted stage set, before the first of the rioters came into sight along the far corner of the quay.

They were soon joined by further groups from the side streets, wary and uncertain in the unexpected stillness and abrupt sight of the beckoning domes of the city, suddenly almost within their grasp across the river. Within minutes the broken, doubtful vanguard coagulated into a solid unquestioning mass urged and spurred forward by unthinking eagerness from behind. Here and there a sword or a bayonet winked in the sunlight and once there was a loud report as if an ancient blunderbuss had exploded in unwary fingers, but chiefly Eleanor was aware of movement, as if the mob were possessed of a life of its own, responding first to one touch and then another, eddying, lunging, contracting, all-absorbing, a wild unwary creature only half harnessed and dragging those who would grasp its reins into its own headlong career.

The first hesitant clusters of peasants began to gather on the bridge itself, peering round uncertainly for the sight of an enemy which would give them back their lost impetus. She saw one of them indicate the Bazaar and the whole of the western bank of the city with a sweep of his hand and held her breath, praying they would go that way although it would mean the ruination of Berdeyev's plans. But there was an angry roar from the greedy rabble behind, who would not have to lead the vanguard into those empty, unknown spaces but would certainly join in the fantastic, undreamed-of-scramble for the loot which lay so closely under their hands.

Still they hesitated, apprehensive and aware of menace in the brooding silence, and still no shot was fired, no glimpse of movement could be seen in the blind, tempting façades whose splintered reflections patterned the ice-lumped river. Suddenly a wild shout sounded across the still air and Eleanor recognized Akim, still carrying his rifle above his head, haranguing the group around him while their acclaim swelled and faded, exulted and sobbed with the tones of his voice, the gestures of his hands. Across the length of the bridge it was impossible to hear what he was saying but his meaning was unmistakable, his enthusiasm such that no man could stand against it and not feel himself shamed.

When he had done, the quays and the end of the Ekaterinskaya were jammed with cheering, shouting, unquestioning disciples, though they also had probably heard no more than a few of his words. Ready again to die for a cause which most neither knew nor understood but which, through him and his *starets*, had become the symbol of their own grievances and possessed again the whole of their allegiance. It was impossible to estimate how many of them there were, for the hard

411

core of Akim's followers from the barracks had been joined by many from the west-bank shacks and hovels. Two or three thousand probably, and instinctively Eleanor looked behind her to where she knew Kirsel and his small remnant were in position, but her eyes were arrested instead by Berdeyev, erect and tense in his saddle, half slewed round as he watched the scene across the bridge, his face full in her sight for the first time, gray and drawn, a muscle in his cheek twitching uncontrollably.

After a moment she found she could not bear to watch and buried her face in the harsh redolence of George's mane, hearing as if from a great distance the terrible menacing roar approaching toward her. George shifted uneasily under the infection of her distress and whickered plaintively, making her snatch at his muzzle, panic-stricken lest at this most disastrous moment her presence should be discovered.

She need not have worried, it was the moment of decision and no one would have noticed if George had trotted over the ice floes drifting placidly downriver. Akim and his fellows were advancing at last in a solid, congested mass, the rifle held aloft with a symbolic potato speared on its bayonet.

Twenty-Eight

For a brief moment there was darkness in Eleanor's recess as Berdeyev urged his horse slowly out from cover, blocking the light as he was framed for an instant in the entrance.

At first, so great was their delirium, no one in the shouting, singing, lusting crowd saw the solitary figure stationary at the end of the bridge until, like the stiffening of a hound who scents his prey, a faint tremor spread from the front ranks, bringing silence and then jubilation in its wake at this first sight of the enemy.

"Kill, Akim! Kill for the purging of our sins!" came in a great chanting roar as the mob swirled and broke in its eagerness to advance.

Very slowly Berdeyev edged his mount forward, his eyes and senses frozen to everything except Akim, perhaps fifty yards away as he leveled his rifle. So very different, this chill offering of oneself up for execution in its most disgusting form to the comradeship which dignified and helped contain fear in the other kinds of battle he had known. But the last time he had seen action five years ago, part of his command had been overrun and he had spent twelve hours with his leg pinned under his horse by a Kazakh lance until Ivan came back to look for him, and the memory of that too rode with him now in his trembling fingers and harsh, uneven breathing. Dispassionately, he considered the chances of a raw peasant hitting his target at fifty or even thirty paces, with an unfamiliar weapon and under such wild excitement as held him in its grip at present, to be almost negligible. He forced himself to discount the possibility and reflected how illogical it was for him to feel more exposed without the familiar weight of his sword at his side.

Damn the fellow, he thought angrily, suddenly aware of the sweat on his face and the leaden sickness in his stomach, will he never fire? Much nearer and even a peasant levy is bound to hit something. Sensing his fear, his horse hesitated, the sudden silence which had descended on the mob shivered into a wild howl of impatience and Akim, flustered, tightened his finger on the trigger, seeing only a blurred shape advancing toward him, his eyes trapped and held by the dull gleam of the rifle barrel, the potato askew on the bent bayonet, the faint smile on the governor's face as he edged up to him, forcing him back and nearly making him drop his precious weapon.

Where the shot went no one could tell, but with its passing Berdeyev was aware for the first time of a faint stirring of hope. Five minutes before he would have considered his chances of seeing another sunrise so remote as to be scarcely worth regarding, but when he saw the way the crowd fell back before him, their normal habits of submission to confident authority reawakened by what they felt to be his supernatural escape from Akim's shot, he knew that instead of a countless rioting mob he had one man with whom to deal. Dominate and shame their leader and the reins of control would fall into his hand; provoke or rouse their wavering will and he would die horribly under the bestial weapons most of them carried.

He was right on top of Akim now, who had made no attempt to reload his rifle, indeed he had probably little idea how it worked. Berdeyev considered fleetingly and then discarded immediately the idea of riding him down; he had to gain their minds and not show how advantage could shift through the death of one man when he himself was in their power. He had no illusions about the impossibility of the task he had given Kirsel: with himself would die the city and province of Kharkov until a punitive expedition could be mustered from among the depleted garrisons of the Empire.

Eleanor, not having Berdeyev's knowledge of untrained Russian marksmanship, waited paralyzed with horror for him to fall from Akim's apparently point-blank shot, unable to believe even when she saw the crowd fall back, leaving the two men facing each other, that he was unhurt.

Berdeyev sat a moment looking down at Akim while the tensions stretched around them into a surface fragile as glass, until at last, reluctantly, despairingly almost, Akim looked up and met his eyes. His head moved from side to side as if he were willing himself to look away, to tell his followers to kill this flimsy barrier between them and their desires. Words had seemed so easy, he had been so confident in the blessing of God which the *starets*' messages had conveyed to him, but now the unexpected turn of events caught him unprepared. The authority which had supervised and directed all his life leashed and drained his resolution, even while his mind fumbled at the task of unlocking his own limitations.

Never taking his eyes from Akim's face for an instant, Berdeyev leaned down and pulled the potato from the end of his bayonet. Amid a groan of horror from those around him, he bit off a small portion and swallowed it. "Now you." He held it out to Akim.

"No!" Akim managed to choke out, his eyes bulging like those of a trapped rabbit. The crowd swayed and was still again.

"You have spread your false beliefs among many, now is the time for payment or for proof. Eat and bring an end to your woman's fables of evil. If one shall die to prove your faith, let it be you who truly believe and not those others who follow; and if you do not die, then your words are but the idle croaking of one whose wits walk the ground with his feet." He held it out again. "Eat."

Automatically responding to an order, Akim put out his hand for the potato and then, recollecting himself, snatched it back. "No!" he screamed, at last managing to tear his eyes away from Berdeyev's and slashing wildly at his arm with the bayonet, forgotten in his hands through all those endless, paralyzed moments.

Involuntarily Berdeyev flinched, his horse sidling and snorting nervously, while around him the silent faces closed in, watchful, pitiless, caressing the feel of their weapons and savoring the drama and the opportunity that was theirs. They had much to avenge and none of it would be forgotten.

The sleeve of his tunic took the brunt of the blow, savage and only half aimed, but the point ripped flesh in a long ugly slash from wrist to elbow. By a miracle

415

he managed to keep hold of the potato and to regain control of his mount, forcing the frightened animal up again to where Akim stood, cornered and dangerous, urged to finish his handiwork in a steadily rising howl of execration from endless vengeful faces.

In that moment Berdeyev smiled, glancing round the dense hostile concourse before returning to Akim, compelling him to meet his eyes again by sheer force of will, dominating him until he could see nothing but the faint smile on his face and the light in his eyes, think of nothing but what was dropped into the confused chaos of his mind by Berdeyev's quiet words.

"It is the judgment of God you have sought, Akim Akimovitch, see how He has answered you." He held out the potato again, the blood running over the back of his hand smearing its innocuous smoothness. "The blood that you would have shed in this city in churlish rejection of one of His gifts returns to you alone; God has spoken, let no one stand against His words." Seizing his brief advantage while Akim stared mesmerized at the miracle so confidently pointed out to him, credulous awe muddling his shocked senses, Berdeyev leaned forward and touched his lips with the horrible object.

A great gasp went up from the crowd, appalled and shocked to the roots of their faith, for though most of them had no religious feelings about the consumption of potatoes, through Akim and his fellow believers that particular potato had become the rallying point and final cause of their rebellion and had acquired a mystical significance for all of them.

Berdeyev dropped it casually onto the ground, too shrewd to insist further on an advantage he knew he had already won, stood up in his stirrups and held his arms wide for silence as those at the back fought to see what had occurred to their leaders. All at once he was unbearably conscious of the heat of the sun on his neck, a brightness in the light which dazed his senses and blurred his vision for an instant, and a fatigue so overwhelming that at first his voice cracked uncertainly

416

when he managed to force his mind to fumble together the necessary words.

"You have been brought here to serve your country and not to weaken her in the hour of her mortal need. The difficulties and discomforts that you are suffering are but a small part of what is being suffered by our armies in the field. I cannot promise you alleviation of your miseries or deliverance from the perils you will soon undergo in defense of our land, but I know that I can promise on your behalf that this will not deter you and you will serve your country well and faithfully. May God grant you a safe return to your homes and your families after your willing service."

He hesitated briefly, wondering whether to refer further to the potatoes which were their inevitable rations until the summer harvest, but seeing Akim, slumped still in shocked incomprehension at his failure, he decided against it. All could yet be lost in laboring what had already been sufficiently demonstrated. A sure instinct made him finish, his voice echoing strongly in sudden emotion across the stilled throng. "We all, you as well as I, serve Russia side by side, it is not for me to thank you for your services. We can only pray for this land which holds our duty, our love, and our trust that under God we will not fail in our task so that a new future may dawn for us and for our children."

He raised his cap above his head and cried:: "May we justify the confidence Russia has in us, may God grant we serve her honorably and not deceive the hopes which rest in us. To you whom I trust! To Russia whom we love!"

There was an instant, a glass moment in time, of complete silence, then tumultuous cheers spread from bank to bank and it could be seen that many of the men were in tears.

. . .

If the Allies by a miracle could have advanced four

hundred miles from the gates of Sebastopol to the gates of Kharkov they would have found there that night no mean foe to meet them, no matter what their shortcomings in equipment and training.

Eleanor chose to ride slowly homeward along the quays to give herself time to recover from a weight of strain that had been almost intolerable. As she traversed the silent emptiness of Rybnaya Square she could see the dense mass of levies streaming back across the Lopàn Bridge into the barracks singing, characteristically, not one of the martial patriotic songs which might have been favored by Westerners at such a moment, but a soft haunting refrain from the steppes, fading and blending with the draining light of evening, caressing the land with their love as it had been throughout the ages: for the abstract of Empire had no meaning for them any more than it had had for their free-roving ancestors.

Out of the tired jumble of her thoughts she was conscious of one which jarred on the deep thankfulness she felt: pulled from its hiding place, she realized it was pity for Akim. Outwitted and bluffed by an experience and judgment far more profound than anything he could hope to understand, his scruples and beliefs exposed to contempt and his resolution tricked from him before a thousand comrades without his realizing how he had failed, she felt deeply sorry for him: and grateful at the same time for his credulous simplicity.

And Berdeyev? She was certain he had not expected to be able to stop the rising as he had, but how many more times would he be able to hold them in check, how long before the ardor he had deliberately invoked festered under idleness into resentment again?

For herself she wondered unhappily whether he would choose to ignore again the love between them which he had acknowledged in the moment of his extremity. She felt she could bear anything from him except apologies. She did not understand the motives which drove him but she hugged to herself the truth of his love for her as the light at the end of a lifelong

418

nightmare, of which this terrible day had been only the culmination, which justified everything, forgave everything, inspired everything.

Now that she wished for time to recover and regain her composure, George moved at a brisk trot and it was only a few minutes before he was clattering over Vossnessenskaya Bridge and she had to pull with all her strength to make him turn into the Traskine courtyard.

Her arrival was hailed with relieved astonishment by Madame Traskine and superstitious reverence by the servants, Theodosia touching her arm timidly to make sure it was not her spirit which had returned to them.

Eleanor pulled off her bonnet tiredly and ran her fingers through her crushed curls. "It is really me! I am sorry I wasn't able to get back before, madame." How trite it sounded, as if she had been buying half a pound of onions at a stall.

"Wherever have you been? We thought you dead or worse in all this terrible rioting, knowing you had gone to the barracks against all my advice. I hope that the government will see that those responsible are flogged until—"

"Please, madame," Eleanor broke in, seeing Theodosia's white face, and she added to her, "Akim is safe and well, I saw him only a few minutes ago and it is all over now."

Theodosia threw her apron over her head, sobbing uncontrollably, until Didi led her away.

"Did you say it was over? May God be praised! What happened?"

Eleanor told her briefly, adding: "I don't know what happened to Dr. Mavurian, I hope someone has remembered him."

Madame Traskine shrugged and then added: "You may tell Theodosia that Akim is well now but I warrant that tomorrow his bones will be picked white by the knout."

"Oh no! He—"

"You don't suggest that such an outrage, not to say

the deaths from your own words of several soldiers and the probable murder of an inoffensive doctor, should go unpunished? That whenever those animals have a fancied grievance they should be allowed to rob and pillage without hindrance or punishment? If I were Nicolai Pavl'itch I would round up a hundred of them as soon as they are safely back in the barracks and shoot them then and there, so that there is no possibility of anyone forgetting such a lesson. That is what he should have done long before this trouble broke out: shoot ten a day so they know who is master, and then there would never be anything to worry about. After today he will no longer be able to ignore his duty."

"Dear God, will this never end!" Eleanor cried despairingly. "He has done today the uttermost any man can do while everyone in the city crouched at home in fear! The peasants have many just grievances, the soldiers who died were doing their duty, Mavurian gave all the skill he had and was reviled, Akim believed in what he did and so did those who followed him. You cannot point to anyone and say he was right or wrong; everyone is right, everybody wrong, and I can't see how it will end."

Madame Traskine looked at her coldly. "Your experiences have disarranged your mind, Ilena Vassilievna. Force is the only thing these people understand or will ever obey. One moment of weakness and you have a reckoning like today's. It was most undignified of Nicolai Pavl'itch to plead with them as you say he has done, anyone with the true feelings of a gentleman would have died if necessary rather than do such a thing. You are excused from your duties until tomorrow so that you may recover your composure away from the children."

Eleanor curtsied thankfully and withdrew, her tormenting thoughts submerged in a blank wash of exhaustion as soon as she dropped onto her bed.

. . .

Someone was shouting in someone else's ear, rocking their bed until she felt quite distressed for them. The night would be so wonderfully peaceful if it were not for that disagreeable person disturbing everything. Eleanor groaned and turned over to remonstrate and then realized it was Theodosia shaking her own shoulder, pleading in an agonized whisper for her to wake up.

"*Barishna!* Oh, *barishna*, please!" she sobbed.

Eleanor struggled into a sitting position, her limbs heavy with sleep and her mouth parched and unpleasant. "What is it? What's the matter?"

"Hush! Oh, please, not so loud or someone else will wake."

Eleanor rubbed her gummy eyes miserably, then swung her legs out of bed and felt her way across to the washstand. The water was icy and after a moment she felt better and turned back to Theodosia. "Now tell me quietly what is the matter. Why aren't you in bed? It must be very late." As if in answer to her words a clock struck three.

But now she was awake Theodosia seemed incapable of telling any more, continuing to wail and sob, muffling the sounds with a towel as best she might, until Eleanor, quite exasperated, went over to the washstand again and threw a complete glassful of water over her and ruthlessly pulled the towel away.

"If you don't tell me at once what the matter is I shall return to bed and not wake up until morning." She smiled to herself, knowing her curiosity quite incapable of letting her placidly return to sleep.

But the threat had its effect and Theodosia's sobs abated immediately. "You—you won't tell anyone else, *barishna?*"

"I can't promise anything until I know what it is," said Eleanor cautiously. "I won't unless I must."

Theodosia appeared to take this as consent, for she hurried on. "It is Akim, *barishna*. Please, you must come with me. He is terribly hurt, and I do not know at all what to do."

"How is he hurt?"

"He—he has been shot," she sobbed again. "I think his spirit leaves him, *barishna*, unless there is some miracle you can do for him."

"Shot! Have many been shot at the barracks?" She had dismissed Madame Traskine's conviction that there would be reprisals as contemptible, convinced that Berdeyev was not capable of shooting down men in cold blood to whom he had publicly given and offered his trust. She was appalled to find that apparently he was capable of it, appalled and betrayed.

She felt ashamed of her doubts the next moment when Theodosia shook her head. "I don't know, *barishna*, for Akim came here to bid me farewell and then fired on himself in his shame at what happened on the bridge. I heard the sound after he had gone and ran along the riverbank after him."

Eleanor dressed hurriedly and followed her silently out of the house and across the shaggy grass of the garden, carrying some hastily torn bandages, a screw of basilicum powder, and a bottle of lotion which were all the medicaments she possessed.

Akim was lying in the muddy track which ran alongside the river beyond the far corner of the garden. The strong moonlight fell in chiseled fragments across the dark surface of the water and by its light she could see at once that there was nothing she could do. The whole right side of his chest looked shattered and with every breath he drew the blood bubbled ominously in his mouth and trickled thinly down his chin. Beside him lay his rifle but when she would have picked it up his hand tightened on the barrel and his eyes fluttered open.

For an instant he stared at her blankly and then his lips twisted and he whispered, "Ilena Vassilievna—it is —droll now—that it should be I—who—seek the— attentions of a—Devil's agent."

She knelt beside him. "Do not try to talk."

"It—will not make—any difference. You said—once that—only God could judge. I have tried—to do His will—and go to Him—for judgment." He choked and closed his eyes again. In the deceptive, indifferent moonlight he might have been already dead except for the painful rasp of his breathing.

"Can't you do anything for his pain, *barishna?*" wailed Theodosia, wringing her hands.

Eleanor laid her arm protectively across her shoulders. "There is nothing anyone can do."

"Ilena?" croaked Akim.

She leaned over and moistened his lips with water. "I am here."

"It will—not always be like—yesterday, will it? I am—I am glad to die—for I did—did—did—" He choked again but, when she made to calm him, he brushed away her hand and continued more strongly: "I was—I failed to follow my faith. When the—test came I could only see—see his terrible eyes—those terrible eyes looking—at me from his horse—and not —not—at all the cause we had—had to fight for. I do not understand—not understand—not under—" A terrible fit of coughing racked him, the blood running out of his mouth while she held him in her arms. Theodosia was shocked and motionless as a painting, a canvas figure doomed to look upon her dying love for the rest of time.

Tremulously Akim managed to touch her lips and run his fingers over her face before his hand dropped back to his side, but she never moved, could not have moved, looked as if she would never move again. As the breath relaxed slowly out of his tortured lungs he smiled, peace on his face as he murmured, "It will not always be like yesterday, Ilena."

"No." Like Akim, she had no doubts. "It will not always be like yesterday."

He smiled again and so, a few minutes later, he died.

Twenty-Nine

The Traskine garden ran down to the Kharkov River and it was one of Micha's greatest joys to lie on the unkempt grass watching the life which passed by its banks. Slow oxen would come to drink, washerwomen to pound their piles of clothes in gossiping groups, city water carts to fill their great wooden-straked containers, and occasionally, in the flood season, whole trees or bushes would float past on the swollen waters. Eleanor thankfully realized on the following morning that there was no chance of her being allowed into the barracks and after a late, leisurely Russian breakfast took her two charges out into the garden and made a pretense at sewing, her broken night and the strain of the day before showing in her shadowed eyes and the sharpness of her tone when she reprimanded Micha, kicking aimlessly at the mud on the river's edge.

"There's nothing to see, Ilena," he whined. "Why is everyone staying at home today?"

"They will be out later on," she replied evasively. "Look at those two pieces of ice there, like a galloping horse and a hunting lion. Which do you think will reach the bridge first?"

But he was not listening, staring back over his shoulder toward the house and then scampering off into some bushes in the far corner of the garden. Surprised, she started to her feet and then saw Berdeyev walking toward her, the sun picking out the red and gold embellishments on the green-blue of his uniform.

"I hope I do not disturb you," he said formally.

424

She smiled at him. "No, of course not, how could you?"

He turned away to look out over the shining water, watching another ice floe until it dived out of sight under the bridge. She hardly recognized his voice when he said at length, in English, "I have no excuse for what I did yesterday, except that I intended no insult and I have wanted to so very much for so long."

She laughed shakily. "Insult, good gracious! When I have been willing you to do it for weeks!"

"Ilena—" He grasped her hand painfully and then dropped it again when he saw Madame Traskine watching them unashamedly from the veranda.

Eleanor glanced toward the house, irritated by his restraint. "What does it matter? I feel I want the whole world to know how happy I am!"

He scrubbed at his face with his left hand—she noticed that he kept his right stiffly in his pocket—and said bitterly, "It does matter. Please believe me, Ilena, there is nothing I would have desired more than to be able to ask you to be my wife, but there are so many things against it that I cannot. Our countries are at war and Suikevsky is pressing so hard upon me that I may not count even my servants safe—you saw yesterday also what Russia can be like and I do not think things will improve." He paused and then added sadly, "I would offer you so much but find that I have nothing to give, not even a sound body."

"Oh, my dear—" She twisted her sewing blindly between her fingers. Unreal and impossible to be talking like this when she longed only for him to take her in his arms. "Oh, my dear, as if it mattered! I love you for the wonderful person you are and it wouldn't make any difference what you had to offer, it is only you I want. You are everything to me, I know that now. I know too what Russia is like, but together I could love it as you do."

He spoke very quietly, not looking at her, switching back into Russian to give emphasis to his words: "I think perhaps you know that my father was accused of being implicated in the Decembrist plot at the accession of the Tsar. It was true up to a point, he knew some of the conspirators, he was a vague idealist who knew there was much wrong in Russia but with little idea what to do if he and his friends had succeeded. After it failed the Tsar interrogated personally all who were accused, among them my father; some were shot, some exiled to Siberia."

He shrugged. "His Majesty never forgave those who gave his reign such an inauspicious start but that was not surprising, the Decembrists knew what they did and the penalty of their failure. My father was exiled to a settlement on the Yenisei River and my mother chose to follow him there. That was in 1826 and they were there for nearly ten years. I wish I could make you understand what my mother endured, nearly a thousand versts from Tobolsk—which is just a squalid village when you get there—with only semi-savage loggers, trappers, and traders for companions, my father sunk in despair and marshy riverbanks the only view as far as the horizon."

He shook his head and Eleanor saw with wonder there were tears in his eyes as he continued: "When my father died my mother applied for transport to Tobolsk; it was refused. She wrote to the governor, to the Ministry of the Interior, to the Tsar himself, explaining how she had gone there of her own free will to be with her husband, but everywhere the answer was the same: no pardon for the wife of a Decembrist once she had shared her husband's guilt. I was a cadet in Petersburg by then and did what I could but His Majesty was unchangeable, the subject was closed, and so there my mother died four years later. I only saw her once more." He touched her cheek and said gently, "I do not wish such a thing for you, Ilena *vozlublenny*."[1]

She turned her head quickly and kissed his fingers.

[1]Beloved.

"But you are no Decembrist! You are a general, a governor of a province, the Tsar has nothing against you!"

"I spent nearly twenty years in Kazakhstan, the Caucasus, and on the Khiva expedition because I was not trusted. I was fortunate four years ago to be introduced to the Tsarevitch[2] in Moscow when I was convalescing and to obtain the attachment to our embassy in London through his interest, where it was thought the doctors might be able to cure my leg. But I was retired from active service because the Tsar would not approve my appointment to higher command and it was only the circumstances of Traskine's death which led to my appointment here. Now the war has made it necessary to retain me for the moment, otherwise I should have long since been posted away to some obscure fort. One of the reasons I am so powerless against Suikevsky is that I dare not complain officially, it is I who would suffer if it came to the Tsar's ears and not he, whatever the rights and wrongs of the matter are. So long as the Tsar lives no one's connection with the Decembrists is ever forgotten or forgiven."

"But surely—"

"It is true, Ilena, I know, it has happened so often."

"Perhaps it was, but not after yesterday! It was only you who saved Kharkov from pillage and perhaps the whole province too. I didn't see Suikevsky or any of his policemen helping you."

"I don't know where he was hiding yesterday, but I do know that today he is writing an official complaint against me for allowing such a situation to arise and for encouraging it to arise again by not executing a couple of hundred of those wretched peasants as an example."

"But you warned them! You told them what would happen! How can you execute anyone now when you don't know which are to blame?"

"It is no good saying 'but,' Ilena," he said wearily,

2The heir to the Russian throne (later Alexander II).

"it has all been said long ago. Any warnings I gave will certainly be conveniently forgotten by those who ignored them, and the question of guilt is not important to the government where reprisals for rebellion are concerned."

She suddenly remembered the events of last night and said cautiously, "What would you do if you caught Akim?"

"He would have to be tried and certainly shot or exiled. I am sorry, my dear, I know he is a friend of yours but I would have no choice where he is concerned. Twelve soldiers were killed or seriously wounded, Mavurian is dead, and so are several of the patients in the hospital." He did not tell her the horrible way they had died, adding wryly: "I cannot afford to let revolutionaries use me as a training school. Next time he would be a wiser and more dangerous enemy if he won his influence back."

She did not smile. "What would you do if you discovered his body?"

Berdeyev's eyes narrowed. "What a remarkable question! Naturally I should instruct my men to bury him. He is dead then?"

She nodded. "Last night he shot himself in the lane there but Theodosia—we—hid his body because she was distraught and swore it would be desecrated and hung up in the barracks for all to see."

"You thought I would do that?" And, yet, God help me, perhaps I would, he thought, revolted. If it would do any good; but it would not.

"No, of course not! But she wouldn't listen to what I said and she was so desperate I had to help her. I'll tell her what you have said and try—"

Berdeyev smiled at her, the old mocking gleam back in his eyes. "You always have to help everyone however undeserving, don't you?"

"She isn't undeserving! And I liked Akim in spite of what he did. He really believed in his faith, enough to kill himself for it last night."

428

"I hope the next revolutionary in these parts is not more dangerous and less likable," he observed caustically. "Next time it will be more difficult to deal with, more dangerous; and the time after that again, and again until . . . I can see no end to it, Ilena, that is what I am trying to explain to you."

"I know; I understand, and as long as I'm with you I don't mind. Akim knew too last night, his last words were 'It will not always be like yesterday.' I'm not blind, my darling, I know there is no peace here, but together I am foolish enough to think we can at least have our love, be it long or short. Nothing else has any meaning."

He gathered both her hands in his left one and raised them to his lips. "You are—sure, *vozlublenny?*"

"I am sure," she said steadily, the certainty of her love unmistakable in the radiance of her face.

"You know that we must wait until the war is over? It must be between ourselves alone until then, not an easy thing for either of us."

She covered her eyes. "Is there no other way?"

"Only for you to petition the Tsar for Russian nationality, but while the war—"

"No," she said positively. "I don't feel myself at war with Russia, your country, my dearest, but I am British and I couldn't—"

"I understand, I couldn't either, and I was sure you would not consider such a thing." They stared at each other in a heavy silence before Berdeyev added bitterly, "It is only a question now of how much the Allies will exact as their price for peace. Two months ago we agreed to discuss the original points the war began over, and with the new campaigning season our position will grow weaker every day. Sebastopol cannot hold out forever."

"When the war is over will something be done for these poor people? There will never be peace here so long as the injustice and poverty of serfdom remain."

"It must come as it should have come fifty years

ago when we still had the strength and stability to withstand such an upheaval. To right a great wrong and emancipate the serfs will not now be enough, too much has been pushed out of sight for too long. I am afraid that when our present rigid control is relaxed people will be horrified at the pressure that has been festering out of sight for so long."

"But they must be freed!" Eleanor cried.

"Of course," he agreed. "But now emancipation will only teach them the strength and justice of their other grievances. A relaxation of our absurd censorship will not teach people a sense of responsibility in what they write. I am only so anxious, Ilena, that you should not be misled by what waits for you here as my wife and a Russian citizen. There is no magic formula which will solve such difficulties in our lifetime. I think that every year things will become more difficult, more dangerous, more wearying, more insoluble. If I remain here as governor I shall often have little time to spare for you and if I do not, as is very likely once the war is over, then with my background the best I could hope for is a posting to the East, which can be very terrible for a woman. At worst—" He broke off and added angrily, "If I had not behaved like a blackguard yesterday, lost to all control and decency, it would never have come to this."

"And you regret it?" she asked, smiling.

"For you, yes! I intended this morning to apologize, to—to make you go, to show you it was nothing but a passing impulse which meant nothing, although in my heart I think I knew you would not believe me, certainly after Suikevsky's efforts the other week. Then I could not speak the lies I knew I had to speak. I cannot think how I came to forget myself in such a way yesterday."

"You thought you were going to die. At such a time there is room only for the truth. Perhaps in a small way it was a miracle of God we found each other at such a terrible time, but now we have, surely it is for me

430

to say yes or no when a man asks me to marry him, and I say yes, a thousand times yes, my dear! Do let us stop being sorry about things we can't help. I keep trying to tell you I am so happy nothing else matters at all, but you are being very difficult about it."

"*Vozlublenny*," he said desperately, very red in the face, all his balance and aloofness swept away. "It is only that I feel a thief to accept such a gift when I know the sum of it and you do not." He added ruefully, "If anyone had told me I should propose marriage, unable to take the lady of my choice and the light of my life in my arms, watched by half a dozen people and interrupted by a crawling child, I should have thought them mad." He watched as Eleanor bent to detach Sacha from the seat he was precariously attempting to climb. "Life certainly makes fools of us all."

She laughed. "It suddenly seems a very nice sort of foolishness to me!" She studied his averted face, by now so familiar to her as a façade, with its thin bones, deeply etched lines, and straight, defensive mouth, but she knew she was only just beginning to understand his thoughts and fears. Not naturally a humble man, she realized now that his pride was deeply and sensitively hurt by what he felt to be the selfishness of his love for her. Upright and generous by nature, all his life he had labored against suspicion, loneliness, and mistrust to find that from her whom he loved he could only accept and not give.

"You were there on the bridge yesterday, weren't you?" he asked unexpectedly.

She nodded. "You saw me standing by the pillar when you came back from speaking to the levies? I wondered whether you had but you gave no sign so I thought perhaps you had not." She remembered his beaten, exhausted face which had forbidden any approach as he rode by as if in a trance.

"I did not remember until afterward that I had seen you. It was as if I was drunk; I stared at Kirsel like a lunatic for God knows how long trying to find the

431

words to tell him to warn Gatchukov and the gate guard not to fire on the levies when they returned to the barracks. I am sorry I did not take you home but I do not remember anything else until nearly an hour later when I was in my office, although I am told I walked into the building quite normally." He frowned uncomfortably at the memory. "Just as well no one saw their governor lost in a stupor of fear while anything could have happened in the city."

"Please don't talk of yourself in that dreadful way, as if what you did was not the most wonderful thing! I would have given anything to have stopped you but somehow I was proud to know I could not." She touched his stiff sleeve. "How is your arm today?"

Berdeyev shrugged and grinned suddenly. "All right, but a damned nuisance with that fool Gatchukov hooking my tunic up all wrong and some idiot with five thumbs shaving me as if he were plowing a field."

Eleanor laughed and with one consent they turned and walked back toward the house, with frequent pauses while Sacha scrambled along behind them. "All the same you should be careful, the bayonet was very rusty, I saw it last night. You must not forget you owe some care of yourself to me now."

"You need not worry about that. In our present shortage of doctors Gatchukov much enjoyed tipping a carafe of vodka over it, which by the feel of it should take care of any little trifles like rust." Eleanor felt her mouth dry at the very thought, but he continued cheerfully, "The poor fellow is in a sad quandary, not knowing whether to continue plotting against me with Marya Fedorovna and Suikevsky, to follow me now and see what he can glean on the way, or to start some more private schemes of his own."

"Surely there isn't the least doubt about it," objected Eleanor, "he couldn't possibly live without schemes of his own." They both laughed, their love and contentment with each other suddenly sealed by the meaningless words.

"I'll tell you one thing, Ilena," he remarked abruptly while they waited for Sacha at the top of a bank. "Even if we are not married by next winter, somehow I am going to give you some proper furs. The sight of you in those miserable cast-off scraps of Marya Fedorovna's and your stupid English cloak has driven me nearly distracted these last months."

"That would be very nice," she said primly, her eyes dancing, and he laughed again, the hard lines of his face relaxing so that he suddenly looked much younger. She wondered how she could ever have thought him cold and unapproachable. "Do you know what made me first wonder whether I wasn't becoming rather too fond of you? When you came to that awful lunch at Nipocritiy last summer and I nearly laughed at Madame Traskine languishing at those officers. I looked up and saw you were amused too. I have missed almost above everything someone to laugh with since I left home."

He held her fingers a moment. "One of these days I am going to kiss you where the dimple comes on your chin when you laugh. I hope—I hope nothing I ever do will make the laughter fade and the lines come to your face." He carried her hand to his lips. "I give you my word, although I hope not to show it again by getting drunk as I did that night, that I have loved you since that afternoon on the bridge of the *Neptune*, each day more than the one before, and I will love you to the day I die whatever may happen or come between us."

"Whatever may happen, nothing will come between us."

"I must go now, my love," Berdeyev said gently. "There is much to be done and I have stayed overlong already. I do not know when I will be able to see you again, we will have created enough food for gossip this morning, although the events of yesterday are some slight excuse for the curious. I have no desire to give Suikevsky more cause than he already has for worrying you."

"Whatever you decide, I will understand until there is peace," Eleanor said steadily. "After that we take our chances together."

He was about to mount when he remembered something. "Would you like me to send someone for Akim's body? Have you hidden his rifle? I cannot imagine where he found it but it is about the only modern weapon in the Kharkov armory."

"I think perhaps I should speak to Theodosia first and send someone with a message to your office. I am afraid I threw the rifle in the river, it seemed to have such terrible evil attached to it and—and perhaps I did not wish it to be used against my countrymen in the Crimea."

He stiffened and then smiled, but this time without humor. "You see, there are still some things between us, Ilena my love."

Thirty

Timidly, uncertainly at first, and then with a pent-up feverish gaiety, the city of Kharkov celebrated its escape. "Levy" soirees and "riot" routs were all the mode and parties of sightseers crowded the Kontorskaya and the quays of the Lopàn, the ladies fluttering their parasols and retreating in mock alarm whenever a temporary bridge of ice was formed before it ground into fragments again with a crash the next moment. For now the early heat of spring had come, gay muslins and light silks were everywhere and the last fragments of ice were melting on the upper reaches of the rivers.

The peasants were flattered by this interest and shouted good-natured jests across the water, their dangerous mood evaporated for the time being by the excitements of their Day, the events of which were happily told and retold, embellished and disputed in every corner of the barracks. No ill effects had been suffered by those who ate the potato rations and as the alternative was voluntary starvation, with the disappearance of Akim there were few who now held out against them.

Under Berdeyev's direction the entire barracks compound was divided into a series of strips, fenced off from each other, a group of levies allotted to each one, and their seclusion from each other enforced as rigidly as possible. Because the fences between them were both flimsy and vulnerable, this would have been impossible had it not been for the friendly co-operation which still characterized the levies since their return to the barracks. They did not understand what they were intended to do or why, but Berdeyev had, temporarily at least, engaged their sympathy and interest and they were willing to try.

So while there was endless visiting between the various enclosures, most of the men returned to their own in between times and the painful business of instruction ground slowly into gear again. The smaller groups thus formed rendered their instructors' task only a trifle less hopeless in the absence of any stiffening of trained soldiers whose methods they could copy and whose knowledge of the difference between their right and left hands would at least serve as a basis on which to build. The training schedule was not improved either by the generally low standard of the instruction officers, most of whom regarded it as a deep insult to be denied the glory of battle and took every opportunity of absenting themselves from duty and devoting as much of their time as possible to more agreeable pastimes in the city.

These pleasures were abruptly shattered by the incredible news of the Tsar's death. Nicholas I, Emperor of All the Russias, the "Gendarme of Europe," had died of a chill and disillusion of spirit ten days before in far-off St. Petersburg, as he saw all he believed he had built during his reign crumbling in anarchy around him.

The news was brought by Ivan, returning as fast as he was able to acquaint his master of events three days before the official announcement was received. Official mourning was proclaimed, a breath-takingly beautiful requiem held in the cathedral, and Berdeyev seized his opportunity to pardon in the name of the new Tsar the remainder of the levies, except for one who, somewhat at random, was convicted of the murder of Mavurian and shot. Unobtrusively too, away at Chuguyev, it was life for Corporal Domovoye. Not even the most trivial victory for Russian arms had lightened the passing weeks but now the accession of a new Tsar provided the excuse Berdeyev sought. Stepàn Karajevitch Domovoye received a dishonorable discharge, papers and money to take him away to safety on the Don steppe together with a stern warning which Berdeyev sincerely trusted he would have the intelligence to interpret as an instruction to keep his mouth shut. Riding back from Chuguyev very late at night afterward, Berdeyev found his thoughts turning toward the future with more hope and confidence than he would have believed possible: love and the incredible warmth of love returned were so unexpectedly his, and now perhaps the chance also to enjoy this gift, if not in peace, then at least with a measure of personal security.

Eleanor managed to hide her joy at the news from her stricken companions, whose personal veneration for the Tsar, whatever his failings, was real and vivid down to the least serf who wept while he swept the cobbles of the courtyard. Although he had not said so, she knew that Berdeyev had felt weighted out of everything he undertook, no matter what his endeavors, so long as the Tsar's animosity relentlessly remembered his connections with the Decembrists. Now after thirty long years the account was closed and with a new reign the shadow of the past could at last be allowed to rest.

Already it was rumored that the new Tsar had made fresh overtures of peace to the Allies. These rumors were received with sullen acceptance by most but to many of the romantic idealists, pouring out their faith in the overwhelming future of the Slav race everywhere, it seemed like a fresh betrayal. To a very few the idea of peace was repugnant for quite other reasons: here and there Eleanor heard the whispered desire that Russia would be totally defeated, her towns and countryside given over to rioting and protest as only by the utter ruin of the past could a new future be born. The fear that nothing would be changed, that everything would be changed, that the wrong things would be changed in a future full of promise and uncertainty and menace all at the same time, unlocked tongues in a wave of unaccustomed, heady speculation. No one knew what the new Tsar was like, what he would do, what he could do; only one thing was certain, after thirty years in which the future, the present, and the past had become one gray monotony of boredom and repression, nothing could ever be quite the same again.

Although she listened eagerly to all the debates which were now rife in every drawing room, Eleanor could think only of one thing: at last peace was near, at last the days of pretense, of longing, of concealment were running out. For she saw little of Berdeyev although she was intensely conscious of every fleeting glimpse she had of him, and each time his name was mentioned she had to bend her head lower over her sewing lest anyone should remark on the light in her eyes.

She did not resent his enforced absence: until the time came when the need for secrecy was past it was better so and her life had not taught her to expect any great regard to be taken of her own inclinations and desires. She knew that when he could come to her he would, and until then they were unable to trust themselves sufficiently to meet with equanimity under the public eye.

During those fleeting days of spring she was happy as she had never been happy before, all her doubts and self-questionings surmounted and finally dispatched. Her contentment spread to those around her, even Theodosia emerging sufficiently from her red-eyed apathy to help her limewash the nursery after Didi had taken out the double windows, always a sign that the long winter was over for another year in Russian households.

Letters from England continued to arrive, despite frequent delays and occasional lost communications. The Postal building was in the Mikhailovskaya Square only a few minutes from the Traskine house and most mornings Eleanor and Micha would walk there in the hopes of finding some letters, for he was as enthusiastic as she, his imagination captured by this fabulous land from which Ilena came, surrounded by sea wider than the Lopàn River, the greatest stretch of water he had ever seen.

Eleanor was surprised, one morning in May, to be handed a letter from her mother, for Mrs. Lovell was a meticulously regular correspondent and it was another six weeks until her turn to write should again come round. Micha grumbled all the way home, for her letters were dull and moralizing; he liked best those from Charlotte describing London where she had spent her honeymoon or John's scribbled notes telling of wagers he had lost.

He was so uninterested that he did not even ask her to read it to him and Eleanor was able to spread out the flimsy sheets in the privacy of her own bedroom. Half an hour later she was still staring at them, sick and cold, numbly trying to comprehend the depths of the disaster written there. The strong, angular writing reached out to her, bringing across the gulf separating her from home the substance of a shadow that had overhung her for so long and now finally shattered her hopes. Flimsy, insubstantial, beautiful, unrealizable dreams they seemed to her now and in her agony she had not even the impulse to fight against her sentence any more.

Dry-eyed she took Micha and Sacha for their afternoon walk, dry-eyed she penned a short note to Berdeyev asking him to visit her as soon as possible, silent and composed she moved through the interminable day, but when night came she felt as if she had been through a great illness and hour after hour stared at the shadowed ceiling, her eyes aching but denied the easy solace of tears. The long years stretching before her were endless in their repelling, lonely bleakness.

The morrow was a Sunday and she went to the Lutheran church as usual, praying for strength to carry through what she knew she must do, for during the night she had determined on one thing: she must leave Kharkov and at once, to stay here now would be beyond bearing.

"You are looking moped up today, my dear, what's the trouble or aren't you feeling well?" Mrs. Braillard accosted her in the porch after the service, the fat contours of her face pouched with concern.

"I'm all right, thank you." Eleanor smiled wanly, trying to escape the old lady's shrewd glance.

"You don't look it! Come on now, what's the trouble? Nothing gained by hiding a niggling tooth or an aching stomach, you know!"

"I'm all right, really I am!" she repeated desperately.

"That's as may be, but I know what I see and it isn't all right! No good nursing it on your own, you are coming home with me as usual, I hope? A good English lunch, none of these Russian gewgaws, and you'll soon see how much better you will feel."

"Please, I—"

But her protests were brushed aside and she found herself borne along unresisting on the flood of Mrs. Braillard's good will, too tired and apathetic to object further.

Throughout the meal Mrs. Braillard kept up a continuous flow of chatter ably backed up, after several admonitory kicks, by her normally silent husband, who speculated hopefully on his chances of delivering un-censored lectures again under the new regime.

"For I hear, mademoiselle, that the new Tsar is a realist; although he doesn't like reforms he will carry them out because they are inevitable, *l'intelligence les demande!*[1] Already the police are more circumspect in case their power is to be less, for no one knows how things will go. The governor will find his tasks easier now." He gave her a sidelong, Gallic glance and if Elea-nor had been less wrapped up in her own cataclysm she would have realized that the Braillards at least had heard some of the gossip which had followed Berdeyev's visit to her, before it was mercifully swamped by the news of the Tsar's death and finally dispelled by their later caution.

Mrs. Braillard kicked him again, warningly, and broke in, "It will take more than the death of a Tsar in Petersburg to make the police circumspect. Circum-spect! With three people arrested yesterday and only two released today."

"All the same, they are being more careful, or per-haps one should say less blatantly illegal. I see by the way, mademoiselle, that the *salaud*—"

"Armand!" shrieked his wife, clapping her hands to her ears.

"Son of a diseased camel if you prefer it, my dear," rejoined her husband tranquilly, and Eleanor, even in her desolation, was betrayed into a faint smile. "—Gat-chukov, has decided he would not be running too much of a risk any longer if he lays siege to Madame Tra-skine and tries to obtain Nipocritiy that way. Now there seems no chance of an inquiry convicting him, more than many others in the province, I expect he feels himself more likely to win by marriage than by the infantile intrigues he has been pursuing."

This plunged Eleanor even deeper into misery, as with poignant grief she remembered the joke over

[1] Common sense demands it!

Gatchukov which she and Berdeyev had shared and how it had seemed then to seal their certainty of each other. She was spared from having to reply by the entrance of a servant who murmured something in Mrs. Braillard's ear. She nodded and beamed. "Show His Excellency into the parlor." Once the servant had gone she turned to Eleanor with a twinkle. "I have a feeling, my dear, that it is you and not I whom our governor wishes to see."

* * *

Eleanor stood a moment in the hall summoning up her courage for what she felt was about to be the most difficult hour of her life. She hoped desperately that Berdeyev would not be too angry with her for asking him to meet her in this imprudent way and with what she had to tell him. In her present state all her earlier fears of hasty words and high temper had returned and when she opened the door she was only holding onto the tattered shreds of her composure.

He was standing with his back to the window, his face in shadow: even with the eye of love it was still difficult to interpret his expression.

He came forward at once, taking her hands and raising them to his lips. "What is it, my love?" he asked, seeing the dark rings under her overbright eyes. At the sound of his voice, with its clipped syllables and accented English, her mouth trembled and she could not speak, fumbling clumsily in her reticule for the letter before thrusting it at him.

"What is it?" Berdeyev repeated, turning the paper over in his fingers but with his eyes still on her face.

"Please—" She gestured at the letter.

Puzzled, he looked down at it, smoothing out the crumpled sheets and frowning over the difficult writing and crossed lines.

Eleanor could not look at him while he read; she moved over to the window and stared out unseeingly at the dreary log-built back yards which the graceful, decorated fronts of the Kouznetchnaya concealed.

She felt Berdeyev's hands on her shoulders as he pulled her round to face him. "Look at me, Ilena."

"Please," she whispered, "please just go, I know it is all impossible now, you—you do not need to tell me polite lies."

He put his fingers under her chin and gently forced it up. "Look at me," he repeated quietly, smiling as he kissed her. "I told you I would kiss your dimple where you laugh at the next opportunity, so you have only yourself to blame."

She clung to him sobbing. "You make it so hard for me! Please, I must go, I—"

He stood away from her. "Where do you think you are going?"

"I don't know! Kursk, Moscow, it doesn't matter where, but I cannot stay here near you when—"

"My little love," he said tenderly, "you did not think this rubbish would make any difference, did you?" He crumpled up the letter and stuffed it into his pocket.

"But it does, it must! And it is not rubbish, it is true, I know it is. It must be, when it explains so many things."

"I think probably it is, but why should it matter? I knew about it anyway."

"*You knew?*"

He led her to an aggressive-looking settle and drew her down beside him. "When we have our own home I refuse to have a piece of furniture like this to sit on in moments of stress!" She made a gesture of protest, blowing her nose defiantly, and he tightened his arm around her. "Listen, dearest, St. Albyn told me his father had always wondered about your parentage because of the way your mother treated you, and from what you yourself had told me, I was not surprised. I had wondered myself. I could not imagine anyone allowing their own daughter to come unprotected to Russia when there was no need for it. I still cannot understand how your father—but that is not my affair. I must be glad for what they did from my selfish point of view, though when I wrote informing them of my intention to marry you I had considerable difficulty in not allowing my opinion of them too free a rein! It may be a little while before they receive my letter as I did not wish it to be censored and had to send it by rather devious means."

"You have written to them?" she said dazedly. "But if you know, don't you mind?"

"Why should I? I am glad you have nothing of your so-called mother in you. From everything I have heard, I should much dislike to marry her daughter."

"But—but the disgrace! It is a terrible thing, you cannot marry a—a—" Her voice broke and then she continued evenly: "A baseborn nobody. You are a count, a governor, a general in the army, I could not bring you disgrace like that. I should feel shamed in myself even if no one ever knew, to think that your wife had not even a name she could call her own."

"Will you listen to me?" he demanded, shaking her lightly. "If we are talking of families, I bear a name which is disgraced enough, our property sequestered and my father fortunate to escape execution. And as to being governor, that with all its disadvantages may not last so very long, so we have decided not to worry about it, and there are hundreds of generals in the Russian army—and hundreds more in the civil service! It is not such an unusual thing to be as it is in England. But you in your generosity have already said it is I you want to marry and the disabilities of my position and the fact that I am—I am neither fit nor young, as you know, has not weighed with you.

"It is you that I want to marry, not your family— heaven forbid!—or your birth, what should it matter to me? On the contrary, I am glad as I told you. I am already contemplating with pleasure the prospect of composing another letter in reply to this in which I can be as insolent as I please."

Eleanor gave a watery chuckle but said wistfully,

"I suppose Christopher told you as one of the reasons he did not want to marry me? I see now he must have known when he came to say good-by to me at Abbotsfield."

"Why, yes, and I told him then it was not a reason but an excuse, and I am not seeking excuses. I wonder whether you realize, my dear, what a compliment Mrs. Lovell paid you in that letter?"

"Compliment?" She blinked at him.

"She may have cloaked her feeling for you in religion, but to me it is more like plain resentment and jealousy. She is angry you have not been defeated by the fate she forced on you, and which she forced on you because she felt defeat was your due. Now she has realized that you are not only undefeated but happy as well, so she has made this last attempt, which she calls her duty, to spoil it all for you again. She knew you well enough to be sure you would tell me, whatever the cost to yourself. She does not even know my name. As I understand it, this is written only because St. Albyn must have sent some indiscreet gossip home to his parents when he reached Riazan and they presumably told your father." That inconsiderate little whelp, he thought, I certainly wasted my time trying to explain things to him. "Any other woman would have burned this letter and said nothing about it, except you, my love."

Eleanor looked up at him shyly. "I am glad I didn't."

He held her tightly and said huskily, "And I, *vozlublenny*," before his lips were on hers and complete joy and understanding were theirs at last.

.   .   .

"I am sorry, did I hurt you?"
"Yes, no! Kiss me again."
"*Vozlublenny!* My very own."

.   .   .

"I wish generals didn't have so much gold braid, it is very scratchy." She rubbed her cheek on the front

444

of his tunic. "If I hadn't seen you those days on the *Neptune* in ordinary clothes I would have thought you were born in uniform like all the other Russians."

He laughed. "And I wish we were not perched on a piece of furniture like a gun limber!"

In the fading light the two figures were as one: through the open windows sounds from the outside world went unheard, the clutter of life unheeded, and time sped by unmarked.

· · ·

"Nicolai. How strange it sounds!"

"Ilena, light of my life."

"Nicolai, how long will we have to wait?"

"It is hard to say, six months, perhaps, or a year."

"It is going to seem very long."

"Very long, but we must still be careful. Now Tsar Nicholas is dead I have applied for a new permit of residence for you under His Majesty's own signature, explaining that you were in difficulties with the police over attentions to the British prisoners here and praising your services to our own wounded—not quite the strict truth, I am afraid, but close enough. I think I shall obtain it, for to this Tsar I am not a personal enemy, but Suikevsky's powers are still very great and his campaign against me unabated. I may now manage to have him removed but even with the new reign it is not something which can be achieved in a hurry: whatever changes or reforms or cataclysms may occur in Russia, you can be sure the Third Section will survive in one form or another."

"Are things very difficult still?"

He shrugged. "Less changes than anyone ever thinks. The levies are restive again, that fool Gatchukov is running around after Marya Fedorovna instead of attending to his duties, Suikevsky questioned two more of my officers yesterday, and there is famine in parts of the province until the new harvest is gathered. There are times when the prospect of exile to a nice quiet fort

445

in the Caucasus seems postively attractive, but you give me strength, dear one, and now some fresh purpose for what I try to do."

· · ·

"Gatchukov will get Nipocritiy at last?"

"If he marries Marya Fedorovna, yes. But I still have what trust the government will allow me for the children, unfortunately, for all that Micha runs away whenever he sees me. I should not let him sell it and I think he will not find it as profitable as he hopes with all the charges it has on it for Traskine's debts."

"And the serfs?"

"Those too he will lose. Now, with defeat and a new Tsar, emancipation must come, God knows how. We will not live to see it, you and I, but one day, my love, this land of ours will be a proud land, one worthy of the love so many have given to it. That I do believe."

· · ·

She had never dreamed she could feel so completely happy: uncomplicated by doubt or reservation, unclouded by fear or loneliness, undaunted by past or future. She was at rest yet eagerly alive as never before; receiving everything yet also giving everything.

· · ·

"Excellency! General Berdeyev!"

A discreet knocking at the door, and when Berdeyev opened it he found Mrs. Braillard hovering outside, bright-eyed and conspiratorial.

"I beg your pardon, madame, for taking over your room in this disgraceful manner for so long." She had never before seen him smile and was astonished by the warmth of his expression. "We had much to discuss."

"Oh, and I'm so glad for you both! You need not fear Armand or I will say a word to anyone until everything is settled!"

"I shall be much in your debt, madame, so long as the war still lasts."

Mrs. Braillard twittered sympathetically and then rushed on. "But I do not mean to intrude where I'm not wanted. There is a messenger come for you, General, and I thought perhaps you would prefer to see him in the dining room."

"Thank you, madame, you are all consideration," he replied gravely, twitching his tunic straight and following her across the hall.

* * *

"I am afraid I must go at once, *vozlublenny*, there is trouble at Chuguyev again. That is one corner of serfdom which cannot disappear too quickly for me."

"Nicolai—"

"I must go, it is not serious yet but unless they are damped at once these things spread with the speed of steppe fires."

"Can't someone else go for a change?" she cried bitterly. "Why must it always be you?"

"Whom do you suggest I send, Suikevsky? Gatchukov? One of those drunken, gambling youths from the training battalion?" He held her very close for a long moment and then released her gently, carrying her cold fingers to his lips. "I will be back, never fear,"

* * *

She heard the receding clatter of his horse's hoofs through the open window as she sat blindly on the discomfort of the settle, absurdly hallowed to her now because he had laughed at it. *I will be back*, she thought. Yes, my love, whatever the difficulties, whatever the dangers, nothing shall keep us apart now. Even the waiting, hard as it will be, somehow will soon pass when we are already truly together.

IF YOU ENJOYED **A SPACE OF THE HEART**, YOU'LL LOVE THESE HISTORICAL NOVELS. ORDER THEM TODAY!

_____**LILIANE** by Annabel Erwin   **$1.95 (79-941)**
The tumultuous tale of a French noblewoman who fled from Napoleon's legions to the uncertain haven of a Virginia plantation—and the two handsome, powerful brothers who vied for her. "I loved it!"—Jennifer Wilde, author of **Love's Tender Fury**

_____**SKARRA** by Henry V. M. Richardson   **$1.95 (89-126)**
Highland lord of a large and noble clan, Skarra is a soldier of fortune, an eloquent scholar and a fiery lover whose fierceness at battle and tenderness at love blaze a legend across 17th-century Europe—and through the hearts of two very different women.

_____**LOVE'S TENDER FURY** by Jennifer Wilde **$1.95 (79-921)**
Over two million copies sold! This is the turbulent story of an English beauty—sold at auction like a slave—who scandalized the New World by enslaving her masters.

_____**GREAT MARIA** by Cecilia Holland   **$1.95 (79-957)**
In violent, dangerous 11th-century Italy two people in love struggle for power against the world—and each other. GREAT MARIA is an enthralling novel of a woman's triumph over the times, over herself and over conflicting male dominance.

 A Warner Communications Company

If you are unable to obtain these books from your local dealer, they may be ordered from the publisher.

Please allow 2 weeks for delivery.

WARNER BOOKS, Dept. PAA
75 Rockefeller Plaza, New York, N.Y. 10019

Please send me the books I have checked.
I am enclosing payment plus 35¢ per copy to cover postage and handling. N.Y. State residents add applicable sales tax.

Name ....

Address ....

City .... State .... Zip ....

___Please send me your free catalogs of new historical novels and gothics.